# Aindreas
# the Messenger

*a novel*

*Louisville, 1855*

# Gerald McDaniel

D1518923

*Aindreas the Messenger: Louisville, Kentucky 1855*

This book is manufactured in the United States. This is a work of fiction; Names, characters, places, and incidents are the product of the author's imagination or are used fictitiously. Any resemblance to actual persons, living or dead is entirely coincidental.

ISBN 978-0-9834144-7-6
Soft Cover
Library of Congress Number 2015948651
SECOND EDITION

Publisher:
Darby Press

DARBY
PRESS
Simpsonville, Kentucky

Author: McDaniel, Gerald
*Aindreas: the Messenger*

*To Kim*

BEAR GRASS CREEK AT PRESTONS LANDING

# 1

LOUISVILLE, KENTUCKY, APRIL 8, 1855

**Aindreas** Rivers lay writhing on the red earth of Preston's Landing. *Maybe death is like this,* he thought in the part of his mind that could still think. *Maybe this is death.* Three steam whistle blasts rolled over him. "Lord have mercy...Christ have mercy," he pleaded.

His limbs twitched out of control, and a burnt taste clung to the roof of his mouth. He flopped from his right side onto his back and saw the inevitable splashes of vomit in the dirt a few feet away to his left. The morning sun was hot and the brightest white, even to his closed eyes, and he jerked his hand above his face for shade.

"Steady, now...don't try to move quickly," a voice above him said.

He squinted at the dark, blurred form standing between him and the sun. Looking between his fingers, he could make out spectacles, a light beard—a face gazing down from the top of the man-shape...a good face, one Aindreas knew from somewhere.

"Think you can sit up now?" The voice seemed somehow familiar, and there was a clipped kindness in its tone.

Aindreas nodded. He covered his twitching right eye with his hand, and swallowed an awful taste. The man folded his coat and laid it across his writing case on the ground, then grasped

5

Aindreas under the arms and dragged him on his backside into the sparse shade of a sumac tree. It was cooler there. Thinking he might have fouled himself, Aindreas reached down and touched at the crotch of his trousers.

The reassuring voice again. "Don't worry…you're all right."

"I had a spell," Aindreas said, then glanced away when the man leaned down and wiped away the spittle from his face and shirt with a large handkerchief.

"I know," the man said, and handed over the handkerchief. "Take this, your nose is running."

"Sometimes I know when it's going to happen, and I wish I could die," Aindreas said, then blew his nose.

Neither spoke for several moments. The boy brushed the hair back away from his forehead. He looked more closely at the man, trying to figure out who he might be.

*Yes. He had seen him before…more than once, and he'd had spells those other times, too. Until today, the man had never spoken.*

Aindreas groaned, shifted his body to get more comfortable against the tree. Images of the things around him were becoming clearer. He glanced back over his shoulder toward the waterfront. The bridge over Beargrass Creek still hung there, right where it should have been, and higher up the bank lay the long row of large brick warehouses strung out toward the west, their windows looking down on the river like a thousand eyes.

A dozen or more steamboats lay tied up in a line along the wharf, and others out in the river glided this way and that, and beyond the boats lay the white water of the rapids, stretching out in the distance. The far shore, Indiana, sprawled silent and green—he'd gone there once with his father once on the Portland-New Albany Ferry, and his father had told him that Indiana was *free*. It hadn't looked different from Louisville except that there weren't any Colored there. Aindreas had later heard that Coloreds were only allowed to pass through there, not to stay—and runaways would be easy pickings for the slave catchers.

Aindreas sat straight up in alarm, pulling a thin package from inside his shirt. "My God, I've missed the *Ben Franklin,* he said, hating the shaking in his voice. He struggled to his feet. "I'm in trouble now, 'cause this won't get to Memphis on time."

"No hurry," said the man easily. "Your boat likely hasn't even arrived."

"What do you mean?"

"A small boiler problem," the man said easily, as if describing something that happened last week.

Doubtful, Aindreas looked down the line of boats. "Are you sure?" he asked. "And how do you know that, sir?"

The man shrugged, then said, "Don't you recall, that boiler has been given them trouble for weeks? I'd guess the *Ben Franklin* will dock near the foot of Sixth Street, somewhere around the usual spot."

Aindreas sat back down and leaned against the tree. He stretched out his legs on the ground; the strength in them hadn't yet returned, and his twitchy right eye must be a sight. He sure hoped this gentleman knew what he was talking about.

The man opened a writing case. Aindreas studied him in earnest: he looked about medium height, not portly, but not skinny either. The wire rims on his eyeglasses looked like copper, his sandy, thin hair was neatly combed, and his short beard had taken on a few flecks of gray. Had to be getting onto middle age, maybe even thirty or so. His clothes looked different but fine cut—not like any Aindreas had seen around Louisville, even the newest things at Walker's Merchant Tailor Shop.

The man propped a tablet on his knee and noted something on a sheet of foolscap with a shaven pencil. He looked up. "Mighty serious mood for a young man just past his thirteenth birthday," he said.

"How'd you know how old I am?"

The man shrugged again. "I know a lot of things," he said, "…but that's not important."

"Like you know what?" Aindreas asked.

"Oh, I know about some of the bad things going on in this town. I know you're Aindreas Rivers, and you have bad dreams."

Aindreas nodded, waiting for more.

"Some people think you are the fool, and some may be too embarrassed even to talk about it," the man continued. He took a pipe and package of tobacco from his coat pocket. "Let's see, you were five-foot two-inches tall the last time your mother marked your height on the edge of the door, and you must weigh about a hundred and ten pounds; you have an older brother and sister; and you're trying to make up your mind whether or not to go back to school. How's that?"

"Jesus, Mary and Joseph!"

"And you won't always have those freckles," the man added good-naturedly.

The boy ran his hand slowly over his face, as if he might be trying to find the freckles. "Do I know you, sir?"

The man lighted the pipe and blew out a cloud of smoke that didn't smell bad. "It might be that I'm nothing more than the far side of those bad dreams."

Aindreas sat silent for a moment, thinking. The man's suggestion didn't seem a disagreeable idea. Then quickly somberness quickly overtook him. "Know what people call me?"

The man made no response.

"I mean, my mother and sister say *Andrew* and my father calls me *boy*," Aindreas said. "But almost everybody else…."

"*Lucky*, isn't it?"

Miserable, Aindreas nodded assent. Still, the name hadn't sounded mean when the man said it. "Even my brother calls me that—and now you know, too."

"I won't repeat it," the man said.

"Wasn't so bad at first," Aindreas went on, "because I didn't know what it meant. People would pat me on the head, ask me dumb questions. One day at school, I found out."

The man blinked.

"They call me that because I have fits," said Aindreas. "I'm different from other people."

The man handed Aindreas a writing tablet and a pencil. "You know," he said, "you should write about these things…every day if you can."

Aindreas mumbled his thanks for the gifts, then put them down. He wrapped his arms around his up-drawn knees and locked his fingers so tightly his knuckles looked white. "Some people think I see things they can't," he said. "Seemed bad enough being a Catholic. I'll probably lose my job when the chief clerk finds out, and we need the money."

"How is your job?" asked the man.

Aindreas rubbed his right leg with both hands. "You mean you don't know?"

A smile played at the corners of the man's mouth. "I can't remember everything," he said.

"I run messages for the Ben Cawthon Furniture Manufactory, at Ninth and Jefferson," Aindreas said. "My favorite part is when I get to bring something down here to the river, to the boats." He sat up straighter, feeling a little proud. "I get all over town, walk mostly. But I try to hitch a ride if I have to go to Shippingport or Portland. I had to walk clear out to the Bardstown Turnpike once, by the old Cave Hill Farm," he added.

"Remember later to write all this down," said the man.

"Two of us, Tim and me, we run," Aindreas said. "South to Oak Street, west out Jefferson past the city graveyard. That's where my uncle's buried."

The man's gaze didn't change; he didn't look away. Most

grownups couldn't do that.

"Yesterday I carried a note to St. Martin's, that new church over in Germantown," Aindreas went on. "Couldn't hardly understand that priest." He paused. "My mother worries. You know, about the packages bein' too heavy. Anyway, I get to see a lot."

"Sounds like quite an adventure," the man said. "Tell me, would you rather be on a steamboat, or learn to run a machine and make furniture for Mr. Cawthon...or go to school?"

"I'm not sure."

"Well, you'll need to be thinking about it," said the man. He put the papers away and knocked the ashes out of his pipe, folded his coat over his arm, and picked up the writing case. "I'm afraid I have to go," he said.

Aindreas felt disappointed. "You're leaving already, sir?"

"Perhaps we'll meet again."

"I hope so," Aindreas said, and got to his feet. "Sure was nice to meet you."

The man ambled toward the suspension bridge over the creek and then he seemed to move across the hundred-foot span so quickly that he might have been borne by a breeze.

"Wait," Aindreas called after him. "You know all about me, but I don't know who you are."

Barely visible now, the man stopped and turned around. *"Knight,"* he said. "Just call me Knight."

Aindreas raised his arm and waved. "Good-bye Mr. Knight."

1

**P**lank boats and finished keel boats with sails glided in the morning breeze through the channel. Some lashed together, broad horn flat boats and barges maneuvered north toward Clarksville, on the Indiana shore. A steamboat backed away from the wharf while another churned slowly out in the river, waiting to take its place.

Aindreas limped from the Point across the shaky suspension bridge over the creek to the main part of the wharf, about half a mile from the place he hoped the *Ben Franklin* would be. He smiled when he noticed that the large black dog lying in the shade of a warehouse building was looking back at him, watching him.

Aindreas shuffled along the sloping plain of cobblestones, past open wagons, covered wagons, and bawling, squealing livestock with flies buzzing all around. Cargoes of machines, cotton bales, wood, barrels, boxes of all kinds, stone, hogsheads of tobacco and tierces of sugar and molasses were loaded or unloaded by grunting, swearing stevedores and roustabouts. Men on horses shouted orders at the laborers. This was just a part of the friction between the river and the land, and the sweat of these Black men and Irish men served as the grease.

Aindreas had to step quickly to avoid wagons rumbling over the stones. After a time, he stopped next to a wagon wheel to scrape the sole of his right boot. He wagged his head, recalling his grandfather's love of horses. "Now, horses leave manure, and you put up with that because they're horses," Grandpa had always said. "With the rest of them, though, it's just plain shit." Aindreas ruefully wished he still had the chance to tell the old man that, no matter how you described it, all of it made the same pancake on the sole of your boot.

Though he needed to find the *Ben Franklin*, Aindreas slowed down to appraise several boats he hadn't seen before. Even a couple of sternwheelers had docked that day. One, a cotton packet, had burlap-covered bales in tall stacks from the very edges of the main deck. You could barely see the boat.

Farther down the line, Aindreas felt relieved to see the *Ben Franklin* near the foot of Sixth Street, right where he had been told it would be. *How could Mr. Knight have guessed that?*

The old side-wheeler looked as good as ever. Wood smoke

had long since turned the white superstructure of the *Ben Franklin* gray, but Aindreas still considered it beautiful. Last year, he'd been on board as a passenger for a day trip to Brandenburg and back. That first day he had delivered a package to the boat, well over a year ago, he and Captain Workman became fast friends. It always felt good to talk river and boats.

"This ain't no Hudson River boat," Workman had told him that very first day.

"The low draft gets us through the shallows, all right, but I have to steer us around the snags and sawyers."

Aindreas gazed at the *Ben Franklin* with approval. A real Western river boat. No space for engines inside that square hull; the engine room stood right on the main deck. Freight usually filled the rest of that deck, and this day was no exception. The boat sat low in the river, the deck surface only a couple of feet above the water.

Aindreas scanned the boiler deck, filled with passenger cabins, and the crew quarters stacked above them. Perched still higher up, between the smoking twin stacks, was the pilothouse. Captain Workman leaned out the window, barking orders to the hands below.

Aindreas waved at him.

"Hello, m'boy!" the captain shouted. "Come aboard as soon as they roll off those barrels."

A moment later, the plank clear, Aindreas bounded onto the deck, then scampered upstairs and ladders to the pilothouse. Out of breath, he gasped. "Did you pass by her on your last trip?"

Their conversation usually began that way. Today, however, the captain seemed preoccupied. "Pass who?" he asked.

The boy felt let down. "The *Eclipse,* Captain."

"Oh, her." The heavy man's voice sounded bored at the mention of the legendary riverboat, but his too-serious demeanor betrayed him. "I did, boy," he said finally, then chuckled. "I wish you could have seen her. A little below Paducah in the middle of the night, out in the channel and lit up like a torch. My lord, she's as big as two boats."

"How close did you get?"

"Close enough for me. She stirs up the water something fierce."

A warm glow settled in Aindreas's stomach, and he reasoned that a world with the Eclipse in it couldn't be as bad as it sometimes seemed.

Workman mentioned that he needed to check on some things below. Aindreas went along, reminding himself that he mustn't forget to give his package to the captain before he got off the boat. They talked all the way down the ladder and the stairs, reluctant to let loose of the floating palace as a topic.

"Twelve boilers, is it, boy?" the captain asked.

"No, sixteen," responded Aindreas. "And is the carpet really from England?"

"Belgium," the captain corrected with mock severity. "And the pantry-ware came from France and the glassware from Switzerland."

"Tell me true, Captain Workman. Can anybody on the river beat that record from New Orleans to Portland, here?"

"No, for certain," Workman said. "Four days, nine hours," he added, then shook his head. "Nobody will ever match that."

They reached the main deck. Workman opened the hatch and eased his bulk down the ladder into the hold. Aindreas followed. He had never been allowed there. He could barely see in the dark, even with the hatch still open above them and the light from the captain's lantern wavering on the black, tapered bulkheads. The hold looked smaller than Aindreas had imagined. The dank river-water smell hung thick in the humid air.

Workman couldn't stand erect. He moved forward in a massive crouch, then bumped his head and swore. The captain eventually saw what he'd been searching for, and pointed to a pile of wood in a narrow space near the bulkhead. "Boy, can you get back in there and hand me about six or eight of those shorter wood pieces? I'm gonna have the deckhands make a few braces."

Aindreas had to crawl the last few feet to reach the wood. He handed out the three and four-foot lengths that the captain wanted, then helped Workman carry them back up to the deck. It occurred to Aindreas that he was overdue back at Cawthon's Furniture, but he didn't want to leave. He followed the captain, who checked and pulled at the lines that secured the freight on the main deck. Toward the rear of the boat, just beyond a pyramid of nail kegs, Aindreas saw black faces and black muscular bodies dressed in hard-time cotton sprawled along the deck. A tall white man with red hair made a sarcastic-sounding remark to the captain…something about the boat running late.

Workman's jaw tightened. "Mr. Cooper, I don't pay much mind to complaints from your kind. If I owned this boat, you wouldn't even be on board."

"That wouldn't be businesslike, Captain, "said the red-haired man, making no effort to conceal his smirk. "We're good pay."

Workman snorted, "I'll run this boat, and you stick to your godforsaken business for Bolton and Dickens."

*So that's what this Mr. Cooper is: a slave trader.*

The captain turned away. The red-haired man turned and whispered to a second white man, who laughed out loud.

Some of the Negro men looked old, and all of them seemed fearful. Strung out in twos, sixteen of them were chained across the stern of the boat in a coffle. Both ends of the center chain were bolted to the deck, each man shackled to the chain by an ankle cuff.

Two young women, apparently part of the group, stood separated from the men. The one in the high-neck dress with long sleeves had skin so light she might have been white. She looked down when Cooper took hold of her arm. The other one, little more than a girl herself, toted a baby on her hip. She wore a calico frock and a kerchief around her head.

As instructed, Aindreas stacked the wood pieces in the narrow place between the nail kegs to the pilothouse and then he fished the mail package out of his shirt and handed it over to the captain. Workman assured him it would be delivered to the addressee's agent at the Memphis Wharf.

"Probably won't be back for ten days or so," Captain Workman added. "If Mr. Cawthon has anything for upriver, just check with the wharf master and catch us when we're here." The big man gave the boy a friendly cuff to the shoulder. "And if you get over to Portland, keep a lookout for the *Eclipse*. She ought to be back in the next few weeks."

The captain stepped on the first rung of the ladder, then turned and said in a low voice, "Forget you saw all this slave business, boy. It's rotten through and through, and I may end up losing a first mate over it."

Workman then climbed heavily up the ladder toward the pilothouse.

Aindreas felt puzzled. *What was that about the first mate, Jack Graham, and what could the captain be thinking to leave those wood pieces stacked where he did?*

Jack Graham, the first mate, stood on the boiler deck staring down at the Negroes and traders. It had to be past time to get back to the factory, but Aindreas climbed the stairs to find out what the captain had meant and to talk with Jack. This was the man who had told Aindreas many stories about how he had started working as a deck hand as a boy on the Mississippi, and how he trained to pilot on the Kentucky River and the upper Ohio. What wonderful tales these were, and how Aindreas loved to hear them. The young pilot spat over the rail and turned, scowling, as Aindreas approached.

15

"Hello, Jack." Aindreas said, keeping in mind that this was the first time he'd seen the *Ben Franklin* carrying slaves downriver. He gestured toward the scene below. "The captain says all this is a rotten business."

Eyes hard, the pilot muttered, "It is that, Lucky."

This was usually a man of such good humor that Aindreas did not even take offense when Graham called him by that awful name. "My da doesn't care much for Negroes," Aindreas said, "but he says slavery is the worst thing that can happen for everybody. He says the English must have something to do with it."

Graham laughed. "Your old man's probably right," he said. "This whole thing will turn out wrong for all of us, but it may be bad for me sooner than some."

"Why?" asked Aindreas.

"Accidents can happen on a riverboat," Jack said, his tone mysterious.

"What kind of accidents?"

"Well hell, you're old enough to hear it," Jack said. He nodded toward the slaves. "You know what's going on down there?"

"Well, it looks like those Negroes got sold down the river."

"Like a bunch of animals," Graham said. "But it's worse than that."

"You mean about the Kentucky people getting rid of them."

Graham nodded. "The cotton people way down south got hold of new land. They want more slaves, and they can pay a lot of money." He indicated the city with a wave of his hand. "In places like Kentucky, the owners round up the farm hands, household slaves, cooks, and stable boys...the Coloreds they always said they loved so much. They smear oil all over them; pluck the gray hairs out of the old ones. Some of those poor devils won't last very long down in Louisiana or Mississippi."

16

"They'll die...won't they?" said Aindreas.

"Most of 'em," said Graham. "But this boat is for hire: we'll ship anything," he went on, smiling crookedly. He looked below. "Those women down there."

"Uh-huh," said Aindreas. "That one looks like a white lady."

"Damn near." Graham said. "A fancy lady. Very valuable. Probably the real reason Bolton and Dickens would send a small group like this down from Lexington. She'll be a toy for some planter. Cooper first, if he has his way."

"Cooper and her?"

Graham leaned back on the rail. "I saw Red Cooper in action before, him and that bastard with him, back when I crewed on some packets on the Mississippi and the Kentucky. Cooper's workin' on the fancy lady now. She's afraid of him, but she's worth too much to damage. If he can't do any good with her, he and his pal will still have the black girl with the baby."

Aindreas felt the flush in his face. "They'll make her do it?"

"If they have to." Graham said. "But she looks scared to death, and she's got that baby. No more than streaked meat and molasses might do the trick. Either way, they'll take turns with her all the way to Natchez."

Aindreas stared down at the deck boards.

"And Cooper will do something even worse," Jack went on. "Can you guess what I'm talking about?"

Still looking down, Aindreas shook his head. "No." he said.

"For liquor, tobacco, or whatever, he'll sell that baby before we get past Memphis."

Aindreas remained silent.

Graham went on. "I thought you needed to hear this, in case you don't see me around for a while. A few stretches down below the Kentucky border, that ole Mississippi has some bad currents. If Red Cooper wanders around by himself after dark he could fall overboard, and I got a feeling he might not be hanging onto any balsa wood when it happens."

Aindreas swallowed.

"So, don't worry if you don't see me around for a while," Graham said. "There's good boats out there on the Missouri, and that's where I could end up."

The boy's hand almost disappeared in Graham's when they shook hands. Graham wrapped his arms around Aindreas and hugged him, then turned him about and shoved him in the direction of the staircase.

"Get out of here; I got work to do."

Aindreas walked down the plank and onto the wharf. He turned and waved toward the pilothouse. Captain Workman responded with several sharp pulls on the steam whistle. The paddle wheels churned the water to light brown as the *Ben Franklin* backed away from the levee, and then the boat swung around and headed toward the Portland Canal.

PUBLIC LANDING

# 2

**Whispers.** More of them. Used to be that Aindreas heard them only when he was sick or when a spell threatened. They might come to him at any time and any place now...right in the middle of a crowd, alone, or perhaps from out of a discarded newspaper, and especially in bed at night. Mean whispers.

*Yes we are pureblooded Native Americans of Anglo-Saxon stock. We aren't Catholic, and we aren't related to such as them by blood or marriage. Wouldn't vote for one of them, either. God save us from those Godless Germans and drunken Irish.*

*There is a certain personage in this land you should get to know. His name is "Sam." Not "Uncle Sam." A stern fellow, he carries in his hand a flag of our country, and enemies of this great nation fly at his coming, like they were kites and crows that saw the eagle ready to swoop. Sam is the embodiment of liberty. He's the one who pointed young Luther to the dust-covered Bible. Yes he is, and he's the one who brought the Bible with him across the ocean on the Mayflower. And he's the one who laid the cornerstone of the first Protestant Church in this land.*

Aindreas delivered an invoice in his own neighborhood, which didn't happen often. He headed toward home to look in on his mother. She had looked sicker over the last months. No one in the family ever talked about how she had grown worse, as if not speaking of her illness would make it go away. He took a shortcut through an alleyway, climbed over a board fence, and went into the yard from the back.

Home was the bottom half of a homely, two-story frame building in the rear of the Travis property. Covered with peeling clapboard, the place had once been used as a storage barn. A water pump stood outside the front door, and a privy behind the building. The Rivers family had lived in the lower level for over five years. As he almost always did, Aindreas glanced up the outside stairs to the newer second story of the building, where Blanche Flowers and her husband lived. Miss Flowers. She had once been Aindreas's teacher and was so beautiful a lady that she made all others seem plain.

His mother, Doireann Rivers, a short, fleshy woman, leaned over the wash tubs. She fished out steaming garments with the tip of a smooth paddle, swung them in a bunch from the boiling wash to a second tub, and then prodded the billowing cotton mass in the rinse water. She paused, hands on hips and breathing hard, as Aindreas approached.

She looked tired, more so than at breakfast. "Wasn't Kirsty supposed to help you?"

Doireann gazed up at the sky. "Clear and warm as it is, I'd best not wait on your sister. If I hurry, the whole mess will be dry on the line in a few hours."

She wrung out a garment by hand, then grimaced and pressed her hand against her side. Aindreas started toward her, but she waved him away. "Don't borrow trouble, Andrew," she said, as she always said.

"You better get on back to your job." There seemed to be nothing he could do, but Aindreas hung around a few minutes to reassure himself that she was managing all right. He walked along the side path toward the front of the Travis property, toward Prather Street, past the sagging log cabin midway back on the parcel. The cabin had probably been there long before the Travis residence was built. Aindreas's treasured friend, Isaac, had lived there for years with his family.

On the front half of the lot stood a handsome, two-story brick home with a small carriage barn to one side—the residence of Squire Travis and his wife, owners of the property. *The Squire,* as he preferred to be called, had been away the last few days. Mrs. Travis had remained; everyone knew she was there, but she couldn't often be seen, except as a fleeting image at a window or in her carriage on Sunday to and from Christ Church. Full view of the squire's wife apparently favored only those allowed inside her house and Episcopalians at Christ Church.

When Aindreas reached Prather Street, he stopped to look at the front of the residence, partially concealed from the street by elm trees. Miss Flowers had told him the house was called "Federal style." It had something called a portico across the front and a large, rich-looking entrance set off by sidelights and a transom, but with all of that, Aindreas had never seen Squire Travis smile.

1

**A** muscular young man in grimy shirt and trousers sat down at the kitchen table and pulled off his boots. "I'm home, Ma," he said.

Doireann Rivers said from the doorway. "Don't call me that, Michael."

"Well then, *Mither mine,* I'm home."

She shooed him out of the chair toward the door. "None of your foolishness," she said. "No mending done, and Kirsty not here to peel potatoes and scale the fish. Your father likes something on the table when he gets home."

"Yeah, yeah…let's all give three cheers for Da."

Doireann frowned. "Get yourself cleaned up and empty out

the wash tubs."

He trudged out the kitchen doorway.

"And fill them up for tomorrow," she said after him.

Aindreas heard them, from just outside, and now watched Michael walking barefoot on the gravel along the side of the tenement.

"Dammit," Michael muttered, as he tipped the first tub.

The splashing water pooled, then began running toward the low place in back of the building. "Pick-and-shovel up and down that damn L&N roadbed all day," Michael said, loud enough for Aindreas to hear, "and the family taking all of me money," he added to drive home the point.

Aindreas knew his brother wouldn't spend the better part of an hour pumping and carrying another fifty gallons of water. Usually, Michael got away as early as he could, to "…hoist a few with the lads and chase 'round after the lovelies…"

Michael began to hum, then winked at Aindreas. "The ladies won't want this old ganconer all tired out. You'll help me out, won't you, Lucky?" Later, the Rivers family sat down to supper. Four of them sat on the shiny hard chairs at the round oak table that Doireann's mother had left her, the proudest possessions in the place except for the cast-iron stove. Aindreas sat on a stool.

Michael looked sullen. "Good old mackerel stew again." he muttered.

Kirsty covered a smile with her hand.

Joseph Rivers scowled at Kirsty, then turned hard eyes on Michael. Gripping his spoon like a trowel in his fist, Michael began to eat. Aindreas had heard it said that the place wasn't big enough for both his father and his brother, that a house could not hold two men.

Joseph Rivers had scrubbed his face and neck pink and combed his wet, light hair straight back. "Did'ya know, Dorrie, we have two mayors now?" he asked between bites. "That's what the newspaper man told me at the store."

"Two?"

"Well, Speed didn't run because his term wasn't up until '56. And the court said he was right about that argument, too. But the Know-Nothings got Barbee on the ballot for that city election a while back. He got the most votes, 'cause Speed wasn't even on the ballot."

Aindreas's mother finished filling her plate. "Don't see how a town can carry on with two mayors, especially if one is a Know-Nothing."

Joseph Rivers grinned wickedly. "The almighty Church carried on, Dorrie, and it had two popes for forty years, one in Rome and one in a little French place called Avignon...and *neither one* of them knew anything."

Doireann waved her hand in dismissal, but the corners of her mouth were turned up. "Don't start on the Church, Joe, not at the table."

Aindreas knew this wasn't going to be one of those serious, bad times. His mother seemed proud of his father, even when he said things that put her off. Joseph Rivers had worked as a laborer since twelve years of age, then at the grocery shop after his back gave out. When they were first married, he had been able to write little more than his name. Doireann had helped him, and now he read every book about history he could borrow. But neither Doireann nor Joseph Rivers knew that Aindreas, as well, had read every one of those books by candle in the night.

Michael shook his head with impatience. "Hey, in my bunch we know they're throwing Speed out 'cause he turned Catholic," he grumbled. "But they better not start any damned stuff down at the rail yards. We'll lay a stick or two over some heads."

Aindreas's father nodded.

Kirsty said, "The Irish and Germans at the market talk like they're worried."

Aindreas joined in. "Two men got beat up today...down on Green Street."

"A fight?" asked Kirsty. "You shouldn't go around those saloons."

"Not much of a fight. Five men, three of them with clubs, beat these two German men all bloody. I ran."

Joseph Rivers glared at Aindreas, but his mother patted his arm. "I'm glad you got away from there," she said. "Joe, Michael, let's finish up the stew."

Aindreas wondered if his father would have approved of him more if he had hit someone with a rock. He volunteered, "Mr. Knight said there are bad things going on in this town."

"Knight?" his father's expression turned quizzical. "Don't know anyone with that name around here."

"Down at the wharf this morning," Aindreas said. "That's what he told me to call him."

Michael grinned. "Was this a real person?"

Aindreas hoped they weren't going to start all that business again. He felt shamed, and only nodded.

"See here, boy, I hope you're not talking about another one of your made-up friends," Aindreas's father said, resting his spoon in his bowl. "I'm not in the mood for it."

Aindreas looked down at his plate. It might have been better if he hadn't said anything at all.

Joseph Rivers sopped a crust in the last of his stew, popped it into his mouth, and got up from the table still chewing. He had that look he always had before he went out for a jar, or maybe to get all-the-way drunk. Maybe it was the mention of Mr. Knight at the wharf that had done it. Aindreas had overheard arguments about him between his father and mother. Once, when she had tried to quiet him down, Joseph Rivers had said, "I've had to show Mike who was head of the house a time or two, but that was a joy compared to dealing with that boy. You can't talk to him like other people, Dorrie. He tells strange stories, that one, always looking off at something I don't see."

Aindreas's mother watched as his father rose from the table. Joseph Rivers didn't look back. "I'm goin' out," he said over his shoulder.

Michael followed a few minutes later.

Doireann cleaned the dishes, then set out the irons on the stove lid while Kirsty brought in the wash from the line. They spread a pad on the kitchen table. His mother looked exhausted, and Aindreas felt thankful that Kirsty had planned to help. Outside, he quietly pumped and carried water to fill the second tub, as he had promised Michael that he would. When he was finished, Aindreas intended to go over to the cabin and talk with Isaac. He wondered if Isaac had found the money. After a last trip to the pump, Aindreas paused near the kitchen door.

"Michael will probably be getting married before long," Kirsty said, "and maybe someone is looking at me."

"Looking, is it? And who might that be?" asked Doireann.

"Nobody you know. I'll tell you more later on."

Aindreas peered through the crack in the door. His mother sprinkled water on a shirt, then stretched the sleeve by the cuff as she pulled the heavy iron over it. "It's certain that we don't have room for another person here, Kirsty. Your cot is folded up in the pantry as it is. And you be sure that 'looking' is all this somebody you're going to tell me about later does. You and your brother both have things to learn, yet."

Kirsty whined, "Oh, I couldn't get married, anyway. You keep all the money."

"We've been all over this, lass. How many times do we have to talk about it?" Doireann put the iron back on the stove and began folding the shirt. "Ten dollars and fifty cents a week it costs us just for the rent, food, and coal for the stove. *You know this.* We have to scratch just to have soap and lamp oil. That's why I've

25

always done the outwork."

Doireann began working on another shirt with the second iron. "Your father would do better, if he could. Sometimes they have work for him on Saturday, but mostly not. He brings in a dollar-fifty a day, and lucky we are to get it with his back in that shape. Mike earns seventy-five cents a day. He gives me most of it, though I have to stay after him. That little they pay you on your maid jobs has helped, too."

"What about Andrew?" Kirsty said.

"Quarter a day, and brings it to me." Doireann said proudly. "Won't keep a cent."

The girl smoothed a pair of window curtains on the pad while her mother reheated the irons.

"That's not what I meant, Mother."

"What, then?"

"Last year, Da said I would have to keep working for the family if Andrew went back to school."

"That's the way of a daughter, miss. Might not be fair, but a father always has the right to ask it."

"Does what Andrew wants count for anything?"

"With me it does," Doireann said. "What did he say?"

"He said, 'Don't do it for me,'" Kirsty responded. "Says he'll figure out a way to learn what he needs."

"I'll talk to your father about it," said Doireann. She patted her daughter's shoulder and sat down. "Thanks for the help, 'cause I couldn't finish this by myself," then she added, "Tomorrow, there'll be a more garments where these came from."

They both laughed.

"Andrew, I heard you filling those tubs," said his mother with a raised voice. "Where are you?"

Aindreas started toward the cabin. "I'm going over to see Isaac."

Aindreas always looked forward to listening to him. Soon after the Rivers family had moved into the old storage barn on the Travis property, he'd taken to hanging around Isaac. Isaac was a man to respect, and Aindreas had chosen him for a friend. Months had passed before the Black man openly trusted him in return.

Isaac never preached or acted as if he were certain about things—even his age; he admitted he only *thought* he was forty-eight years old. But Isaac was smart, maybe smarter than anyone Aindreas had ever met. They had learned some things together, even swap, but Aindreas knew he had been taught more than he could ever give back. Isaac truly knew how things fit together, and why they did. He knew. He must have always known, but had never attached pride or words to it. He'd kept it quiet. That's how he had managed to think all those years and not lose his life for it; how he had managed to survive so long he had forgotten his mother, father, and the rest of the old folks; long enough to meet and marry Tempie and father two children.

Isaac sat hunched on a stool at his usual warm-weather spot outside, in a patch of light near the cabin window opening. Aindreas paused and watched. A crescent of shine moved about the bald crown of Isaac's head when he bobbed up and down at his work. He peered down at a pair of shoes. His hands moved slowly. This deliberation came of necessity; three fingers on Isaac's left hand were gnarled and twisted.

"Who are the shoes for, Isaac?" Aindreas asked.

"Tempie." Aindreas hunkered down. "Did you find the box?" he whispered.

Isaac seemed not to hear him. There had been a noise near the back of the Travis house.

"You hungry, young Andrew?" Isaac said. "Go tell Tempie

you want some kush. It's mighty good."

Aindreas went inside the cabin and squatted near the hearth. Smells of wood smoke, hot cornmeal, onions, and ham juice filled the room, along with the low, steady sound of the juice sizzling in a skillet. Tempie and the children were sitting around the table. Aindreas smiled and shook his head *no* when she offered to dish food on a plate for him.

He watched them eat and mused about his friendship with Isaac. The swapping of ideas between a slave and a white boy surely would have surprised Squire Travis, and maybe scandalized a lot of others in the town. Aindreas figured it didn't matter because most people thought him as a fool, and treated Isaac as though he were as dull as they believed any Colored to be. In fact, the contacts between the two had been simply practical, the kinds of deeds and words sane friends exchange in a time gone mad.

Isaac had told Aindreas about his Georgia roots, how he'd been separated from his family when he was still a child. About how crude tools and cast-off materials had been his best teachers and friends while he aged and learned. Before Isaac reached twenty years old he'd been given to Squire Travis's father, Hiram, as a gift from a Travis relative in Georgia. Isaac had grown up doing masonry and carpenter work, and had gotten good at it—so good he became one of those slaves-for-hire who made money for their masters by the contract work done for others. When old Hiram Travis died, his son Squire took to hiring out Isaac more and more and, for reasons of his own, letting Isaac keep a small part of the pay for himself. Isaac had married Tempie five years ago and had dreamed of buying his freedom one day.

Aindreas went back outside the cabin, sat down in the dirt near Isaac, and drew up his knees. The crickets started a racket.

Isaac shaved at the edge of the hard sole leather on one of the shoes with a short, curved knife. His slight nod signaled that whatever he earlier heard no longer worried him. He chuckled. "Yes, I found that box. Tempie didn't know I'd wrapped it up in a pile of rags, and she'd shoved them over in the corner."

"Did you count it?"

"Nine-hundred and forty-two dollars, and a few extra coins."

"My God, I can't even think of that much money, Isaac. I wonder if it's enough, though."

"I got to find that out. Things keep changin', and I got to know that."

Aindreas squirmed. "Did the squire ever say that he was going to do it?"

"No, but it's in my mind." Isaac said. His voice became even softer, "The squire spends more time out at the racetrack."

"You mean Oakland."

"Yeah. And he favors whiskey and women. Mrs. Travis know some things; some she don't. They carry on with each other sometimes. Tempie knows. She heard, too. They holler at one another about money." Isaac held up the shoe in the light and turned it all about. Apparently satisfied, he put it down. He placed the second upper on a thicker piece of leather and traced the outline of the shoe on the sole leather with a pointed knife. "Young Andrew, the squire gamblin' too much money."

"And that's what made you think that he would…"

"Me or Tempie, or the children or maybe all of us. Maybe he'd sell us in a bunch, and tell them to keep us together. Could he do that?"

"I don't know."

"Try to find out, 'fore I go crazy. And something else. You said that boy, Tim, you work with asked you one time to walk to the nigger pens with him. I wished you'd look around there, Andrew. You know I can't. Traders hangin' around. I know they's one place up on Second Street near the Galt House, and another over on First."

Isaac sawed through the leather with the knife, carefully putting the scraps into a pile. "I've got that money, but I don't know," he said. "Find out what one old as me would bring." Isaac shook his head when he held up his wounded left hand to the light. "And I got this," he said.

Tempie hummed inside. Isaac grimaced. "Them traders like women like Tempie. And the boy may bring more than the girl child. I don't know these things, but I got to."

Intensity burned in those dark eyes, and Aindreas looked away. He would do anything to help this man, but what if he did something wrong, and caused trouble for Isaac?

"You gonna help me?" Isaac asked.

"Yes, I'll try to find out."

Isaac's frown softened. He hunched down over his work again. "You know, I been thinking on the time I first knew your daddy, back when he was young as you," he said "Want to hear 'bout it?"

Aindreas nodded. Da never talked about those days. In fact, he almost never mentioned Isaac's name.

"Scoopin' out that canal went on maybe three years," Isaac began. "Old Hiram Travis sent me out on it. Hired out slaves made up most all of the masons, and the Irish did the diggin'. We worked side by side."

Aindreas watched Isaac's hands.

"That old ditch stretched out almost two miles. One boss told us there was two-thousand men working on it. They called it the Shippingport Canal then, but now they call it the Portland."

Isaac smiled. "Your granddaddy, John Rivers, used to talk to me sometimes."

"Back when he first came here?" asked Aindreas.

"Yeah, after his wife died while he was workin' up on the Erie Canal," Isaac said. He held the shoe sole up in the light, then cut a bevel along the top edge. "See how I'm doing this, Andrew?"

Aindreas nodded.

"The Irish used to talk 'bout how the Erie was the longest anywhere. Told it stretched out like a river. It went from the Hudson clear over that place where the big falls is, on over to Lake Erie. When the work ran out, a bunch of them came down here to dig. Your granddaddy left a couple of young'uns with a sister, but he brought your daddy with him."

"And Da was about my age then?"

"Uh-huh. Old John Rivers used a pick and shovel every day, and young Joe carried bricks or a water bucket or grub...he was a hard worker."

"Must have been stronger than me," Aindreas said.

Isaac blinked assent. "But some of them workers was bad people, and you had to step careful. Whites was the worse. A few of them commenced to give your daddy misery, said they would beat him up. Said he wasn't on time with the grub, such as that. Looked like he walked around scared all the time."

Aindreas had never thought of his father as being afraid.

"This one white mason worked near me hit your daddy once," Isaac went on. "Made me mad, but nothin' I could do about it. In that same bunch, they had this big free Colored, a mean one. Been a driver down the state somewhere...you know the kind I'm talking about, the ones they use to make the other niggers work faster. Well, this one just naturally didn't like me and I didn't like him. He'd been gettin' all close to that white mason, so he tripped your daddy down one day. I told him private it looked dumb to start trouble with white folks, even the poor ones. Besides, he was too big to be pushing around boys."

Aindreas surged with pride at his friend's courage. "Did he get mad?"

"Oh, did he? Thought I'd have to fight that big man right there," Isaac said. "The boss told us to cool down, but they got me later." Isaac put down the shoe, and gestured with his hands. "See,

I was spreadin' in some mortar under a block wedged up by a wood piece, like this. That white man I told you and the free Colored was movin' a big stone to a spot next to mine. They rammed the block that was already there, and it came over on my hand. The boss raised all hell with those two, but they claimed it just happened."

Aindreas had always found it painful to look closely at Isaac's left hand.

"They both got run off the job, but it didn't do me no good. Old Hiram Travis's doctor talked the longest time 'bout cutting off my hand, but he never did. No more mason work for me, or canal work either."

"How did my father feel about what happened to you?"

"Don't know," Isaac said. "You best ask him 'bout that."

Aindreas got to his feet. "I'd better get home, or my mother will be yelling for me."

Isaac went back to his work.

Aindreas walked toward the tenement building through a veil of sinking coal smoke and the smell of soap and sour water in the grass. A deep dog bark echoed in the distance.

Joseph Rivers had gone to bed, Kirsty to her bunk in the pantry room, and Michael hadn't come home yet. The ashes from the stove had been set out. Aindreas's mother knelt on the kitchen floor, blacking the oven.

"Mother, shouldn't you go to bed?" he asked.

"Just have a few more things to do, and Michael hasn't come home yet," she said without looking up. "Take out the ashes for me?"

Aindreas took the bucket out back and emptied it. He paused, looking out into the darkness. König was out there somewhere, closer now.

He went back to the kitchen. *God, how she loved that stove.* She wiped off the top and the lids, around the cooking holes and the surfaces of all the fancy gingerbread work. Then she pulled a rag over the tip of an awl and inched the point through the grooves of the nickeling, the curlicues, and the scrolls. The quick movements of her hands made him half dizzy.

His mother seemed not to notice when Aindreas picked up and folded a paper with fish scraps and bread crusts. She hugged him and gestured toward the small room that he shared with Michael. "Go on to bed, Andrew. I'll only be a while longer."

### 3

Her side hurt bad and Doireann felt sick to her stomach. She doubled over for a time. It happened almost every day. Dr. MacIntosh had told her it would come to this.

Once she caught her breath, she made herself a cup of tea and then sat down by the table to admire her handiwork. Doireann felt proud. Not many women such as her owned a cast-iron coal-burning stove. One like this cost six dollars or more, extra for delivery. She had come by the stove through Mrs. Travis, of all the unlikely people. It had been in the Travis basement, part of a wagon-load of fancy things inherited from an aunt. In one of the few times the woman had spoken to her, Mrs. Travis had asked if Doireann would like to buy the stove.

Doireann sipped the tea, remembering the thrill when she found it could be had for a dollar and a half. Joe and Michael and two other men had strained and cursed when they set the three-hundred-pound miracle in place. But she felt as if her heart would break when the stove proved to rock unsteadily with the least nudge. Two of the legs were shorter than the others. Damaged. Probably always had been. Furious, Joe had said that a fire would be dangerous in the thing. They would have to return it and try to get back the money from Mrs. Travis.

Doireann recalled how Aindreas had run to see Isaac, later returning with a ball of clay. Joe and Michael and the men laughed at him when he made molds of the gaps between the stove footings and the floor. She had been so upset she pulled him to the back room and scolded him to quit fooling around with serious business. But Aindreas ran off to the river and got back to the house before she had worked up the nerve to talk with Mrs. Travis. He had brought two flat-looking rocks. He worked and jammed and hammered, first one and then the other a certain way under the short legs of the stove. She had cried when the stove stood steady as a boulder and nobody could make it move one way or other, even pushing hard against it. She had never forgotten that, though Joe and Michael never mentioned it again.

Sleepy, she walked over to the front window and looked out. Still no Michael. She sat down again, her arms cushioning her head on the table as she drowsed. She thought of all the things she and Joe had gone through together. How they had been happy, once. How would he get on without her? Sleep was coming as she pictured a time when they had lived with Joe's father in two rooms in Portland, back before Kirsty and Aindreas were born. She and Joe had made sweaty love under a comforter, with baby Michael asleep beside them.

4

Aindreas stood by the open window with the food scraps, listening. König would come. König. Aindreas had a picture in his mind of Mr. Ostertag, who used to run a tobacco shop at Second and Main Streets. König may have been the old man's only companion in those last years of his life. Whenever Mr. Ostertag was out in the city, the huge black dog walked along right beside him. *Where could an animal like that have come from?* Tim, Aindreas's co-worker, had said he heard the old man owned some kind of precious vessel, a dish of some kind, and he needed that fearsome dog for protection. Sometimes, Tim's stories sounded hard to believe.

Mr. Ostertag had died a few months ago and now König lived in the streets on his own. Stories went around that he was a killer, had always been a killer. More than once, men with guns searched for him.

Aindreas saw the dog many times on the street, often bleeding fresh from a wound on his right foreleg. Aindreas had felt ashamed of being afraid, but he feared this dog, who stood nearly as tall as he was—and must have weighed a time and a half as much. But after a while, he stopped crossing the street when he saw the dog coming, and he began leaving scraps of food whenever König followed him, and if a pump was nearby, he would make a fresh puddle of water for drink. *What day had it begun?* Aindreas couldn't remember the exact date, but König became a shadowy part of his life, always somewhere nearby.

Amber eyes glittered in the darkness. Then a large, silent shape appeared beneath the window. Aindreas climbed quietly out the window and dropped to the ground. He squatted beside the bear-like dog and laid out the greasy paper with the scraps. König loved fish more than anything else.

"I only saw you once all day," Aindreas whispered, stroking the thick ruff around the dog's neck and the white patch on his chest. "But I knew you were there all the time."

The dog ate quickly, nosed the paper about, and then lay down. The wound above the right foreleg had opened again.

THE MARKET

THE CUSTOMS HOUSE

# 3

**Always** a bustling place, Ben Cawthon Furniture Manufactory grew even busier the following weeks. Each day, Aindreas and Tim divided the morning pile of messages, invoices, and packages for delivery, knowing there would be more by midday.

Tim would complain, "Damn, don't it ever let up?"

All day, every day but Sunday, Aindreas and Tim ran. All over town in the hot May sun—all over the tenth-largest city in the country.

SATURDAY, MAY 12.

Aindreas stood waiting in the factory office. Earlier that morning, he'd hoped to have time to stop by the slave pens but hadn't felt well. A hint of roses hung in the air, and a sense of dread nearly made him moan inside. It always started after he noticed that smell. He leaned against the wall, embarrassed at the dark splotches of sweat on his shirt and trousers. The crisp sound of paper came from the high, slanted desk where the chief clerk's long fingers creased and folded invoices and bills of sale, then stuffed them into envelopes.

Aindreas had the impression that he was shrinking. He knew that couldn't be right. No, the office had to be expanding. The room went on growing and swelling until it was as big as the factory, and that made him feel afraid. The chief clerk glanced down from his tall stool.

"Something wrong with you, boy?"

Now no more than a mere speck in the vastness of the room, Aindreas steadied himself against the baseboard of the wall. "I'm OK," he said quickly.

"Well then, look like you're awake and get over here." The clerk, apparently unaware of what had happened to the room, casually held up two envelopes. "This one's for East Market Street," he said. "And when you come back down Jefferson Street, drop off this tax bill at the county clerk's office."

Aindreas nodded that he understood.

The clerk held up the second, smaller envelope. "Don't lose the money in this one, or I'll have your hide."

By the time Aindreas reached the street, he could concentrate enough to keep his eyes directly on the path ahead. He felt less shaky when he achieved a steady pace, but images of shouting men and fires kept leaping into his mind without warning. Not letting the words escape his lips, he tried talking to himself. "Least on this trip, I'll be on limestone streets. Can't be more than a half-dozen of them in the whole town. Count 'em up: there was Water Street, nearest the river, and Main Street with all the brick buildings. They're paved, and so is Market Street."

The city looked as if it had a kind of design. In truth, it had just grown up that way. On Water Street, facing the river, the buildings were tied in with the river traffic. One block higher up the bank, on Main Street, the wholesalers' warehouses began, those big, expansive buildings. Only a few retailers around there. Most of the shops were located on Market and Jefferson Streets. Still farther south of the river neighborhoods began, and there were homes, churches, grocery stores, schools and the like. The schools were for other boys, not for him.

It seemed as if a hundred pins pricked at his face. He began to talk silently again, as if he were acquainting a stranger with the city. "Then the only other hard streets are Jefferson, Green, and Walnut, that's it. All the rest are dirt—shin-deep mud when it rains. It was the same with the gas lights; the city only lighted up the *big* streets."

Off in the distance, in the middle of wide Market Street, stood one of the large enclosed produce houses. Aindreas went well around the stray dogs and pigs that were picking at a greenish mound of garbage as high as his waist. Gagging, he held his hand over his nose and mouth, but he had seen worse. Slops and refuse had always been drained and dumped in the streets, sometimes the garbage mounded so high that it covered half the street, and even a dead animal might lie in such a heap. Maybe it would rain soon and wash some of it away. But it should be a gentle rain. Aindreas knew better than to wish for a storm, because if that happened the streets would flood, and hordes of rats would swim and crawl all over the place.

He could hear himself breathing and his legs weren't entirely under control, so he stopped at a horse trough. He worked the pump handle, holding his face under the faucet. The cool water felt good on his eyes, and he sagged to the curb. Though his eyes remained open, the light dimmed and the sounds of the clopping horses and the grind of the wagon wheels against the limestone got softer; people quickly looked away when their eyes met his. Disconnected scenes from the past came to him and then evaporated   just as quickly from his mind. Women pushcarts, men, children, store windows melted into a single, many-colored and pulsing thing—and there in the middle of Saturday market, his body wanted to draw up into a ball. An argument began a few feet away and Aindreas became a part of it; he was the seller and then the customer...then they both disappeared. A lost child whimpered close by him. Aindreas drifted. A dream took him over.

*S*pring. Hurry, trying to finish the deliveries before sundown. Have to go down into the inner city, that scary place that sprawls between the low bank of the river at Water Street on up to the high bank at Main Street, then spreads west for blocks from Second Street—a squalid, damp and gray place with low, mean places jammed together, chandler's stores, grog shops, and bawdy houses. No place to be after dark. Walk as fast as you can through those narrow streets and alleys, past the darkest places. The smells, even the sounds, are bad.

Never told anyone about the night two men step in front of me in an alley. I try to run, but one of them grabs my arm and pulls me almost to the ground. The other man is bigger and carries a heavy stick. He smirks. His face has a knowing expression. I never saw him before, but he asks, "What's in the package, me lucky boy?"

The man holding my arm makes little sniffling sounds, as if he had a runny nose that never stopped. Their faces seem ugly, now. Their intent was to hurt or to kill. No one would ever have found me. They joke to each other, laughter private in some way. It must be fun for them to see how afraid I look, and considering what they are going to do.

A guttural sound, like a shallow cough, comes from somewhere in the dark. A low growl follows and then silence. The sound comes again, deeper and longer; something is out there in the dark. Two close-together crescents of shiny crystal. Are those eyes? These men must see them, too, and the hold on my arms loosens. I pull free and step away.

The one with the big stick mutters, "What in hell is that?"

40

They both draw back a step when a long, black, wolfish shape edges into the dim light. The ears droop forward at the sides of the broad head; the eyes are narrowed and the teeth bared. Head low, it crouches taut, the shadow stretching back into the darkness. The most fearsome creature I've ever seen.

I back away from the men. One of them picks up a stone and throws it hard at the animal. The stone barely misses and makes chinking sounds as it skips down the alley cobblestones. The animal doesn't flinch or move. The men make low sounds to each other, fear in their voices, and begin moving sideways toward the near edge of the alley; the smaller one curses when the animal silently darts forward and cuts off their pathway.

The big man waves his club and yells, "I'll knock your head off, you black sonofabitch!"

The animal pays no more attention to the stick than it did the stone. It moves forward, the large plumed tail curled over its back.

Great God, it's König.

The dog toys with the men, making low, feinting moves, as if to attack. The big man takes a vicious swipe with the club. As if in different kind of time, König without effort moves under the stick and rips open the man's arm from the elbow to the wrist. The man screams in pain, his loose shirtsleeve flapping, dark with blood. The dog circles the men, reins them in, keeping them from separating. The shiny wetness is there in the dark coat, all around a wound just above the right foreleg.

The growl can barely be heard now. König's head is low and moving. He intends to take them both, and has only to decide which one he will bring down first. The lives of these terrible men are in my hands. I could run

41

*and leave them to die.*

*Another man appears just at the edge of the darkness.*
*I remember now, that was the first time I'd ever seen him.*
*It was Mr. Knight, I know that now. He shakes his head*
*no, and I realize what I must do.*

*I hold up my hand. "König, nein!"*
*He stops, only a few seconds, long enough for the men*
*to bound the few steps to the other side of the narrow*
*alley and inside a door. An instant behind them, König*
*hits the closed door with a heavy thud and paces back*
*and forth a long time before I can persuade him to leave.*
*Mr. Knight has already gone.*

## 1

Aindreas sat upright with a start, sharp traffic sounds all around him. He got to his feet, wiped the saliva from his chin, and walked toward his East Market Street delivery location. He felt stiff, sore and the sunlight hurt his eyes, so he walked through the market houses along his way. A brisk trade went on in the produce stalls as well as at the meat and fish counters. Ladies and gentlemen, servants and farmers, hucksters—they had all turned up to play their parts in the lively bustle and bargain that civilized custom required.

"These're good…you want me to weigh 'em?"

"Nineteen cents a dozen, since you've got a bag."

"No ma'am, we don't have none of those."

"Fifteen cents a pound—seventeen if you want me to cut it."

Aindreas listened also to the silence. The fish on the ice fixed him in frozen stares, dark rivulets ran in low places beneath dripping red slabs of beef and pork, and the only birds in the air were strung up by their feet, their wings bound with twine. He walked faster, out into the sunlight, having noted all the requirements of civilized custom he could stand for one day.

After he delivered the invoice to the tobacco shop on East Market, Aindreas altered his return route so he could go by the T&J Arterburn Negro Depot on First Street and, a block farther, by Matt Garrison's Slave Pen. He hoped Isaac hadn't lost faith in him. After all, he had promised to get information about the prices being paid for slaves, but he hadn't been able to attend any actual sales. Every time he had gone to the pens, he had been told there would be another sale "next Thursday noon," or some other time when he couldn't be there. This day turned out to be no different, and neither of the pens had any sales scheduled.

Disappointed, Aindreas plodded in the direction of his other delivery. Passing the courthouse, he couldn't fail to notice a mass of people, maybe fifty or more, milling around the southwest corner of the lot. Many of them were well dressed, like patrons in a theater line.

Inside the county clerk's office, Aindreas handed the tax bill and the money to the man behind the counter. "What's going on out there in the yard, sir?" Aindreas asked.

"They're waiting for the master commissioner to start the courthouse sale...to settle an estate, I think."

"Will they sell any slaves?"

The clerk stamped the bill and winked. "You look a little young to be buying a slave, sonny, but I do believe they will."

Aindreas hurried outside and worked his way to the center of the crowd. Within moments, the sheriff led a small group of Negroes into the cleared area and made them stand near a table, three adults and two children. Aindreas moved on to the front of the crowd and sat down on the grass. A heavy man wearing a hammer-tail coat stood in the open area in the center. He joked with people in the crowd and fanned his florid face with a broad-brimmed hat.

The sheriff rapped the table with a mallet. "Let's quiet down, ladies and gentlemen."

The heavy man pushed the hat to the back of his head and began to speak. "I'm Tad Englender, the master commissioner of the Jefferson Circuit Court, and this sale involves the Estate of Horace Spencer," he announced. He sounded very official. "There's personal property and real property to be disposed of. I intend to get right to it, but first we have to get one item of business for the county out of the way."

His thumbs hooked under his suspenders, Englender paced in front of the crowd. "Some of you are dealers and traders, or maybe you've read the public notices. For those of you who don't know about such proceedings, any sale is on a credit of sixty days, the buyer to give bond with approved security. Sheriff, bring that buck on over here."

A short Negro man, his gaze downward, shuffled forward in leg irons. His shirt was open, and his pants were held up by a rope belt.

"Ladies and gentlemen," the commissioner said, "this is *Jolly*." A few in the audience laughed.

"He ran away from Mississippi, and the sheriff caught him here in Jefferson County," Englender continued. "We tried to contact the owner but didn't get a response. The county has kept ole Jolly for six months now and that's about long enough. We're going to get our costs back." The master commissioner rubbed his hands together in a sort of glee. "Sheriff, strip off his shirt."

At a touch of the sheriff's cane, the Negro quickly removed his shirt. The crowd appraised his well-muscled upper body and some craned their necks, apparently looking for lash scars. The black man stared back at the crowd, his eyes slits of wariness.

Englender shifted the rhythm of his words to a sort of singsong. "All right, we have this buck, Jolly. Twenty-three years old, he tells us. Fine constitution—meant to do hard work—and it looks like the vinegar has been pretty well knocked out of him. Let's start at five-hundred dollars."

The traders in the crowd proceeded cautiously, the bids usually raising the figure no more than twenty-five dollars. While the bidding continued, Aindreas scanned the semicircle of people around the table. Startled, he recognized the tall, red-haired man. It was Cooper, the slave-trader. He was holding one arm close to his side, his hand wrapped in a heavy bandage, and his face was bruised and discolored. Someone was with him, but it wasn't the same person Aindreas had seen on the *Ben Franklin*. There had been talk around town that several slaves had escaped on that trip downriver. Aindreas hadn't seen Captain Workman for weeks and wondered whether he or Jack Graham had anything to do with it.

A trader from out of town eventually bought the black man called Jolly for nine hundred and fifty dollars. The Negroes who had waited in the rear were prodded forward by a deputy. An old man came first, tall and gray, dignified. A young woman followed with two young boys, five or six years old, hanging close to her.

The commissioner continued, "Now, ladies and gentlemen...the Spencer estate. We'll dispose of the personal property first, then the real property. The sheriff will have the furniture in here in just a few minutes. I must tell you that the survivors of the decedent requested that these Negroes be sold as a group, as a family. But I see my first duty as being to the creditors. I'll hear bids on them as a group and then as individuals, and I'm going to sell this property the way that makes the most money."

Someone in the crowd yelled out, "Tad, that is admirable, and not one thought about your own commissions."

Raucous laughter erupted. The commissioner rolled his eyes, and the Negro woman pulled the children closer to her.

Englender resumed. "First, we have old Nap. Step on up here, Nap. He's fifty-eight years old...at least that's what they tell me."

More guffawing from the crowd.

"A house servant, stronger than he looks," the commissioner said.

The old man stepped back.

"Then we've got a twenty-one-year-old wench, Josephine, Nap's daughter. She cooks, has worked as a field hand and around the house. Good health and, as you see, she can make children."

The sheriff gestured with his cane. The two boys looked up at their mother before finally stepping forward. "Last, we've got these two likely young niggers: Henry, seven years old, and little Nap, five," said Englender.

The bidding began. The commissioner seemed to enjoy his work and kept a running line of jokes going through the process. True to his word, he first took bids on the group and then on the individuals. It ended quickly. Old Nap went for two-hundred dollars to a local man. A Lexington couple bought Josephine for eight-hundred and fifty dollars, and Red Cooper bought the two boys for four hundred dollars each.

There was no time for words. The sheriff and his deputies moved in and separated the family. Nap's expression didn't change; he stood tall, resigned. The sheriff took hold of the young woman's arm. Her limbs were jerking as if she were a marionette, and she began to screech. Two deputies wrestled her to the ground.

Aindreas felt sick and his right eye began twitching. He edged away through the crowd and finally reached the open. He walked faster and faster and then ran, trying to outdistance the screeching that he could still hear. With the urgency of a thief, he fled between the wagons and carriages and down the middle of Jefferson Street.

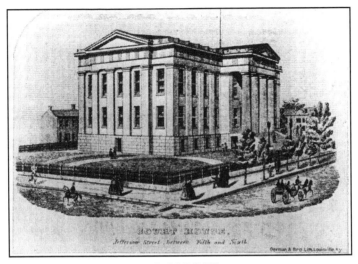

COURT HOUSE

Aindreas sat in the corner of the office dejected but at least glad to rest his legs. Some of the office employees of Cawthon's Furniture were gathered near the front of the chief clerk's desk. Their voices were low at first, but the words became progressively more heated. Last week during the magistrates' election, the German Sag Nichts, the Say Nothings, had taken control of the polls in the First and Second Wards. Brawls had erupted in the streets. The candidates of the American Party, the Know-Nothings, won overwhelmingly, but they certainly hadn't done at all well in the First and Second Wards. The junior clerks disagreed as to which candidates should have won.

The chief clerk ended the discussion. He said, "Everyone seems to have an opinion, but I have no use for all this talk. One thing I do know: Louisville doesn't have polling places for everybody to vote, and unless the city council takes care of this, we could have some real trouble one of these days." With that, he motioned the rest of the clerks back to work with a wave of his hand. "But the most important thing you young men should learn is that business people shouldn't waste their time talking about politics," he chided them. "It's filthy, and you shouldn't soil your minds with it."

2

That afternoon, Aindreas carried a letter bound for Lexington to the post office in the ground floor of the customs house on Green Street. When he came back out the front door, a dozen people or more stood talking in a circle. They weren't dressed like laboring folks and they took up the whole sidewalk, paying no attention to those who had to walk out into the street to get around them.

Aindreas paused and listened.

A prosperous-looking couple held center stage, the man cradling a hat box against his middle. He made little nods, and periodic "hmmmf" sounds of approval came from him while the woman spoke. She closed a small fan and tapped it in her palm for emphasis. "…and to come back to Louisville after six years and find it overrun with these people, and to hear all those wild and radical things and dangerous abolitionist talk from these Catholics and other foreigners," she said. "We're just heart-broken." The woman's husband nodded vigorously at that, and others murmured assent.

A short, round man responded. "I'm not a radical, madam—not even a Catholic. But the way I hear it, the abolitionists claim that slavery has to stop because it's simply wrong. Does this make them dangerous?"

It seemed an awkward moment. The fan lady looked at her husband, as if at a loss to respond. A gentleman stepped in to stand close beside her. Silence, as quiet as thought cloaked the crowd; no one looked directly at the man or seemed to pay any particular notice to him, but his presence settled over them all. Aindreas had seen this gentleman around town from time to time, though he'd never looked at him closely until that instant. A

48

gaunt fellow, tall and loosely constructed. Aindreas had always thought of him by a nickname...*Mr. Bones.* This man didn't perspire in the heat, and his brown broadcloth dress coat looked immaculate. His nearly white hair was parted in the middle, old-style; this, and his fair complexion and pale blue eyes gave him a ghostly aura; those eyes, expressive and grave, seemed at odds with stingy thin lips and a very wide mouth. *Could he manage a whistle with such a mouth?* Tied off with a heavy black neck cloth, his tall, starched collar touched his ears, and his boots had a soft shine. In short, he seemed the kind of man Squire Travis had wanted to be, pretended to be, all his life, and also the kind of man Aindreas's grandfather would have called "an elegant bag of bones."

The round man regained his voice. "I meant no offense, madam, but many members of Congress themselves say slavery no longer has a place in this country. Are these people also dangerous?"

A man in shirtsleeves, maybe a shop-keeper, patted the round man on the back and said, "I agree with your sentiment, by God!"

The fan lady didn't reply.

Mr. Bones took a pair of spectacles from his coat pocket as if to put them on, but he only held them. There was a tremor in his hands, but his voice was clear and expressive. "These abolitionists. With them the rights of property are nothing. The incontestable powers of the states mean nothing. Civil war, a dissolution of the union, and the overthrow of a government mean nothing! Is that what you want?" Mr. Bones paused. "Is it?"

The fan lady smiled comfortably, along with others in the gathering. Aindreas could almost hear the minds changing, as clearly as if they had said in chorus, *"Yes, such people are dangerous, and they would bring us all down."*

Aindreas felt uneasy. Wasn't someone going to say that one person just didn't have any right to own another person?

The round man responded, his voice less ringing than before. "No matter what you say about danger, you have to agree that Congress has the right and the power to get rid of slavery if it wants to."

Mr. Bones pointed with his spectacles. "The powers of the Congress are few, my friend, cautiously limited. Above all, it has no power over slavery." Bones walked now into the vacant space at the very center of the group, his eyes boring into the shopkeeper. "The Constitution of the United States never could have been formed upon the principle of giving the government in Washington power to abolish slavery at its pleasure, and the Constitution couldn't be continued for a single day if the federal government tried to claim that power."

A murmur of approval rippled through those listening. The shopkeeper looked down. Had he bowed his head?

The round man hadn't given up. He said, "I can't believe there is one of you here in 1855, for God's sake, who believes a human should be a piece of property."

Mr. Bones smiled wanly. "That *is* property, my man, which the law declares *to be* property," he responded, his patience as weighty as granite. "And don't you know that kind of property is diffused throughout all classes and conditions of society? Owned by widows and orphans, by the aged and infirm, as well as the sound and vigorous?"

The round man wagged his head miserably. He gave a hollow laugh and mumbled. "So much for notions of liberty."

His long hands spread in placation, Mr. Bones moved so smoothly he seemed to glide toward the round man. Aindreas felt an arm go around his shoulder; perhaps it was so with every shoulder there, and Bones's marvelous voice grew soft as a lute. "The searcher of all hearts knows that every beat of mine is high and strong in the cause of civil liberty. Wherever it is safe and predictable, I desire to see every portion of the human family in the enjoyment of it." The voice seemed to come even closer now to Aindreas's ear, and he shivered at the utter charm of it. Even passers-by who had stopped now leaned in to listen. Bones said, softer still, "But I prefer the liberty of my own country to that of any other people. And the liberty of my own race to that of any other race."

The round man, then the shopkeeper turned and walked away separately and alone. The majority broke up in satisfied, amiable partings. Some of the crowd drifted into the customs house. Mr. Bones slipped away with the rest, and Aindreas wondered about him into the afternoon.

3

As Aindreas walked on Seventh Street, a bell began clanging loudly. "Fire!" someone shouted. The street suddenly came alive. People came out of shops and houses. Aindreas hurried with the rest of them toward the next intersection.

He spotted fire-fighting equipment when he got to Market Street. It was the German company; he knew them by sight. At one time or another, like most other boys, he had run with the machines of all eight volunteer fire companies serving the city. Thrilling races occurred when one company would try to pass another on the way to a fire.

A fancy hose carriage led the way this time, a hook-and-ladder wagon close behind. There wouldn't be any race between these two; members of the same company never competed with each other. Ten men or more pulled each piece of equipment, some holding onto the tongue of the wagon, while others pulled on long hemp ropes strung out in front. Wheeling fast toward Eighth Street, less than half-a-block away, they must have been close to their limits with that kind of speed. Aindreas began running alongside them. It felt good. He looked up ahead, searching for smoke, for some kind of direction, and for the next water source.

Usually, the first unit arriving at a fire put their intake hose into the nearest water supply, pumped the engine box full, and gave their output hose to the next unit to pass the water along and they, in turn, would pump it to the next unit. Sometimes these volunteer fire companies tried to "wash" another unit, to pump them so much water that the unit couldn't keep pace, and its engine box would overflow. A company felt disgraced if another one washed their hose unit or passed them on the way to a fire.

Aindreas thoroughly enjoyed the prospect of watching another pumping duel, but by the time they all passed Eighth Street, something didn't seem right. Both wagons slowed to a stop, and the firemen looked around in confusion. No sign of a fire. It must have been a false alarm. Quickly, a howling wave of men swarmed out of a mid-block alley and attacked the German fire company. Aindreas recognized the blue helmets of the Relief Company among them and the uniforms of the Rescue Company. He'd heard about bad blood between the Germans and the Relief Company, but this was looking like much more than a brawl between rivals.

"Kill that kraut bastard!" someone yelled. "Chase those stinking Catholics outta the state.

*Know-Nothings.*

The trap had been laid well, and the fight turned out to be uneven, savage. One German after another went down, with two or more on him. Several tried to run, but Aindreas didn't see anyone get away. Some of the mob turned their attention to the Germans' equipment and went at it with hammers and axes. They knocked the whale-oil torches off the wagons and broke the oaken brake handles on each end of the hose carriage. Others unrolled the brass-riveted leather horses and chopped off the wheels. Piece by piece, they smashed the polished wood surfaces, the underside, and the engine box of the hose carriage, while laughing onlookers carried off axes, chains, buckets, and the wall and ceiling hooks.

The crowd that formed around the melee cheered it all, even the most brutal acts. When it ended, only a few bloodied Germans could stagger about. The rest lay broken in the street. The victorious mob, howling victory, pulled the battered equipment down toward the river. First the hose carriage, then the hook-and-ladder wagon clattered over the cobblestones into the water. The crowd ranted and cheered for a moment or two, then headed back toward Market Street in celebration.

Alone, Aindreas remained on the river bank. No matter where he went or what he did, he couldn't seem to get away from this madness. The debris swirled in the muddy water at river's edge. One by one, the shattered pieces drifted into the current. For long moments he could make out the shape of the ladders as they floated downstream.

# 4

Isaac and his family had gotten home from church only a short time ago. Every Sunday, he and Tempie took the children to the Second Colored Baptist Church over on Fifth Street. Hard as it was to believe, Squire Travis had never told them they couldn't. They had started going there a little over a year ago, soon after Aaron was born. Isaac wondered these days and nights whether he could give up such precious times.

At church, Tempie had told him, "I better tend to Miss Travis's flowers, get some water on 'em. They dry out...be hell to pay. If it don't rain soon, they may be bad anyway. Pump water won't keep up big roses like that. Unh-uh."

Not a cloud in the sky. Little Aaron rolled around in the grass, under the eye of four-year-old Sarah. Isaac gazed toward the Travis house, where Tempie was working at the soil around the rose bushes below the parlor windows; she moved duck-like, without rising, from one bush to the next. Isaac smiled. *Got to have good legs to do that.*

Satisfied that he'd split enough wood for the week, Isaac stopped and wiped his forehead with the back of his hand. He stacked some pieces by the hearth and came outside for more when he saw Aindreas trudging toward the cabin.

"You go to church this morning, young man?" Isaac asked with mock severity

"Yep, I've been waiting for you to get back. Your church go all day?"

Isaac laughed. "Oh, I wish it did, Andrew. When the preacher lines out the songs and we all together, I'm happy." He rolled his eyes. "Now, Tempie say she wants a dress for church. This boy I know, Calvin—his mistress lady gave Calvin's wife some clothes, more than she need. He's goin' out with a pushcart this evening to make a little money. If he got a dress for Tempie, I'm gonna buy it. Want to come along later over to the church and help me make up my mind?"

"I can't. Mrs. Travis invited Miss Flowers for a visit, and I'm supposed to go along," said Aindreas, pleased that his friend would have asked such a thing. "But I do need to talk to you," he added quickly.

Isaac stooped to pick up more wood. He glanced toward the Travis house. A familiar figure stood at the back window. After a time, perhaps satisfied that Mrs. Travis was more worried about her roses than his talk with Aindreas, he moved toward the cabin door and motioned Aindreas to follow.

They sat down at the table. Some time had passed since Aindreas had been in the cabin, but it hadn't changed. A crude bench, the only other piece of furniture, stood near the hearth. Straw ticks and rough blankets in the far corner lay on wood pallets, just inches off the floor. Jars and gourds, some full, some empty, were piled along one wall, and a small mirror hung on another.

Isaac's voice sounded anxious. "You find a sale?"

Aindreas nodded. "At the courthouse," he said.

Before he could say any more, Isaac got out of his chair and walked over to the hearth. He picked up a long wooden spoon and absently stirred the supper pot hanging over the embers. "Sometimes I think back when I first came here. You know, I near put a whole new floor in this place, scrap at a time. Ain't much, but it's better'n dirt."

Aindreas looked down at the planks and smaller pieces that

made the floor a patchwork of age and decay. If any man on earth deserved more than this, Isaac White was that man.

Isaac returned to the table. "Tell me what you heard," he said.

"They sold five. The first was a runaway, then an old man, his daughter, and her two boys."

Isaac sat silent, his arms folded.

Aindreas felt a drop of sweat running down his forehead. The dread of this moment had stuck on him so tight that he hadn't slept for more than an hour the night before. He idly stared at Isaac and Tempie's household belongings: two tallow candles, a few knives and spoons on a stack of four plates, and a lamp with a spidery crack down the glass chimney.

"They was kinda a family, like us," Isaac said. "Did they try to sell 'em in a bunch?"

Aindreas nodded sadly. "I don't think they tried very hard."

"Was they split up right there on the spot?"

Squirming in his chair, Aindreas ran his hand through his hair. "Don't know, Isaac. I had to leave quick as I heard the prices."

Isaac raised his eyebrows, as though he might have doubted this last thing Aindreas had said. "How much they bring?" Isaac asked.

"Some local man bid two-hundred dollars on the old man. The daughter brought eight-hundred-fifty, and the two boys four hundred each."

Isaac's lips moved silently as he quickly added figures on the table with his finger. He winced at the invisible total. "Near twice what I got," he said. "You think me and Tempie, the children bring that much?"

"I've figured some on it, Isaac, and can't see how it would hardly be less. I think Tempie would bring as much money as that woman, and Sarah and Aaron maybe less than those two boys—but you'd bring a lot more than that old man."

Isaac paced back and forth from the doorway to the stack of gourds. He tapped his forehead again and again with the fingers of his good hand. "One-thousand eight-hundred and fifty. Save all I could, but I ain't got half of that. What am I goin' to do, my God, what?"

Isaac swiped his palm across the table, as if to wipe out the figures. Aindreas rose from his seat to go. It felt bad to see Isaac in such a state.

"I'll get some help somewhere, Isaac," Aindreas said, and put his hand over his heart. "I promise. Just don't get the squire or Mrs. Travis down on you."

1

That afternoon, Aindreas lay in bed, miserable. He looked out the window once and saw König napping. It might have helped to talk with Captain Workman and Jack Graham about Isaac's problem. But most of all, Aindreas wanted to see Mr. Knight again—to tell him about his mother, to ask what to do about Isaac, to demand that he try to explain the whispers that seemed to be everywhere, and maybe even to ask that he explain "Sam."

His parents had gone out for a walk, and Michael and Kirsty had been gone for almost all day. Aindreas knew that he needed to get cleaned up, but it was hard to get moving. His mind wandered as he lay there and finally his thoughts settled on Miss Flowers, once his teacher at the Fifth Ward School; how she had cried when he told her he had taken the job at Cawthon's Furniture and probably wouldn't be going any further in school. She'd probably ask him again tonight whether he was going back to school in the fall term. It came up nearly every time he saw her.

The family needed any money he could make, but he wished he could do something that would please Miss Flowers. Her feelings were important to him. He didn't feel that way just because of what she had taught him from books. She might have

57

come out of a book herself—maybe one of those goddesses.

Aindreas finally rose from the bed. A wipe off with water and a coarse towel wouldn't do this night. He pumped and carried half-a-dozen bucketful's of water to the stone sink in the kitchen, then sliced curly shavings from the heavy yellow soap his mother saved for washing clothes. Maybe she wouldn't notice.

He stared down into the sink water, his mind going back to that time last winter when they didn't have any money to buy soap. His mother was desperate, and decided she would have to make enough soap to tide them over.

*A cousin had told them fat was there for the taking at the small dams across Beargrass Creek. Aindreas agreed to go there with Michael, somehow not knowing that the owners of the slaughterhouses and tanneries had those dams built, and these men thought of the creek as simply a drain to carry away the offal.*

*On an early Sunday morning, he and Michael rode to the creek in a friend's delivery wagon. They found a clear, level place for the wagon and no one chased them off. Ice had crusted here and there on the creek. They saw a seam of whitish fat bobbing along the edge of a dam, so he and Michael waded in. The water came up to his chest and once he nearly fell. The creek water didn't feel like water; foul and sluggish, it clung to him, chilled him and stung like pins sticking in him. His legs brushed against things under the surface. When he couldn't stand the smell of it any longer he gasped a few times through his mouth and could taste the rottenness.*

*They ladled globs of fat into the tubs they had carried there and finally rode home shivering in the wagon. His mother knew how to render their find and she did make soap, but he vowed never to go near that creek again.*

He stared. The water in the sink looked pure and clear, yet he hesitated. His shirt covered him nearly to his knees, but what if someone walked in? They would see him without anything on. The fear of such an event had grown on him over time. Not only his own pale, skinny body he disliked, but the notion of anybody's being naked... even in a holy picture. He gritted his teeth and pulled off his shirt, then scrubbed and splashed in such a frenzy that it was necessary to mop the floor after he'd washed and was back in his shirt. Though his eyes burned and his skin felt raw and smelled of strong soap; he felt clean enough to see Miss Flowers.

Aindreas kept a watch on the outside stairs from the kitchen window. Michael had come in, but his parents didn't return until past six o'clock. His father smelled of whiskey. Mother said she wasn't feeling well and went to lie down.

2

The next time Aindreas looked out the window, he saw Miss Flowers waiting.

"There you are, Andrew," she said, her voice sounding like music. "Shall we go call on Mrs. Travis?"

His heart actually did beat faster when she talked to him. "Going with Miss Flowers," he said over his shoulder, and grabbed his cap on the way out the door.

Miss Flowers was holding a small purse in her hands; she might well have been waiting for a well-dressed gentleman in the lobby of Mozart Hall. Her long, auburn hair, parted in the middle, had been drawn back with a strip of white lace, and the collar ringing her flowered dress had more lace. She wore no jewelry other than a slender silver bracelet. The mere sight of this beautiful green-eyed woman of twenty-four years, still taller than he, filled him full. Aindreas pulled on his cap and quickly rubbed the toe of one boot and then the other on the backs of his trouser legs. Blanche Flowers looked at him approvingly. She rested her hand lightly on his arm as they walked past Isaac's cabin and around to the front of the Travis house. Aindreas held his breath when they passed near the rose bushes.

Tempie wiped her hands on her apron when she answered the door. She looked surprised to see Aindreas waiting on the porch.

Arms outstretched, Mrs. Travis appeared in the hall, a small woman in hanging ribbons and curls. "Hello, Blanche," she cooed. "We *never* see you anymore." Emily Travis had a pretty, round face, but the lines around her mouth made even a smile seem hard. Her kiss brushed past Miss Flowers's cheek. Aindreas could read her lips when she whispered: "Thanks for bringing the ragamuffin along."

Miss Flowers looked away from her and spoke to Tempie. It occurred to Aindreas, when Mrs. Travis turned toward him, that his corduroys might not be clean enough. He took off his cap and inclined his head slightly.

"How nice," Mrs. Travis said. "Most young men don't make their manners any more. Andrew, is it?"

"Yes, ma'am."

"We've seen you with Isaac. What *do* you all find to talk about so much?"

Behind Mrs. Travis, Tempie looked tense. "Just talk, ma'am… maybe the weather…maybe anything," Aindreas said. "We're friends."

"Oh?" Her eyebrows were more sharply arched than church doors. "Well, we don't want to keep him from his work, do we?"

"No, ma'am."

Mrs. Travis's attention shifted when Miss Flowers volunteered how much she admired the oriental rug in the entry hall. Never having been inside the house, Aindreas looked around. He gaped at the tall, elegant case clock in the corner and the lamps along the papered walls. The entire place was ablaze with light.

For an instant, Mrs. Travis seemed undecided whether she wanted to send Aindreas to the kitchen with Tempie or take him on down the hall with Miss Flowers into the parlor. Squire Travis folded his newspaper, rose from his chair and came forward to greet them. Such a dandy figure in his close-cut jacket and a buttoned vest made more prominent by his rooster-like walk. The squire's aim was better than his wife's; he actually did kiss Miss Flowers's hand.

Aindreas had not been inside a room like this for any longer than it took to hand someone a parcel. Uneasy, he sat down on a footstool. Large mirrors reflected the light of four lamps and the parlor seemed as bright as the entry hall. Aindreas thought of his father's sitting close by their lamp at home, reading at the kitchen table. Tempie put down a tray of refreshments covered with a napkin, then returned to the kitchen. Mrs. Travis identified portraits on the walls for Blanche. The two of them made low, clucking sounds over the mourning pictures of Mrs. Travis's parents, done by the squire's niece.

They were talking so fast that Aindreas, drowsy and thirsty, didn't follow the conversation entirely. The soft sound of Mrs. Travis's voice was interrupted now and again by the deep gruff of her husband's. Squire Travis shifted from one pose to another, and he seemed to be flirting with Miss Flowers. He talked and laughed close to her ear and touched her shoulder several times.

The squire reminded Aindreas of someone. Who could it be? A velvet collar set off his jacket, and pearl buttons adorned his vest. He wore loud plaid trousers, a shirt with a turned-down collar, and a satin cravat tied in a thick, wadded bow. Mr. Knight and Mr. Bones both dressed oddly, but Squire Travis wasn't like either of them. Nor did he resemble Captain Workman or any of the men at Cawthon's. Certainly, he didn't look like Aindreas's father. *Red Cooper!* The squire reminded him of the slave trader

Cooper. *And with a hammer-tail coat,* Aindreas thought, smothering a laugh, *the squire might even have made a master commissioner.*

"Well, ladies," the squire said after a time, "let's see what Tempie made to tempt our appetites."

Mrs. Travis busied herself with the tea and cakes on the tray and then finally addressed Aindreas. "We're having a party in a few weeks, and I have so many things to do," she said. "I'm never able to get the kind of help I need. Miss Flowers mentioned that you were a bright boy, and I asked her to bring you along tonight."

Miss Flowers ruffled his hair. "And since Johnny is out of town, I wanted you to escort me."

Aindreas peevishly turned his head away. The notion of Miss Flowers being married to anyone, even an agreeable sort like Johnny Flowers, filled him with anger.

Smiling thinly, Mrs. Travis kept her eyes on him. "Well," she resumed, "we have invitations for friends in town and I need someone reliable to deliver them. Could you do that?"

"Yes, ma'am. I know my way around town."

"Very well. I have some jars of string beans and corn that Tempie helped me put up that Mrs.—that your mother might want." She poured the tea and put several cakes around the cup on his saucer. "Here, don't spill this," she cautioned.

The cup and saucer were decorated with oriental scenes. Aindreas had never seen such dishes. He surveyed the parlor again, a room the chief clerk at Cawthon's might have described as "fancy." Most of the furniture looked like mahogany, and a square pianoforte stood near the back window. Expensive-looking engravings and knickknacks were on every wall and wedged into every corner. Satin covered the sofa and chairs and he silently thanked heaven he had sat down on a stool with heavy, dark material. Or had Mrs. Travis directed him there?

"What a lovely jacket," Miss Flowers exclaimed.

"Oh, this old thing," said Mrs. Travis. She made a pouting expression, then turned back and forth, putting the hanging ribbons into motion. "I just make do with what I have. Squire never takes me to the places I need to shop."

"Now, Emily, don't be telling our lovely young friend how deprived you are," Squire Travis said, and slipped his arm around his wife's waist. "Why don't we have some music?"

Mrs. Travis smiled. She seemed to brighten with attention more than anything else.

*Earlier, Isaac had decided to surprise Tempie, who would be serving at the Travis home for several hours. He took the children along to look at the clothes Calvin wanted to sell. Isaac went north on Fifth Street, carrying Aaron, who made talk sounds the whole way. Sarah walked beside Isaac, solemn in the dark.*

*"Maybe we'll buy your mamma a dress," he told her.*

*Calvin told him that morning he would bring his pushcart to the front of the church. Isaac didn't see Calvin yet, but he heard something and glanced back over his shoulder.*

3

Mrs. Travis played several songs, including *Old Folks At Home,* and sang in a tremulous voice. She flushed at compliments from Miss Flowers and the squire. Tempie brought another plate of small cakes and cookies and refilled the cups. As she started back to the kitchen, she gave Aindreas a sly wink.

Squire Travis took a large envelope from a cabinet and handed it to his wife. Mrs. Travis took out the papers and examined them. "Oh," her voice sounding as excited as a young girl, "it's a new Stephen Foster song."

The squire spread the papers before his wife on the music desk. He glanced at Miss Flowers and said, "It's called *Dreaming the Happy Hours Away.* Won't be for sale to the public for several months."

Mrs. Travis played a few chords uncertainly, then struggled with the beginning again. She motioned for Miss Flowers to sit on the bench beside her and tried once more to get the opening notes right. Flustered, she said, "I don't know what in the world is wrong with me tonight." She turned to Miss Flowers. "Blanche, do you think you could play this for us?"

*Isaac noticed the two white men who had stopped across the street. They stood idly, smoking cigars. He and the children got up from the curb as Calvin approached with a pushcart piled high with clothing. The white men came across the street, toward the wagon. They wore suits, like storekeepers. The tall and heavy one wore his hat pulled down near his eyes. The other had mutton-chop side-whiskers. He spoke first, to Calvin. "What's your name, and where'd you get all this?"*

*Calvin whipped off his cap. "I'm Calvin, sir," he said. "This stuff belongs to my wife. Our mistress gave them to us."*

*The man with the side-whiskers sorted through the garments. He picked up a nightgown and held it up against his body, then turned toward the other man. They both laughed. He tossed the gown on the wagon and turned to Isaac and the children. "Who are you, boy?" he asked. "You another married man?"*

Apparently, no one in the room had any prior notion that Miss Flowers could play so well. Aindreas sat mesmerized. She sight-read the melody through with very little hesitation, then played it a second time with sureness. Something like a smile froze on Mrs. Travis's face. The squire clasped his hands behind his back. His mouth slightly open, he looked utterly smitten. Tempie lingered in the doorway as Blanche Flowers sang in a fine clear voice.

Soft is her slumber…Thoughts bright and free…
Dance through her dreams…Like gushing mel-o-dy…

Aindreas's father sat alone in the kitchen, drinking beer. His wife had gone to bed. He doubted that she waited in anticipation for him. He could faintly hear the music through the Travis parlor windows.

*Now, Calvin looked frightened. He told the white men he would just as soon take his cart on home. Isaac put Aaron in Sarah's care and separated himself from the children. He felt angry with himself for having them there, worried that Sarah might not remember the way home if she had to.*

*The tall, heavy man backed Calvin between the handles of the cart. "Now, I want to know what made you two think you could sneak around the streets all night and do whatever comes into your heads."*

*Calvin mumbled the start of an apology, but the white man cut him off. "And I don't give a damn if you are some kind of 'free Blacks,' or whatever you call yourselves," he said. "You're not going to be out here in the city streets after dark."*

*Calvin nodded, "Yes, sir. Time to be gettin' on home."*

*The man with the side-whiskers flipped open a wallet to show his badge. He grabbed Isaac's wrist. "How about you, boy? Time for you to be gettin' on?"*

*Isaac fought against his rage. This was wrong. Wrong, right in front of the church he had been in that very morning—and for an instant he forgot one or two of the lessons of his lifetime. "We ain't doing no harm," he said, "I come to buy a dress for Tempie... my own money, my own business."*

Aindreas flushed with pride at Miss Flowers's voice, the purity of it. If only he could have the kind of dreams she was singing about.

She finished the closing lines of the song in a strong, musical voice, "in visions bright redeeming…The fleeting joys of day…"

*"You Goddamn nigger," the policeman snarled. "Empty out your pockets right here on this cart."*

"Come where my love lies dreaming…"

*The blow smashed into Isaac's face, knocking him against the wheel of the pushcart. Sarah whimpered. The second man grabbed Isaac's arm.*

"Dre..a..ming the happy hours away."

4

Aindreas's father and brother were sitting at the kitchen table finishing their beer when Aindreas came in and sat down.

Michael punched him on the arm. "You and your lady friend have a nice time?"

Aindreas didn't respond.

"Seems like," his brother went on, feigning a leer, "she'd want somebody grown up with her…a fine woman like that."

Joseph Rivers said, "You watch your mouth, boyo."

Michael glowered, then left the table.

The two of them sat in silence for a moment. Aindreas felt odd sitting there alone with his father, who had always seemed to avoid him.

"She after you to go back to school?" Joseph Rivers asked.

"Yes."

"You want to go?"

"If I can work, too, and make some money," said Aindreas. "I won't do anything until I ask you about it first."

This seemed to please Joseph Rivers. Then his smile faded. Red showed in his eyes, but he didn't slur his words like he did when he had too much to drink. "I should go on to bed, but I wanted to make sure your mother was asleep first," Joseph Rivers said, absently rubbing his face. "We had a row this afternoon. I forgot it's about the time of year for her to start acting up again."

"About what?"

"Marcus."

"Oh." Aindreas couldn't think of anything more to say. He wondered why Da had decided to talk to him now, especially about Uncle Marcus. The only cause Aindreas could imagine was that his father needed someone, anyone, to listen.

"You're too young to remember all that happened," Joseph Rivers said, then swallowed the very last of his beer. "You and Kirsty went to live with your Aunt Mary for a few weeks. It's been five years since he died, but some things don't ever end."

Aindreas dipped some water for himself, then filled a cup for his father. It occurred to him this might be the time would find out why the subject of Marcus was nearly a forbidden one, one that almost never came up.

"If there was but a drop of whiskey in this cup...ah, what a terrible waste of water this would be," his father said, then took a drink and grimaced. "You know, I always joshed your mother about her bunch of Scots. She was a McFate, remember...country people that was your mother's family." Never had his father sounded fond of Aunt Mary and Aunt Margaret.

Aindreas decided to risk a question. "Did you get along with her family back then?" he asked.

"Her father had died before I met her," replied Joseph Rivers. "Her mother stayed on that little farm. Dorrie had two sisters,

Mary and Margaret, and this…this little brother. He was only four years old when I married your mother.

"Uncle Marcus," Aindreas said.

"Marcus McFate. Where in hell did they come up with a name like that?" Joseph Rivers's face darkened. "Sounds like a man who threw dice at the foot of the Cross."

"You never liked him, did you, Da?" Aindreas said softly.

Joe Rivers got up and paced, hands in his pockets. "I guess I hated him before the end," he said bitterly. "Marcus wasn't the common cut of cloth, that's for certain."

Aindreas smiled at a picture in his mind. "What I remember about Uncle Marcus, it's mostly about how big around he was."

His father's tone quickly changed again. "Short and stout as a post," said Joseph Rivers, sounding almost sentimental.

Aindreas remembered a face his uncle used to make, and laughed. Joseph Rivers smiled and sat back down at the table. They began to talk rapidly, exchanging small memories. Giddiness nearly overtook Aindreas when he realized that his father was talking to him as if he were a real person.

"Did he always wear eyeglasses?" Aindreas asked.

"Yeah. He called them *specs.*"

"And he always had a book with him."

"A book? He'd carry three or four, some of 'em in Latin."

"I remember Mother always tried to cook something extra when he would come to see us."

"Lord, you couldn't keep food on the table," Joseph Rivers declared. "Once, he ate the most of a turkey somebody gave us for Christmas."

Suddenly, without apparent cause, Joseph Rivers slammed the table hard with the heel of his hand; the very air in the room changed. He shook his head. "You see. Here he is again, the center of everything like he always was. We talk like he was some famous man and so does everyone who knew him, but he's dead, and he was barely eighteen years old when he died."

The muscles in Joseph Rivers's jaw rippled. "Your mother practically raised him. Fifteen years older, she was. Thought the sun rose in the morning with him. But I didn't feel like a father to him. I wanted no part of that."

Aindreas recalled feeling safer near Uncle Marcus than with anyone else. "Why did you hate him?"

"Because your mother acted closer to him than me," his father snarled. "Because he could tell you if it would rain and be right—because he knew more at age ten than I do now. Because I don't think he even cared for women, and they fell all over themselves around that fat little..." His voice quavered. "Because with a little luck he could have run the whole damn world, even though sometimes his right eye crossed and he drooled behind his handkerchief."

Aindreas winced. "Why didn't he run the world?"

"Cholera," Joseph Rivers said. "Over a hundred died on that one day." He rose from his chair and went to the cabinet. He took dishes out for no reason, wiped them with a towel, and began to order the shelves. "Marcus tutored in his rooms over near the university. Hottest day of the summer, that's when it happened. He'd been found on the floor that morning, they told us, but he got sicker and sicker as the day went on. That's the way it always worked, and I hope to God it never comes through here again, so you have to find out. When somebody got it, he'd start cramping. Once the diarrhea and vomiting began...it wouldn't stop until he died."

Aindreas looked down.

"Someone over at the university sent your mother a message. She went over there and stayed all afternoon. A doctor came, but he couldn't help. I got there toward the last, and I've never been worse scared than that, just being in that room as he was dying."

Aindreas watched his father at the cabinet carefully putting away each cup and plate. "I searched all over town, and they had run out of coffins," Joseph Rivers said hoarsely. "Insane fear got a lot of people down. I wasn't the only one. Damn priest didn't even come to say words over him. Dorrie went crazy, claimed I didn't care about what had happened. She said my fear hurt her, and that some things about Marcus I wouldn't ever know because I was too afraid to hear." Joseph Rivers covered his eyes with his hands. A big vein to the side of his neck stood out. "The landlord was screaming at us to get the body out of the building. Your mother wanted to hold a wake. I couldn't make her understand that I didn't want to take him back to where we lived. Nobody would've come anyway."

Joseph Rivers mopped at his sweating face with a ragged cloth. "It must have been four o'clock in the morning before I got hold of a wagon and a couple of men. Dorrie was still sitting in that stinking room. She had cleaned up the body and wouldn't let us touch him without a priest. She was screaming like a banshee, wouldn't stop. I had to hit her, had to pin her arms."

His shoulders sagged. The pause was so long that it seemed as if he might be finished, but he went on. "They sewed him up in the bedclothes. Dorrie and me rode beside him in the back of the wagon down to the cemetery. You know where it is. They had closed and chained the gates. A crowd of people stood out there crying and moaning. It seemed like Hell. Coffins lay piled up outside, some of 'em half open. The rest of the bodies had only been wrapped up in bundles. Three men from the cemetery took him from us. Your mother wouldn't look away, even when they swung him up on that pile like a sack of meal."

Joseph Rivers placed the last cup in place and closed the cabinet door, finished. His voice had become flat. "Father Quinn, from over on Fifth Street, had been there most of the night, and he said words over all of them. Cholera got him the next year, rest his soul. I told him Marcus's name. I didn't tell the Father how he

70

felt about the Church or any of the rest of it."

Joseph Rivers opened the bedroom door part way and peeked in. Apparently satisfied his wife had gone to sleep, he turned to Aindreas. "A fine woman, your mother, but she never forgave me. She thinks I'm a coward."

# 5

**Aindreas** lay half-asleep. Sometime in the night, he thought he heard voices from the kitchen. It had sounded like Tempie, of all people, and his mother. The voices stopped just before he drifted off into a bad dream that he couldn't quite remember after his father shook him awake the next morning. Aindreas felt surprised when a mug of tea and hot slices of bread were set in front of him at the table.

"Is Mother sick?" Aindreas asked, rising from his chair.

"Sit down, boy," said Joseph Rivers. "She went over to the cabin and ought to be back soon. Shouldn't be gone at all, but she told me when she left to be sure you ate somethin'."

"The cabin?"

"That damn Isaac musta got hurt."

Aindreas's mouth felt dry.

"I told you to sit down and I mean it," Joseph Rivers said harshly.

Overnight, things had gone back to the way they had been. His father was angry with him again. Aindreas tore off a piece of the heavy, dark bread and dunked it in the hot tea. No matter how much he chewed, the crust would break down to no less than sticky little wads

"What happened to Isaac?" asked Aindreas in as matter-of-fact tone as he could muster.

Joseph Rivers moved toward the door. "Here comes your mother now."

Aindreas watched Doireann Rivers walking slowly across the grass. Da took the rags and bottles from her at the door. She sat down at the table, and Aindreas poured her a cup of tea. Joseph Rivers lingered and seemed undecided whether or not to leave.

"Thanks for waitin', Joe," she said, and nodded at the plates. "I would've worried if the two of you had gone off without something in your stomach."

Joseph Rivers stroked her shoulder. Worry lines creased his face. She waved her hand and said, "None of that, now. I'm fine, and I'll lie back down as soon as you're gone."

Da leaned down and kissed her on the cheek. "Be on my way, then, machshla, only be fifteen minutes late if I hurry." He made a comic show of hitching up his trousers as he went out the door.

She smiled after him, then turned to Aindreas. "You need to hurry, too," she said, "but I know you're not going to be leaving until we talk a minute."

"What happened to Isaac?"

"He was...well, he was beaten up."

"Who did that?"

His mother only shook her head.

Aindreas fought against a sickness in his stomach. "Is he hurt bad?"

His mother pressed a hand to her side. Pale, she looked as if she might topple over. She sipped the tea and breathed deeply.

"I have to go back to bed and you'll be late, so I'll say this once and you listen: don't go over there now—you have to go to work. Do you hear me, Andrew?"

"Yes, ma'am."

She looked relieved. "Squire Travis will surely have the doctor come by and look at him."

Furious that such a thing could have happened, Aindreas wanted to leave, get outside and walk.

He kissed his mother on top of the head. She didn't look at

him but reached out and took his hand. "I know you're sick about this because Isaac means a lot to you," she said. "He's been hurt, but he won't throw up his hands. People who care hang on til they're done with it."

She reached behind Aindreas and pushed him. "Quarter till eight. You can still make it."

Once out the door, Aindreas began to run. If he kept an even pace, not too fast, he wouldn't be late. He consoled himself with the idea that he could see Isaac tonight. *What had his mother meant about people who care hanging on until they're done?*

1

By twelve o'clock, Aindreas had returned to the office from morning deliveries.

The chief clerk tossed an orange to him. "Eat that," he said, "and come on back to my desk in about twenty minutes."

At midday, along the side of the building where some of the office people usually ate and smoked, Aindreas and Tim squatted near the wall playing mumblety-peg and watching the comings and goings on Jefferson Street. Aindreas won two games in a row. He peeled the orange and ate it one section at a time.

Tim Lytle, a couple of years older than Aindreas, recited a shady limerick. Two clerks, who were maybe as old as twenty, smirked in his direction. Sometimes Tim became the brunt of jokes. Rumor in the office had it that he collected and sold rags while he was still on the clock for Cawthon Furniture. As long as Aindreas had known him, Tim had spun stories of his romantic adventures. He would describe females of various shapes and ages who had been his partners, and now and then he would actually point out a young woman on the street he had *done it* with. Aindreas could only guess how much of this to believe. Wiry and strong, the boy stood a head taller than Aindreas. Tim's frame was bony and his face, fair-skinned and sharp, seemed always broken out with something or other. Sometimes he picked at the bumps on his face and that made Aindreas nervous. But Tim usually carried a good nature, and they had worked together at Cawthon's without any arguments. The only thing likely to put Tim in a mood to fight was reference to his protruding ears.

Tim turned his back on the others and described to Aindreas the time he and a girl named Constance did it for two hours behind the big scale at the DuPont Paper and Rag Warehouse. The clerks broke out laughing near the end of the story. Red-faced, Tim held up a grimy middle finger in the air.

The taller of the clerks frowned. "Can you stand up straight in the wind with those ears?" he asked.

Tim jumped to his feet, and the two young men got up from their seats at the same time. No part of this argument did Aindreas want, especially since his size fell well short of the rest of them.

"Tim, if you're gonna get into it, will you try to be finished by the time I'm done talking to the chief clerk so we can split up the deliveries?" he asked.

Tempers cooled all around at the mere mention of the boss. Tim took on a hurt expression. Perhaps he thought Aindreas had somehow denied him the right to defend his honor. Moments later, Aindreas stood before the high desk with his hands folded behind his back.

The chief clerk glanced up from his work. "What is it?"

"Uh, you said…"

"Oh yes, Rivers. I told you to come back here."

Aindreas looked directly at the chief clerk for an instant, then nervously glanced away.

The clerk's quill pen made sharp, scratching sounds on the ledger.

"I've been watching you, Rivers, and I've had a word with Mr. Cawthon." Aindreas mouthed a quick, silent prayer to stave off the loss of his job.

"Starting next week, your pay will be thirty-five cents a day," the clerk said. "But you'll have to pick up the pace, you understand—get out there and hustle."

"Thank you, sir," Aindreas said. He felt goose flesh across his shoulders despite the warmness of the day. "I'll work harder, a lot harder," he added. "Thank you very much."

Backing away from the desk, Aindreas nearly bumped into the clerk's assistant, who sidestepped him. The man said, "Hey, kid, walk frontwards."

Aindreas's chest swelled as he retraced his steps back outside. He wouldn't mention the increase in pay to anyone at Cawthon's, of course. Tim had been working there longer and still made twenty-five cents.

*A person could do a lot with thirty-five cents a day. The family could use the extra. How would he tell his mother? She'd done outwork for years and somehow made or stretched the money to do for what the family needed. But she wasn't able to do that kind of work anymore, especially those heavy loads of wash.*

2

Crowd noise was washing down Market Street so loud that Aindreas heard it a block away. On each side of Sixth Street, tough-looking men handed out large folded papers. He took one, opened it, and saw the title: the *Manifesto*, by the Union of Free Germans, 1854. *So this is what it looks like.* His father had mentioned the *Manifesto* more than once, and the wagon drivers at Cawthon Furniture had talked about it from time to time. Aindreas traced down the sheet with his finger to the comments under the heading "Religions," while he walked toward the corner.

"...we therefore hold the Sabbath laws, Thanksgiving days, prayers in Congress and Legislature, the oath upon the Bible, introduction of the Bible into the schools, the exclusion of atheists, etc. as open violations of human rights as well as of the Constitution, and demand their removal."

He turned the corner onto Market Street. A speaker had mounted a makeshift platform, which stood surrounded by men who stood with locked arms and with eyes straight ahead. Aindreas paused in front of a hat shop. An audience of a hundred or more milled around in the street, and passers-by moved into and past the gathering. The actual members of the audience in front of the speaker changed from moment to moment in the heavy traffic of Market Street, yet the group stayed the same size; it all looked like a hill of sand in a moving stream Aindreas had once watched—parts of it were pulled away by the current around it, yet new grains from upstream were constantly pushed onto the same hill by that same current.

The speaker, a small man with thinning blond hair, raised his arms. "The most important change for our state Constitution," he said, "is all elections directly from the people!"

Cheers drowned out the catcalls. Some Irish had come and roared their approval of this declaration. Aindreas mounted the base of a lamppost and scanned the crowd. He couldn't miss that those dressed like working people cheered the speaker, while the rest booed or stood cross-armed and silent. He could have sworn that for a second or two he saw Mr. Bones watching the speaker from the edge of the crowd.

Aindreas wound his way into the mass and paused next to a man with heavy side-whiskers who smoked a cigar. The man simply watched, showing no outward reaction to the speaker's words. Right beside him, a tall, heavy man with his hat pulled down nearly to his eyes made notes on a pad.

"No extension of slavery to the new territories," the speaker continued with spirit. "All laws in support of slavery, especially the Fugitive Slave Law, must be abolished."

Food scraps and wadded papers sailed from the crowd just before some men tried to break through the protective ring around the platform. The speaker ducked to avoid a projectile, then he shouted, "And slavery must be abolished where it exists."

Aindreas would have loved to have cheered that one, but the side-whiskered man had glanced at him several times. The uproar took several minutes to subside.

The blond man's straining voice went on doggedly. "And these measures for the welfare of the people: first, free public lands to settlers; second, make the admission of citizenship as easy as possible."

"Tell 'em, lad!" an Irishman shouted. "Spread that blarney all over their square heads."

Angry men and women exchanged frowns. "Did you hear what that kraut sonofabitch is sayin'?" one man in front of Aindreas asked another.

"Third, a minimum wage."

At that, the mood of many in the crowd grew more hostile. Aindreas sensed the listening was about over.

"Fourth, a maximum workday of ten hours."

Hisses and boos came louder. Others began to chant, "Lo-co-fo-co...lo-co-fo-co...lo-co-fo-co..."

"You won't shut me up, my friends," the speaker shouted over them, his fist in the air. "Fifth, free schools," he said, "and sixth, free justice."

Those two men next to Aindreas moved in the direction of the platform. Aindreas followed in the wake of the tall, heavy man.

"Rights of women," the speaker went on. He could barely be heard above the ruckus. "The Declaration of Independence says all men are born equal and endowed with inalienable rights and to these belong life, liberty, and the pursuit of happiness. We believe that women, too, are among all men."

The cordon around the speaker began to give way, then a number of men broke through. The speaker was screeching, while the police pulled him down, "...the rights of free persons; the color of skin cannot justify a difference in legal rights."

The Germans were vastly outnumbered, and men from the audience gave the police more help than they appeared to need in subduing the Free Union men. The police didn't drag anybody but Germans off to jail. The show ending, the crowd in the street began to lose its shape and break apart. Aindreas recognized that wide, thin-lipped smile on a face among the well-dressed ladies and gentlemen standing to the side.

3

Mrs. Travis had instructed Aindreas the previous night to come by her house during the afternoon to pick up the first of her party invitations for delivery. He decided he'd best go there before he went home or saw Isaac. Mrs. Travis, herself, answered the door. Aindreas could hear the squire's voice in the background.

"Wipe your feet and come in," she said. "You may as well...I've had Tempie's pickaninnies underfoot all day." She pulled the door closed behind him. "Just stand right here and don't you move. I have one or two more envelopes to address."

She walked down the hall toward the parlor and Aindreas waited in the entry hall. Squire Travis's voice came from a small sitting room near the front door, and there came also another voice, a deeper one, apparently belonging to a Mr. Jones.

"That's the way I see it, Squire," the deep voice said. "Can't see where benefits are payable in a situation like this."

"Goddamn it, Jones, this boy got chewed up," the squire said. "Course, he had no business fooling around that damn Colored church. Don't know why in hell I ever let him go in there the first time."

"Uh-huh."

"He won't be any good to me for weeks, maybe months," said the squire in a whining tone. "Tell me, why do I pay Knickerbocker for an insurance policy on my man if it doesn't pay when he's down?"

"Do you have Isaac hired out right now…or did you have him on the job in the last few weeks?"

"No."

"Then you don't have a loss that can be proved."

Travis snorted.

"Squire, listen," Jones went on. "Maybe you shouldn't have bought the policy, but you wanted it and I sold it to you. You're just not into outside business like Hiram…like your daddy was. You made some money on Isaac before, but now he's starting to cause you trouble."

"That's for damn certain."

"You and the missus don't need that, and you don't need those two little ones on the place. A troublesome nigger ain't worth a helluva lot. If it was me, I'd get rid of the pack of 'em while they got some value."

"How do you expect me to run this house?" the squire asked.

A chair scooted on the floor. Mr. Jones apparently had gotten up. "You can hire a Colored good at handyman-work real cheap, and get yourself a healthy young Irish girl for the house," he rumbled. "That's what I did."

Whispering, then laughter. "Know what I mean, Squire?"

Mrs. Travis came down the hall with a large envelope. "I have ten invitations in here," she said. "Make sure to wash your hands before you handle them."

Aindreas looked directly at Mrs. Travis. Her lips were moving, but he couldn't get the words of this Jones man and the squire out of his head. *Was time running out to help Isaac?* Mrs. Travis's voice broke in sharply. "Are you listening to me? Standing there with that dreamy look on your face."

"Uh, yes, ma'am, I am."

"I expect you to get these delivered by the middle of the week," she said. "Come back on Friday and pick up the second bunch."

When he got home, Aindreas took the party invitations to his room, then returned to the kitchen. His mother reached into the oven and poked at the sweet mickeys with a fork. Doireann wore her best apron, the one with flower stitching around the border. She looked much better than she had that morning.

By the time they finished supper, twilight had come. His right boot had rubbed a blister on his foot, so Aindreas walked barefoot toward the cabin. He stepped carefully on the sharp grass blades. He felt worried but consoled himself with the idea that maybe Isaac hadn't been hurt as bad as the two men said. Then there came to mind that other thing. *Wasn't Isaac entitled to know what had been said at the Travis house earlier?* Aindreas shook his head. No, he wouldn't bring it up—at least not now. He paused in the open doorway of the cabin.

Tempie sewed at the table, Aaron in her lap. She waved Aindreas inside. "Come on in," she said in a flat voice, and then she pointed. "He's over there, maybe sleepin." She held out the lamp for Aindreas. "You kin have this. I don't need it."

Little Sarah with the bright eyes moved to the other side of the table as Aindreas came near. He leaned down and spoke to her, but she turned her head away.

Holding out the lamp before him, Aindreas walked over by the pallet in the corner. Seconds passed before he realized that Isaac was looking right at him. Aindreas set the lamp on the floor and dropped down on one knee. Isaac groaned when he turned onto his right side and raised himself on his elbow. He wore only trousers. From the waist to the chest, his body was wrapped in a wide strip of bed sheet. His face hadn't much shape. Aindreas could make out the right eye, but a mass of swelling covered over the other.

"Hello, young Andrew," Isaac said.

The words sounded garbled, as if whoever had done this to him had broken some of his teeth or maybe knocked them out.

Aindreas's throat tightened. He couldn't make out where Isaac's mouth began and ended. *Men who would do a thing like this—what do they look like?*

"Hello, Isaac," Aindreas responded hesitantly. Then he blurted, "Does it hurt?"

Muffled laughing sounds came from the pallet. Isaac grimaced and held his sides. "Tempie say my head look like a brown pumpkin, and you ask if it hurt."

Isaac laughed again, and Aindreas joined in. Tempie took a scolding tone. "What you all doin' over there?"

A moment later, she brought over a bowl of soup. Very patient, Tempie couldn't get more than two or three spoonfuls into his mouth. She finally gave up and went back to the table.

"Your mamma did a good job on me," Isaac said. "The doctor told me she did." Pride made Aindreas glow.

"You know how sick she is, Andrew?" Aindreas could do no more than nod.

Isaac let himself down carefully to lie flat on his back again. He lay silent for a time, so quiet and still he might have been asleep.

Aindreas leaned in close and whispered, "Did they take any money?"

Isaac whispered, "Bout thirty-five, forty dollars."

"Oh my God...did you tell Squire Travis? He could report it to the police watch."

Isaac chuckled. "They *was* the police, boy." He motioned for Aindreas to move closer. "Made up my mind on something,'" said Isaac.

"What's that?"

"Don't know how I'll manage, but nobody gonna do this to me no more."

4

Business slowed on Saturday morning. Early in the afternoon, the chief clerk told Aindreas and Tim that they could go home at three o'clock if the deliveries had been made.

Aindreas felt almost carefree when he headed home early. His mother hadn't had any bad sickness the last few days, and Isaac looked a little better. Only three more of Mrs. Travis's party invitations remained to be delivered, and he took care of that on the way home. König trotted along in front of him most of the time, then went off exploring.

Doireann Rivers and Kirsty were working in the kitchen when Aindreas arrived. His father and brother hadn't gotten home from work. Aindreas carried out the ashes and brought in water. He stretched out on his bed and had nearly fallen asleep when he remembered: Miss Flowers had asked him on Thursday to clean and put her books in boxes the first chance he got. Because of that fire a while back at the Fifth Ward School, the teachers had been forced to store the books at home for the classes they taught.

Aindreas raised himself and sat on the edge of the bed. Miss Flowers had asked him for help with odd jobs, now and then, and he always felt glad when she did. He would have done anything Miss Flowers had asked simply because she asked it. Johnny Flowers often traveled with his job, and maybe sometimes she just wanted to talk. And Miss Flowers wasn't like Mrs. Travis, Miss Flowers always paid. He had once spent part of a Sunday afternoon helping her move light furniture and things from one room to another, and she gave him twenty-five cents.

He had said, "Ma'am, are you sure? This is what I get for the whole day at Cawthon's."

And Miss Flowers had told him, "Keep it...you earned it."

83

Generous; it seemed fitting that this ideal woman be so. Blanche Flowers was simply a perfect fact. In her, Aindreas saw what a woman should look and act like, what a woman should be.

It troubled Aindreas that Miss Flowers was married to Johnny Flowers. She'd told Aindreas that she grew up in Cincinnati. There she had met Johnny Flowers, a drummer for the Great Western Hardware Company, and they moved to Louisville when the company assigned him a territory in Kentucky and southern Indiana. Doireann Rivers often mentioned how well-groomed Johnny Flowers looked. Truth to tell, both she and Kirsty seemed taken with his good looks. A dark, slender man of medium height, Johnny Flowers had shiny, black hair and a thick mustache that curved around the corners of his mouth. Always in a good humor, he seemed to have a new joke in every pocket. Most people liked him, but at times Aindreas had uneasy feelings about the man, feelings he couldn't quite put into words. Johnny was as handsome and well-dressed and as smooth a man as one would ever see, no argument about that. On the other hand, no one seemed more aware of this than Johnny Flowers himself.

Why had she married this man? It had to be one of those grownup situations Aindreas didn't understand. He carried his mother's broom, some rags, and a water can up the outside stairs. When the building in which Aindreas's family lived had been converted from a storage barn to a dwelling house, a large room had been left unfinished on the upper level. Squire and Mrs. Travis stored several trunks and some odds and ends of furniture there. Miss Flowers also used it to store books.

The outer door stood ajar. Only a couple of feet inside the short hallway, Miss Flowers's door stood to the right, and straight ahead down the hall another door led to the storage room. Aindreas knocked on her door.

Her voice sounded strained when she saw Aindreas. "Oh," she said. "You're going to box up the books in the storage room today?"

"Yes, but don't worry, Miss Flowers. I'll sprinkle water around on the floor to hold down the dust."

She looked like a picture of an angel in her light-blue robe, and a dressing gown of the same color. Her braided hair made her high cheekbones even more prominent.

"I hoped Johnny would be here by now," she said, a little sadly. "He should have been back in town this morning."

She accompanied Aindreas into the storage room, pointing out which boxes and books needed moving and where he should put them. It looked like the job would take a while, but nothing looked too heavy to handle.

Miss Flowers handed him twenty-five cents. "I'll be next door, in case you need me," she said. "Be sure the outside door is closed tight when you leave, so the wind doesn't bang it around."

Daylight winked through cracks in the wallboards. No wonder the place got so dirty. Aindreas wiped away the thin layer of soot on the storage room walls and the cobwebs that had grown in the corners. He then got the textbooks in the order she wanted and worked steadily for perhaps two hours—carefully wiping off the books and putting them into clean boxes. It went so well, he figured to be finished before long. He stopped only long enough for a drink of water. After he had pushed the boxes into a row, he began sweeping the floor.

He stopped when he heard loud words. A man and a woman, words loud enough to come through the thin walls. Aindreas opened the door and listened. Miss Flowers and Johnny. The door to their apartment stood partially open. Maybe she had forgotten he was working in the storage room.

"And if you don't want to be here, don't come back here," she said.

"I don't know what you're so upset about," he said. "I told you I had to catch another train because of an extra appointment.

You didn't have any business looking at that note, Blanche. Doesn't mean a thing, anyway. It's from a customer's wife, a thank-you note."

"Johnny, don't treat me like a fool. When the note fell out of your coat pocket, I didn't even look to see who wrote it. But it doesn't smell like a thank-you note."

At least Johnny Flowers wasn't being rough or threatening with her. Aindreas wouldn't have known what to do if that had happened, but he would have done something. *Why did things get like this between grownups? He felt nervous, the same helpless feeling as he had late at night when he heard hard words, slammed doors.*

He resumed his sweeping. The voices grew softer, and then faded away altogether. Finally done, Aindreas stepped into the hall and pulled the door closed behind him. He abruptly stopped. Sounds came from the apartment, sounds he knew. A sense of panic came over him, but he couldn't stay there. His sister would soon be yelling for him to come to supper. The hallway presented the only way out. The door to the apartment hung open maybe a foot, no more. If he stepped softly and carefully, maybe he could get past it without being seen.

Aindreas padded silently toward the outer door. He had started to raise his hand to open the outside door when he glanced
to his left, then froze. Only a few seconds passed, he knew later, but it seemed much longer. Miss Flowers looked up from the floor, through the door opening, her face turned slightly toward him. The man was kissing her neck and shoulder, his shiny black hair in stark contrast to her pale skin. She mouthed silent words, as though speaking to Aindreas. Her light blue robe lay strewn across a chair, the dressing gown of the same color had become a wadded band around her waist. The man's hands moved over her, his body pressed against her.

86

Sick, Aindreas darted out the doorway. He made it down the stairs without making any noise but threw up in the open lot back behind the privy. When he went into the kitchen his mother asked, "What's wrong with you, Andrew?"

"Nothing."

"It certainly doesn't sound like *nothing,* and you look terrible. Better get to bed right after supper."

"I'm not hungry," he said.

5

Michael hadn't come home, and Aindreas lay alone in the room. What he had seen flashed across his mind over and over. *Had it really happened? Would he ever be able to face her again?* How he wished Johnny Flowers was gone, or dead.

After a time, Aindreas realized that she might not have actually seen him in that darkened hallway. There was relief in that idea, but the hurting fullness where his ribs met wouldn't go away. He woke long before dawn, soaked with sweat, thankful to God that Cawthon's Furniture stayed closed on Sunday. The upstairs scene kept coming back into his mind. He couldn't shut it out, and he was horrified that it also gave him a dark, cutting pleasure. He decided he must be an evil person. Excitement of that kind had to come from some evil power.

He tossed and turned, resisted. Even prayed once. Hating it, he always hated it when he did that. He took hold of himself and became both watcher and doer in the scene before him. Spasms of breath raked through him. The picture of Miss Flowers and Johnny was clear for a time but changed before he wrung himself out completely. Johnny Flowers had gone. Miss Flowers remained … and Aindreas.

# 6

The sky showed gray streaks of dawn before Michael finally came in and lay down on his bed. By the time Aindreas returned from a quick trip out to the privy, his brother was back up—pacing between the window and the door. Michael's hand-rolled cigarette smoldered, the curls of smoke wafting a whiskey smell. His voice seemed loud for the hour. "Ah, Lucky boy," he exclaimed, laughing. "It's been a large evening."

"Hey, quiet down," Aindreas cautioned. "You want to wake everybody?"

"Got things to do," said Michael more softly. "If Da or Mum should ask, tell 'em...uh, what time did they go to bed?"

"About ten o'clock."

"Tell 'em I came in before midnight and had to go out early to haul some furniture. Eh?"

"Okay."

"Promise?" Michael asked.

Aindreas put his hand over his heart. "Promise."

Michael stretched and yawned. "I owe you."

"I know."

Michael climbed out the window into the darkness. Aindreas whispered after him, "Watch where you're goin' out there. If you barge into König, you'll wish you hadn't."

"Oh, Jesus! I see him," Michael said, then skirted well around the black shape and glowing eyes. "Keep an eye on him for me, will you?"

Aindreas finally went to sleep. His mother and Kirsty had already returned from church when he woke. A bowl of porridge was placed in front of him at the table. Every Sunday morning as far back as he could remember, steaming bowls of rice porridge appeared on the table—if his mother could manage it. Aindreas loved the tradition, but, in truth had never liked rice. He drank tea and ignored the bowl.

Doireann Rivers seemed in a bright mood. One of her sisters, Margaret, had invited the family over for Sunday dinner. About noon, Uncle Theodore was to come with the wagon to carry them there.

"I'd better not go with you to Aunt Margaret's," Aindreas said.

Doireann Rivers eyed him closely. "You don't look good, Andrew, but we couldn't just leave you here."

"Leave the boy be, Dorrie," his father said. "Rather not go, myself. I've heard enough of Theodore Herdrich's stories, and I've eaten enough of his sauerkraut, too."

Doireann's eyes flashed.

"But I'll go," Joseph Rivers added quickly. He dipped a spoon in the jar and sprinkled sugar over Aindreas's porridge. "Now, eat the rice and make your mother happy."

Aindreas ate some of the porridge. His father and mother both smiled when he told the story about Michael's helping a friend haul furniture that morning.

"Are you sure you want to stay home?" Doireann asked, and squeezed his shoulder. "I couldn't forgive myself if we ran off and you needed us."

How little strength he felt in her grip. Aindreas knew she didn't see her sisters as often as she wanted to. "I'll be fine, and the visit'll be good for you," he said.

Later, he watched as his mother, father, and sister walked toward Prather Street to meet the wagon. They had not noticed the scent of roses clinging to the walls. Aindreas waved after them, uncertain whether he would see them again. There wasn't much time left; he knew he would fall.

Aindreas carried a half-full bucket of water to his room and undressed. He washed out his mouth, then soaked a towel and cleaned himself and combed his hair, believing that to do those things now might relieve someone else from the job later. He slipped back into his trousers. The bucket stayed in the room in case he had to throw up.

It was coming. Yes. At least his family didn't have to watch this time and maybe this would be the last time. Tiny dust particles floated in the sun rays slanting upward from bleached puddles of brightness on the floor. He wondered aloud. "I never thought about dying on Sunday afternoon before." He moved over by the window.

Mother is getting worse. Isaac may never be the same. A lot of people in this country are just plain bad, or I'm crazy. They say one thing, but they do something else. I'm bad, too. That thing about Miss Flowers.

Maybe Sunday afternoon is as good a time as any.

Weak, he felt as if he were floating. His arms and legs became useless things extending from his body. The window and the walls seemed farther and farther away from him. Aindreas watched it all happen, in a room as dull gray as stones in a graveyard. His head and the window frame collided, then dark-red splatter hung in the air over Aindreas as he fell.

Later, his throat squeezed every muscle to let the air pass, to suck in more. *Those uncontrollable jerks and spasms. Whose were they? Was that his left side, his body that had ground the rough floorboards? How long had he been there?* Such thoughts were not entirely welcome. He had expected to die, perhaps even wanted to, but he had not.

His senses came to him, as did the hurts. Something smelled

and tasted burnt. A stickiness clung to his face. Aindreas grabbed the side of the bed and pulled himself up to sit. The room around him took on the blunt shapes and colors of the place he knew. He stared at the Madonna picture over his bed. Strange that he had never noticed it before. Her face had darkened to a shade black as char.

He hadn't thrown up after all. The bucket rested only a few feet away. He crawled to it and ducked his face in the water. It turned red, tasted of iron, of blood. He reached to his brother's nightstand and grabbed the mirror. The image in it frightened him. Blood, thick and dark, covered the right side of his face. It was hard to wipe away and the water in the bucket grew deeper red each time he rinsed the rag. Hands shaking, he probed through his hair with his fingers. He found the place, finally, a gash above the right temple. He pressed a clean cloth against the wound.

He sprawled against the side of the bed, feeling alone. No sounds at all; even the leaves on the tree out back hung dead still. Mute heat waves wiggled up from the baked ground in the distance. A tree branch just above the window flashed red, and a cardinal jumped along a limb. In a moment its mate arrived. Aindreas watched as one, then the other, moved from branch to branch down the tree in some bird version of leapfrog. The birds set up a racket when a squirrel started climbing the tree—but then thought better of it and retreated. Aindreas scanned the tree upwards. Yes. Up near the top, a nest.

He found another clean rag and wiped the blood from the window frame. Out back, someone was coming, carrying his coat over his arm, walking across the bare ground of the large vacant lot behind the Travis property. A remembered figure, even at a distance, who was taking the same path Aindreas always used to return home by the back way. König roused and shook himself, then loped out of the shade toward the trespasser.

"Stop!" Aindreas shouted to the figure. "Stay where you are. I'll come out."

The man seemed not to hear, and continued straight on. He pulled up short only when König cut in front of him. To Aindreas's surprise, the dog lay down on its belly, his brushy tail sweeping up puffs of dust. The man leaned over and rubbed König's head, then appeared to examine the draining abscess above the dog's foreleg before he straightened up and continued toward the house, the sunlight sparkling on the metal rims of his spectacles.

Aindreas felt a great sense of relief. "Am I glad you're here," he shouted out the window. "I've been watching everywhere for you."

"Good to see you again, Aindreas," Mr. Knight responded, then wagged his head in mock severity, "But I must say, you look a mess."

"I'll put on my shirt and be right out."

"No," Knight said. "Now, hold up and listen. Find your father's razor, a mirror, and that dark bottle your mother keeps around for cuts and bruises."

Aindreas grimaced. "The stuff that stings?"

"Right. Bring those things, some water, and clean rags."

"I'll be right out," Aindreas said, and started to turn away.

"And try the door," Knight added, then laughed. "You're a little young yet to have to climb out of windows."

Aindreas brought out the needed items. While he sat very still on an upturned crate, an old towel draped over his shoulders, Mr. Knight shaved the hair around the cut on his head.

"This is closing well and I don't think it needs sewing up," Knight said. "Now, turn your head a little more to the side so this stuff doesn't get in your eyes…that's good."

"Ouch!"

"It's not that bad," Knight said, and replaced the cork in the bottle. He folded a strip of old bed sheet into a bandage. "I'm making this as narrow as possible so your mother doesn't faint when she sees you." He wound the cloth around Aindreas's head. "There," said Mr. Knight as he tied off the wrapping. "You look like a true man of action, maybe even a pirate."

Aindreas lightly touched the bandage with his fingers and felt around the knot tied in the back. Satisfied, he said, "I need to talk to you."

Knight pulled a handkerchief from his coat pocket and blotted his forehead. "Why don't we get out of this sun?" He moved the crate into the shade and sat down. Aindreas rested on the ground, propping himself against the tree trunk.

Knight lighted his pipe. "Carrying the world on your back, are you?"

"Everything's going wrong," Aindreas said. "I'm afraid somethin' will happen to my mother—she's sick and doesn't get any better."

Mr. Knight's voice sounded kind of stern. "You're not a stupid boy."

Aindreas shook his head, as if he didn't understand.

"Try that on someone who believes it," Knight said. "You suspect that your mother's time has run out, and that's something you won't allow yourself to think."

Aindreas felt his throat tighten. "I guess so."

They sat in silence. König watched them with his big, sad eyes and the cardinals chattered their own concerns.

"Why don't you talk to her, Aindreas?" asked Mr. Knight

"Maybe she wants to know that I'll be all right…but that isn't much."

"When you give it some thought," Mr. Knight mused, "it's more than she has ever gotten from anyone."

Aindreas wept, there in the mottled shade of a maple tree. Mr. Knight looked away and tapped the ashes out of his pipe.

Aindreas's breath was coming in catches. He swiped under his nose with the heel of his hand.

"Did you know that my friend, Isaac, got hurt?"

"So I heard," Knight said, his head still turned away.

"I want to help Isaac."

"Now that's better, my boy." Knight gazed back at him, now, smiling a very kind smile. "What would be help for Isaac?"

"I've thought about it," declared Aindreas. He absently scribbled letters in the dust with his finger, then said, "I know this much: Isaac and his family have to get away from here, so far away that Squire Travis or a bounty hunter couldn't find them…or even if he did, he couldn't bring them back."

Aindreas looked at the ground. Though he had written the letters in the dust, the words there startled him: *Indiana,* and *New Albany,* and *Indiana* once again. Mr. Knight didn't seem to notice.

"If Isaac and his family went away, do you think I would ever see them again?" asked Aindreas.

"Those are questions for another day," Knight said. "Right now, you must try to help Isaac get away and that will be risky and tough enough."

For long seconds, Aindreas gazed down at the words in the dust. He said, "I thought I was going to die today."

"And I suppose after these last few minutes, you might wonder why you didn't."

Aindreas smiled ruefully.

"I'm glad you're still around," said Knight. "Trouble is coming, and you could be of aid."

"To my mother and Isaac?"

"Yes, and others as well." Knight sounded a little excited. "Now, about Isaac, why not speak with your friend, Captain Workman? He may know more about this sort of thing than he lets on. The *Ben Franklin* will be at the wharf all day."

"I'll go see him."

"Anything else, Aindreas?"

"I need to know about these whispers I keep hearing, about people like George Prentice and *Sam,* and what's a Locofoco?"

Knight's brow arched. "Well, at least you asked one easy one. Come on, I'll go back toward the house with you."

Aindreas gathered up the things he had brought out, and they started toward the footpath beside the house. "Do you know Mr. Prentice?" Aindreas asked.

"Met him once, then only for a moment," said Knight. "A nasty man."

"Is he really as smart as they say?"

"Depends on what you mean by smart," Knight said. "He was playing the hail-fellow-well-met along Fifth Street one morning when I stopped him and introduced myself. I asked him if he really believed all those things he'd written in *The Louisville Journal* about foreign-born people in this country. He jumped back from me as if I were a leper, gave me a look of absolute hatred. A lot of fear in those eyes. The great and powerful Mr. Prentice scurried away and didn't look back."

Aindreas fumbled the bottle and dropped it on the path, but it didn't break. He stopped to pick it up, then scurried to catch up. "Does Mr. Prentice have anything to do with Sam?"

"It's the other way around, Aindreas. *Sam* stands for the way some people think about people different from them, like foreigners, Catholics, Negroes, and Jews. Famous men like George Prentice may prance about and do some mischief, but eventually they go away or die. *Sam* endures."

"That's because *Sam* isn't a real person," agreed Aindreas.

"Very good, Aindreas...*Sam* is an idea, but more powerful than any real person," Knight said. "An idea that represents some of the worst in all of us."

They arrived at the kitchen door. Aindreas asked, "Will you

come in, Mr. Knight?"

"I'd like a drink of water, and there will be just enough time to answer your easy question."

"Locofoco?"

"Funny-sounding word, isn't it?" asked Mr. Knight. "That's why Prentice and others use it to make fun of people with little power to fight back." He took a pamphlet from his coat pocket and handed it to Aindreas. It was written in German. "Get your friend, Georg Adler, to read this to you. In a nutshell, one of the incidents mentioned involved a bunch of people in New York who got together in a meeting hall. Up to something foolish or visionary, no doubt. The Tammany Hall thugs turned out the house lights, leaving them in total darkness. Some in the group had those large phosphorous-head matches, called locofoco matches, and they kept the hall lighted up enough to carry on with the meeting. Ever since, when anybody speaks up for the losers he gets called a lot of names, and 'Locofoco' is among them."

After saying his good-byes, Knight walked toward the Travis house and Prather Street. Aindreas thought about catching up to him to ask about that thing with Miss Flowers but decided against it.

Knight paused, half-turned and waved. Aindreas shouted, "Promise you'll be there when I want to talk!"

Knight put his hand over his heart. "I promise," he said, and was gone.

1

The doors of the shops and mercantile houses were shut, the streets nearly empty. Though four o'clock had come and gone, the air still felt hot and close. His shirt sticking to him, his head still throbbing, Aindreas walked north toward the river. But he felt a purpose in his walk now; he hadn't died and now he didn't intend to. *What could Captain Workman do to help Isaac and him?* Aindreas reached Main Street. The wholesale warehouses and hotels stood like sentinels in the fading light and muted sounds of Sunday afternoon. He paused and looked at the familiar crescent formed by the river from the north to the west. His grandfather had shown him when he was a small child that, down near the river, most of the horizon was Indiana.

A sudden, cool gust chilled the sweat on his face. Tight black clouds, flat as a tabletop, sliced through the sky over the sandstone knobs on the far side of the river. Aindreas counted eleven boats docked at the wharf. Those on the river moved along without any sign of heading in. The *Ben Franklin* rested near the far end of the line of boats, below Pearl Street.

Two men plodded up the incline from the Wharf master's office, which stood midway down the cobblestone-covered levee. As they came closer, Aindreas thought he recognized one of them, the bigger man. Though he wasn't wearing a uniform and seemed somehow different, it definitely was Jack Graham. Aindreas waved. When Graham saw him he spoke to the other man, who continued on up toward Water Street. Jack Graham dashed over, grabbed Aindreas under the arms, and actually lifted him in the air.

"It's been weeks, Lucky. Hey! What happened to your head?"

"I tripped and fell," lied Aindreas. "It doesn't hurt."

Graham ran his hand over his short beard and grinned. "What do you think?"

He looked distinguished. Aindreas said, "It looks okay."

"Maybe you heard, I'm under suspension," Graham said. "It's because of that night back in April. Remember Cooper and those slaves?"

Aindreas nodded. "Then, you're not the first mate on the *Ben Franklin* anymore?"

"It's hard to explain. You going down to talk to Cap'n

97

Workman? I know he'd be pleased."

"I was hoping to see both of you," Aindreas said. "You all were gone a long time."

"Well, come on," Graham said. "I'll go with you."

They started down toward the foot of the levee.

Graham said, "You know, we were scheduled to be back here in a couple of weeks."

"That's what I thought," said Aindreas.

"They held us down in Memphis for an investigation."

*Investigation?*

"Gonna be working for the wharf master during this suspension," Graham went on. "I know most all of these packets, and Cap'n Workman must have put in a word for me. I'll probably be here in Louisville for a couple of months."

They continued on across the wharf toward the boat. The black clouds dipped lower and slid more rapidly along the Indiana shore. The pace of their walk quickened.

"You remember I couldn't stand those things Cooper always did," Graham said. "Guess I must have been waiting for the chance to do something."

Aindreas remembered that Cooper had looked beaten up at the commissioner's sale by the courthouse. "I figured you would," he said.

"We weren't much past Owensboro when they started their usual business with the slaves. They whipped a couple of the men for no reason I could tell, then went after the women. Cooper must have scared the hell out of the fancy lady. She came around. He kept her to himself in his cabin. She kept him so busy he didn't ever have time to sell that baby. Cooper's helper, a rogue called Raskin, fooled around with the young girl with the child."

For an instant, Aindreas thought of Miss Flowers, and looked down at the cobblestones. "Uh-huh," he said.

He glanced toward the far shore. The dark clouds hanging

98

over the river had merged into one, and the black mass had begun to hook south toward Louisville.

"We had to hold up for some freight, and I thought we'd never get out of Paducah," continued Graham. "About as bad a situation as I'd ever been in." Aindreas cast a nervous glance at the sky. Oblivious, Graham went on, "That third night, you know how we handle the wheel—on watch four hours and off four. Cap'n Workman doesn't take a turn at night anymore. It must have been near twelve-thirty when the other pilot relieved me."

Aindreas and Graham were still about a hundred yards from the *Ben Franklin* when the wind whipped in fresh off the water. Aindreas felt pinpricks on his face. He and Graham found themselves reeling in a dazzling world within a cloud. Tiny hailstones swirled from every direction and rebounded crazily from the ground. Aindreas leaned into the wind and covered his face with his hands. In seconds, it seemed, the wide crevices between the cobblestones overflowed with shiny pieces of white.

Aindreas felt a tug on his arm. "Let's go!" Graham urged. They lurched in the direction of the *Ben Franklin*. In no time at all, the ice along the levee was over an inch deep. The boats tied up at the wharf pitched and bobbed, yanking at the lines holding them. Aindreas had never seen anything like it. A line on one boat separated, and the aft section swung in toward the wharf. Fortunately, nothing lay in its path. The boat leaned heavily when the hull scraped the shore, and then the wind swallowed up the grinding sounds.

The hail stopped as suddenly as it had begun, and Aindreas became clear witness to the anger of the great Ohio. As far as he could see, deep, muddy water and dirty froth whipped up into whitecaps taller than a man. The water came in like sea rollers up the lower levee, over the tops of his boots, leaving the icy hailstones the color of dark chocolate. Aindreas and Graham slogged aboard the *Ben Franklin just* before the deck hands pulled in the plank. Captain Workman perched on the hurricane deck, holding to the edge of the cabin roof with one hand. He bellowed down to the hands on the main deck, "At three bells, start letting out the lines, and don't tie them off until you only have a few feet left!"

Aindreas could feel the engine vibrations in the handrails and under his feet as he followed Graham up to the pilothouse.

Captain Workman shouted out the window to the engineer below and yanked on the bell pull three times. He smiled when he saw Graham and pulled him up to the wheel. "You have better nerves than mine, Jack. Back it away some, or we'll rip out the hull on the levee. We've got about seventy-five to a hundred feet of line. Take her straight back and turn up river, then try to hold steady."

The *Ben Franklin* pitched and rolled as Graham backed the boat away from the wharf. He turned the wheel slowly with his strong arms and shoulders.

"Hold her straight as you can," yelled the captain.

Hard rain pounded the small pilothouse. Aindreas joined the captain near the back window. Workman pointed down river, toward the west horizon. Back in the southwest, from down near Portland on the Kentucky side of the river to New Albany on the far shore, the black tabletop cloud curled like a huge question mark. The top of the hook loomed directly over them.

"Forgot to tell you, I'm glad to see you, boy. You know, you look like a damn pirate with that bandage," the captain said, and ruffled Aindreas's hair.

"Oww," Aindreas said, and ducked his head. Workman looked up at the huge hook. "If that closes, we've got a cyclone, and this boat will be in one hell of a mess. Are you scared?"

"No sir," replied Aindreas. "Just glad I'm still alive so I can come down here on the river."

"Well, I'll be damned," the captain said.

The wind streaked the raindrops across the pilothouse windows. Each end of the boat came out of the water more than once, but Graham held the *Ben Franklin* against the current. Two of the boats tied up at the wharf raked over the stones. Aindreas cringed at the sight, hoping no one had been hurt.

The captain and Aindreas continued to watch the sky and the river. Late afternoon sun broke through, covering the world in a yellowish cast. The hook cloud did not close, and within an hour the black mass sailed northeast, along the Indiana shore.

"Take her in, Jack," Captain Workman said. "This old river spared us for another day, but Cincinnati may play hell tonight."

In Workman's cabin, the captain poured drinks for Jack Graham and himself. One of the hands brought in a mug of tea for Aindreas. Workman seemed very pleased. Not so much as a keg had been lost overboard. Some of the other boats at the wharf looked to have sustained real damage. Workman and Graham took turns recalling scary details. Aindreas got the chance to tell them about one packet he had watched while they were both occupied at the wheel. The boat was listing badly and looked for a time as if it wouldn't make it but battled to shore at Jeffersonville.

"I'm beholden to you, Jack," said the captain, and he nodded at Aindreas, "And you, too, boy. We were all in that together."

Aindreas sat proudly on the edge of a bunk, his hands around the warm mug.

Jack Graham said, "I was telling Lucky about that night we had the trouble, but the weather went bad before I could finish."

"I see," responded the captain.

Graham flipped open his pocket watch and glanced toward Aindreas. "Well, I'm meeting a friend for some supper, and I only have a few minutes," he said. "As I told you, I got off watch about twelve-thirty and figured to have a smoke before I turned in. Then I heard some kind of commotion aft and started back to find out what had happened."

101

Aindreas listened intently. Captain Workman sat back in the chair, his eyes hooded, as if he might be thinking about something else.

"About midway back, Cooper came at me out of the dark, swinging a club. He kept screaming, 'I knew you'd try something like this, you sonofabitch.' He whacked me across the shoulder, and I was flat on my back before I knew what happened. I grabbed his ankle and brought him down with me. We wrestled over that club and rolled into the rail. That's what broke his arm, I think. He lost control of the club, and I punched him in the face a few times pretty good. Might have done more, but two of the deckhands pulled us apart."

"What did he think you did?" Aindreas said.

Graham rose to leave. "That's the crazy part," he said. "I'd been brooding about Cooper, but I hadn't done a damn thing. Turned out his helper had disappeared. Later, we guessed the slaves ganged up and threw Raskin right over the rudder before some of them escaped. I've really got to go," he said, glancing at his watch again. "Maybe Cap'n Workman will tell you the rest."

Graham shook hands with Aindreas and Workman and said good-bye. The captain made certain the door closed securely behind him. Aindreas wanted to hear more, since the story could have a lot to do with Isaac.

"What else happened, Captain Workman?"

Workman sat back in the chair, his hands folded on his stomach. "Young Jack described his experience well. What else do you want to know?"

"About the slaves, Captain."

"It appears that several pried themselves loose somehow, subdued Mr. Raskin, and made their escape." The captain sounded near bored. "Evidently, Mr. Cooper was occupied in his cabin at the time and found out only when he took a respite from his labors. He brutally beat two of the slaves still chained and attacked my first mate, Mr. Graham. This is what I told the proctor—he's a lawyer—when he took my statement in Memphis two days later."

Aindreas asked, "What really happened, Captain?"

"As I told you, boy."

"Didn't Mr. Raskin carry a club and gun?"

"I presume he did."

"Then how did the slaves take him down?"

"My own theory—private, mind you—is that they got hold of several boards and beat Raskin unconscious, pried themselves loose, then dumped him overboard before they jumped for it." The captain poured a little more whiskey into his glass. "Many didn't try, including that young girl with the baby. They remained, and given the odds against swimming to safety, I'm glad she did."

Aindreas recalled the lengths of wood he and the captain had brought up from the hold and left between some nail kegs and the bulkhead, where the slaves might have been able to reach them. "Where did the slaves get the wood pieces, Captain?"

"Can't imagine," Workman said, and smiled. "Later, I found several pieces with blood on them and took it upon myself to throw them overboard."

"Did Mr. Raskin ever turn up?"

The captain shook his head. "An unconscious man in the channel of the Mississippi in the middle of the night? Not likely."

"How many slaves got away?"

"Six. Bounty hunters captured one a few days later. The others escaped, or they died in the river."

"What happened to the fancy lady?"

Workman poured himself another taste of whiskey, chuckling, perhaps enjoying the recollection. "Mr. Cooper needed medical attention," said the captain. "The doctor gave him something for his pain, and he slept late the next morning. I understand the fancy lady walked right down the plank and over the Memphis levee looking good as new money."

"Did you see her leave?"

Workman laughed. "Hell, boy, I tipped my hat to her when she asked permission to go ashore."

Aindreas stretched and stood up. "Jack Graham will get his job back…won't he?"

"I don't know. The owners of the *Ben Franklin* acted unhappy with me, too, but they won't do anything until the proctor files his report. I told them no good result could come out of slave trading, and if they felt determined to be involved, they should at least insist that Bolton and Dickens send competent people to look out for the slaves. They didn't like what I said, but I'm still captain …up till now, at least."

Workman looked tired. He rose from his chair and said to Aindreas, "Need to stretch my legs. I have the feeling you've been waiting to ask me something else all along. I'll walk up the levee aways."

Captain Workman eased his bulk down the plank ahead of Aindreas. They moved carefully across the levee stones, still slippery from the river bath. The air smelled fresh.

"Look at those stars, boy. Who would have imagined this a couple of hours ago?"

They moved up toward Water Street. Aindreas tried to think of the best way to bring up Isaac's plight.

"All right," Workman said. "My wife and I raised two sons, and I've seen that expression often enough. What's on your mind?"

Aindreas talked without stopping for some minutes. He told the captain about Isaac and Tempie and the children, that the black man was his best and oldest friend, about Isaac's beating and robbery by the police. Workman listened intently, nodding several times. Aindreas explained why he feared Squire Travis might sell the family to the traders. Finally, he stopped and took a deep breath.

Workman asked, "And what do you want from me?"

"Can you help me get them out of here?"

"On the river, I can take care of myself," said the captain, frowning. "It's illegal, what you want. Do you know what you're asking me?"

Aindreas gulped, then took the risk. "Yes," he said, "and I feel like you're the one I'm supposed to ask." They walked on, without speaking, to the edge of Water Street. Aindreas recalled the words in the dust. He asked, "Would *New Albany* and *Indiana* have anything to do with it?

Captain Workman looked hard at Aindreas. "Well, maybe if you mean what we were just talking about. New Albany used to be a whole town full of Presbyterians," he said. "One of their churches, a big, beautiful place, backs up to within a hundred yards of the shore. Over the years, I've heard that those people keep a station for runaway slaves."

"Do you believe it, Captain?"

Workman nodded.

Aindreas tried to keep his voice from breaking. "Please help me get Isaac and his family to that church."

Workman removed his cap, then stared at the ground for a time. "Wish my old friend, Major Krauth, was here," he said. "I could use his advice."

Workman looked decisive and stern by the time he pulled his cap back on. A little like the general in a picture Aindreas remembered from school.

"This Isaac. He strong enough to pull the oars on a ship's yawl, when he's well?" the captain asked.

Aindreas said, "Sure he is."

"And his wife. Could she pull, too?"

"Oh, Tempie's plenty strong."

Workman glanced back toward the *Ben Franklin*. "One way I've thought about it," he mused. "No promises, now, but you let me know when this Isaac looks fit to go. I'll see if I can make some arrangements, then."

Aindreas stood very straight, flushed with pride. "Yes, sir," he said.

"Now get on home, boy," Captain Workman said. "With all this rough weather, your mother probably wonders where you are.

BEN FRANKLIN AND VIEW OF LOUISVILLE KENTUCKY

# 7

June nearly gone, Isaac did small jobs around the Travis place, refinishing blistered wood on the trunk of the case clock and scraping the inner hearths and firebacks of the fireplaces. He looked more like himself in these last few weeks, and much of the swelling had disappeared from his face. Still, Isaac grimaced even when he bent down to pick up his toolbox. Aindreas only went to the cabin after dark these days, when eyes from the Travis house windows couldn't see him.

Isaac seemed nervous. He fidgeted with a loose leg on the table. "What kind of help you talking about?" he asked.

"You have to get away from Louisville, from Kentucky," Aindreas said. "I'm getting help for that."

Isaac glanced at Tempie and his children. "If I go, we all going together. Ain't nobody gonna stay here."

"That's right, Isaac. You all have to go."

Isaac looked doubtful. "How me and Tempie carry children away from here?"

"I can't tell you."

"Why not?"

"I don't know yet."

Little Aaron lay asleep in Tempie's lap, his head nestled in the crook of her arm. Tempie said nothing. Her eyes shifted back and forth from her husband to Aindreas as they talked.

Muttering to himself, Isaac began pacing along the discolored walls of the cabin. Tempie simply nodded to Aindreas out of trust or intuition, she seemed to know he wouldn't make empty talk about something as dangerous as running away. Aindreas hoped Tempie would keep Isaac steady and not let him do anything out of line until the time came.

Worry about Isaac faded from his mind as Aindreas trudged back toward the tenement. His mother shriveled each day Isaac grew stronger. Dr. MacIntosh had paid several visits, leaving medicine each time.

Kirsty fired the stove now, fixed the supper, and cleaned the house. Doireann Rivers lay in her bed, staring at the whitewashed ceiling boards. No more sewing and tailoring for her. No more washing and ironing. No more problems with making peace and soothing hurts. All that was finished. But her presence seemed larger than ever.

Life in the family had changed for always. Joseph Rivers slept on a pallet in the kitchen. Aunt Margaret or Aunt Mary came every day with a freshly washed nightgown. Never before had Doireann Rivers possessed three nightgowns. Aindreas and Kirsty tiptoed about the place when their mother slept, and Michael and his father hadn't yelled at each other for days.

By unspoken agreement, Doireann had been declared entitled to the peace she had always wanted—and peace was freely given, now that she no longer had the power to bargain for it.

Aindreas spent the best part of an hour late Wednesday afternoon in the shops on Jefferson Street, searching for something special for his mother's birthday on July fourth. Up and down the aisles, he squinted into the glass-covered display cases. Nothing special enough could be found, at least not for a price he could pay. He consoled himself that he still had a week, time enough to find the right thing. But already, a wide banner hung between the Jefferson County Courthouse columns, with a red, white, and blue proclamation.

## HAPPY 79ᵀᴴ BIRTHDAY
## TO THE THIRTY-ONE UNITED STATES

Aindreas calculated that this final birthday for his mother would be her thirty-eighth. Not half as many as the Union.

He walked home and went in the front way, past the Travis house. Hard to get used to the idea that Kirsty worked there three days a week as a maid. Tempie spent most of her time cooking and tending the garden. Isaac managed to be seldom seen. When Aindreas came into the kitchen, he heard Kirsty's voice from his mother's room. "Can you imagine it?" Kirsty asked.

His mother's voice sounded grainy, husky. "My heavens, that's terrible."

"Poor Blanche," Kirsty added. "To come home and find out that way."

Aindreas paused at the open doorway. His mother had become so thin her coverlet looked flat, except the part that covered her bloated middle. The swelling looked bigger than last week. Aindreas looked away and spoke to his sister's back. "What did you say about Miss Flowers?" he asked.

Kirsty turned to him wide-eyed. "Johnny Flowers has gone!"

It took a moment for Aindreas to make sense of the words. Finally, he attached the name to his picture of the man Blanche Flowers was married to. He felt odd and a little guilty. *Hadn't he wished for Johnny Flowers to be gone?*

"Where?" he asked.

"Just gone." Kirsty looked flushed, and her voice betrayed a hint of enjoyment, excitement. "When Blanche Flowers came home from a teachers' meeting yesterday, Johnny's suits, shirts, all his clothes had disappeared."

Doireann coughed in her handkerchief. "There must be a reason," she said. "Who is that company he works for? Great Western Hardware? Maybe a sales call."

"He didn't take a trip," Kirsty insisted. "Blanche sent a telegraph message to them in Cincinnati, and they answered back that he quit his job last week. They wanted to know about some samples he was supposed to return."

Doireann Rivers closed her eyes. "That poor girl."

Aindreas and his sister each put an arm around their mother and helped her to a sitting position. Kirsty fluffed the pillows Aunt Margaret had brought, and they let her back gently.

Kirsty sauntered toward the door. She said over her shoulder, "I bet she'd like to come down and talk to you, Mum."

"Maybe I'll feel better tomorrow," Doireann said. She looked at Aindreas. "She's so fond of you, Andrew. Why don't you go upstairs and see her?"

Aindreas mumbled, "No, I don't want to."

"She's been asking where you been lately," Kirsty teased. "What's wrong? I thought you were *sweet* on her."

"No. No, I wasn't," said Aindreas, and brushed past his sister out of the room.

1

Allison, one of the wagoners at Cawthon's Furniture, apparently had a bad hangover Saturday morning. He repeatedly threw up behind the factory building. In a rare gesture of mercy to such a sinner, the chief clerk let the man go home at midday. One of the three delivery wagons lay thus idle.

Aindreas and Tim had finished their deliveries by mid-afternoon. Preparing to sweep the office, they sprinkled water on the dry floorboards and got their brooms from the closet.

"Rivers, Lytle, get over here," the chief clerk said.

"Yes sir!" Aindreas and Tim responded in unison. They leaned the brooms against the wall and hustled between the writing tables to the clerk's desk by the window.

"Can either one of you drive a wagon?"

"I can," Tim said. "Hauled rags in my uncle's wagon a lotta times."

A little envious, Aindreas remained silent.

The chief clerk smiled thinly at Tim. "Now that you mention it, you've been seen on a rag wagon during working hours for this company. We'll talk about that when I have time."

Tim gazed toward the window.

The crisp paper snapped when the clerk folded and creased two invoices. Aindreas had never seen or heard anyone who handled paper to such an effect. Papers made up the man's life.

The clerk said, "I need both of you on this." He wrote the address on the outside of the papers. "Two desks that should have been delivered this morning are out on the wagon. Take them to Saint Martin's, on Shelby Street. You'll have to find out whether they go to the church or the school." The clerk put the invoices into an envelope and handed it to Aindreas. "Get to it," he said, and resumed writing in his ledger even before they turned to go.

Aindreas and Tim walked through the noise, the sawdust, the reek of turpentine inside the factory. Each at its own tempo, many saws ripped wood. Tim scowled, his lips moving silently. Aindreas wondered whether his friend might be telling off the chief clerk or saying a prayer, and then he bit his lip to keep from laughing at the notion of Tim at prayer.

A large gray horse stood hitched to the loaded wagon resting by the freight dock. They climbed aboard. Aindreas suggested they go by way of Gray Street to avoid traffic. Tim disagreed. Perhaps he wanted to be seen by as many people as possible at the reins of the wagon with the Cawthon name painted on its side panels. Aindreas took note of the way Tim braced his feet, and he did the same. Tim slapped the reins on the big gray's rump, and the wagon lurched onto Jefferson Street, into a quarrel of hacks, carriages, wagons, and shoppers afoot.

Aindreas's ears burned. Along the way, every driver and every walker, even children, swore loud and often at Tim. He seemed determined to drive the wagon faster than traffic would allow. After urging the horse to a near gallop, he then had to pull up sharply to avoid a beer wagon at Third Street. Unused to such treatment, the big gray snorted, then tried to back up in the harness, bumping the shafts with its flanks and ribs. Finally, Tim let the horse set its own pace.

All the while, Aindreas sat on the far right side of the driver's box, his hand on the brake lever. He looked back once and saw König following at a distance. They got off Jefferson Street, at last, without a collision.

On rutted Shelby Street, the wagon swayed and groaned. Tim abruptly swung the wagon around a hearse drawn by two black horses and passed it. Aindreas knew Germantown: he knew the names, the smells, and the ways. These were good people. His aunt Margaret lived nearby. From up in the high seat of the wagon, the storefronts looked so different from the times he had walked the neighborhood. They rolled past Meier's Coffee Shop, Dorrn's Saloon, Strasser's Cabinet Shop, Schweitzer's Bakery, and grocery stores—Klotter's and Bassler's and Berghold's. The new Saint Martin of Tours Church loomed ahead, the cross atop its gray-green spire higher than anything else around. Saint Martin's wasn't huge, like the cathedral on Fifth Street, but Aindreas always felt thrilled when he saw it. The eight-sided tower began clear down at ground level, the rear half of it merging into the church building itself. Large sawtooth molding accented the roofline between the top of the tower and the spire. Sometimes when he drew near the church, Aindreas had the sense that someone might be watching through the slits of the louvered windows below the tower clock.

Tim Lytle sharply brought the wagon to a halt in front of the church, and jumped down. "Wait here," he said with the tone of a seasoned wagoner. "I'll find out where these damn things go."

Aindreas consoled himself that, at least, the wagon hadn't been wrecked. He leaned back and stretched his legs, watching the sun and shade play on the lancet windows. A sound of horses' hooves behind him grew louder, and the hearse they had passed earlier pulled in close behind the wagon. Two men took a small casket from the hearse and carried it through the portal on their shoulders. The idea of a church funeral seemed foreign to Aindreas; aside from his grandfather, no one close to him had died. Some of the Irish he'd grown up around might not have been able to afford such a thing.

A small, thin man came rushing out of the tower. He frantically waved his arms at the Cawthon wagon, as though trying to ward off a bad vision. "You can't be here!" he screeched.

"We'll be gone in a few minutes," Aindreas responded.

A muscle in the man's jaw twitched and he stared steadily at Aindreas with a dark, hostile expression. It made one itch just to look at him. Sweat salt trailed along the seams of the man's faded shirt. He carried a dirty look about him, something in his complexion, the sly set of his eyes, the short and unkempt graying beard. Doireann Rivers would have said of such a man, "A thousand baths wouldn't change the way he looks."

The man said in a shrill voice, "This is *verboten.*"

"The driver will be right back," Aindreas said, nervously looking around for Tim.

Men and women wearing Sunday clothes and black sashes came together in twos and threes at the church door. They murmured and embraced before they went inside. The dirty-looking man trailed after the mourners for a few steps, as if to go inside, then abruptly whirled about. He looked so wildly furious that Aindreas had no idea what he might do. Fortunately, Tim came hurrying around the side of the church, alongside a heavy man wearing an apron.

The dirty man whined to the new arrival, "I told him, Adler. I told him he couldn't be here."

The heavy man shook his head and untied his apron. His shirtsleeves were held up with garters, in the manner of a barkeep. "Finkel, I said you could call me Georg," he replied. "If you use my last name, it's *Mr.* Adler."

Finkel glared, then stared down at the gutter. How different, these two men. This Georg Adler looked like an aging pink cherub, lithe in spite of his weight, and Finkel was the very picture of a sullen scrag.

Adler pointed to the place in front of the school, just south of the church. "You," he said to Aindreas. "Move the wagon in front of that building."

Startled, Aindreas stared dumbly.

"Well, go on," Mr. Adler said, obviously put off that a boy didn't do as he was told.

Aindreas gripped the reins tightly, hoping the horse wasn't holding a grudge over that trip from Cawthon's. He carefully released the brake and made clicking noises with his tongue against the roof of his mouth. The gray horse pulled in the harness, and the wagon moved slowly forward.

Slow seconds passed before Aindreas pulled back gently on the reins. "Whoa," he said. The wagon came to rest right in front of the schoolhouse door. He set the brake, pleased.

Georg Adler climbed up on the wagon bed to examine the freight. "This one is for Brother Arsacious," he said, pulling a blanket cover off a drop-lid desk. He pointed, giving direction. "This should go right in the front door."

Aindreas helped Adler scoot the desk to the rear of the wagon, into the hands of Finkel and Tim. Finkel's knees shook as they lowered the desk to a dolly. Aindreas started to jump down and help him hold the weight of it, but Adler stopped him. "No, no," Adler said pleasantly. "Finkel is strong."

Tim and Finkel rolled the dolly to the front door of the

school. They had to turn the desk on its side to get it through the doorway. Cursing and tugging, they finally got the desk inside.

Adler appraised their efforts from the wagon. He took an apple from his pocket and sat on the edge of the wagon's side-panel. His voice sounded clear. It was almost a musical voice. "Well, you know I'm Georg Adler. Who are you?"

"Aindreas Rivers."

"Ah, I thought something like that. Irish or Scot, or both?"

"Irish."

"What was your mother's name?"

"McFate."

Adler laughed deep in his belly. "You're both, and just as bad as people who speak German. You know, Bavarians and Prussians don't claim each other, either." He took a bite from the juicy apple. "Marta, my wife, is from Baden." He wiped the apple juice from the corner of his mouth. "Her people didn't want to die in the army, so they came to America. Many of your Scots and Irish did the same thing. Who could blame them?"

"Are you from Baden, sir?"

"My parents were. I'm from New Jersey."

Tim and Finkel returned to the wagon. The second desk, it turned out, had been ordered for the church sanctuary. Adler apparently assumed Aindreas to be the wagoner and Tim the helper, so he instructed Finkel and Tim to take the desk back to the rear door of the church. Aindreas would have liked to help Tim, but he felt hesitant to correct Mr. Adler.

"Let's go in," Adler said, "I'll show you the organ and the altar Father Streber had sent all the way from Munich."

They quietly entered the nave of the church, into the muted light and sounds so different from the world outside. Through the stained-glass windows, the afternoon sun splotched melancholy colors on the walls, benches, and faces. Deep, somber organ chords rolled over the balcony railing. The funeral Mass had ended. For no reason, Aindreas thought of his mother's thirty-eighth birthday.

The men from the hearse carried the casket back up the aisle. Men and women dressed in black followed. There weren't many of them. By the look of their clothes, these couldn't be rich people. They would probably walk to the cemetery, Aindreas reckoned, maybe a long way, but the dead child would ride. He thought again of his mother. With all her heart's sorrow, thank God she had never had to take such a walk.

The building lay empty now but for the two of them. Mr. Adler had been the caretaker of the church since its dedication last August and knew a lot about it, though he gently made it clear that he himself was not a Christian. Aindreas listened to him as best he could, trying to concentrate in spite of an almost paralyzing sense of sadness.

They went together up to the high altar. Adler whispered and pointed out the artistic details in plaster, wood, and gold. Holy things confused Aindreas more and more. The Madonna in his room at home had turned black, and the Christ hanging on the high altar crucifix looked German.

Aindreas followed Adler back to the wagon. Tim sat sullenly in the driver's box, reins in his hands. Adler signed copies of the invoices and retrieved his apron.

"Hey, Aindreas," Tim said, "I'm gonna go by my house on the way to Cawthon's. They won't expect us back in the office. Why don't you just go on home from here?"

Aindreas wondered if Tim might do something with the wagon that would cause problems. "You think that's a good idea?" he asked.

"A helluva good idea," Tim responded and then, without another word, turned the wagon around and headed north on Shelby Street.

Across the street, König watched. He sat like a lion, paws as big as Aindreas's fists, his long, pink tongue lolling from the side of his mouth.

Adler seemed transfixed. "What a wonderful-looking animal," he said. "Is he yours?"

"We look out for each other," said Aindreas. "He used to be with Mr. Ostertag, but he doesn't belong to anybody."

"Ah, so that's him!" Adler said. "After old Ostertag died, that dog killed a huge, mean hog down by one of those garbage heaps on Market Street."

Aindreas tried to sound surprised. "He did?"

"Men with guns went searching for him. Called him an outlaw," Adler added with a smile, perhaps deciding that Aindreas was aware of these details all along. "What do you call him?"

"His name is König."

"Would you bring him by so my Marta could see him? She would love it."

"Where do you live, sir?"

"East…across Beargrass Creek, below the hill."

"I know that place," Aindreas said, "near the Bardstown Turnpike. They call the low street Underhill, and the high one Overhill."

"Yes, yes." Mr. Adler seemed pleased that Aindreas would know that. "You must get home, I know, but take a few minutes for yourself. Marta bakes sweet things on Saturday. Bring the dog and join us for something to eat."

2

They walked together over the creek bridge. Adler, apron slung over his shoulder, looked back several times to be sure the dog was following. He explained that besides his work at Saint Martin's, he did part-time carpentry, part-time wagon driving, and tended bar part-time at Dorrn's Saloon. He patted his stomach. "Marta says I drink beer better than serve it."

Aindreas asked, "Where did Mr. Finkel come from?"

Adler wrinkled his nose. "Ach, Herbert Finkel. I used to work for him at Herzog's Feed Merchants. He was a cousin of one of the owners. The place burned down over a year ago, and we all lost our employment. Only God knows why, but when I got the job with the church, I arranged for him to help me."

"Is there, uh, something wrong with him?"

"Same thing that's wrong with that damn George Prentice, though I don't think the two of them would agree on much."

"Mr. Prentice of the *Louisville Journal?*"

"Ya. Too much education, those two, and maybe a little crazy. They both studied law, each says he's a poet, and each thinks he's smarter than anyone else."

Adler waved to a woman sweeping in the street. Toward the end of the block, they stopped in front of a substantial, rough-timber house with a central chimney. "Here we are," he said.

Aindreas breathed in a delicious smell of baking bread.

Adler cupped his hands around his mouth and called out, "Marta, come out and see *der hund.*"

A large, pretty woman with braided blonde hair came to the doorway. The bare arms below the puffed sleeves of her dress looked soft and strong. She had the largest bosom Aindreas had ever seen.

"Say hello to young Aindreas Rivers," Adler said.

Marta Adler ruffled Aindreas's hair. "How skinny he is," she said. Then she poked her husband in the middle with her finger. "And how fat this one."

Adler gestured toward König, who lay by the edge of the street. "Remember, Marta, when I told you about the outlaw dog."

"Oh, *Mein Gott,*" she exclaimed, and covered her mouth. She took several steps toward the dog. "So huge…is he part wolf?"

"I don't know," Aindreas said. He whistled softly and said, "König...*kommen.*"

The dog plodded to within perhaps ten feet, then lay down again. Marta made cooing sounds. König watched her impassively. "Could I touch him?"

"No, I'm sorry." Aindreas said. "Only I can, and Mr. Knight."

"What does he eat? Marta asked, clasping her hands together. "I'll give him whatever he likes."

Aindreas said, "Anything, but he likes fish most of all."

Marta shooed Georg and Aindreas on through a parlor room with rows of knickknacks on the shelves, past a staircase to the loft, and into the kitchen. Adler and Aindreas sat on benches at the heavy table. Marta returned from the pantry room with a sack of fishmeal. "The king always eats better than the rest," she said, then held up a huge platter heaped with food. "See this, Aindreas? *Krautflecken*—boiled cabbage and noodles fried in bacon grease." She scraped some into a bowl and mixed it with the fish meal. "Here," she said, handing him a full bowl, "take it to the king. Plenty more for you when you get back and some *kuchen*, with apples and onions."

Aindreas set out the bowl of food for König, then hustled back to the kitchen. A mug of milk sat by his plate. Georg and Marta had glasses of dark beer. The noodles tasted wonderful, and Aindreas couldn't refuse chunks of brown bread still warm from the oven.

Mr. Adler told how he met Marta over twenty years ago, a widow with three daughters, and relatives who farmed down here in Jefferson County. Marta had thought Georg might make a farmer, so they had come to Louisville about nine years ago. He hated farming, it turned out, and had worked at a lot of jobs.

Georg and Marta bantered with each other. Aindreas had never seen married people laugh so much. After some beer, Mr. Adler became more serious and began to talk about how life changed so fast in Louisville. "Those who came here from Germany don't get credit for what they've done, Aindreas. Charity work in all eight wards of the city, and forming the unions for the cabinetmakers and the cobblers."

Marta laughed. "Don't forget the saloons, and the time the deacons over at Saint Boniface got into that squabble with Bishop Spalding over a cemetery," she said, then threw her hands in the air. "And the whole thing ended up in a brawl after Mass. And the newspapers fighting each other," she went on. "And that wild bunch in the Turner movement. They put on their red kerchiefs and white jackets and they'll fight anybody. The Irish don't have anything on the Germans when it comes to getting into fights, young man."

Adler waited, patient and amused, then resumed talking the instant his wife stopped to take a breath. "That city council, they're all Know-Nothings. Won't even let people drink in peace. They shut down the Sunday business, and last year all the taverns had to close by ten o'clock. People just getting started, then," he said indignantly. "Why, it's barely dark."

"At least I know you'll be home not much after ten," Marta said.

"This is a good Irish boy, Marta, and he needs to know about people who speak German. You're not helping."

Adler turned back to Aindreas. "But it's true what she said about the German newspapers. Only three left in Louisville now. The *Anzeiger*, a Democrat, and the Democrats amount to a damn bunch of slavers. The *Beobachter* has turned Whig, and I don't want to get started on that. And Karl Heinzen and those radicals at the *Herald* are going broke. All three papers get after each other every day, arguing and accusing. Seems to be mainly about what's going on in Germany since the revolution went sour."

Adler swigged his beer and wiped his mouth with the back of his hand. Marta rolled her eyes and handed him a napkin.

"A while back," Adler said, "it got talked around that the *Anzeiger* editor went to whorehouses. Well, he heard enough of that and paid a visit to Karl Heinzen and whacked him with an oxgoad. But Heinzen took it away from him and punched him good." Adler laughed so hard his face reddened. "This kind of thing goes on all the time."

Aindreas felt stuffed, but Marta scraped the last of the noodles and cabbage onto his plate. "Eat, boy, you look like a clothesline pole."

"You heard of the Union Band?" Georg asked. "They played at Elmtree Garden and Woodland Garden."

"I think maybe I saw them once in a parade," said Aindreas.

"And the German Theatrical Company," Adler went on. "I did work for them, even performed a few times. Last year…well, have you been to the stage in Jacob's Wood?"

Aindreas shook his head. "My mother and father went there once with my aunt and uncle," he said.

"Last year, they must have put on a hundred shows," Adler said. "Something every night. Dramas, comedies, light operas. I worked backstage on a lot of them, carpenter work, putting scenery together. I painted a backdrop for *Die Rauber* so beautiful they let me sing in the chorus the next musical performance."

"Did they do the shows in German?" Aindreas asked.

"Uh-huh, and a lot of people in the city wouldn't go because of that. They don't speak German—but say they don't like German. It's madness."

Marta said, "Now, don't get on your high horse, Georg. Next, you'll start about Yiddish."

"It's crazy," Adler insisted. "A few years back, P. T. Barnum brought that Swedish singer here…you know, Jenny Lind. Everybody with the price of a ticket crammed into Mozart Hall for two nights, and most of 'em didn't understand a damn word."

Adler reached to poke Aindreas in the chest with his finger. "Barnum made twenty-two thousand dollars and left the city eighteen dollars and fifty cents for the poor."

"Georg sings in the *Liederkranz.*" Marta said. She pinched her husband's arm. "He sang tenor when we married, and now they call him a baritone. My oldest daughter says I made a man out of him."

Georg Adler grinned. "All right, Marta, if we're going to talk like that, I'm going to ask the young man a German riddle."

Marta giggled. "You shouldn't tell these things in front of me."

"Do you know what a cow can do that a woman can't?" Georg asked.

Marta made a clatter as she cleared the dishes from the table.

"No," Aindreas said.

"She can wade in the water up to her tits and never get her ass wet."

Aindreas chuckled, and Marta rolled her eyes.

After she stacked the dishes, Marta came back to the table. "Well," she said, "this young man's mother probably wonders why he hasn't come home to supper, even if he's now too full to eat. Before he goes, why don't you tell him about the time even that cow you joke about was smarter than you and Dembitz."

"Everybody forgot about that," Adler moaned. "I wish you would."

Aindreas hoped they would tell what happened. Georg poured another half-glass of beer.

Marta said, "Your whistle already looks wet enough. Tell him."

"A couple of years ago," began Georg, "a few of us had a custom to stop at Frankel's Saloon. Marta thought there were women in the group, but there absolutely weren't." He smiled at his wife. "No more than a couple. When it got warm enough, we

122

would go down near Willow Bar and swim in the river."

"You mean when you had drunk enough," Marta put in.

Georg gave her a wave of the hand. "Dembitz was a good swimmer, too, and I guess we tried to outdo each other. We got out too far, and the rapids got hold of us. Dembitz yelled and screamed. A man named Poschner, who used to be an artillery officer back in Austria, jumped in after us. The rapids grabbed him, too."

"I tell you, Aindreas, I was going mad when they told me this," Marta broke in, "nine-thirty at night and those jackasses pounding on the door. Told me Georg had been carried over the falls. I didn't sleep all night. Went down to the river the next morning, and by the time I got back home, he had already gone to bed."

"Everybody thought we were done for," Adler resumed. "The news traveled all over town. I guess I believed it, too, at the time. Felt like a leaf sailing in the wind and got rolled under a couple of times. All I could do was stay afloat and keep my hands out in front so I wouldn't get mashed on the rocks. Turns out Poschner caught hold of a rock that stuck out of the water. He hung on till a boat came out from Jeffersonville and picked him up. Dembitz and I both ended up all the way past Clarksville." He laughed. "Each of us wondered if the other was dead."

"How did you get back?" Aindreas asked.

"It got dark, thank God. I hid in the bushes, without a stitch on, near the ferryboat landing."

Marta laughed hard and slapped Aindreas's knee when Georg wrinkled his nose.

"I guess I must have sat down on some poison ivy, but that's another story," Adler said. "Anyway, the ferryboat came in the next morning, and the crew had a good time about it. They lent me some pants and a shirt that covered about half my belly and brought me back over to Louisville."

His sides sore from laughing, Aindreas got up from the table. Georg and Marta each had an arm around the other as they walked with Aindreas to the door.

Marta said, "He doesn't have to worry about drowning anymore because I told him if he ever goes to the river with women again I'll kill him."

Outside, late dusk grew darker by the minute. König walked on ahead, leading the way, west on Prather Street toward home. For a time Aindreas had forgotten about his mother, and he felt guilty about laughing so much. He would talk to her when he got home, while there still was time.

# 8

Aindreas passed through the kitchen doorway into a gray, quiet room. Michael and Kirsty sat at the table, heads down, as though listening for something.

"She was screaming, before," Michael reported, when he first noticed Aindreas.

His sister came around the table and put her arms around Aindreas. "I think Mum may have gone to sleep," Kirsty said, near tears. "The doctor is still in there."

Aindreas peeked into his mother's room. She lay asleep. Joseph Rivers stood by the bed and listened to sad-faced Dr. MacIntosh.

"...of opium," MacIntosh was saying. "I'm leaving two bottles. Don't give it to her unless she needs it, but when she does..." Joseph Rivers rested his shoulder against the wall. His face looked flushed, and Aindreas guessed he'd been drinking. The doctor's expression gave no clue that he knew or cared.

"Haven't had any money for a time," Joseph Rivers slurred. "How much is our bill?"

"Twenty-seven dollars," said Dr. MacIntosh. "You might want to talk to your priest. The churches keep a fund to help out at a time like this."

"To hell with priests," Joseph Rivers grumbled. "Only met one of 'em in me life worth a damn, and he's dead."

The doctor shrugged. Aindreas's father shook his head

gravely. "But I guess you're tired of waiting for your money."

"I'm not pressing you."

Joseph Rivers reached down and took his wife's hand. "She can't go on and on this way, Goddamn it."

Dr. MacIntosh picked up his black bag. "She won't, sir."

Aindreas hurried back to his room. He knelt down by his bed, put his arm through the hole in the mattress, and fished around in the straw until he felt the small cloth sack hidden there. He pulled it out, untied the string, and counted out the contents: twelve dollars and seventy cents in coins. Aindreas returned the money to the sack and then hefted it in his hand—the savings of his life, every last penny of it. He had added to it whenever he could, certain he would know when to spend it for something that could not be done without. Earlier, that had seemed to be a special gift for his mother's birthday, but things had changed. Now, that something was the certainty Dr. MacIntosh would be there when Doireann Rivers needed him.

When Aindreas came out of his room, MacIntosh had left the house, headed toward his carriage. Aindreas caught up with him near Isaac's cabin.

The doctor put down his bag. He had a rumpled look and smelled of stale tobacco. "What is it, young man?" he asked.

Aindreas handed over the sack. "I want to pay this on the bill."

MacIntosh took off his hat and ran his fingers through his thin, light hair, then counted the coins in the dim light from the cabin. "A lot of money, Aindreas. Where did you get it?"

"It's mine. I saved it."

"I see," said the doctor.

"Will you still come when my mother gets bad?" asked Aindreas.

"I always come," said the doctor, and wearily rubbed the side of his face. "As long as she needs me."

"We'll pay it all," Aindreas assured him. "We always pay."

"I'm not worried about that," Macintosh said, and smiled tiredly. He wrote on his notepad, tore off a page, and held it out. "Here's your receipt."

Aindreas stuffed the paper in his pocket and returned to the house. When he reentered the kitchen the hushed talk between Michael and Kirsty stopped. Aindreas felt sorry for them. Only now did they seem to realize how bad Mother had gotten, and they may have thought their silence protected him.

His father had gone out again. Aindreas went into his mother's room. She lay on her back, thin arms folded over her stomach. Hair lay flat against her head in wet ringlets, as if she had been caught in the rain. Aindreas watched her, listening to her rasping breaths. *What would happen when her chest grew silent? Would she see a place better than this?*

He slumped in the chair by the bed. Maybe tomorrow he could talk to her.

1

The next morning, Sunday, it rained. Cool air blew through the house. Joseph Rivers put more bedcovers over Doireann and closed the window in the room where she lay. Kirsty cooked the rice porridge, but Doireann awoke confused and refused to eat.

Aindreas was sitting alone at the table when Tim Lytle rapped at the kitchen door. Tim seemed on edge, red-eyed and sleepless-looking. "Come on, Aindreas," said Tim. "We gotta go down to Cawthon's."

"On Sunday? Why?"

"I got the wagon back late, and the night watchman had been told to be on the lookout for me. That damn chief clerk must have set it up," Tim said bitterly. "The watchman told me we both had to come in at one o'clock today."

Aindreas's hands and feet felt cold. "What time *did* you go back to the freight yard?"

Tim shrugged his shoulders. "I don't know, maybe nine-fifteen. What of it?"

Aindreas grabbed his cap and stalked out the door, afraid and angry, realizing that he might lose his job because of Tim's showing off.

Walking behind, Tim said, "Don't act so high and mighty. You're in as much trouble as I am."

Aindreas didn't respond. He trudged all the way to Cawthon's, eight blocks of rain, without speaking a word.

Soaking wet, Aindreas and Tim finally stood in front of the chief clerk's high desk. "I believe you gentlemen were about to sweep out the office yesterday before you went on your little adventure," the clerk said in his usual measured tone. "Finish that now, before we have our talk."

Aindreas and Tim went to the task with anxious industry, even shifting the desks around to be sure they got at the entire floor. It took nearly an hour to finish. Then they waited for their work to be inspected.

But the chief clerk gave the floor only a brief glance before he began. "I'm told that you didn't get back with the wagon until after nine o'clock. Is that right?"

Tim said, "I don't think it was that late."

The clerk looked at Aindreas. "What time?"

"I don't know, sir."

"Why don't you?"

"I went home from Saint Martin's, or rather from Mr. Adler's house."

The clerk's tone took on an edge. "Who had the wagon all that time? One of you had better speak up."

Tim gnawed at his lip. "I had some things to haul, so I took it by my house," he said, then nodded toward Aindreas. "Rivers didn't care. I told him to go on home, 'cause we didn't finish with those desks until about four-thirty. He wasn't much help, anyway."

The clerk glanced at Aindreas. "You finished at four-thirty?"

Aindreas nodded.

The clerk tapped on the window for the watchman, then turned back to Tim. He said, "You're fired, Lytle."

Tim sagged. He stood silent for a time, then squared his shoulders. "Tomorrow is…payday," he stammered, "I'll want my money now."

The watchman, Clark, came inside and closed the door. This big man with a florid face and a thick mustache turning to gray walked toward them, leaving dark footprints on the dry wood floor.

The clerk gestured toward Tim. "This young man, Lytle, is no longer one of our employees. Should he come around here again, have him arrested."

Tim said, "I want my pay."

"You'll get your pay when a court says we owe it to you," the chief clerk snapped. "Now get out of here."

Clark watched impassively, water dripping from his coat into small puddles around his feet. He put a large hand on Tim's shoulder and said softly, "Come along now."

Tim shrugged the hand from his shoulder, then turned and shoved the watchman to the side. "I ain't leaving till I get my pay!" Tim shouted. "What do I have to do, throw a goddamn brick through the window?"

Clark's punch traveled a short distance—with his shoulder, his weight and all his experience behind it. The clean suddenness of it, the sound of fist and flesh and teeth, shocked Aindreas. Tim Lytle pitched forward to the floor as if his feet had slipped from under him. Pulled to his feet, the boy wobbled. Blood dribbled down his chin.

"You shouldn't have made me do that," Clark said. He pinned

Tim's arm behind his back and half-carried him out the door to Jefferson Street.

The chief clerk closed the ledger book on his desk. "You're still on the job, Rivers, but I'm going to be watching you," he said, pulling on his coat. "And I hope that you learned something from this."

"Nothing I didn't already know," Aindreas said flatly.

The rain finally stopped and the sky began to clear in the southwest by the time Aindreas got home. Kirsty kneaded dough on the counter. His father and brother were out somewhere. Neither of them had been around the house much these last weeks.

"Mother talked a little," Kirsty said. "Why don't you go in and see her?"

Aindreas smeared some butter on a slice of bread and ate it as he walked into his mother's room. Doireann Rivers opened her eyes when Aindreas sat down by the bed.

"Where you been, Andrew?" she asked. "You had breakfast?"

"It's after three o'clock, Mother. Kirsty made porridge earlier."

"That's good." She gazed at him uncertainly, as if she couldn't quite fix his image. "You sitting with me awhile?"

"Yes." He leaned forward and righted the pillows behind her.

Doireann glanced down at the middle of her body. Her voice was faint, "You know I'm awful sick, don't you?"

"Yes, I've known for a long time."

"You figured it out," she said, and gave him a sad smile. "I'm glad you did. I dreaded to tell you, but nobody else in the family has the blood for it."

Kirsty looked in and told them she would be working for Mrs. Travis for a few hours. Aindreas remained sitting by the bed. His mother grew very quiet, then dozed for a while. He watched through the window as tree shadows climbed like vines up the

130

Travis house. Her eyes were still closed, and he started when she spoke. "I've thought on it, Andrew," she said. "I'll be gone before my dreams die. It's best that way."

"Don't say that," Aindreas responded, though what she had said made the best of sense.

Doireann wagged her head. "God, the troubles. They never stopped after the yard doctors and the midwives with their whiskey stews started on me. Old Dr. Kalbrier, he's dead now, called it 'hysteria,' year before last. Can you imagine that? He bled me, poured that awful calomel down my throat." She sighed. "Almost a year ago, Dr. MacIntosh told me…said I might not last six months. I did last, but I'm tired, Andrew."

"Rest, now," Aindreas said. "I'll fix some tea."

In the kitchen, Aindreas stirred the coal embers to a glow, then set the kettle on the stove lid. He sensed someone in the room behind him and turned around. Mr. Knight was standing in the open doorway.

"I'm fixing tea," Aindreas said, swiping at his eyes with the back of his hand. "Do you want some?"

Knight nodded, and sat down. He held in his hands an object wrapped in velvet.

"It's hard to do what you told me to," Aindreas said.

"I know," Knight said, "but you'll do fine."

Aindreas scoured the cups with a towel and filled them with dark tea. Only a little sugar remained in the canister. Knight declined with a wave of his hand, so Aindreas poured it all into his mother's cup.

Knight placed on the table the object he had brought. He removed the velvet covering and held it out. "I found this not far away, buried in rubbish…a bason, I think they used to call it," he said. Perhaps as large as a middling platter, the vessel's edges curved upwards from a flat bottom, more like that of a shallow dish than a bowl. Knight added, "I heard the old German,

Ostertag, had it once."

Aindreas took the precious vessel in his hands, brought it close to his face. It felt cool in his palms. Colors emerged, dim patterns showed through tacky brown film and tarnish. This thing he held seemed very old, yet it was somehow familiar to him. The more you looked at it, the more was clear to you. It was, plainly, the stuff of lore that had always been beyond his reach. "What is it called?" he asked.

"What does it mean to you?" asked Knight.

"I guess what I have always searched for," Aindreas said, running his fingers along one edge. "I've never had anything so wonderful, but I don't know if I could make it look grand again."

"You'll find a way," Knight said. "And why not give it to your mother on her birthday? She deserves much more, but you have nothing else."

The notion of such a gift made his chest pound. "Yes," said Aindreas.

"Take your mother her tea," Knight said. He reclaimed the bason, wrapped it again in the velvet cover, and placed it on the table. "She has things to tell. It may trouble you, but you must listen—no one ever has."

Aindreas hesitated, still holding her cup of tea. "Should I go for a priest?"

At the door, Knight said, "No, you don't have a lot more time. You must be the priest."

2

**A** persistent red bird carried on from the tree near the window. In that crease between waking and dreaming she heard his call and from her bed dimly saw a holy man in the doorway, his collar gleaming white in the late afternoon sun.

"Tempie…Tempie."

She swung her heels to the floor and rubbed her eyes. It was

Reverend Cole, from the church.

"Sorry to wake you up, Tempie," the reverend said. "I came to call on you all."

Embarrassed, she smoothed out her dress as she got up from the pallet. Caught napping while Isaac worked. What would the reverend think of her? The tiredness seemed to come on her when she didn't expect it, just like the other times. "Isaac's over back of the big house, Reverend," she said, then pulled a chair out from the table for him.

"Sit down, I'll git him."

Moments later, she returned with her husband and the children. Isaac and Reverend Junior Cole embraced, and Tempie poured their guest a cup of water.

"Glad to see you healing up so fine, Isaac," Cole said. "Haven't seen you and Tempie for weeks."

Isaac said, "We're doin' all right, Reverend. You know, Squire Travis wasn't none too happy I got hurt over by the church. That's why we stopped coming on Sunday."

Reverend Cole drained the cup and smacked his lips. "Hope he'll change his mind. You want me to try and talk with the squire?"

Tempie looked down.

Isaac said, "Don't know if we have the chance to get back, but we sure was happy when we got to come there."

Reverend Cole kept his eyes on Sarah and Aaron, playing on the floor by the fireplace. "You're fixing to run, ain't you?" he said in a low voice.

Isaac and Tempie didn't respond.

Cole got up from the table and shook hands with Isaac. His expression remained very serious, but his words came out loud and cheerful. "Well, God bless you, and we be expectin' you the first Sunday you can make it."

"Hot as it's been, how could I be cold?" Doireann asked, then shivered, holding onto the cup in both hands. "Some people say sickness is punishment," she said, her voice trailing off. "I heard that more than once."

Aindreas wondered about his own sickness, and all the bad things he'd done.

"Have I always been sick?"

"No," she declared. "Small you were and not so strong as the others. I'm not sure that fall you had caused it, mind you, but the spells didn't start till after that."

A few times, Aunt Margaret had mentioned a fall. No one else in the family ever talked about it, and Aindreas had no memory of such a thing happening to him. "How did I fall?" he asked.

"You were with Marc."

"Uncle Marcus?"

Doireann seemed not to have heard his question. She handed him the empty cup. "That was sweet and tasty," she said. She rolled to her side, pulling the bed covers up under her chin. "A boy like him had no place out on the farm, so he spent time here in Louisville with some teachers," she began. "They wanted to help him because he was so smart. You heard about that."

Aindreas nodded.

"Read Latin when only a little thing, and he could say pages out of a book from memory," Doireann said. "I always thought he'd be called to the Church, but he never cared about that."

"Did he live with us then?"

"He boarded at the school. But he came to see us a lot, back when we lived on Main Street."

"So how did it happen—the fall?"

"Two years before Marc died; he was sixteen," said Doireann. "You were just six, and little at that. He would carry you around on his shoulders sometimes, and you'd cry when he had to go. He loved you so much because you never acted like he was different."

Faint, dark pictures played for an instant along the edges of Aindreas's mind, an image of a round face with fearful, bulging eyes, a body heaving and gasping for air.

"Somebody hurt him, didn't they?" Aindreas asked. "Who did that?"

"A gang of thugs that used to hang around between Main and Water Street."

"Why?"

"A lot of people hated him," Doireann said. "Maybe some of them feared him. So round and heavy, and his eyes. He couldn't...control himself some ways. You remember. When it got talked around that he was some kind of wizard...well."

"That day, he came by and took you to a sweet shop. Some of those no-goods threw rocks and made fun of him. When they looked like they wanted to beat him up, he grabbed you and tried to run, but they caught up to him. Maybe a rock hit you, or your head got hurt when he fell to the ground. We thought you were dead when he carried you in. You didn't come to for a day and a half. Some people blamed Marc, especially your father. Joe raved every time he saw Marc after that."

Aindreas recalled his father's admitting his feelings for Marcus. "Do you think that's really why Da hated him?"

"No, it started a long time before that," said Doireann. She wiped at her suddenly damp face with a corner of the sheet. Aindreas fetched a jar of cool water from the kitchen. Settled down again, she asked, "Where was I, Andrew?"

Aindreas felt unsure about asking any more questions about his father and Uncle Marcus. "You told me about the fall," he prompted.

"The terrible gash on your head took the longest time healing up. Dr. Kalbrier said the skull had been broken. The spells started soon after that. The doctor would feel around so carefully on your head. Said there was a depression there. He thought he found one, once, but then said he couldn't be sure."

"What did the doctor *do*?"

"Nothing…he wanted to see if he could find something pressing at the brain," said Doireann. She sobbed. "He wanted to cut open your head with a thing he called the 'elevator.' I'll never forget that. I knew you would've died, and I wouldn't let him do it."

Aindreas ran his fingertips along the short scarred crevice on the back of his head nearly covered by the hair. He said, "So everybody blamed Uncle Marcus."

"You never did," Doireann said. "Besides, it was my fault from the start, and I'll be judged for it."

4

Emily Travis waved her handkerchief out the front window. "Blanche," she cried. "Oh, Blanche!" She waved again. "Yes, here I am. Won't you come in?"

Emily hurried to the front porch. She always enjoyed the sweet anticipation of even small triumphs. What a shame the altar society-meeting started in thirty minutes. A chairwoman should be early, but beautiful, musical Blanche Flowers had walked right by the window, and Emily hadn't had the chance to talk to her since hearing all that news about Johnny Flowers. Emily opened the door. "There you are, Blanche. Do come in."

She did not intend to lead her guest to the parlor, and it amused her that Blanche looked a little awkward just standing there in the hallway. Emily felt a warm glow in her middle. Lovely Blanche needed to learn what awkwardness felt like. "I'm so sorry that I only have a minute," Emily said. "I would offer you something cool to drink."

"That's quite all right," Blanche said, "I need to get back to my rooms."

"The first of the month, already," Emily said, smiling. "You and Mr. Flowers have always been so prompt."

"Mrs. Travis, perhaps..."

"*Emily*, please."

"Yes, Emily, possibly you hadn't heard that my husband is away. I'm not sure when he'll be back."

"Isn't that just like a husband? And I'd wager the irresponsible fellow didn't even leave the money for the rent."

"No, I'm afraid not." Blanche said, returning Emily's gaze. "School will begin in a few weeks, and my salary will start again. In the meantime, I've written to my parents, in Cincinnati. As soon as I have money on hand, the rent will be paid...as it always has been."

"I wasn't the least concerned about it, my dear," said Emily.

Walking stick in hand, Squire Travis sauntered up the brick walkway. Emily Travis put gloved fingers to her lips, affecting surprise. "Well, here's my squire, in the nick of time for both of us," she said, and impatiently tapped her closed fan against her purse. "Squire, I'm late for my meeting at Christ Church. Where has that Isaac gone with the carriage?"

Squire Travis glanced toward Blanche, then gave a slight bow toward both women. He said, "I saw him hitching up the horse." The squire stepped back out the door and craned his neck, looking. "There, I see him. He's bringing the carriage around now, dear."

"Good," Emily said. She felt wonderful. After a brief appraisal of her face in a hand mirror, she kissed her husband on the cheek and opened the door without looking at Blanche Flowers. "I must hurry. Blanche is unescorted. Would you mind taking her back to the guest house?"

A moment later, the carriage proceeded down Prather Street, providing anyone who cared with a glimpse of Emily Travis.

His wife underway, Squire Travis looked again at Blanche. "I'll walk along with you."

"There is no need to inconvenience yourself, Squire."

He patted her arm. "I insist."

When they walked past the cabin, the voices of Tempie and Sarah could be heard in one of their singsongs:

Run nigger, run, it's almost day;

That nigger run, that nigger flew,

That nigger tore his shirt in two;

Run nigger run, the *patroller catch you…*

Squire Travis rolled his eyes and smiled. "To think that otherwise sane people claim the Negroes should be free," he said. He gazed down at Blanche with an expression of concern. "I hope you won't mind my broaching the subject, but I heard that John Flowers has gone. Should you need help, I would be offended if you didn't let me know."

"That's very kind," she said. "But I assure you everything's fine." Shortly, they arrived at the outside stairs to Blanche Flowers's rooms. Squire Travis wanted very much to think of some way he might talk with her in real privacy. *He could tell her he needed to go upstairs and look at the storage room. No, better not.* The front window of the Rivers's flat was only a few feet away. *It would probably be tough to collect the rent from that Rivers bunch again, with that woman dying. Maybe it would be best to just throw them out and be done with it.*

Hands in his pockets, the squire scuffed the toe of his boot in the dust like a boy. "Please don't think me forward, but it's hard to imagine John, or any man, doing anything like that to a person as…as charming as you."

Blanche colored. "Please," she said, "I must go now."

He pressed her hand. *Perhaps he had tried to move too quickly, but it made his head spin standing close to the beautiful Blanche Flowers.* "Don't be offended. I am very fond of you, and hope we will know each other better as time goes by."

She turned to leave. "Thank you, Squire, and good day."

As she climbed the stairway, he watched her take each step, all the way to the top, imagining the movements of the body beneath the dress and the crinoline.

5

Doireann said she wanted to get up. But she could barely stand, even with Aindreas's help. A man and woman talked outside the window as Aindreas draped his mother's quilted robe over her shoulders.

Having finally made it to the kitchen, she slumped out of breath into a chair. She stared out the window as she spoke. "There is something I need to tell you. Someone…. once someone killed my daddy's dream, and he didn't care a damn after that. I was fourteen, a little slip of a thing, and I watched him wither away like a stalk."

Aindreas leaned against the sink. His mother's face was outlined in the twilight.

"Who did that to him?" asked Aindreas.

"My daddy's youngest brother, William," she said. "The fairest McFate."

"What did he do?"

"William was the father of Marc, the one you children called Uncle Marcus." She sighed and lowered her head. "My own Marcus."

These words filled all the space in his head, and for an instant he had no understanding of them. Then he had to clasp his hands together to keep from shaking.

"Daddy never spoke to his brother again, never saw him," Doireann went on miserably. "But that didn't help Daddy. You see, William had always been the one in the whole family who made life seem worth living."

"Did Aunt Margaret and Aunt Mary know what happened?"

"They did, and a few others. I went with Mamma when she went on a long visit with her sister down in Tennessee. We brought the baby back with us. Daddy didn't last a year after that. Pneumonia got him."

"What happened to William McFate?"

Doireann laughed bitterly. "Once, they elected him a state senator."

Aindreas wished with all his heart he had not heard any of this.

"Marc was different, even as a baby," said Doireann. "I helped with him all I could, always, but nothing could ever wipe out the way that child came to be." Her words became mixed with sobs. "Your father and I never talked about this. He couldn't. I gave him a hundred chances. Still, I know that somewhere in his soul he always held it against Marcus and against me."

Aindreas helped her from the chair and back to her bed. When she settled in bed, he said, "You had no fault...God knows you did nothing wrong."

She gripped his hand. "How can you be so sure He knows that?"

"God isn't a fool."

Doireann's breathing seemed easier. "Thank you," she whispered.

Aindreas went to the kitchen and returned with a burning sliver of kindling. He lit the lamp, turned it up bright.

"What will happen to you when I'm not around, Andrew?" she said. "I worry about that. I think about the July rent, too, and I wonder how the doctor will ever get paid."

Aindreas said, "I'll be all right." Only a second later, he lied again. "And Da told me he has a way to get the money for the rent."

"Really, Andrew?"

He nodded, dug down in his pocket for the receipt MacIntosh had given him, then handed her the crumpled paper. "And look at this payment on the doctor bill."

Doireann looked at it and blinked in wonder. "I don't know how you did this, but I won't need anything to help me rest tonight."

In a few moments she closed her eyes and drifted off to sleep. Aindreas looked down at the paper that had so pleased her, then held it up closer to the lamp. It read:

JULY 1, 1855

*On account of Doireann Rivers, received the sum of $27.00. Paid In Full.*

   *Dr. J. A. MacIntosh*

# 9

Isaac pursed his lips, as though that might help him see more clearly, then held out the bason at arm's length in the fading sunlight slanting through the cabin window. "No, young Andrew," he said, inspecting the underside for some mark of the smith who had made it. "I never seen nothing like this. What you gonna do with it?"

"It's going to be a gift," replied Aindreas.

"It was mine, I'd sure enough want to keep it," Isaac said, and ran his fingers over the smooth, rounded edges. He shrugged. "But if you gonna give it away…well, you know what you want to do."

"Could I make it shine the way it must have before?"

"Can't tell," mused Isaac. "It's so old, and got three …four kind of metal in it, and maybe some sort of glass." He thought for a moment. "One thing we might try." He knelt and rooted in a heap of burlap sacks beside the wall and produced a cloth sack. He opened the drawstrings so Aindreas could see inside; the sack, about a third full, contained powder that looked like coarse, white dust.

"It's pumice, all ground up. Old Hiram Travis, the squire's daddy, brought it back from Boston. But then he told me not to use it, 'cause he was scared some of his wife's fine pieces might get all scratched up." Isaac grinned. "He didn't know I mixed it with the polish when I had to. Never scratched nothin'."

Aindreas rubbed a pinch of the dust between his thumb and fingers. Soft as face powder at first, the feel of the underlying grittiness made the skin on his face prickle. Isaac gestured toward the bason. "Who you giving this to?"

"My mother. It's for her birthday."

"That's good. I was gonna help, but I guess you want to do this by yourself."

Aindreas nodded.

"Here's what you do. Get some polish like they use on silver, and mix in a little water." Isaac grabbed a rag and stretched it tight over the first two fingers of his good hand. "Now, you don't rub in the hot sun with no polish. You work it in with little circles, like this."

Aindreas watched closely. "I see," he said.

"All right." Isaac pointed to the worst discolorations. "Add just a little bit of the powder. About this much…see? Don't press down too hard, but keep the pressure even." He chuckled. "Time you finish Andrew, your fingers look like you been teasing 'round with snappin' turtles."

Though Aindreas hung around the cabin a while longer, his friend didn't ask anything about an escape plan. That worried Aindreas. With all that had gone on, running away couldn't ever have been far from Isaac's mind.

Aindreas carried the gift back to his room. Aunt Margaret and Aunt Mary had come for a visit with his mother. He went into her room and stayed with them for a time.

He had once seen a jar of silver polish in the pantry and finally found it behind some old bottles. Why his family would have such a thing was hard to imagine, since they had nothing for which to use it. *Maybe his mother had saved it for this.* The thick, smelly paste thinned out with a little water. He turned his head away while he stirred it. Not a whole lot of time. It was already Monday, but he still had tonight, and tomorrow night he had to help Tempie and Kirsty at the Travis party, then it would be Wednesday, the Fourth of July, his mother's birthday. There had been a rumor that Cawthon's Furniture might close at noon for the Independence Day celebration. That would help. He wound a rag tight around two fingers and went to work.

1

William Williams, younger brother of one of the clerks, had been hired to replace Tim Lytle. Aindreas worked alongside this new boy Tuesday morning to show him the ropes. William didn't sound as if he knew much about the streets and neighborhoods. He would certainly learn the hard way on this job, Aindreas figured. William did ask a lot of questions, and he seemed curious about how the first two fingers of Aindreas's right hand had gotten so discolored.

Nobody had been able to tell what Tim Lytle might do at any time, and that sort of unreliability had gotten him fired. William Williams was different. This fair-haired, lanky boy with a prominent nose and cheekbones turned out to be eighteen months older than Aindreas. William positively reeked of the desire to do the proper thing every minute; he did exactly as told and sought favor from anyone at Cawthon's who ranked above him, and that was everyone. Aindreas was uneasy with him from the start. Near noon, a delivery took them down Water Street. Aindreas saw Jack Graham up ahead and ran to catch up with him.

"Haven't heard a word about my reinstatement," Graham reported. "Did you know the *Ben Franklin* will dock here this afternoon?"

Aindreas's heart skipped a beat. *The captain might be ready to talk about a plan for Isaac.* "I didn't know that," Aindreas understated.

"Cap'n Workman will lay over a couple of days, so try to get

144

down there to say hello," Graham said. "Hey, remember that storm the last time? You held up like a real riverboat man."

Aindreas smiled and looked down.

William stood open-mouthed, obviously impressed by his colleague's friendship with a real river pilot.

"I'm on my way to the Wharfmaster's office, Lucky," said Graham. "Come on by when you get a chance."

Aindreas assured Graham that he would.

When Graham went on his way, William asked, "Why did he call you Lucky?"

"No reason," Aindreas said, feeling the warm color in his face. "Just a name."

At lunch time, William decided to stay inside the office and eat with his brother. Aindreas had brought along the gift to the office so he could work on it, should time permit. He removed the bason from the file cabinet where he had hidden it, then went outside and sat down by the side of the building, where Tim used to spin stories about his romances. Aindreas had stopped by the cabin on the way to work, and Isaac sounded even more taken with the bason than he was before and couldn't imagine where they could make things like that. Aindreas unwrapped the bason, inspected it again. The tiny etched circles along the edges and underside, and the stars, squares, and triangles were becoming clear. It seemed the more Aindreas put into it, the more an inner brightness shone.

He dipped the rag into the polish and rubbed not too hard in small circles, the way Isaac had told him. When he looked up once, Tim Lytle, or someone who looked like him, was walking past on the other side of Jefferson Street. Aindreas stopped and held up the oval, studying the shapes and colors spread across the flat bottom. Would he ever understand all this? Such colors: nearly purplish blue, green, silver, and deep copper-gold. It didn't look like a landscape in a painting; the scenes coming out of the bason were deeper, drew you in. Trees, and mountains, sea, sky, and fire. It had all been created with mixed and overlaid metals in such a way that no shape or color had worn more than the rest. Color and shape were one.

A noise broke his concentration. An instant passed before he realized that he had heard shattering glass. A heavy, gray-haired man hurried away on Jefferson Street. Then again, the sound of breaking glass farther away.

Someone shouted, "You, there: stop!"

Immediately, Cawthon's workers on their dinnertime milled about the place, confused, pointing this way and that. Aindreas ran to the front of the building. The Jefferson Street office window had been smashed, and long glass shards hung from the top of the frame. He went inside the office; on the far side of the room, the window on Eighth Street had also been broken. Juniors crowded around the chief clerk's desk. He looked dazed, and his face was bleeding from several cuts. William Williams showed hunks of brick he found on the floor to anyone who would listen to him.

"Let's get some brooms and boxes up here, and get this glass cleaned up," one of the juniors urged in high-pitched earnestness.

Everyone in the office talked at once. Finally, a common understanding formed: somebody had thrown bricks through both windows and then gotten away clean as a whistle.

"Who would want to do a thing like that?"

"Think this has anything to do with the election coming up?"

"Oh, hell no. Mr. Cawthon doesn't care about politics."

"Bet it was one of those German or Irish drunks."

"A drunk wouldn't hit both windows, you dummy."

Splinters of glass lay scattered across the desks and the floor. Aindreas swept some of the smaller pieces into a pile. Had he really seen Tim Lytle on Jefferson Street? If so, Aindreas wondered whether the chief clerk had learned something from all

146

this.

*The gift.* He had left it outside. Aindreas dropped the broom and ran out of the office to the side of the building. A number of men, including several policemen, were still tramping all around the building exterior. A miracle. The gift still lay shining in the sun, right where he had set it down by the wall. Footprints lay in the dust all around it. Aindreas took a deep breath and picked up the bason. It had become as valuable to him as anything in the world, he realized. Others would think it had worth, too, and some of the people who hung around Jefferson Street would steal things simply for the pleasure of doing it—yet no one had noticed it or cared, being caught up in the excitement. Caught up in the excitement. Just as he had been. He must try not to be so childish again.

2

**L**ater that afternoon, on a return trip to the factory, Aindreas and William made their way along Ninth Street, between Market and Main. Angry voices could be heard up ahead. William hung back.

"C'mon," Aindreas said, and waved his hand.

A washtub, some clothes, a chair, and a few pots and pans had been piled along the sidewalk in front of a listing two-story tenement. Sweaty men carried out a battered table and put it beside the disreputable-looking pile of things. Neighbors hung about; men and women passing on the street paused to watch.

William said, "Let's stay on this side of the street."

"No, I need to find out what's happening," Aindreas said. He crossed the street, Williams following along, and found a spot close enough to listen.

A tall woman stood in the center, holding the hand of a broad-faced little girl with skinned knees and a runny nose. Two shirtless boys, a couple of years younger, were half-hiding behind the girl.

147

The woman's face and arms were raw red, and her hoarse voice sounded the same. "Before God, think of what you're doin', Mr. Pritchett," she said.

The man at whom she nearly shouted stood only a few feet away. His coat over his arm and a tall hat still perched on his head, perspiration ran down his double chin onto his shirt. He poked the air with his finger and said, "I've thought all I need to, Mrs. Greene. Now, we don't want a scene here, do we? You need to get these children on down the street."

A murmur rose from the crowd when Pritchett's men pushed their way through the onlookers and dumped soiled sheets and straw ticking by the rest of it. Perhaps the gawkers felt sympathy for Mrs. Greene, or maybe they were just reacting to the dirty bedding.

Mr. Pritchett paced about, nervous and twitchy. He grasped the arm of one of his men. "How much left up there?"

"Two or three more trips, Mr. Pritchett...some bed rails, junk from the kitchen, a few other things."

"What about the sheriff's deputies?"

The man shrugged. "They was supposed to meet us here at three o'clock," he replied before he started back up the stairs.

Three men carrying lunch pails brushed past Aindreas into the center of the group. They stopped and talked in whispers with Mrs. Greene. All three men wore corduroys and coarse cotton shirts; Aindreas figured they probably were laborers from the nearby Louisville & Portland Railroad. One of them, small and muscular, and with hair so curly it looked like wire, patted Mrs. Greene's shoulder.

The man glared at Pritchett. "At it again, are you?"

Pritchett didn't answer. Several deputies arrived. "About time," he chided the one nearest him.

Mrs. Greene was crying as if her heart would break, and that made Aindreas very sad. "He knows my husband went to

Lexington to look for work," she said to the man with curly hair.

William touched Aindreas on the arm. "Let's go."

"Not yet," Aindreas said, "Maybe you need to see this, too."

The railroad men stared at Pritchett, who seemed to stand taller in the presence of the deputies. He had grown bolder as well, and glared back at the railroad men.

"How long has she owed you?" the man asked.

"She didn't pay for June, and now it's July. Besides, it's none of your business."

Mrs. Greene wept more quietly.

"Her husband's looking for work," said the man.

Pritchett snapped, "Why don't you shut up and get out of here?" Perhaps seeking moral support, he smiled toward a cluster of men in coats and ties, women in clean dresses. Pritchett glanced at Mrs. Greene. "You people are always *looking* for work, but you never seem to find it."

Several of the men wearing white shirts and neck cloths laughed, and Aindreas heard William snickering behind him.

The curly-haired man scowled and took a step toward Pritchett, who backed away. "It's easy enough for some of you to laugh," the man said, turning to the crowd. "Those who laughed likely don't have to find work." He turned to Pritchett. "Where do you think this woman can go?"

The deputies cleared the way for Pritchett's men, who brought the bed rails out to the pile by the curb. One deputy tried to break up the crowd. "Move on down the street," he ordered.

Only a few onlookers left.

The curly-haired man stood his ground, and the two other railroad workers stayed right behind him. His tone was insistent. "I asked you a question, Pritchett."

Two men, newly arrived, moved in beside Pritchett. One had mutton-chop whiskers and smoked a cigar and the other was tall and heavy, wearing a hat pulled down near his eyes; Aindreas remembered them from the Free German Union rally.

Pritchett's confidence apparently had returned. "You're some kind of union agitator, aren't you?" he asked.

The man snorted, then gestured toward the pile of Mrs. Greene's belongings. "What I do at the shop has nothing to do with this."

Pritchett flushed. "It has everything to do with it," he snarled. "Work made this country great, and now we take in the loafers from all over the world. You Irish and Germans floated over here like rubbish, and now you think you can run the whole place."

"I work every day," the man said. "What do you mean calling me a loafer?"

Pritchett waved a hand in dismissal. "Ever since your sort came, we've had nothing but trouble. The Know-Nothings have called you a bunch of Communists and Papists, and they're right. Nothing but lazy, immoral people, the lot of you, and I've had enough." His rage growing, Pritchett boldly wandered a few steps from the police. He motioned toward Mrs. Greene. "This woman's husband doesn't work, and that's just too bad for her and for those children she was improvident enough to bring into this world."

Aindreas started at the quickness of the curly-haired man, who grabbed Pritchett by the collar and pulled him so close that their faces touched. "You fat little pig," the man said. "You never worked a damn day in your life."

Pritchett wriggled furiously; the bottom edges of his fine coat dragged the dirty sidewalk and the tall hat toppled. His nearly bald head, sparsely covered by long hairs combed across the top, looked pink in the sunlight. He didn't look much taller than Aindreas.

The policemen pulled Pritchett free, then looked around nervously, perhaps concerned the situation would get out of hand. One of the policemen signaled the deputies, who brandished their clubs and pushed the people down the sidewalk or into the street. A few onlookers, reluctant to leave the show, stepped back only far enough to be out of reach of the clubs—but the crowd was scattering.

The police kept the railroad workers separated from the rest. "Do you three want to talk with Judge Joyes? Maybe break stone for ninety days at the Cave Hill Quarry?" the man with the side-whiskers asked. "I can fix that and I will, if you're not out of here in one minute."

The railroad men grumbled and swore but picked up their lunch pails and walked away. Aindreas and William trotted back across Ninth and walked toward Jefferson. Aindreas looked back: only Mrs. Greene and her children remained, consoled by two old ladies the police hadn't bothered. *The old axiom proved true again: only the poor help the poor. And every day, another ugly thing to see, more ugly whispers to hear.*

As they approached the factory, Aindreas remembered that he had to help Kirsty and Tempie at the Travis party that night, and he picked up the pace. He would have to get home from work as soon as he could.

Pulling up nearly even with Aindreas, William Williams said, "That one man told the God's honest truth."

"Which man?" asked Aindreas.

"Why, Mr. Pritchett. That woman and her children look like trashy good-for-nothings. My father and mother told me about people like that."

Aindreas looked away. He decided that he would never call this new boy by his first name again. "Shake a leg, Williams, we haven't got all day," he said.

### 3

Kirsty was out in the kitchen, ironing Aindreas's corduroy trousers on the sink counter. "I'm glad you didn't get these dirty."

Louder, she asked, "Did you put on your other shirt?"

"Yes," he said from the back room.

Aindreas brushed his boots as he waited for Kirsty to finish. Standing around without his pants on made him seem like a child.

Kirsty put away the iron and prepared to leave for the Travis house. Pulling on his pants, Aindreas called after her, "I'll be along in a minute."

His mother had called for medicine earlier. Aindreas went to her room. His father sat by the bed, his gaze toward the window. Doireann Rivers slept, her breathing shallow and rapid.

"I have to go," Aindreas said to his father. "Do you want anything?"

Joseph Rivers continued staring out the window. After a few seconds, Aindreas turned and left for the Travis house.

4

He stood just inside the kitchen door. Eyes flashing, Emily Travis pranced into the room in a long, green dress. "Tempie, don't you dare put those puff shells in the oven until I tell you," she said. "You hear me?"

"Yes, Miss Travis."

Aindreas gaped. Trays and serving dishes filled all the counters and the table. Chicken, ham, and cold beef. Bowls of potatoes, corn, tomatoes, squash, strawberries, watermelon, covered dishes, bread, relishes and sauces, cakes and cookies with chocolate all over them. *Never saw anything like it outside one of those hotel restaurants.* Kirsty moved the food to the dining room or the parlor as directed.

Mrs. Travis spotted Aindreas. "There you are," she said, and crooked her finger. "Come over here and let me have a look at you."

She looked him up and down. He felt glad he had cleaned up

and combed his hair.

"...a shame." Her voice sounded almost wistful. "You're not really the worst-looking youngster."

For an instant, Aindreas sensed that Mrs. Travis wanted to touch his face. He felt relieved when she withdrew her hand.

The edge had returned to her voice. "Is that the only pair of trousers you have?"

"Yes, ma'am."

"Well, that shirt will never do," she said, then made a face. "And, my word, have you been digging in the dirt? Look at your fingers. You'll have to wear gloves."

Kirsty was in and out of the kitchen, carrying trays of food. Each time she came back in the room, she gave Aindreas a nervous glance.

Mrs. Travis ducked into the pantry and brought out several white cotton jackets. "Here," she said, "Try on this smallest one."

Aindreas pulled on the jacket.

"Tempie, find those gloves Isaac used when he waited table last year," Mrs. Travis said. "That trunk, in the hall closet."

Mrs. Travis checked the fit of the jacket, smoothed the shoulders. "This will have to do," she pronounced. Then her tone became sugary sweet. "For delivery of the invitations I intended to give your mother some put-up things from the pantry, but I guess you'd rather think of money."

Aindreas made no reply, unsure as to where she was headed. Mrs. Travis, in turn, watched him with an amused expression. "I'm going to give you seventy-five cents for delivering the notes and another fifty cents for your help tonight...credited against the rent your family owes us, of course." Her eyes fairly sparkled when she smiled. "I assume you agree that's fair?"

Aindreas swallowed. "I didn't expect anything else," he said.

"Good. Now, you will clear out the dishes after the guests use them, and bring them back here to Tempie. You will not talk to any of the guests. If anyone should speak to you for any reason, you are to respond with *Yes, ma'am,* or *Yes, sir.*"

He nodded.

"We have a man here to handle the spirits. But if someone should ask you to bring something, you may take it to them on a tray; but for God's sake don't spill it."

Tempie returned with the gloves, and Aindreas put them on.

It didn't matter that they were too big because the jacket sleeves nearly concealed his hands. The guests would be arriving within minutes. Aindreas wandered into the parlor, where a man busied himself at a makeshift table near the liquor cabinet. The white jacket, held by a single button, barely closed over his round middle.

Aindreas bowed elaborately. "Good evening, Mr. Adler."

Georg Adler looked up and grinned but put a finger to his lips. "Shhh. They think they got Dorrn," he said, "but he was suddenly taken drunk this afternoon. Let's keep quiet about this Adler person."

Aindreas couldn't stop his laughter altogether. "Okay."

Mr. Adler lined up the glasses alongside an ice bucket. "So, a young wagoner does this kind of thing on the side?"

"Just carrying dishes," Aindreas said. "First time for me." He thought for a moment before volunteering, "Squire Travis owns the place where we live." Aindreas pointed toward the back windows. "Right back there."

Adler's eyes twinkled. "Ahh. Is *der hund* out there?

"Yes, sir. I'd imagine König is watching that window right now."

There came loud conversation from the hall. Mrs. Travis greeted the first guests at the door.

Adler said, "Stop by and talk to me later, if you can."

"Let me know if you need any help, Mr. Dorrn," Aindreas said loud enough for Mrs. Travis to hear, and went back toward the kitchen.

The work went slowly at first. Plates, cups, saucers, glasses, and silverware were used and set aside by the guests. Aindreas carried them to the sink in the kitchen. Tempie turned out to be a good dishwasher, and quick. Aindreas would dry and stack the clean dishes alongside the food trays, to be used again. There must have been more than thirty people eating. The gentlemen usually set down their food and drink on any flat place they could find, even the fireplace mantles, but the ladies always balanced their plates primly in their laps if a chair-side table wasn't handy.

Between trips, Aindreas stopped and listened to the trunk clock in the hall chime the quarter hour. Nearly eight o'clock. He felt awkward doing this kind of thing, but at least he hadn't found himself totally among strangers. Tempie and Kirsty, of course. And while he didn't care for Squire and Mrs. Travis, he did know them. Other familiar faces, also. Mr. Pritchett ate hungrily near the parlor doorway, the crown of his head covered with an ill-fitting brown wig. A younger lady, who seemed very nice, stayed close to him. She didn't look at all like Pritchett, so maybe she wasn't his daughter. Blanche Flowers sat near a window. An attentive group of gentlemen hovered around her. Aindreas thought she waved at him, but he acted as if he hadn't seen her. And, elegant as ever in a light linen suit, Mr. Bones worked the parlor and the hall. Wineglass in hand, he effortlessly drifted from one group to the next, his charm and presence falling over the guests as easily as a silk scarf.

Sometime later, it shocked Aindreas to see Captain Workman in the hallway. After the conversation he and the captain had about Isaac, he wondered why Workman would be at Squire Travis's house. After he thought it over, Aindreas became less anxious; Captain Workman probably had no acquaintance with the host. A military officer and his wife accompanied Workman. Mrs. Travis addressed the officer as Major Krauth. *Ah, the captain's old friend.*

Numberless conversations made for a din in the parlor. It seemed as if everyone in the house talked at the same time, and Aindreas wondered if anyone was listening. While he retrieved dishes among the guests, he heard certain points made time and again: that drunkard Franklin Pierce should never have been made president; business was tolerable but could be better; womankind deserved better than the curse of garters; and one could not find or keep good help.

Emily Travis conversed with a lady who wore huge round earrings and smelled like lilacs. Mrs. Travis said, "I prefer to eat in a civilized manner at the table, like family, but Squire has to invite all his cronies, you know."

When the woman nodded, the earrings waved crazily above her shoulders.

Later, Squire Travis played the host on the far side of the parlor, his thumbs hooked in the watch pockets of a blue satin vest. He shrugged his shoulders in a helpless gesture, saying, "Emily always has to have her friends from the church." The men near him murmured sympathetically.

Later, with a stir near the front door, Mrs. Travis rushed into the hall. "Look, everyone, she said excitedly. "George Prentice managed to come after all."

Squire and Mrs. Travis staked out their positions on either side of a man of medium height, with a slight stoop.

The mood of the entire gathering had been charged by this new arrival. The guests, many still eating, craned to look at him. Aindreas maneuvered his way to a table between the couch and a chair and collected two plates left there. The spot provided a clear view of this latest guest. Prentice, definitely not a handsome man, had an impressive forehead, wide and high, with wavy, dark hair that had begun turning gray. Dressed like a preacher, he wore a dark suit and vest, a thick, black neck cloth under a starched upright collar. The lines in his clean-shaven, fleshy face furrowed in smiles as he greeted one guest after another. But there were no smile lines around his eyes.

"Thank you, thank you very much," he said dryly to one. He inclined his head to another. "The pleasure is mine, ma'am." Not a man limited to simple transactions, Prentice nodded and gave the appearance of listening when suitors sought his attention, and all the while he was looking here and there over the room as though for someone else he expected to see. He did this several times, checking carefully, missing little or nothing. Prentice's gaze eventually came to Aindreas, who shuddered at the look of those small, cold eyes. The man had a menacing, dangerous aura, even more than König. Prentice turned away, returning his gaze to the men and women who sought it.

After a time, the guests finished eating. Aindreas and Kirsty dried and put away the rest of the dishes Tempie washed. The guests drank and talked and played charade games. Mrs. Travis played a succession of Stephen Foster songs on the pianoforte: *Oh! Susanna, Camptown Races, Old Folks at Home, Jeanie with the Light Brown Hair,* and finished up with a song called *My Old Kentucky Home.* Some who knew the words joined in the singing. Others obviously didn't know the words but warmed by Adler's libations, they sang anyway.

> *The young folks roll on the lit tle cabin floor,*
> *All merry, all happy and bright:*
> *By'n by Hard Times comes a knocking at the door,*
> *Then my old Kentucky Home, good night.*

Captain Workman stood way over by a back window. Aindreas felt a little afraid at the idea of bringing up the subject of Isaac but decided he would try and work his way over to the captain when he could.

During a lull, Aindreas stopped at Mr. Adler's table. "Well,

157

my young friend, I'll bet you've never seen so many tight stays and bodices in your life," Adler observed.

Smiling, Aindreas shook his head.

"My God, if my Marta tried to bind herself up like that, there'd be an explosion."

Aindreas smothered a laugh with his hand.

"Guess you saw Prentice," Adler said, and wrinkled his nose. "Isn't he a beauty?"

"Yes," Aindreas responded, thinking he had begun to understand more about some of the whispers he heard.

Squire Travis and his wife moved to the center of the room. The squire motioned for silence. "Ladies and gentlemen, I know you share our delight in having George Prentice with us."

Most of the guests applauded.

"After all," the squire went on, "one doesn't rub elbows with a legend every day."

Prentice smiled, and glanced down at his glossy shoes.

Mrs. Travis took over. "A few moments ago, Squire and I talked with Major Krauth and his lovely wife, Libby. They're literary people. The major wanted to talk about that awful Herman Melville and *Moby Dick*. But I told him we had always thought Hester Prynne was so much more interesting than a gang of silly old whales." Amid the laughter, Emily Travis covered her face with her fan, as though to hide a blush, and Major Krauth waved a white handkerchief, as if in surrender. Mrs. Travis held out her hand to Prentice. "Perhaps we can convince George to recite his wonderful poem, *The Closing Year*."

Prentice said, "Really, I…"

Adler whispered to Aindreas, "He's probably got the damn thing in his pocket."

After more pleading from Mrs. Travis and encouragement from the others, Prentice took several folded sheets of paper from his coat pocket. Adler winked at Aindreas. Shortly, Prentice began to read in an arid voice.

Aindreas padded along near the wall, behind the guests, toward the spot where Captain Workman stood. The captain needed to know he was in the house of the man who thought he owned Isaac.

Prentice went on.

> Remorseless Time!
> Fierce spirit of the glass and scythe'
> What power
> Can stay him in his silent course, or melt
> His iron heart to pity' On still on,
> He presses and forever. The proud bird,
> The Condor of the Andes, that can soar
> Through heaven's unfathomable depths...

Aindreas collected a stray saucer along the way, hoping Mrs. Travis wouldn't notice him talking to Captain Workman. The captain smiled when he saw Aindreas clearing a couple of cups and saucers from the window ledge. Aindreas motioned to the captain, who walked over to the window near him. At least partially hidden from the view of Mrs. Travis, they now stood side by side. Aindreas pointed out the window toward the cabin, perhaps a hundred feet away. A man stood alone in the doorway. Two children played on the floor inside.

Aindreas whispered, "Isaac."

Workman looked stunned. "Go get me a drink...whiskey."

Prentice went on reading.

> And bathe his plumage in the thunder's home,
> Furls his broad wing at nightfall, and sinks down
> To rest upon his mountain crag; but Time
> Knows not the weight of sleep or weariness;
> And Night's deep darkness has no chain to bind
> His rushing pinion.

Aindreas returned with the whiskey. His hand was shaking when he handed the glass to the captain.

Workman downed half the drink in a single gulp. "Thank you," he said.

Aindreas's voice quavered. "Now that you've come here and have met these people, will you still help Isaac and me?"

Workman nodded in the direction of Squire Travis, whose rapt attention was locked on Prentice. Aindreas hadn't earlier seen still another late-coming guest. On the other side of the squire stood Samuel Cooper...Red Cooper, the slave trader from the *Ben Franklin* and the slave auction.

Captain Workman chuckled. "I never had any doubts, my boy, but the friends Travis keeps make it all the sweeter." Workman swirled the remaining drink in his glass. "I thought if I'm to help steal away what the law says belongs to him, I may as well drink his whiskey, too."

Prentice picked up the pace in his reading, winding toward the finish.

*...Gathering the strength of hoary centuries,*
*And rush down, like the Alpine avalanche,*
*Startling the nations...*

Major Krauth smiled as the guests applauded at the conclusion of the reading. By the window, Aindreas could see Isaac in the cabin doorway, could see König watching the Travis house from down by the rosebushes.

The major began to speak. "Ladies and gentlemen," he said. "We've heard Mr. Prentice's verse about time...at least, I think it concerned time." The major lifted his glass. "And I salute his audacious efforts."

A woman on the couch giggled, then abruptly stopped when Squire Travis glared at her.

The major, his face flushed, looked a little unsteady. "Libby," he nodded toward his wife, "grew up in Louisville and has known the charming Mrs. Travis for a long time. But we now live in another part of the country. In New York, recently, I became acquainted with the work of a man named Walt Whitman."

"My Lord, he's worse than Melville," blurted the woman who smelled like lilacs.

The major joined in the laughter. His wife nervously clutched his arm. He patted her hand and continued, "But the hour grows late, and we must soon say good night. We thank you for your hospitality, and our farewell will be a verse from Whitman."

Aindreas gazed out the window again. Isaac still stood in wait for Tempie in front of the cabin.

Though Major Krauth held out a paper before him, it seemed as if he actually recited the verse.

*The runaway slave came to my house and stopped outside,*
*I heard his motions crackling the twigs of the woodpile,*
*Through the swung half-door of the kitchen I saw him limpsy and weak,*
*And went where he sat on a log and led him and assured him*
*And brought water and fill'd a tub for his sweated body and bruised feet,*
*And gave him a room that enter'd from my own, and gave him some coarse clean clothes,*

Aindreas listened in amazement. *Did the major know about Isaac?* Aindreas watched the faces around the room. A frown creased Mr. Prentice's face even more deeply. Mrs. Travis and many of the guests looked grim. Krauth went on.

*And remember perfectly well his revolving eyes and his*

161

*awkwardness,*
*And remember putting plasters on the galls of his neck*
*and ankles,*

Prentice's brow arched, his lips pressed together hard. He shook hands with Squire Travis, who seemed to try to hold onto his hand. Prentice stalked out of the room. Other guests had risen from their seats and were leaving in a group.

The major recited the last lines.

*He staid with me a week before he was recuperated and*
*pass'd north,*
*I had him sit next me at table, my fire-lock lean'd in the*
*corner.*

The party not so much ended as collapsed. The Squire and Mrs. Travis looked anxious saying their goodnights to the departing guests. Major Krauth's wife looked a trifle embarrassed, but Captain Workman gave Krauth a pat on the back.

Aindreas lingered by the window, his eyes still on the cabin. Perhaps he wasn't the only one who knew things he had no business knowing. Major Krauth may have known something about Isaac after all, though he didn't know this particular Isaac. And Walt Whitman knew him as well, in another place and time. Perhaps even such a man as Stephen Foster, in his too-sweet way, had known Isaac.

Aindreas got a tray and began picking up the last few glasses the guests had left around the room. As soon as these had been washed and put away, he would get home. Tomorrow would be his mother's birthday, and he had a wonderful gift for her.

# 10

*Family* members and others are telling tales around a blazing fire. Death sits among them, spinning stories with the rest. Such an ordinary looking shopkeeper, his high apron partly covers his chest like a woman's gown. His smile, more like a smirk, gives him away—but that is seen too late, and he carries Doireann Rivers off with him.

Aindreas bolted upright in bed, fists clinched. He held his head in his hands until her screams finally broke into pieces and disappeared. Another bad dream. He rose from the bed and looked out the window at the high, wind-streaked purple clouds creasing the dawn sky. Silence, except for Michael's snoring across the room. The window casing shuddered when an explosion ripped the air, making the black Madonna picture hang crooked on the wall. A second blast followed and then another.

"What in goddamn hell…." Michael muttered, and pulled the blanket over his head.

Seconds later, the violent sounds began again. Aindreas figured out the source and where the troopers might be located. Kirsty appeared at the doorway, a shawl clutched around her shoulders. "Did you hear that awful noise, Andrew?"

"Nothing to worry about," he said. "Is Mother awake?"

"I think so…and she's probably scared," Kirsty said. "Da has already gone."

Aindreas felt a little angry at Kirsty's attitude of ignorant innocence. When the two of them had gotten home from the Travis party after midnight, the pallet on the kitchen floor where their father slept lay empty. Kirsty could not have failed to see that, but Aindreas didn't remind her. He only said, "I'll go in and check."

He smoothed out the wrinkles in his shirt and pants. Maybe his mother wouldn't notice he had slept in his clothes again.

Doireann Rivers lay surrounded by pillows. Her hair dripping wet, hints of mischief played at the corners of her mouth like that of a child enjoying the excitement.

Her voice sounded girlish. "Who's getting blown up, Andrew?"

"Nobody. Army troopers are firing cannons…three of 'em, I think." He gestured toward the window. "Must be over there in Jacob's Wood."

She giggled and tugged at a strand of hair. "I hope Mamma gets back in time to hear them. Will they do it many more times?"

"I'd bet they'll stop at thirty-one," he said, hoping his expression wouldn't betray his alarm at the state of her mind.

She looked blank. "Thirty-one," he repeated, "one round for each state." He leaned down and hugged her. "It's the Fourth of July, Mother. Happy birthday to you."

She smiled and looked like herself again.

1

From appearances at the office, Cawthon's Furniture might have been under siege. Flush pine boards covered the window openings on Jefferson and on Eighth Streets, and a watchman with arms crossed stood outside the front door.

The chief clerk looked like a stage performer made up for a performance. Here and there on his face, little white plasters covered the cuts he'd received from the flying glass yesterday. "It's hard to take, but they tell me it'll take several weeks to replace those windows. We'll just have to keep our chins high and get the job done," he said to the office employees gathered around his desk.

"We'll go blind in here with no light from windows," a junior clerk said, wiping the thick lenses of his spectacles.

"Now listen, all of you," the chief clerk said. "The normal amount of business won't get done today. This town has nearly closed down already. Mr. Cawthon told me our doors could be locked at noon, provided all the work is caught up."

Aindreas beamed. This would give him the extra time he needed. The clerks yelled and pumped their fists in the air.

"All right, get to it," the chief clerk exhorted.

The young men scattered to their tables, each to his own dream of how the holiday would be enjoyed.

"Williams," said the clerk, "you and Rivers sweep the sidewalks on Jefferson and Eighth. A parade will come through here tonight, and Mr. Cawthon wants the place to look clean as can be. You can do the office floor after the rest of the boys have gone."

"Yes sir," William Williams said with his usual excess of cheer.

It hurt Aindreas's feelings that instructions had been given to the new boy rather than him. Had the chief clerk forgotten that Tim had broken the rules, and not him?

Outside, the two of them agreed to decide by a coin toss who would sweep which sidewalk. The new boy flipped a shiny new dollar his father had given him in celebration of the day. He won, gave Aindreas a smug grin, and chose the Jefferson Street sidewalk. That would be the shorter, cleaner job. "Don't get into contests with me, Rivers," said Williams. "You couldn't beat me at anything."

Aindreas carried a wide, straw push broom and a small crate

down the Eighth Street side of the building and began the task. It made dusty work on a hot, dry day, but at least the sweeping took his mind off his resentment toward Williams. In the distance, a brass band played *The Star Spangled Banner*. Aindreas reckoned that the band had to be placed near the speaker's stand, recently put up at the corner of Seventh and Jefferson Streets. He'd seen the workers covering the rails and sides with flags and strips of bunting that morning. Handbills and flyers advertised a ceremony at twelve o'clock, and he intended to stop there on the way home.

Working steadily, he scooped up the larger pieces of dirt and refuse and emptied them into a crate, then he swept the sidewalk clean. The band played a stirring version of *Hail Columbia*. Neighborhood children were already raising all the Cain they could manage, and every few minutes he would hear a staccato rat-tat-tat from another string of firecrackers. Puff-clouds of acrid, blue smoke hovered just above the mud crust along the gutters.

The slow strains of *Home Sweet Home* carried through the air. Aindreas shoved the crate ahead with his foot. His mind wandered as he worked. *Would the family hold together after his mother was gone?*

No sooner had Aindreas thought of the question than he saw Mr. Knight, leaning on a walking stick at the edge of the street. He looked so dignified in his dark coat.

"Music does bring on memories, doesn't it?" Knight asked, then tapped his hat brim with the stick. "I didn't think we'd meet again so soon, but I heard that song and here I am. Enjoy that fine old English piece, do you?"

"You mean *Home Sweet Home*?"

"Yes, I thought you might remember hearing about its origins in school," Knight said, and smiled devilishly. "Tell me about the gift for your mother."

"It's ready." Aindreas held up his hands. "Look at my fingers."

Only about twenty feet of sidewalk remained to be cleaned before reaching the corner. Down Jefferson Street, the band launched into *Old Dan Tucker*. Aindreas resumed sweeping. "Strange to see you without your writing case, Mr. Knight," he said. "At night, I've been writing about a lot of things, myself."

"Good for you. As for me, I have no need for notes about this day. I know it by heart."

The bright sunlight made Aindreas squint, as he puzzled over what his friend might have meant. "I worked at a party last night over at the Travis house," he said.

"Did you enjoy it?" asked Knight.

"Well, I learned some things. Captain Workman came, and Georg Adler. And Major Krauth read a poem about a runaway slave. For a moment, I thought he knew something about Isaac and me."

Knight nodded. "I know that feeling."

"And I saw Mr. Prentice and lots of people," Aindreas added, "but I didn't see you."

Knight shrugged. "True, but I do plan to attend the festivities down by the courthouse a little later."

"Me, too," Aindreas said. "Prentice is supposed to speak."

Knight nodded. "I'd wager he won't read any poetry."

"Last night, I felt odd when he looked at me…a little scared," said Aindreas.

"Let's see whether you feel any different at the speech today," Knight said, his brow arched. "Will you give your mother her present this afternoon?"

"Yes…yes, I will," Aindreas said, and managed a wave before Knight vanished in the crowd down Eighth Street.

Aindreas and Williams finished their respective sidewalks and met at the corner of the building as the band was playing *Oh! Susanna*. They relaxed for a moment, leaning on their brooms.

More firecrackers whistled and popped.

"Were you with somebody around there?" asked Williams. "I thought I heard you talking once, but never saw anybody go by."

"A friend," Aindreas said, and led the way inside.

Nearly all the desks had been cleared, and only the chief clerk and Williams' brother remained in the office. Aindreas and Williams began sweeping the aisles between the desks.

"My father and mother are coming down to hear George Prentice, and I'll meet them down there by the bandstand," said Williams. "My father says Mr. Prentice is a genius."

"I've heard of people who said that about him," replied Aindreas.

It seemed surprising how much more sure of himself Williams acted. He nearly swaggered these days.

"I liked listening to all those songs," he said, and snickered. "Course, you probably couldn't even hear the band back where you were."

"I heard the music," said Aindreas, "and I…"

"My mother loves those real American songs," Williams interrupted, "and she plays them all on the piano."

Aindreas heard his own voice speaking the words but had the sensation of someone else thinking them. "Those weren't all American songs," he said.

"I heard every one of them…American," said Williams, his eyes narrowing. "What do you know, anyway? Somebody told me that you have fits."

Aindreas didn't respond, though he wanted to punch Williams. He held himself silent for a few seconds. "Want to bet about the songs?" he asked finally.

"You couldn't beat me even if your life depended on it," crowed Williams. "How much?"

"That dollar in your pocket?"

Williams looked Aindreas up and down. "Do you even have a

dollar?"

"I have one at home," Aindreas lied.

"It's a bet," Williams said, "The chief clerk will be the judge."

Aindreas nodded his assent. Everyone in the office knew the clerk and his wife went to concerts; he surely would know a lot about music. After the office floor had been swept clean, Aindreas and Williams stationed themselves in front of the tall desk.

The chief clerk ignored them for a time, making more of those rapier strokes of his pen on a ledger book. "What is it?" he finally asked without looking up.

Williams recited the names of the songs that the band had played. "All of them American songs—right, sir? Rivers says they aren't."

Aindreas stared at the plasters on the chief clerk's face, wondering whether he realized that it was probably Tim Lytle who had done that to him.

The clerk cleared his throat and glanced toward Williams's brother, a junior. The chief clerk had never seemed reluctant to play the authority, but he looked uncomfortable this time. "Well, several of them might be open to question, but I know at least one of them might not be called strictly American," he said.

William Williams frowned. "How can that be, sir?"

"Oh, really, Williams. A lot of our songs came from someplace else," the clerk said. "*Home Sweet Home*, for instance, came from an English opera." Shrugging, he asked, "What possible difference can it make?"

Williams's face flamed. He shuffled his feet, turned away. "Let's go outside," he said to Aindreas in a low voice.

The chief clerk and Williams's brother glanced back and forth between the two boys.

Aindreas shook his head no. He figured Williams had earned the humiliation, and so he thrust out his hand. "Give me the dollar."

Williams fished the coin from his pocket. He didn't look directly at Aindreas when he handed it over. The clerk's eyes showed a guarded amusement. Aindreas smiled thinly back at him, pocketed the dollar, and walked out of the office onto the cleanly swept sidewalk.

Even from more than a block away, the crowd around the speaker's stand looked big. A stream of men and women, dressed in Sunday clothes, carried or pulled their children down Jefferson Street toward the courthouse. The noon sun blazed down on the believers from nearly straight overhead.

Banners for Know-Nothing candidates plastered every wall and lamppost along the way.

*William V. Loving for Governor*
**THE AMERICAN PARTY**

*For Congress*
*Elect Humphrey Marshall*
**THE AMERICAN PARTY**

*Our next Attorney General*
*James Harlan*
**THE AMERICAN PARTY**

A bell rang faintly in the distance, then all became quiet as far as Aindreas could hear. The chime had sounded so far away, it might have come from Saint Martin's in the east, or as far west as Saint John's Episcopal, down near Twelfth Street. And then bells from other churches began to ring. *My God—it sounded like all of them, even the Catholic churches.* The German Evangelical Lutheran on Preston Street, the Colored Baptist churches, Saint Boniface, the First Christian Church, and the large Baptist church on Walnut Street, the African Church, Second Presbyterian on Third Street, Christ Church, the cathedral on Fifth Street, and others. Apparently, all of them had joined in.

Aindreas covered his ears. *None of this made sense.* He had read the Declaration of Independence in school and talked about it with Miss Flowers. *The notion that white men should run everyone else's lives seemed strange enough. Now, the Know-Nothings were saying that only certain kinds of white men should do that. And bells were now chiming in celebration! What did the churches have to do with all this?*

He searched the faces around him to see if anyone else seemed as confused as he felt but got no help. From all appearances, everyone was savoring the day, nodding to one another with knowing glances, while their children hung onto them with mouths open, perhaps numbed by the discordant thunder of the bells.

Determined to stay long enough to hear what was said this day, Aindreas started through the crush of elbows and knees and picnic baskets toward the speaker's stand. "Excuse me, sir," he said as he wormed his way in. "Sorry, ma'am." All the time he was looking for Prentice on the speaker's stand. The band played *My Old Kentucky Home* and men were taking off their hats. Surprised, Aindreas did not remove his cap.

"LADIES and GENTLEMEN!"

Samuel Cooper, the red-haired slave trader for Bolton & Dickens, stood front and center at the rail on the speaker's stand. After thundering bells and a brass band, the crowd still shuffled around noisily, slow to respond to a mere voice. Having wound his way through the crunch, Aindreas finally reached the front of the crowd and stood directly in front of the platform.

"Please let me have your attention." Red Cooper held up both arms to quiet the crowd. He appeared to have pretty well recovered from his injuries at the hands of Jack Graham. His slicked-back hair glistened in the sun, and his clean-shaven face conveyed, at a distance, a babyish, innocent quality.

"Distinguished guests, ladies and gentlemen," he said in a

strong, clear voice, "We have with us members of the city council." Cooper turned and motioned for the councilmen to rise. A smattering of applause acknowledged them, and they promptly resumed their seats. "And, of course, the Honorable John Barbee," Cooper said, "Mayor of the city of Louisville."

No mention had yet been made of George Prentice, who sat with Mr. Bones just to the right of Cooper. The dry-goods merchant, Barbee, stepped up to the front of the stand.

Aindreas studied him. So...this was the soft, puffy-looking man who took the office of James Speed in an election many still called illegal. His dark hair had a meticulous part down the middle, and he indeed dressed like a mayor, with his freshly pressed coat, his shirt brilliant white in the sun, and a broad, gold watch chain hanging between the pockets of his vest. Hands clasped in front of him, Barbee looked out over the crowd with a benign expression. As it turned out, Mayor Barbee did nothing to rouse the crowd. He spoke briefly in a soft, placating voice about the necessity of electing several of the American Party candidates, then returned to his chair.

"And now," Cooper said, "I give you the man who will introduce our speaker. I've known Tad Englender several years. A successful lawyer and one of our rising stars in Jefferson County, Mr. Englender still takes the time to be active in public service. For the American Party, of course."

Cooper laughed, and some of the crowd joined him, then began applauding as Englender took center stage. Aindreas remembered him, the commissioner at the slave auction by the courthouse. Englender smiled, looking more moon-faced than when Aindreas had seen him before. Again, Englender was fanning himself with his hat.

"My fellow citizens of the sovereign state of Kentucky," he began. The crowd cheered the "sovereign state" reference. "Our Union has never been in greater danger than today. Fortunately, real Americans prepared us for these times: Yes...the Harpers, of that great publishing family; Lyman Beecher, father of that woman Harriet Beecher Stowe; and Samuel Morse, inventor of the telegraph and the Morse code. Wonderful people such as these anticipated the dangers years ago. It doesn't matter a whit whether they chose to be active in the Order of United Americans or the Supreme Order of the Star Spangled Banner. What does matter is that they led thousands of us in every one of the Sovereign States to find the path, to see *Sam*."

George Prentice smiled amiably, perhaps amused by Englender's oratorical delivery. When Prentice scanned the crowd, Aindreas met his gaze once again. This time, Prentice didn't look away, and his eyes fixed Aindreas in a malevolent, defiant stare.

"...and that's what we are here to celebrate today," Englender said. "Now, it's my pleasure to bring on our distinguished speaker. Some of you may know he came to Kentucky twenty-five years ago, penniless and unknown. He came to write a campaign biography of our own *Harry of the West*, the great statesman, Henry Clay."

Loud applause waved through the crowd at the mere mention of Clay's name. Mr. Bones grinned, and patted Prentice on the shoulder.

Englender's manner suggested slyness. He kept lowering his eyes to check the small cards he held at waist level, and Aindreas wondered why the man didn't just read the notes and quit pretending to speak from memory.

"George Dennison Prentice was born fifty-three years ago in Connecticut," said Englender importantly. "A child prodigy, he loved reading everything by the age of four years—and he translated Horace before reaching the age of fifteen."

Aindreas thought of Marcus McFate, his tragic half-brother, and how different can be the paths that prodigies might take.

"A graduate of Brown University, he also studied law and became a brilliant editor of the *New England Review* before he came to Kentucky."

Prentice inclined his head and now appeared to be listening to Englender with more attention.

"Then he founded the *Louisville Journal,* and the rest we know well. We all remember his warfare with other newspaper editors around here, particularly Shradrack Penn."

Men behind Aindreas cheered at mention of this. One of them yelled, "You kicked his ass, George."

"As happened in the case with poor old Shadrack," Englender continued, "most battles between George Prentice and other newspapers turned into routs."

He glanced toward Prentice. "Someone told me that about four-hundred daily newspapers go to print in this country. Well, none better than the *Journal.* We're glad he joined with us back in April."

Prentice gave a slight bow of his head to Englender.

"It seems hardly necessary to mention that Mr. Prentice has been called one of the finest wits of the age. A well-known poet, he is quoted all over this country and Europe."

Prentice pushed forward to the edge of his seat. Maybe he knew what the man at the podium was going to say. Maybe he had written every word Englender had said.

"So, without further ado, I give you George Prentice."

Aindreas heard a few hisses and boos behind the speaker's stand, but hundreds cheered Prentice, waving their flags and American Party placards. The *Journal* editor barely shook hands with Englender, then stepped around him to greet the mayor and the city councilmen with handshakes and embraces. Applause continued until Prentice raised his arms for silence. A few people left. Maybe they had come to hear the usual Fourth of July American self-flattery and now realized this was to be a celebration of a different sort.

"Ladies and gentlemen, we at the *Louisville Journal* have been involved in a crusade and made powerful enemies as a consequence," Prentice began. "We had a good many Catholic subscribers, and the loss of a large portion of them is precisely what we expected. We acted in the faithful discharge of what we considered a great and patriotic duty. But what we asked, and thought we had a right to ask, from the members of the American Order and from the Protestant community generally, was that they would not permit us to suffer pecuniary loss on account of our fearless devotion."

He paused to smile. "The Catholics, as we presumed they would do, made organized movements against us," he continued, "but our Protestant fellow-citizens, unwilling that we should be injured on account of our opposition to the influences of despotism, are sending us at least ten new subscribers for every old one that is taken from us."

Those behind Prentice on the speaker's stand stood and led the thunderous applause from the crowd. Prentice raised his arms in acknowledgment.

"The simple purity of our present system of government is seriously menaced by an immense influx of people unfit by birth and training to take part in the management of our governmental affairs," he went on, chopping at the air with his hand for emphasis. "And from this foreign element, we find Abolitionism procuring its greatest strength. From it have sprung and by it have been fostered Mormonism, Turnerism, Fourrierism, and all the other impious doctrines which threaten to trample all laws, to substitute lustful licentiousness for constitutional liberty, and mob-violence for peace and order."

Men with yellow badges on their hats or pinned to their chests surrounded the speaker's stand. They began a slow, rhythmic hand-clapping. The audience joined in, and the sound of it became deafening.

Prentice signaled for silence. "Are men fit to hold office in this country who yield obedience to the Constitution only by the sufferance of that miserable old despot in red stockings who holds out his toes in Rome to the longing lips of his devotees?"

"No...no...no," the crowd shouted. Next to Aindreas, a young woman held a sleeping baby. She went on saying "no" longer than the rest.

Aindreas felt the sting of accusation. The idea of kissing anyone's toes seemed a stupid one to him, but he wondered if in her dreams this sleeping baby hated him because he had been Catholic from the cradle.

"The Chief Pontiff," Prentice said, "and his cardinals, nuncios, archbishops, and bishops compose, in the aggregate, a vast overshadowing anti-republican hierarchy that abjures and anathematizes the right of private judgment which lies at the foundation of every American Constitution. In our view, religion is a thing strictly between the *private* individual and his maker. But it is not so with the papist."

The baby woke and began to cry. Spectators close by in the audience made shushing sounds and directed hard looks at the woman.

"Catholics, if true to the teachings of the church whose faith they avow, are necessarily the determined enemies of religious liberty, bound to crush it if they have the power. Every native-born Protestant father and son throughout Kentucky should remember. The allegiance of Americans to a Roman potentate is not the allegiance of an American citizen."

The young woman tried to quiet the baby, but the crying grew louder. She began to make her way toward the rear of the audience.

"Our friends," Prentice made sweeping gestures toward the men seated behind him and those out front wearing yellow badges, "must so organize as not only to be able to cast their own utmost strength at the polls, but to mark and exclude every fraudulent voter, no matter who he may be or under what pretext his vote may be offered."

Prentice sipped water and wiped perspiration from his upper lip. The bright sunlight made deep shadows under his brow and nose. His small eyes looked black. "Every American in the state should watch and work from now until the day of the election to see that the ballot box be protected." He pointed into the audience again and again, as he said, "And I mean you, sir...and you...and you...and you.

"This is no ordinary contest. Not only to Kentucky, but to the whole country, to the maintenance of our Union and the preservation of our liberty. Nothing is to be hoped for by the South from any party in the North except the American Party. If that party cannot save the Union, the Union is doomed."

Arms raised high over his head, Prentice bellowed, "Shall Americans rule America, or must they be ruled by foreigners?"

The audience screamed and stamped. "Americans! Americans!" they chanted.

Aindreas turned to leave.

Prentice held up his hand to quiet the crowd. "They tell us that the American Party skulks from human observation. Just take a view of it tonight. We hope that our distant friends, if they see a bright glare upon the sky over Louisville, will not suppose that the city is burning up. There will be a blaze a mile long. If there are any who have never seen *Sam*, let them look out of their windows and doors tonight. Or, if they choose, they can take a walk with him."

3

Doireann Rivers lay alone in her room, her face swollen and red. Aindreas knew she had been crying earlier. He checked her medicine; the remaining clear liquid barely covered the bottom of the sticky bottle. He retrieved the half-dark, cork top and the spoon from the floor. His mother's eyes no longer favored those of an excited little girl listening to the roar of cannons. Her eyes looked hurt and old.

Standing by the bed, Aindreas cradled the bason in the crook of his arm, wrapped once again in the dark velvet cloth in which Mr. Knight had brought it to him.

"Dr. MacIntosh is supposed to come by in just a little while," Aindreas said, "but I'll go find him right this minute if you need more medicine."

She shook her head no.

Aindreas heard voices in the kitchen. It sounded like Kirsty and his aunts. He set the gift down on the edge of the bed beside his mother. "Look, I have something for you.

Her voice was a soft gurgle. "Thank you," she said, and ran her fingers over the velvet. "Pretty," she murmured, then dropped her hand.

After a time, she said, "Open?"

Aindreas removed the velvet covering, and the sight took his breath. Though the sky had become cloudy and the room lay in shadow, the bason glowed in a soft light of its own.

Aindreas's mother lay curled on her side, looking into the gift as if it were a living vista…as if in it she could see forever. She briefly raised her head and gazed deep into changing scenes and light within the bason. "Oh, so beautiful," she said.

She rested for a moment, silently. "I will see you there, one day," said Doireann Rivers, finally.

"Yes…yes," Aindreas managed, and could say no more.

Aindreas knelt by the bed and took her hand. Her mouth grew slack, her breathing shallower, and her eyes half closed. He held onto her hand for some time after he knew she had died.

König set up a mournful howling out behind the tenement. Aindreas got up, moved just inside the doorway to his mother's room, and looked out into the kitchen. A food basket, covered by a checkered cloth, sat on the table. Aunt Mary, Aunt Margaret, and Uncle Theodore talked with Kirsty, who poured coffee at the stove. They chatted and laughed. A moment later, Kirsty went to the door to let in Dr. MacIntosh.

Aindreas knew he couldn't spare them any longer, and he walked into the kitchen. At the first glimpse of him, Kirsty and Aunt Margaret threw their arms around each other and Aunt Mary shrieked and collapsed in a chair. Dr. MacIntosh hurried past Aindreas to the room where Doireann Rivers lay. He returned to the kitchen and nodded to the family.

Kirsty whimpered.

"I knew I should have come this morning," said Aunt Mary.

MacIntosh pulled Aindreas over to the light, and peered closely at his eyes. "How do you feel, Andrew?"

Aindreas said nothing. *It didn't matter how he felt. A great soul had passed on the journey and those left would have to get by on what remained. Now, the rest of them would have to get by with what they had left.*

The doctor put an arm around Aindreas's shoulder. "You're not going to fall down, are you, son?"

"No."

"Good," he said, and turned to the others. "Please stay here. I have a few things to do in the other room. When I'm finished, you may go see her."

Uncle Theodore nodded, his hand under Aunt Margaret's elbow. Kirsty and Aunt Mary held their embrace, like lost children.

MacIntosh turned his attention back to Aindreas. "Listen, you're not needed for what comes next. Get out of here for a while and take the dog with you. Don't be in a hurry...go see the carnival that just came to town...watch the parade."

Aindreas shook hands with the doctor, then left the house without speaking to the rest of them. *What would be the use?*

He walked. Nothing seemed real. The ground looked ten feet down. God, he hoped he wouldn't have a spell. König at his heels, Aindreas wandered aimlessly for a time.

# 11

A huge tent sprawled on Fifth Street, just south of Prather, with large, painted boards propped up all along the front. Aindreas left König on the north side of Prather Street and crossed over to the carnival.

Torch light wavered over the strange creatures in the pictures in front of the tents, some hideous, all of them fantastic. A barker in a tall hat paced on a stage before the growing crowd of adults and children. He urged them not to be timid, to step up and buy their tickets.

Though Aindreas felt that he should be home to do what he could, he decided to follow the advice of Dr. MacIntosh. Grown-ups, at least those in his family, didn't know grief until it jumped at their eyes. They would have to see it their own way.

The barker tried to shame the crowd. "You should not miss, ladies and gentlemen, and for the education and benefit of your children, you *cannot* miss the fabled unicorn, the one-horned rhinoceros."

Mr. Knight, smoking his pipe, stood in front of a billboard near a presently silent brass band. Aindreas walked toward him, grateful that he had thought to be with him. Knight acknowledged Aindreas's grief with a solemn nod.

The loud nasal voice of the barker carried on, "Come inside to see the mocos, the dromedary, the little Shetland pony, the llama, the Africa pelican and the gnu—the horned horse."

"Should we go inside?" Knight asked.

"No need to," Aindreas said. "I overheard two of the workers talking. This whole outfit got mired down in the mud outside Frankfort, and half the animals the barker is talking about haven't even arrived yet."

"Then I suppose they'll drag out everything they have in front of these people, and try to lure a few more customers inside," suggested Knight.

"Without half the show being here?" Aindreas said. "That's cheating, isn't it?"

"It's illusion…and it's July Fourth in the United States of America," said Knight. "They do go together, don't they?" He pointed to some people in the front row of the crowd. "Watch over there."

Listening to the spiel of the barker, a man and woman each held the hand of a small boy. The man wore a suit, white shirt, and shiny, well-heeled shoes. His wife had on a splendid blue silk dress, and a lace mantilla covered her hair and shoulders. A heavy, broad-shouldered boy, maybe sixteen or so, bumped into the man nearly hard enough to knock him down. Brushing at the man's coat, the boy apologized loudly and at length. In the meantime another lad, small and lithe, had filched the man's wallet and watch, vanishing in the crowd like a fox. The victim appeared to have no idea what had happened.

"Shouldn't we do something?" asked Aindreas.

Knight put his hands in his pockets. "What would we do?" he asked. "The thieves are gone. And are you sure the well-heeled fellow is worth a great deal of sympathy?"

"Well, the pickpockets are the bad ones…aren't they?"

"Let's keep watching, Aindreas."

Aindreas and Knight threaded their way a little farther through the audience to stand quite near the man and his family. Two swarthy characters in scarlet silk shirts pulled out a wide cart from the tent, while the barker invited the attention of one and all to the Dancing Turkeys. "An act seen in New York and in the nation's capital," he said with almost comical import.

One of the scarlet-shirted men placed three turkeys on the flat top of the cart; the other man struck up a reel on a mouth-organ. The birds began to jump about, as if in time to the music. The well-heeled man and his wife laughed and pointed at the clumsy attempts of the turkeys to dance. The man lifted his laughing son up on his shoulders so the boy would miss none of it.

"Tell me what's wrong," said Knight. "Why don't they fly away?"

Aindreas replied, "I believe that maybe their wings have been clipped...like those ravens at the Tower of London."

"Probably," conceded Knight. "But have you seen what makes them...*dance*?"

Aindreas gestured toward the threads of vapor-like smoke rising from the rear of the cart. "Maybe I'd try to dance, too, on a surface as hot as that must be," he said.

Mr. Knight turned to go, but Aindreas held him by the arm.

"Have we more illusions to come?" asked Knight.

"I expect so," Aindreas said. "Besides, I have nowhere else to go."

The band played a fanfare, and the ragged carnival company passed in review across the stage. The audience exclaimed each time a new attraction claimed attention.

"Well, I never," a woman snickered to her friend.

An old grandfather said, "Look at that, Johnny."

A man in tights juggled rings and balanced spinning plates on poles. A giant, thin as a nail, stood next to a short, fat lady with sparse chin whiskers. A scary-looking man captured in the Amazon Valley uttered savage noises. His face lacked a nose and ears, and his head had no hair, even eyebrows. A young woman locked her legs behind her head and rolled over and over like a ball.

A number of people bought tickets and went inside the tent. The skeptics, those who needed more than catch-penny lures to spend their money, stubbornly stood their ground. But even their sense of excitement grew sharper at what came next. A broad-shouldered gentleman with a carnation in his coat lapel lugged two carpetbags across the stage. With a confused expression, the man hesitated and peered all about, then set the bags down on a table at the very front of the stage. "Are we still in Frankfort?" the man asked the audience.

They shouted back, "Noooo."

The children laughed out loud when voices came from the carpetbags.

A small voice demanded, "Let me out of here, Louis."

"Help," said a voice from the other bag. "I've been kidnapped."

Louis unbuttoned one of the bags, and out came a tiny soldier, standing no more than two-and-a-half-feet tall. He sparkled in a black uniform with silver buttons, shoulder boards, and medals on the chest. "Colonel Wellington here," this tiny man squeaked, saluting.

The children now shrieked, and the audience pushed forward until those in front were nearly pinned against the stage.

The second bag yielded the colonel's wife, Lady Jane, who had a face as pinched as a new born baby's. Bigger than the colonel, perhaps three-feet tall, she looked younger as well. Her purple dress, replete with bows and flowing ribbons and scarce bigger than a doll's, made up as glorious a miniature as Colonel Wellington's uniform. She kept her hands in a muff covered with the same material as her dress. The little woman linked arms with her hero and leaned her head coyly on his shoulder.

Aindreas asked, "How did they fit in those little bags?"

"Very painfully, I should think," responded Knight.

With a broad smile, Colonel Wellington paraded Lady Jane

184

around a table. He introduced their manager as 'Mr. Louis Vill.' Even that got a laugh from the crowd, but Aindreas sensed that these little people hated their manager.

The colonel mounted the table and waved his arms at the audience. "You young people come on inside, so the little lady and me can sing and dance for you," he said.

Lady Jane winked at the boys and young men, flirting outrageously. The colonel stepped in front of her in a jealous and protective manner. "We have a show to put on," he said, and asked the well-heeled man, "Do you have the time, sir?"

The man reached down to his watch pocket. Though his expression betrayed confusion when he found that pocket empty, the color drained from his face when he patted his coat pocket and found his wallet missing as well.

Lady Jane had leaned over the apron of the small stage and was cooing at the child. Perhaps the boy had never seen a muff. He grabbed it away from her, then flung it to the ground. The crowd gasped. It almost looked as if claws had somehow been attached to her wrists. Each stubby, long-nailed finger stuck out rigid as a spike from the thick nubs of flesh that were her hands. Panic in her face, Lady Jane tried to conceal her hands in the folds of her dress. She began to cry and turned her back to the audience.

The well-heeled man again patted up and down his body in search of his watch and wallet. Failing, his glances shifted frantically to here and there all around him, as though his valuables might be hanging in the air.

Finally he bellowed, "Goddamn it to hell!"

The colonel pointed down at the child. "You are a wicked little bastard," he said.

The boy began to bawl. His father slugged the colonel in the chest and the tiny man skidded on his rump across the table, landing on the stage in a plop. Without pause to assure the well-being of his meal ticket, Louis dove onto the outraged victim of the pickpockets. The two men rolled and grunted in the dust.

"Time to go," said Knight, and nudged Aindreas toward the rear of the crowd.

When they reached the sidewalk, König loped across Prather Street to join them. Aindreas saw the lights coming from blocks away, torches five or ten abreast, stretching off into the west. They were coming.

Knight asked, "Would it be best for you to go on home?"

"No," responded Aindreas. "I have the feeling this will be the longest night of my life."

Knight gestured toward a boy selling lemonade. Using part of the dollar he had won from William Williams that morning, Aindreas stood treat.

"Aaah," Knight exclaimed a moment later, rolling the cold, half-empty tumbler between his palms, "what would the Fourth of July be without lemonade and a parade?"

The marchers were coming east on Prather Street. Onlookers, some still toting picnic baskets, had gathered five or six deep along the sidewalks. The color guard carried more than a dozen American flags. Two ranks of drums and fifes followed closely. Aindreas shrank from the savage tattoo of the drums.

"Scots," Knight observed. "Only people I've ever heard make sounds like that."

König's warrior eyes glittered yellow, and a terrible urge to action resonated through his bones. He pressed his shoulder against Aindreas's knee, as if to reassure by his close presence.

Shiny buckles on their shoes, the first formation of men looked fresh out of a picture of early patriots on the march eighty years and more ago. They wore old-style knee breeches and stockings, hats with three corners, and bandages with red stains. Aindreas had forgotten who was putting on this parade, and his melancholy lifted for a moment. Even Mr. Knight's eyes misted over when the fifes and drums struck up *Yankee Doodle.*

More than a hundred men carrying torches came next. These were tough-looking men, simply plodding along, out of step with the drums and with each other. Their place near the front of the procession might well have been chosen to insure against any chance that someone might try to interfere with the parade.

Aindreas stood balanced on the corner of a water trough, his head above those around him. He gazed down the street at the torches and lanterns strung out into the distance. The flow of torch fire waved and rippled like a hellish river.

"They go all the way back to Eighth Street," Mr. Knight said. "Must have turned south off Jefferson Street, next to Cawthon's."

"More than a mile of them," said Aindreas. "I see, now—they marched just far enough west to taunt the Irish, and now they're headed east to mock the Germans."

Only men marched in the parade, certain kinds of men at that. All others watched, along with the women and children. Except for one rowdy bunch made up like Indians, the marchers looked Anglo-Saxon or Celtic to the man, as ordinary as any Aindreas had ever laid eyes on. "I see what you meant," he observed, "when you told me that *Sam* isn't a real person at all."

Knight smiled. "And I'd wager any one of the characters in this parade thinks he is more *American* than you."

Billowing banners nearly as wide as the street advertised the names of Louisville and Jefferson County, as well as the Indiana towns of New Albany and Jeffersonville. While the marchers had obviously been lined up in some kind of order, no other names had been displayed.

"Do you think they are in groups of some kind?" asked Aindreas.

"Clans," Mr. Knight responded. "They are called Clans of the Supreme Order of the Star Spangled Banner."

On and on came the marchers. Many carried lanterns that

produced transparencies of pictures and slogans. One message repeated itself again and again: *Americans Should Rule America.*

Later, a wide gap opened in the procession. Space for the fireworks. Rockets fired from rolling wagons exploded in colored falling stars. Spectators made excited sounds at the Roman candles, Bengal lights, Chinese fire, Italian suns, fairy bowers and crowns of Jupiter. Louisville skies likely had never seen anything like it. Members of the carnival company came out of the tent and watched. The dwarfs sat on their manager's shoulders. Lady Jane held on to a fistful of Louis's hair to steady herself.

Placards bobbed on poles, a forest of them, promoting candidates on the American Party ticket. Aindreas couldn't read them all but recognized some of the names:

LOVING for Governor
HARDY for Lieutenant Governor
HARLAN for Attorney General
REVEREND MATTHEWS for Superintendent of Public
Instruction

Clan members passed out leaflets for the American Party along the sides of the street and showered handbills over the crowd. Grown men and women actually scrambled for these scraps of paper.

"More illusion," said Knight. "These Know-Nothings do it better than the carnival people, maybe even as well as the pickpockets."

Dispirited, Aindreas was growing weary. He sipped his lemonade and the marchers kept coming. They looked so much alike he could have sworn that he had seen some of them earlier. He closed his eyes and thought suddenly of his mother and the months of her wasting. Sadness cut him so deeply he lost his balance and would have fallen from the water trough if Mr. Knight hadn't steadied him. Sooner or later, he had to go home.

How he dreaded it. The good-bye to his mother had been the best he could do, and it had wrenched his soul. Now, custom would make him live it again through the night and tomorrow and after, and stir the family's grief into his own. He opened his eyes.

"I think I know what's coming next," said Knight. "Have you heard of the Drummond light?"

Aindreas nodded, his fading interest newly piqued by mention of the light that was supposed to be the brightest anywhere. He heard ugly sounds in the background, bone against flesh, and moans. He craned his neck and looked in all directions but couldn't locate the place where someone was being beaten.

A wagon with streamers hanging from the side panels rolled to a stop in the middle of the street. The driver jumped down and held onto the horses' reins. Knight pointed toward two men in white coats, who attached bags to a pipe at the base of a massive glass lamp sitting on the wagon bed.

Aindreas said, "I've heard they can make a piece of lime incandescent."

"Right" agreed Knight. "As long as the oxygen and hydrogen hold out, we may see more clearly…or more, at least."

Clan members and parade-watchers alike shrank back from the wagon, uncertain what might happen. One of the white-coated men struck a match and carefully lit a flame at the tip of the blowpipe inside the lamp. The lamp began to glow. Within seconds, it cast more light than the biggest lamp Aindreas had ever seen. The wagon horses shied uneasily in their harness. The driver made soothing sounds, hanging onto the reins and bridles.

The lamp became brighter yet, then gradually many times brighter. Aindreas turned his back to the light. It seemed like noon, as though the sun lay in the street instead of the heavens. König hunkered down behind the water trough. The carnival giant, towering over the other spectators on the sidewalk, cast his thin-as-a-nail shadow up the side of the tent and clear off the top.

All within a city block froze in place. Everything and everybody. Aindreas could see things and places that had been in the dark, and it was amazing—but part of what he could see clearly before now lay concealed in shadows. On a bench to his left, a young woman pushed away the hand of a young man, her beau perhaps, and hastily buttoned up her blouse. The man rose uncertainly and looked all around at those now plainly in his view, looking as shaken as if he had been suddenly dropped naked in the middle of it all. The young woman watched after him as he walked away. The intensity of the light diminished subtly, almost imperceptibly.

"Will she go after him?" said Aindreas.

Knight shrugged and said "Who knows?"

A woman wailed by the street curb. Two clan members were holding up a carnival man by the arms, and another clansman turned away from the victim. They had beaten this man for some reason and had stopped only because of the brightness of the light. The two holding him abruptly let go of his arms, and the carnival man dropped to his knees. Blood from his nose and mouth streaked his shirt a darker scarlet. The intensity of the light diminished again. It now seemed more like a late afternoon but still quite bright enough to expose this savagery of the dark. The clansmen shuffled their feet, casting uneasy glances at each other, like caught children. One of them stuck his hands into his pockets.

The light grew dimmer. On the far side of the street, the broad-shouldered heavy boy and his lithe confederate had stationed themselves next to a portly shopkeeper and his wife, poised to move on them when the light had gone. Such an unlikely collection of statues in this strange gloaming, each of the four aware of the others—curious, each looking at one another.

*What might the shopkeeper and his wife be thinking?*

A stunning, brilliant flash and the light went out. Aindreas could see nothing but the torches. He listened as the sounds of bodies moving and of voices changing in the darkness. Torches had no more use in such darkness than smoking candles round a coffin.

"So," Knight whispered, "did you see more clearly in the limelight?"

"No," said Aindreas. "And you?"

"The same."

# 12

**Though** the sun had set nearly two hours before, the air was no less muggy. Aindreas walked home, his shirt sticking to his back. He saw no one when he passed by the Travis house and the cabin. In front of the tenement where Aindreas's family lived, Isaac's son sat drawing in the dirt with a stick. Sarah, a straw-stuffed dolly under her arm, watched over Aaron with serious eyes.

"How come you and Aaron are back here?" Aindreas asked.

"Miz Travis say Miz Rivers laid out," Sarah said, and pointed toward the kitchen door where black ribbons dangled from a black bow. "Me and Aaron can't go in there."

"Your mamma and daddy inside?"

Her expression solemn, she nodded.

Aindreas went in the back door to a smoky kitchen filled with people. He stayed near the door, listening to sounds from everywhere in the room—but not the voice he wished that he could hear again and would not.

Aunt Mary, short and heavy like his mother, came and put her arm around him. This good woman had been a widow for years. What would this death of a younger sister do to her?

"We dressed Dorrie the way she had told us," Aunt Mary said. "And we asked for a priest." She surveyed the crowded room and pulled Aindreas to the sink-counter covered with cups, bottles, and dishes of food. Rinsing off a plate, she handed it to him and said, "Eat something."

Aindreas's gaze fell on a pie. A piece had been cut from it, and the juice seeped and pooled at the bottom of the open space; the edge of the pan were dark and sticky. Blueberry, so stuffed with filling that the top crust had broken in a dozen places. Tempie must have made it. He admired the wonderful creation but felt no appetite, and it would be a sin to gag on something as wonderful as Tempie's pie.

"I hope those boys over there in the corner don't overdo the whiskey," Aunt Mary observed. "They work down at the yards with your brother."

Three of them. They looked like Michael, with their hard faces across the room. "That couple with their grown son, over there talking to Kirsty," she went on, "used to live near you all on Main Street, and some neighbors came from over there on Seventh Street."

Isaac and Tempie hung close by the elbow of Emily Travis, who was speaking with Aunt Margaret. There seemed little chance for Aindreas to have any sort of exchange with Isaac.

Four men, and a woman with pockmarks on her face, sat with his father at the table. Aindreas asked, "Those people his friends, or did they come from the store where he works?"

"Both," said Aunt Mary, and pursed her lips. "That woman's name is Lila. Her husband owns the store."

Aindreas shook his head wearily. *Was this the woman who had already replaced his mother?*

One of Michael's friends played Irish airs on the harmonica. The sadness and sentimental talk made an unexpected harmony with the music. A Celt was gone; one would have known this without having any knowledge of Doireann Rivers.

Joseph Rivers began telling an old story about Aindreas's grandmother. His voice rose loud enough that everyone in the place must have heard him. "You see," he said, "Margaret had already married Theodore Herdrich, and Mary had gotten hitched up to Frederich Zimmer, God bless 'im.'"

Joseph Rivers turned up his glass as if in memory of Fred Zimmer, an uncle who had died so long ago that Aindreas had no memory of him. The story had always seemed innocent enough to Aindreas, but his mother had never liked it, and why would his father tell it tonight?

"Well, I'd been chasing around after Dorrie, but I seen some clod buster named Muller hanging around the back door all the time. *Muller*, can you imagine?

Lila, the woman with the pockmarks, laughed.

"I didn't have a job, then and I didn't know how Dorrie's mother felt. So I hung around a little later one night, till after the old dear took her glass of elderberry wine, and I asked her what she thought of this Muller."

Aunt Margaret and Aunt Mary stood, unsmiling, by the stove.

"Mother McFate thought about it," he went on. "She said," and here his voice sounded a little like that of a tipsy old woman, "I think the Div'll owes me a debt, and he's payin' me off in Dutch son-in-laws.'"

The recitation brought on a lot of laughter.

Aindreas felt he could not delay any longer. He went to his mother's place and stood beside her. She lay on a wide board supported by two chairs. Beneath her, ice blocks filled a washtub, and more ice, chunks of it, had been set here and there around her body. On the arms of the chairs had been placed four tall, white tapers. He consoled himself that no pain had etched itself on her face. She had been dressed in a white cotton gown, with stockings on her feet. The bason, not quite so bright as it had been, lay close beside her, and in it nestled a single rose.

Aindreas felt a touch on his arm. "I'm so sorry, Andrew," said Blanche Flowers.

He couldn't look at her squarely. "Thank you," he mumbled.

As she had done many times, Miss Flowers stroked the hair back from his forehead. Aindreas flushed and turned his head away. Given the occasion, he resented her beauty, and there was a beauty even in her touch.

"You put up the candles, didn't you?" he said.

"Yes," said Blanche Flowers. "Let's go ahead and light them. These people will go home soon enough."

Aindreas brought a burning splinter from the stove and lit the tapers. "And you put her birthday gift beside her?"

"Yes."

"Why did you use a rose?" asked Aindreas, then turned away spitefully and blew out the splinter without waiting for an answer.

The squire and Mrs. Travis came forward. Mrs. Travis didn't greet Blanche Flowers but spoke directly to Aindreas. "Well, young man, things won't be so easy for you from now on."

"No, ma'am," he said.

The squire mumbled something to Miss Flowers, who looked ill at ease. Then he swiped at Aindreas's arm with his gloves in a gruff gesture of acknowledgment. "Too bad, boy," he said. "Too bad."

Isaac and Tempie remained behind the squire. They had not been allowed to come and pay respects to their friend. They had been packed up and brought along, the way Tempie's blueberry pie had been brought along.

Blanche Flowers moved around the others and spoke to Isaac and Tempie. The squire followed her with his eyes.

Mrs. Travis stared at the bason, apparently fascinated. She leaned over and picked it up. "Where did your mother get this?"

"I gave it to her," said Aindreas.

"Really? And how did you come by it?" asked Mrs. Travis.

"A friend."

Her voice sounded colder than usual, no less petty. "You know, Andrew, it isn't good to say things are yours that really belong to someone else."

The squire turned away from Miss Flowers. "What's all this, Emily?" he asked.

"Look, Squire." She held up the bason. "This has to be one of my mother's pieces, the one with the painted scenes on the inside."

The squire knotted his brow. Aindreas clenched his hands into fists. How he would have loved to pound on them both.

Examining the bason, the squire shook his head. "No, Emily. That thing from your mother's mantle was bigger...and it certainly didn't have all the detail this one has, or the light in it. My recollection is that you hated that piece so much you threw it out years ago."

Aindreas held out his hands for the bason, but Mrs. Travis did not give it up. She looked down at Doireann Rivers.

"Her sisters did wonders with her hair," she said, her voice turning coy again. "Don't you think she looks more like she used to?"

He firmly grasped the bason, took it from her, and returned it to the place beside his mother. "I think she looks dead," Aindreas answered.

Mrs. Travis stared at him, stone-faced.

A priest had arrived. The squire and Mrs. Travis decided they would leave. Aunt Margaret walked with them toward the door.

"We need to talk," Aindreas whispered to Isaac.

Isaac nodded. "If they let me, I'll go to the graveyard with you in the morning."

Joseph Rivers made a point of turning his chair so that his back faced the proceedings. The priest was short, round, and balding, possessed of startling blue eyes. He'd come from the Cathedral on Fifth Street. Aindreas walked over to him, by the place where Doireann Rivers lay.

The priest had a kind voice. "I'm Father Joseph Callaghan.

You're one of her sons?"

Aindreas liked the man right away. "Yes," he said.

Father Callaghan glanced over at the table, then said in a low voice, "As I understand it, your father did not want a mass in the church. Someone else in the family sent for me."

*Had the priest ever done this in a kitchen?*

About a dozen people remained, including Aindreas's father, who remained camped at the table. The men with him earlier had left, but the woman had not gone. Michael and his friends moved to the table and sat down.

When Uncle Theodore returned from making arrangements for the coffin, Aunt Margaret put her arm around him and thanked him for all he had done.

He chuckled and said to Aindreas, "A friend of mine knows you."

Aindreas made no response.

"A man named Georg Adler," Uncle Theodore continued. "I went looking for this one cabinetmaker people tell me works cheap, if you can find him sober. He usually hangs around at Dorrn's Saloon, where Adler tends bar, but the man hadn't been there tonight. Not at home, either, and nobody knew where he'd gone. I was starting to worry. It was getting late, and I still had to go to the graveyard."

Aunt Margaret handed him a glass of beer.

"Turns out Adler does all kinds of work," Uncle Theodore went on. "Said he'd make the coffin; already had some sawed-out pieces in his shed. He'll bring it over in the morning."

The priest's voice carried over the room.

*"They shall rejoice in the Lord, the bones that are brought low in the dust."*

Uncle Theodore leaned closer. "I told Adler we couldn't afford nothing but pine. We got to talking, and when he found out it was your mother who died, he told me he wouldn't take any money. And he's going to stain the box to look like rosewood!"

Aindreas smiled, then quickly glanced toward the table when he heard his father's angry voice.

Joseph Rivers pointed at Michael. "You never showed proper respect for your mother," he said.

Uncle Theodore shifted his feet, uneasy. "Adler will go with us in the morning, so we'll have two wagons," he went on. "A wagoner shouldn't have to walk, Adler told me. What did he mean by that?"

Aindreas shook his head, as if he didn't know, but Mr. Adler's comment warmed him. He winced, seeing the thin line of spittle running down his father's chin.

"No respect at all," bawled Joseph Rivers. "I don't care a damn what you say."

His head inclined, eyes closed, the priest continued.

*"Have mercy on me, O God, in your goodness; in the greatness of your compassion wipe out my offense."*

Several people rose from their chairs and left; a couple of others stayed just outside the doorway and watched. Uncle Theodore went to the table and pressed Joseph Rivers back down in his chair.

*"Thoroughly wash me from my guilt, and of my sins, cleanse me."*

Michael's face looked dark, furious. Kirsty hovered close by, hands clasped.

*"Indeed, in guilt was I born, and in sin my mother conceived me."*

Michael motioned toward the woman with his father and said, "Mum lays dead, old man, and you bring your whore in here and talk about respect."

*"Turn away your face from my sins, and blot out all my guilt."*

Joseph Rivers sprang from his chair, shook off Uncle Theodore's hand, and went around the table. He said, "Take that back, you worthless bastard."

*"Free me from blood guilt, O God, my saving God; then my tongue shall revel in your justice."*

Michael was still struggling to get up from his chair when Joseph Rivers punched him hard in the face. Uncle Theodore grabbed Aindreas's father from behind, and the woman at the table held onto his arm. Two men Aindreas didn't know stepped into help keep father and son apart.

*"O Lord, open my lips, and my mouth shall proclaim your praise."*

Holding a hand to his eye, Michael said, "I hope you rot in hell, you wicked sonofabitch."

"Get out of this house, and don't come back," snarled Joseph Rivers.

*"Eternal rest grant unto her, O Lord. And let perpetual light shine upon her."*

Michael's friends pulled him outside. Kirsty sobbed. Still enraged, Joseph Rivers struggled to get up from his chair. The woman with pockmarks stroked his face. Aindreas felt grateful that his mother would never have to bear witness to this kind of thing again.

*"They shall rejoice in the Lord, the bones that are brought low in the dust."* The priest closed his missal. "Let us pray," he said. *"Our Father, who art...*.

The candles had burned down to stubs no higher than an inch. From the board where Doireann Rivers lay, melting ice dripped into the washtub below. Aunt Margaret and Aunt Mary apparently had decided to wear out their rosaries and fingers all night at the church. Uncle Theodore would go get them on toward morning and bring them back to the house.

Aindreas had gone back to his room a moment earlier and looked out at a sky still black as ink. He had not slept but had kept watch. His mother needed nothing more. Once, well after midnight, Aindreas saw Mr. Knight watching, too, from the doorway.

Miss Flowers sat at the table, drowsing, head resting on her arm, and Aindreas's father snored in the room where his wife had died. Kirsty cut black cloth into strips. All the others had gone.

Aindreas said, "It's nearly dawn, Kirsty."

"You told me that an hour ago,"

A muffled oath came from outside. Aindreas saw a light moving near the cabin. Clearer this time, a man's voice exclaimed, "Finkel, why can't you put one foot in front of the other?"

Aindreas recognized Mr. Adler's voice, then saw Marta Adler in the lead, lighting the way to the door. She stepped aside with the lantern. Adler and Finkel carried the coffin into the kitchen. Miss Flowers roused from her chair. She and Kirsty stared at Finkel as though he were a Moor. Georg Adler removed the coffin lid.

Enveloped in the calm of Marta Adler's hug, Aindreas felt her soft heartbeat in his cheek, his eyes and his lips. She said, "We know your uncle, Theodore Herdrich, and we felt sorry to hear about his wife's sister. But we knew we must come when he told us this wonderful lady who passed away was your mother."

Georg Adler propped the coffin lid against a chair. "Go stay with the wagon," he ordered Finkel.

In came Uncle Theodore, Aunt Margaret, and Aunt Mary wearing solemn, exhausted faces. In vestments, Father Callaghan trailed close behind, followed by his even younger assistant, carrying a thurible.

Joseph Rivers had awakened. Bleary-eyed, he leaned against the sink. Kirsty tied a strip of black cloth around Aindreas's sleeve. The rest of them put on their armbands.

The family admired Adler's work, and Father Callaghan

sprinkled water over the coffin. The deep-purple wood had a hint of red. It didn't look like pine at all.

Aunt Mary touched one of the handles with delight. "Oh, it looks like rosewood," she said.

Aindreas gave thanks that it didn't *smell* like roses.

Soft white cloth lined the inside of the coffin, and the same material covered a pillow at the head. Adler said softly to Aindreas, "Marta made that for your mother."

"Thank you," said Aindreas, who felt like his collar would choke him.

The first rays of the sun crept through the open doorway and across the floor; the time had come. Georg Adler, Uncle Theodore, and Aindreas acted without words. Joseph Rivers watched dully. The two men gripped under Doireann Rivers's shoulders and knees. Aindreas lifted her feet. He knew why but was still shocked at how stiff she had become. When they picked up Doireann Rivers from the board, her head lolled backwards. Joseph Rivers, roused from his stupor, hurried over and held up his wife's head while they placed her inside the coffin.

A brief, sad smile came to Adler's face. Then, serious and workman like, he secured the lid in place. Nail holes had already been drilled out, two on each side and one at each end. BAM-BAM...BAM-BAM...BAM-BAM. Only two raps with the hammer for each nail.

Father Callaghan's healing voice carried over the noise. *"May the Angels take you into paradise; may the martyrs come to welcome you on your way, and lead you into the holy city, Jerusalem."*

His teeth clenched, Joseph Rivers seemed stunned by the words, or maybe it was nothing more than the clean, blunt sound of the hammer blows. Aindreas could think of nothing he could do to help. Adler was mercifully quick. BAM-BAM...BAM-BAM... BAM-BAM. The last nail was in.

*"May the choir of Angels welcome you, and with Lazarus, who once was poor, may you have everlasting rest."*

Aindreas held onto the handle at the foot of the coffin with both hands. They lifted it and carried his mother on the footpath toward Prather Street. König stayed close beside him.

Isaac and Tempie waited outside the cabin. From behind them, their children peeked at the procession. Isaac turned his head slowly from side to side, signaling that he couldn't come. Aindreas blinked, his jaw clenched.

Black streamers hung from the side panels of both wagons. They hoisted the coffin and slid it into Adler's wagon. Father Callaghan and his assistant, sitting on a bench near the front, seemed taken aback when König vaulted into the wagon and lay down near them. They probably had no idea how safe they were, Aindreas thought, as he secured the tailgate.

The rest of the family and Miss Flowers sat or stood in the other wagon. Aindreas climbed into the driver's box with Georg and Marta.

"I know this is a sad day, but you must drive the wagon" said Adler. "It's the right thing."

Aindreas started to object, but Adler handed him the reins.

"Ready?"

It took a second to recall how Tim Lytle had held the reins. Without waiting for an answer, Adler nudged his wife, who released the brake. "Follow your uncle," Adler said. "He's already starting up."

"Get up!" said Aindreas, and flicked the reins. The horse pulled the wagon away from the curb in front of the Travis house.

Uncle Theodore drove deliberately, thanks to heaven. Aindreas tried to keep the distance between them the same, even when the front wagon needed to slow or stop. They rocked along slowly. Not yet eight o'clock, the sun already brought out wetness on their faces. They moved past the Louisville and Nashville

Railroad yards, where Michael worked. Aindreas questioned where his brother might have spent the night and wondered what would happen to Michael now.

The further west they drove, the smaller the homes became. The procession passed by shacks with pigs and goats in the yards. König maintained his dignity, making no response to the barking dogs. Georg Adler and his wife chatted in low voices. Just before the Elizabethtown Turnpike, Uncle Theodore swung his wagon north on Eighteenth Street. Aindreas pulled gently at the reins, and his wagon turned smoothly behind the other.

"So nice and easy," observed Adler. "You're a good wagoner."

A thousand wagons and more had gouged this street into dusty ruts. The procession had come to the end of the city, where mostly Irish lived along with a few Germans. Women and children watched from their front yards, and men took off their hats at the sight of the wagons with black streamers.

After a time, the wheels clumped over more railroad tracks, this time the Portland and Louisville Railroad. They rolled to a stop, finally, in front of the flat land of Saint Mary's Graveyard. Wooden crosses and stone grave markers stood here and there without apparent pattern over the land—over the soil where, when they all went back to their homes, his mother would remain.

"That will be six dollars," the man at the gate told Uncle Theodore, and waited for it to be counted out before he would allow the wagon to be unloaded.

By the grave site, two grimy men with shovels removed their caps. The priest sprinkled water on the yawning cut in the red earth and paced around the grave with the smoking thurible.

Adler pressed a dollar into the hand of one of the gravediggers. Aunt Margaret wept, and so did Aunt Mary and Kirsty. Miss Flowers cried as bitterly as if Doireann Rivers had been her mother.

"...*in your kindness bless this grave.*

*Entrust it to the care of your holy Angel, and set free from all the chains of sin the soul of her whose body is buried here, so that...*"

Aindreas held onto one of the ropes. At the proper moment he released it, hand over hand in harmony with the others, until she disappeared into the ground.

"...*remember our sister, who God has taken to himself from the trials of this world.*"

Aindreas pressed his hands over his ears to shut out the dull, thunking sounds of red clay raining down on the coffin lid. *Lord have mercy. Christ have mercy. Lord have mercy.*

# 13

**Some** things didn't change at all in a week. Cawthon Furniture Manufactory had demanded its six of the seven days. In fact, Aindreas had gone from the burial of his mother on to work for the rest of that day. The streets remained filthy because it hadn't rained in some time, and the air stayed hot and foul from sunrise to dark. Sometimes a breeze stirred at night. A towel cloth wrapped around his middle, Aindreas paced the room. Something new. He felt uncomfortable now when he hadn't washed up or if his clothes looked dirty. In only seven days some things had changed.

"Are you back there, Andrew?" Kirsty asked from the kitchen.

"Yes."

"Are you dressed?"

"No."

"When you are, come to the kitchen," said Kirsty. "Aunt Mary came to visit, and we're going to eat."

"I'll be out in a minute."

Aindreas pulled on the double rope he had rigged between the window frame and the tree nearest the house. He unfastened his shirt and trousers from the line and put them on. Pulling on his boots, he left the still damp wool socks draped over the edge of his bed.

Aunt Mary, seated at the table, smiled when he came into the kitchen. "It's about time," she said.

Kirsty set out a plate with bread, slices of pork, and cheese.

Aindreas sipped the hot tea.

Aunt Mary seemed to take no notice. "Kirsty tells me you've taken to washing your clothes, most every night."

"You can't tell him anything," Kirsty interjected, as though Aindreas weren't there. "I told him I'd wash his things, same as Da's."

Aindreas ate a thick slice of the bread Kirsty had baked that morning but didn't touch anything else. "Where'd you get all this?" he asked.

Kirsty glared and filled her plate.

"Boys don't have to wash clothes," said Aunt Mary, oblivious to the looks exchanged between Aindreas and Kirsty.

He nudged the meat platter with his thumb. "Did you sneak this out of the Travis house?"

"Who cares?" she snapped. "This food would be thrown out. Your precious Tempie would have taken it, too, and so would anybody else."

"Don't do anything like that for me," said Aindreas.

Kirsty stuck out her tongue.

"Andrew, your father talked to me about keeping house here, living here with you," said Aunt Mary. She reached across the table and squeezed his hand. "Would you like that?"

Aindreas gently pulled his hand from Aunt Mary's.

Kirsty brought the kettle from the stove and poured more tea water. "All of us can't be as perfect as you, Andrew," she said in a spiteful singsong. "Mother liked it when I brought things for her to eat." Aindreas's face burned. He hated it when Kirsty twisted things around like that, using the memory of their mother to make something bad look perfectly clean and good and fine.

"I wouldn't have even thought about it," Aunt Mary began again, "but I don't know what will happen to this family. Your father grieves; your brother has gone." She cupped her hand and scraped crumbs off the table into the other hand. "And now a boy washes his own clothes," she concluded sadly.

Aindreas countered, "I thought you liked living near Aunt Margaret."

"Yes, we help each other out," Aunt Mary said, and absently ran her hand over the table searching for more crumbs. "But I'll come and live here if I'm needed."

He rose from the table and took the mug of tea with him. "Please don't do that on my account, Aunt Mary," said Aindreas.

Back in his room, he felt more at ease. Unhappy with himself for possibly hurting Aunt Mary's feelings, at least he could take some solace in the privacy of this room—now his. While he hoped that nothing bad had happened to Michael, Aindreas had to admit that he didn't really miss his brother like he had thought he would, and it felt good having the space to himself. He needed aloneness to think. The bason and the black Madonna were safe there and they kept him safe, even though the bason did not glow as much as in the last hours of his mother's life. And bad dreams still woke him at night, in some with Isaac being carted away chained to a wagon. A person with bad dreams needed space to flee and needed time alone to heal.

Kirsty and Aunt Mary continued their conversation in the kitchen. It would be dark soon. Aindreas intended to meet Captain Workman and Jack Graham at the *Ben Franklin,* then stop by Isaac's cabin and speak with him on the way home.

A moment later, Aindreas heard Miss Flowers's voice in the kitchen. He didn't want to see her, but he couldn't think of any way to avoid it. If he climbed out the window, Aunt Mary would be certain to come to his room later, knocking at the door. The only approach that made any sense was simply to march through the kitchen as quickly as he could.

Kirsty was pouring a cup of tea for Blanche Flowers when he walked in. Miss Flowers sat hunched over the table.

Her face was pale. "Hello, Andrew," Miss Flowers said.

Aindreas nodded. Her hands shook when she picked up the cup of tea. He paused; something was wrong.

Aunt Mary leaned closer to Miss Flowers. Their heads nearly touched. "What's wrong, dear?"

Miss Flowers began to cry. "I'm afraid I've had some bad news."

Kirsty leaned down and put an arm around Blanche Flowers's shoulder.

"I don't have a job anymore," said Miss Flowers.

"What happened?" Aunt Mary asked.

Miss Flowers began sobbing in earnest. She shook her head and pressed her lips together, trying to regain her composure. "The school board met yesterday, but I didn't find out about it until this afternoon."

"Everybody says you're a fine teacher," said Kirsty. "Isn't that right, Andrew?"

Aindreas shuffled his feet. "Uh-huh," he mumbled.

Aunt Mary persisted. "Did they find out that you're married?"

Miss Flowers dabbed at her eyes with a handkerchief. She seemed nearly as wounded as when Johnny Flowers disappeared. "All I heard is that Catholics and teachers born in some other country won't be rehired for the fall term," she said.

"My Lord!" Aunt Mary said. "What will you do?"

"I don't know...I don't know."

Aindreas could think of nothing to say and left without speaking. After a miserable walk to the river, he waited on the levee for Jack Graham. He stood staring down at the yellowish water that barely rippled in the lights from the *Ben Franklin*. Low and sluggish, the river had been that way for days.

He thought about the motion and the change in his life over these last days. Things with little rhyme or sense had happened and kept on happening—like this new business with Miss Flowers. Nothing and nobody stayed in place long enough to figure it or them out. Maybe he had been foolish to expect that things would ever be any different; only Mr. Knight could make things stand still for Aindreas.

Jack Graham emerged from the Wharfmaster's office. Hello, Lucky," Jack said, and clapped Aindreas on the shoulder. "You sure look pensive this evening."

Aindreas barely nodded. "I think I think too much."

Graham chuckled, and they started down the levee toward the *Ben Franklin*. "I told Captain Workman I'd seen you the other day and that your mother passed on," he said. "The Cap'n said he was real sorry to hear it."

When they arrived at the boat, Captain Workman stood waiting on deck. He shook hands warmly with them both, then led them back to his cabin. Workman sat down at his writing table, a bottle and some glasses on a tray close at hand. The wall shelves behind the table were lined with books, and more lay in uneven stacks in the chairs and on the floor. Other than in school, Aindreas had never seen quite so many books in one room. Maybe Major Krauth had given some of them to the captain. Aindreas made up his mind to ask Captain Workman one day which were the very best books.

"Will you and your family be all right, boy?" asked Workman.

"The family…well, I'm not sure. But don't worry about me, Captain, I'll do okay."

"I'm certainly glad to hear that last part. Has Jack Graham had the chance to tell you his good news?"

Graham grinned and smacked his hands together. "I'm going to be reinstated, m'boy. The papers should come through in the next few days."

"You'll be first mate again?"

"Right."

Graham paused and glanced at Workman. "Lucky, me and the Cap'n got a surprise for you. We hoped you would take a trip downriver with us in the fall. Work your way as a deckhand, of course…earn your keep."

"You mean, to New Orleans?"

"New Orleans," echoed Captain Workman.

Aindreas felt so excited he forgot for a moment that he had come down here to ask about Isaac. Jack Graham went on about how Aindreas just might be a natural river man, and then he suggested a toast. The captain smiled and poured a lot of water and tiny bit of whiskey into Aindreas's glass. They clinked their glasses together.

It tasted awful, but Aindreas tried not to let it show. *Maybe he could be a river man.*

Workman leaned back in his chair, serious now. "It will take some time yet, but I haven't forgotten about my promise for your friend. Isaac, is it?"

Graham confirmed it with a nod. He and Workman must have talked about Isaac.

"It seems the people I dealt with years ago still operate over there in New Albany," Workman said. "I wanted to do something sooner, but we haven't stopped here much in these last weeks. Truth is, I wasn't sure I'd still be captain of this boat until they dropped the charges against Jack."

There came a knock at the door.

"Yes, what is it?" Workman asked.

The engineer, Mr. Brickhouse, handed paperwork to the captain. Brickhouse glanced around the room, perhaps curious about the closed door. He peered through thick eyeglasses down at Graham and Aindreas. No one spoke for a time after Brickhouse left, pulling the door closed behind him.

Workman snorted and said, "Good man, but he has more damn curiosity than a cat."

Aindreas set the glass back on the tray. "When can we try to get Isaac out?"

"The next few weeks we'll haul freight mostly downriver," said Workman, "between Paducah and Natchez, and your friend certainly doesn't want to go in that direction." The captain put on his spectacles and retrieved a long ledger book from a cabinet. He flipped through the book, found the place, and ran his finger down a particular page. "Here it is. We pick up a load for Memphis on the first of the month in Cincinnati. That's definite." He dipped his pen in the inkwell and made a mark on the page. "We ought to return here that weekend, even with some stops, wouldn't we, Jack?" Workman asked.

Graham, who had been watching over the captain's shoulder, grunted agreement.

"You check with us on Saturday or Sunday, the fourth or the fifth of August," the captain said to Aindreas. "I'll tell you then exactly what Isaac and his family have to do. We'll leave on Monday or Tuesday night, depending on the cargo we have to pick up here."

Graham said, "You know, that first Monday in August is Election Day. With all the excitement going on, that might be a good day to try it."

"We'll think about that, Jack," replied Workman.

Anxious to tell Isaac the news, Aindreas rose to leave. The captain walked with him to the door. "We'll talk between now and then," Workman said. "In the meantime, keep your friend out of trouble—don't let him do anything to call attention to himself."

Aindreas hurried back to Prather Street. Light shone through the curtains and the screen door in the front part of the Travis house, but the rest of the place looked dark. Aindreas watched the back of the house for some time and saw no sign of anyone at the window. He knocked softly on the cabin door.

At the window, Isaac squinted into the darkness. "Young Andrew...that you?"

"Yes. Can you come out?"

Isaac whispered for a moment with Tempie, then came outside. Aindreas walked with him to the side of the cabin that couldn't be seen from the Travis house.

"I've been meaning to come by and talk, Isaac, but it seems like someone is always around. Didn't want to cause you any trouble with Mrs. Travis."

Isaac looked at the ground. "Glad you did, 'cause I was going to try and see you later on tonight."

"Tonight?"

"Wouldn't leave without saying good-bye to you and the big dog."

*So here it was. He had decided to run.* Aindreas had worried that something like this might happen. Now that he had actually heard the words, they sounded flat and dull. Aindreas tried frantically to figure out something of his own to say. He felt afraid of what could happen. Bounty hunters, sheriffs, bloodhounds. What could Isaac be thinking of?

"Believe me, Captain Workman will help us," said Aindreas in desperation.

"Can't wait no longer."

"You're just going to run off like a crazy man, without any plan?"

Isaac grimaced. "Things ain't the same as they was," he said. "I heard about a few that got across up by Cincinnati. Maybe we can do that."

Aindreas asked. "Can I talk to Tempie?"

Isaac nodded. "But Tempie and me's the same on this."

They walked quietly back around the cabin. Tempie, waiting by the window, waved them inside. The children were asleep in the corner.

Isaac plopped down wearily on the stool.

Aindreas squatted by the hearth. "What happened, Tempie?"

he asked. "Why did you change your mind?"

"Take a long time to get safe, Andrew," she replied.

"I know; Captain Workman told me you would have to travel for months."

"She won't be fit past October," said Isaac.

Tempie gently touched Aindreas's shoulder. "Maybe Christmas time, I'll birth another baby," she said.

For long moments, the only sounds were whimpers from little Sarah, who stirred restlessly in her sleep. Isaac jumped up from the stool as if he heard a sound outside. He looked out the window toward the Travis house, then came back and sat down.

Tempie pulled over a chair and sat beside Aindreas. She picked and smoothed at the wrinkled dress bunched in her lap. "We don't know where our people is, Andrew, neither one of us. Maybe we won't ever know, even if they alive or dead."

Isaac murmured agreement. Tempie tilted her head and looked up, her dark eyes speckled with light from the supper-fire-embers. "The Lord wouldn't like it if I let the white folks do something like that again," said Tempie, "to Sarah and Aaron and," she patted her stomach, "whoever this be."

Aindreas got to his feet. *They had made up their minds. Where was Mr. Knight with all his ideas when he needed him?*

Aindreas stared hard at Isaac, trying to shame him. "Wait three weeks. Besides, Tempie will need help," he said.

Isaac expression didn't change. "We got to try now."

Aindreas tried to come up with some reason that would make Isaac and Tempie give the idea more time. *What would Mr. Knight say?* Words tumbled out before Aindreas could even think about them. "If they catch you, there won't ever be another chance—they'll split up the family right then and there," he said, ashamed that he was making the prospect sound as dreadful as possible.

Tempie glanced at Isaac, who looked away.

"It's not the right time," insisted Aindreas.

Isaac asked, "Why you so sure?"

"I dreamed about it. I, uh…"

Piercing shrieks from Sarah cut him off. She was standing on her pallet, hands over her eyes, quaking. Tempie picked the child up and held her.

"Dogs, dogs," Sarah cried over and over.

Someone pounded heavily on the door. Aindreas dived into a dark corner among the gourds and burlap sacks and lay still.

The squire shouted, "Isaac, open this damn door." Once inside, Squire Travis moved over near the fireplace. He glanced around. "Don't know why you have to keep that latch on the door," he complained. "And what was all that carrying on in here?"

"Sarah had the bad dreams."

Puffing on his cigar, the squire snickered. "Sometimes even a little wench like that knows more than we think," he said.

Aindreas didn't move. It wouldn't do for him to be caught here. The harsh smoke burned his eyes. He pinched his nose, afraid he might sneeze.

"I've got to get to the train station in the morning," the squire said. "Mrs. Travis forgot to tell you that I'm going to Cincinnati. Have the carriage ready by six-thirty."

Aindreas clamped both hands over his face, certain that any second an explosive sneeze would bring the squire down on his head.

As the squire went out the door, he cautioned Isaac not to be late with the carriage. Aindreas listened as the footsteps faded away. He remained in the dark corner for several minutes, sneezing again and again.

"If we left now…" Isaac said, then shaking his head. "I don't know. Maybe tonight wasn't no good."

Aindreas felt relieved at Isaac's second thoughts.

Before he left, Aindreas asked them once more to hold off until they could get out with Captain Workman's help.

Isaac heard him out, then said, "Maybe we be here in the morning, but that don't mean we will the day after that."

"Just wait until Election Day," Aindreas pleaded. "By then, everything will be fine."

# 14

The next day, Thursday, Aindreas saw Sarah and Aaron outside the cabin playing by the woodpile. It relieved his nerves to see that Isaac and his family hadn't left. But he felt uneasy each following morning until he smelled fresh smoke from the cabin chimney or saw one of the family stirring around. A week passed before he learned what had scared Isaac so much that he had earlier decided to make a wild run for it.

The squire hadn't yet returned from Cincinnati. When Mrs. Travis glided down from her porch into a lady friend's carriage, Aindreas could walk on over to the cabin without worry.

The fear in Isaac' voice painted the room. "Last Wednesday, that's when the squire brung 'em back here."

Tempie rocked young Aaron.

Aindreas tried to sound unconcerned. "The squire has always been a braggart. Suppose he was just showing off for his friends around that beautiful garden Tempie made."

Isaac glared. Tempie wagged her head no.

"Who were these people with him?" Aindreas asked.

Isaac drummed the fingers of his good hand on the table.

"One of 'em I never seen before, but I know that other one."

"C'mon, Isaac," Aindreas said, hoping that his impatience didn't show. "Who?"

"That Mr. Cooper."

Aindreas felt a chill on his skin.

"They looked all around," said Isaac. "The squire pointed at this and that. Yeah, he did take 'em to the garden, and they did some laughing and carrying on the whole while."

Aindreas asked, "Did they say anything to you?"

"They didn't say nothing," Tempie put in. "But it was us they come to look at."

1

That afternoon, Aindreas finished all the deliveries he had been assigned by two-thirty. Williams hadn't come back yet, and Aindreas got started with the sweeping.

The chief clerk waved him over to the desk. "Ever been to New Albany, Rivers?" he asked.

"A long time ago my father took me," said Aindreas.

"We're shorthanded, and we need Allison to make another run with his wagon after this one," the clerk said. "I want you to go with him. He'll drop off a load of furniture at the Portland ferry. You stay with the load on over to New Albany, and come on back after the customer picks up the merchandise on the other side."

Aindreas scratched his head. "That might take the rest of the afternoon."

"Don't worry about it," said the clerk. "Allison has the papers, and he'll pay the ferryboat pilot for your ride back over."

Aindreas hurried to the freight dock. By the time he arrived, Mr. Allison had already loaded the three oak kitchen tables and most of the chairs onto the wagon.

Aindreas helped with the last few chairs. When all the things had been placed on the wagon, there still remained unfilled space. Aindreas had to admire the way Mr. Allison arranged a load of furniture.

A big, heavy man with dark rings of sweat on his shirt and a wad of tobacco in his cheek, Allison assured Aindreas that he was glad to have some company for the trip.

Allison steered the wagon smoothly out of the freight yard and into the stream of traffic. He drove a wagon ten times better than Tim. On the way to Main Street, Aindreas relaxed, free to look at all the painted signs over the shops and storefronts gliding past. Coal was for sale all along the street, and books and boots and sarsaparilla beer. Sellers who weren't hawking wares in the aisles of their shops waited outside, thumbs hooked in their braces.

Mr. Allison turned the wagon west on Main. He chided the horse, "Come on now, Belle, we'll sleep when we're done." Allison handled the wagon with such confidence, and he knew how to humor the dark bay mare through the traffic. "No need to race, love," he cooed, then added, "Those people don't have no manners."

Allison must have noticed his passenger's close attention and told Aindreas he could hold the reins for a while, later, if he wanted to.

"She's a good horse, Mr. Allison. Strong," Aindreas said admiringly.

"They say she has some Morgan in her," said Allison.

Aindreas couldn't help but laugh. His grandfather had told him once that horse people would claim that any four-legged animal that could put one foot in front of the other had some of the Morgan strain. Allison laughed, too, evidently amused that the boy understood the joke.

The wagon rolled past manufacturers of straw goods, buggies, and cigars. It seemed Louisville changed every day. Like toadstools in damp woods, new enterprises sprouted on vacant lots the moment they became so. Here, a brass foundry Aindreas hadn't seen before, and there a fitter of gas fixtures and water closets.

Then came Quinn's Row and strings of other tenements. Women chattered from their windows at the children and a smell of cabbage hung in the air, blue with smoke from cooking fires. Irish lived here. The men worked on the Portland Railroad or the canal, wherever a willing, strong back could earn a wage.

Aindreas said, "We used to live near here."

"Didya now?" said Allison. "I still do...over on Chapel."

"Oh, Chapel Street." Aindreas hoped his voice hadn't betrayed his surprise at the mention of that infamous street.

Allison chuckled. "Me and the missus make do...still got kiddos at home."

They turned onto Twelfth Street. When the wagon began tossing to and fro in the ruts, Allison glanced back to check on the load. Aindreas hoped they wouldn't get onto any rutted street while he was holding the reins, and it wouldn't be long before they would reach the Plank Road to Portland. An article he had read in the newspapers a few days earlier came to mind. "What was that trouble up this way a while back?" he asked Allison.

Allison chuckled. "This here's the Eighth Ward, boy. Which trouble you talking about?"

"Gunshots, and I heard several homes got busted into," Aindreas said.

"Vandals paid by the Know-Nothings did that. Claimed the Irish were hiding guns." Allison spat a brown stream into the dusty street. Mark my word, there's gonna be trouble all over the city with this election coming up. I won't even try to vote."

When they reached High Street, Aindreas looked back. They had traveled farther and farther away from the bustle of downtown Main Street. Across the river, patches of afternoon sun speckled the knobs beyond New Albany, hills that never seemed to change. But there had been changes a plenty nearby. The river practically flowed right over the nude and gouged remains of Corn Island, the place where the settlers had first stopped with the intention of staying. And just the other side of the canal lay the spot his father had described as once the most promising in

219

the whole area—Shippingport. But the canal had cut Shippingport off from the rest of the land and turned it into an island. Except for the big mill and some homes, little more than weeds and vacant lots remained. A steamboat moved through the Portland Canal west toward Sand Island and Portland, toward the place where the canal emptied back into the river channel. The boat didn't even slow down for what was left of Shippingport.

Allison slowed the horse to a stop. He climbed back and retied the ropes securing the furniture. Soon after they started moving again, the wagon lurched up onto the apron of the Plank Road. Mr. Allison made good his promise and allowed Aindreas to take the reins. Rolling along, the wheels rumbled like drums on the corduroy surface.

The horse behaved so well that Aindreas had to do little more than hold the reins in his hands. Before long, Portland lay just ahead. Spreading up and over the high bank, it still had the look of a river town in its own right. The warehouses and the chandlers' stores didn't look as big as those at the Louisville wharf—but a hotel stood nearby, and merchant offices, shops, tradesmen, even a tailor and an apothecary. The town had finally been absorbed into the city only three years before, but the old rivalry still smoldered between Portland and Louisville.

Aindreas made a quick count of the nine boats docked at the wharf. Allison didn't reclaim the reins until they approached the levee on Water Street. The side-wheel ferryboat *Alicia* let loose a blast from her whistle.

Allison slowed the wagon to a stop. "Still got time to put on a load for this trip?" he shouted to the pilot.

The pilot waved for them to come on board. Aindreas helped Allison carry on the tables and chairs. Several wagons and maybe thirty passengers had already staked out their own space on the rounded deck. Once the charges had been settled, Allison got back up on the wagon. He waved back at Aindreas as he began the return trip to Cawthon's Furniture.

The ferryboat apparently was ready to get underway. Aindreas leaned back against the railing, a mixture of uncertainty and anticipation fluttering in his middle. He shielded his eyes from the sun and peered up the wharf toward the coffee shop supposedly owned by a giant, but today no one especially big stood anywhere in sight. Aindreas had never actually seen the giant, in truth, but he believed there was one. He would try to remember to look again when he came back across the river.

The pilot backed the *Alicia* away from the wharf and swung her around toward the Indiana shore. Crossing wouldn't take very long since the river stretched no more than a quarter of a mile wide at this point. Side wheels churning, the boat seemed to be headed somewhat up river of New Albany. Probably to allow for the current. Aindreas enjoyed the ride at first, but after a time an anxious feeling took him over. His breathing became harder, and his tenacious grip on the rail lightened his knuckles.

*What could all this be about? No reason to be afraid.*

At that instant he saw a golden ball over the treetops on the far shore, as high as the tallest building in Louisville. It transfixed him. While it might have come within his vision from a far distance sometime or other, he'd never really taken notice of it. He dashed over to a deckhand and gestured in the direction of the tower. "What do they call that?"

"Call what?"

Aindreas pointed again. "That tower, with the shiny golden ball way up at the top of the steeple. Is it a church?"

"Yes," the man said. "The Town Clock Church."

"What kind of church is it?"

The man squatted, coiling a line. "Presbyterian… the Second Presbyterian Church."

Aindreas remained at the rail for the rest of the short crossing. The wide brick church grew even more imposing as the boat neared the shore. It began to look as if the church stood only a short distance upriver from the ferry slip.

The other passengers went ashore when the ferryboat tied up at the New Albany landing moments later. Aindreas waited for the furniture dealer. After a time, the tables and chairs from Cawthon's were the only freight left on the deck.

The pilot came down to the deck. He propped his elbows on the rail, then packed and lit a weathered-looking pipe. "Haven't come yet, eh?"

Aindreas shook his head.

"No hurry," the pilot said. "This time of day we only go across once an hour, unless we get a whole boatload of people."

Aindreas gestured toward the church. "That's some church spire."

The pilot nodded. "Every boat that sails this river uses that brass ball for a landmark," he said. "I've used it myself with dark coming on."

Only the upper half of the Town Clock Church could be seen from the river bank. Aindreas figured that the church fronted on Main Street. He knew that much about the town, at least; they called the high bank Main Street, same as Louisville.

Two men from Hoeck Furniture arrived a short time later and loaded the tables and chairs on the wagon. The deck of the ferryboat finally clear, the pilot knocked the ashes out of his pipe and started for his cabin. He stopped, then peered down at his pocket watch. "Kick around a little if you want, young fellah," he said. "You still have over half an hour before we go back across."

Glad for the suggestion, Aindreas went down the boarding plank, then turned and walked along the shore. He passed below a few houses located halfway up the bank, then paused to study the church. Only a couple of low storage sheds stood between the back door of the building and the river. It looked to be about two- or three-hundred feet from the water up the slope to the rear of the building. *Yes. This had to be the church, the one Captain Workman was talking about.* Aindreas shivered in spite of the heat.

His boots made soft, dry splashes in the powdery dust as he trudged up the incline. He sauntered past homes on Main Street and peered in the shop windows. Tattered shreds of an ancient poster clung to an alley wall, advertising a long ago speech by Henry Clay.

He admired the church at closer range. It looked like a picture of a Greek temple from the front, but the bleached belfry and clock tower stuck out on top like a decoration on a fancy cake, and he soaring steeple gave an effect unlike anything Aindreas had ever seen.

Aindreas glanced up and down the street. It seemed strange; not one single person of color. A cluster of white men and women stood across the street from the church. Aindreas walked toward them, thinking he might have the chance to pose one or two careful questions about the church. But as he drew closer, their accusing stares stirred up a kind of guilty feeling in him. It seemed like a good idea to reverse direction, but when he turned around, he found himself standing face-to-face with Mr. Bones. Aindreas took solace in the notion that maybe he wasn't the one who'd been the target of those hostile stares. But when Aindreas stepped off the sidewalk to get around the shadowy figure, Bones grabbed the back of his shirt collar and spun him back around to face the advancing people.

A tall, graying woman stood at the front of the group. Her voice sounded hard, metallic. "Did you come searching for runaways?" she asked.

Bones gripped Aindreas's collar tightly. He tried to yell, but no sound came from his throat. The gray woman should be made to know that she had it backwards, that he had a plan to help Isaac and his family run away, and that only today he had discovered the place where they must begin their journey.

"I came here with hesitation and reluctance," Mr. Bones replied, resentment in his every syllable, "because I apprehended the motives of my journey might be misconceived and perverted."

"Stop all that fancy talk," a man yelled from the back of the group. "You keep slaves on the other side of the river, and they should be free."

Aindreas couldn't pry himself free from Bones's iron grip. His body was nothing more than a shield, he realized, but for which side?

Mr. Bones's delivery sounded more conciliatory. "Suppose you had been invited to Kentucky, and that I employed such means to demand that you relinquish your farm or other property. What would you have thought?" he asked. "Would you have deemed it courteous and according to the rights of hospitality?"

"I don't have a farm. Besides, we stand for abolition," the gray woman said, "so let him go!"

Bones, holding Aindreas in front of him, pushed closer to his tormentors. He nearly spat out the mocking words that followed. "I know well that you deny the right of property of slaves. But then you and your associates are not the lawmakers for us, and until the law is repealed, we must be excused for asserting the rights...yes, the property in slaves."

The abolitionists moved slowly forward, narrowing the distance still more.

Aindreas felt himself pulled back a few steps by the retreating Mr. Bones, who talked as he moved. "In no society that ever did exist or ever shall, can the equality asserted among humans be practically enforced and carried out."

"We don't want to hear that hogwash," said the gray woman.

"There are portions of it," Bones smiled malevolently at the woman and went on, "women, minors, insane, culprits, that will probably always remain subject to the government of others in the community."

Some members of the crowd picked up and threw clods of dirt. One hit Aindreas squarely in the chest and knocked the breath out of him. Bones gasped as though he were the one who had been hit. The angry abolitionists looked all the more menacing, ready to close in.

Only then did Aindreas notice the sheriff standing there just to one side. Hands on his hips, the sheriff smiled curiously. Two snickering small boys behind him were holding clods of dirt. Aindreas wondered why the sheriff didn't try to help him.

Still backing up, Mr. Bones scolded the abolitionists. "Go home and mind your own business, and leave other people to take care of theirs," he said. "Limit your benevolent exertions to your own neighborhood. You will be better and wiser than you have shown yourself this day." With a great effort, Aindreas yanked himself free. He fell to the ground, scraping his knee, then scrambled to his feet and ran all the way to the ferryboat. No one came after him, but he stayed right in the midst of the passengers until the *Alicia* cast off for Portland.

His knee burned. Worse, his trousers were torn. Aindreas leaned over the rail and looked down at swirls in the brown water. Reflecting on the strange happenings back there near the church, he wondered how it was that little people like him always ended up in the middle of deadly quarrels between big people. Perhaps, he thought, it was in the nature of the game big people always liked to play.

The ferry hadn't gone halfway across the river when the engine vibrations slackened nearly to a stop. Aindreas squinted toward the low sun hanging over the river, sighted a huge boat, then hurried up the ladder to the pilothouse. The pilot turned the bow into the current to hold a line for the Kentucky shore.

Aindreas coughed.

The pilot looked around, pipe clenched in his teeth. "What is it?"

"May I come in and watch, sir?"

"May as well," the pilot said without turning his head. "Guess you must have seen her, too."

Smoke pouring from her stacks, an enormous white boat swung wide from the channel toward the Portland wharf, and Aindreas couldn't take his eyes away. He had never been this close to the *Eclipse*.

"Forty years, there's been many a steamboat up and down this river but never one like that," the pilot said in awe. "Got a crew of a hundred and twenty. Built right back there in New Albany."

"That's what I heard," said Aindreas.

The ferry narrowed the distance to the wharf. The closer they got, the more impressive the looming *Eclipse* became. Long as a city block, in the setting sun its superstructure looked the color of cream.

"See the name painted on the wheelhouse, boy?" the pilot asked.

"Uh-huh."

"Well, each letter is as tall as you."

Aindreas said, "How I'd love to go onboard."

The pilot made a harrumping sound. "Hell, sneak on there," he said. "That boat is so damn big they won't even know you're around."

The *Eclipse* blocked the fading light when they passed near. The ferry glided into its docking place in near darkness. Aindreas started down the ladder for the main deck.

"Sneak on, boy, that's what I'd do," the pilot said after him.

His right knee had bled through his torn trouser leg, and Aindreas silently swore for not having a rag in his pocket. He limped out on the dock alongside the huge boat. Some passengers were coming ashore. Others still strolled on the decks, and a few sat on chairs in front of the cabins. The ladies wore light dresses with puffy sleeves and carried bright parasols. A loud man on the cabin deck fanned himself with his hat and talked to friends on the shore, telling them about the afternoon excursion.

*No telling when another chance might come.*

Aindreas decided to do it, to take the advice of the ferryboat pilot. If the officers caught him, they could only put him off, maybe nothing much more than that. *They couldn't have him arrested, or could they?* He waited. When the officer stationed near the boarding plank turned away and began talking with several ladies in feathered hats, Aindreas sprinted onto the main deck and kept right on going. He didn't stop until he crouched down near the smokestacks. No sign that anyone had taken notice of him.

He wet a finger and touched one of the stacks. Still hot. Most of the sprawling deck was empty of freight, but even the partial load onboard looked like a lot more than the *Ben Franklin* could carry loaded full.

Working his way back past barrels, bags, and stacks of lumber, Aindreas found the door to the engine room open and went inside. He couldn't resist counting the boilers. Captain Workman hadn't fibbed. Sixteen of them. What an inferno the place had to be when the paddle wheels were turning and the firemen burning a hundred cords of wood in a day. The huge wheels hung silent and still, each of them over forty feet across, Captain Workman had told him, and they looked every bit that big. Aindreas slipped back outside before anyone could notice him.

Concealing himself in the shadows when he could, Aindreas explored for over an hour, careful to go the other way whenever he saw the uniform of a crew member. He managed to cover a good deal of the huge boat's exterior. The door of one stateroom hung open, showing a river scene painted on the inside of it. He peeked inside. Lots of lamps and furniture. Aindreas thought the room looked every bit as well furnished and as comfortable as those he had seen in the Travis house.

Stewards were carrying dishes out of the main cabin. He watched them for a while. Captain Workman had told him that the main cabin looked as splendid as anything in the Galt House or the new Louisville Hotel. It would be a shame not to see it before going ashore. Over the door hung paintings of Louisville and New Orleans, patron cities of the *Eclipse.* Aindreas studied the New Orleans likeness with keen interest, since he might have a chance to visit there.

After a time, when crew members had stopped going in and out, Aindreas summoned the nerve to open the door and look inside the big cabin. The long room was now apparently empty, the lights dimmed and its tables and chairs stacked in rows along the sides.

When his eyes adjusted to the dim light, he saw that the place hadn't completely emptied. An older black woman silently washed the floor.

He went on inside. The woman, on her hands and knees, looked up at him but said nothing when he walked slowly along one wall. The captain's description had not been overstatement, yet Aindreas still hadn't been prepared for anything quite like this. Massive chandeliers, six of them, hung in a line down the middle of the room. He'd seen stained glass before and skylights as well, but never the two of them together. It would be wonderful to tell Mr. Knight and Georg Adler what he had seen, but he wouldn't know the proper words to describe the fancy work on the walls, the arches, or the paintings on the ceiling. He paused near a bronze bust at one end of the room. No name had been inscribed on the base. The nose, the lines in the face, and the swept-back hair of the figure reminded him of pictures of someone he had seen before.

The scrubwoman had worked to a spot nearby. She gazed up at him again.

"Excuse me," he said, pointing at the bust. "Do you know who that is?"

The woman rose slowly to her feet and wiped her hands. She walked unsteadily toward him. It had been a silly question to ask. She seemed so old, probably had no idea what he was talking about, and Aindreas felt sorry to have bothered her.

"That's old Andy Jackson, young man," she said, and cackled. "'Surprise' you didn't know."

Embarrassed about his misjudgment of the old woman, Aindreas could say nothing more than, "Oh."

She gave him a near-toothless smile, her eyes twinkling with mischief, and pointed toward the wall at the opposite end of the room. "Know that one?"

He hadn't noticed the second bust. Careful not to walk on the part of the floor she had cleaned, he padded to the far end of the cabin.

Only a quick look at the bust made him feel shaky inside. *No need to have a name on that one.* Jackson's face, on the other bust, had been rough, full of angles and lines. The face on this one was smooth. Beneath the high forehead, the hard eyes reflected the light in a bronze stare. The thin face had a passive expression, devoid of any outstanding features except high cheekbones and thin lips over a very wide mouth. *Mr. Bones.*

Aindreas turned and walked quickly toward the door. The scrubwoman watched him. "I know that one," he said as he passed her.

He closed the door behind him, wanting to get off the *Eclipse* as soon as possible. In haste, he turned in a different direction than he had come. He realized his mistake in seconds, but before he could get turned around, a crew member spotted him.

Aindreas wheeled around and ran.

"Hey you, come back here!"

He ran faster, hearing footsteps behind him. The double door to the main cabin was off to his right. He skidded to a stop and went in. Breathing hard, he stood with his back against the door.

The old woman, carrying a bucket, came to the door and shooed him out of the way. She put a finger to her lips. "Shhh."

Aindreas heard the footsteps of his pursuer. The woman opened one of the doors as the officer approached.

"Oh, it's you Dicey," the man said. "You seen anybody sneaking around here? A ragged looking boy wearing a cap?"

She wagged her head. "Ain't seen nobody. Jus' fixin' to get clean water."

"Well, you keep your eyes open, you hear?"

She nodded.

Aindreas remained against the wall until the footsteps in the hall faded. The old woman led him across the cabin to the outside door. She pointed to the left. "That way," she said. "Now you git on home."

Out on the deck, Aindreas scurried along the rail. He ran down the boarding plank and started up the levee. He heard a man's voice, a gruff voice he knew. Aindreas stopped and looked around, then gazed up toward the second deck. A man was standing next to a beautiful lady. Squire Travis spoke again, and the lady laughed, a wonderful, musical laugh. He was standing close to her and pressed Miss Flowers's hand in his.

TOWN CLOCK CHURCH

ECLIPSE

# 15

A foul haze hung over the rooftops day after day. Angry women smacked their children and hissed at each other in the vegetable markets; men cursed and fought in the streets. The whole town thrashed about in some kind of premonition of evil to come.

Aindreas moped through late July and early August, his feelings for Miss Flowers broken beyond fixing. He hoped that one day he would understand why she didn't turn out to be the person he had believed in. Desperate for answers, he kept on the lookout for Mr. Knight but hadn't seen him since the night of his mother's wake. One positive thought sustained Aindreas: he could still help Isaac and Tempie, if they would let him. He kept an eye out for the chance to meet with Isaac again, but couldn't manage it without being observed. The squire seemed to be tramping around the property at all hours of the day and night, and Mrs. Travis sat by the back window more than ever. *Did they suspect something?*

FRIDAY, AUGUST 3, 1855.

As he had done every morning for over two weeks, Aindreas counted off the days. Four left, at most. Captain Workman had told him that Isaac and his family could make a run for it on Monday or Tuesday, depending on which day the *Ben Franklin* left for Memphis.

Aindreas arrived for work thirty minutes early. Even before he reached the open doorway, he could hear voices from the office. Another argument? There'd been a number of those lately.

The clerks and some men from the factory were apparently into it about the coming election. One of the voices was Mr. Allison's. When the disagreement became still louder the chief clerk, his brow arched, looked up from his ledgers. Tall, lanky Tom Williams, older brother of the new boy, leaned against a file cabinet. Evidently, he was the spokesman for the clerks. "...and one of my father's friends told me the Americans will do whatever they have to keep the riffraff in line," he said with assurance.

Some of the clerks nodded.

Mr. Allison's eyes flashed, and his usual placid expression disappeared. "The people you call *Americans* amount to Know-Nothings," he said, shifting the tobacco wad in his cheek. "And this *riffraff* you talk about are all Germans or Irish, like me."

Tom Williams started to respond, but Allison held up his hand. "And to keep us *in line* means they don't want us trying to vote."

"I wasn't talking about you," Tom Williams protested.

Mr. Allison spat in the sawdust near the young man's feet. Williams cast a startled glance down at his shoes.

"I'm beggin' your pardon," Allison said. "Even if you say I'm not one of those *riffraff* your father's friends talk about, I hope I haven't *got out of line*."

Two of the factory hands chuckled.

Tom Williams turned to the factory hands, his expression of superior amusement in place again. "You claim you don't like slavery," he said.

They grunted in agreement.

"Well, then, how in the world can you people vote forDemocrats? They're a whole party of slavers, and proud of it."

"Not all of 'em," a carpenter retorted, sounding less than convinced.

Williams rolled his eyes. Those siding with him nudged each

other in appreciation of how cleverly he had turned the tables.

"The Know-Nothings ain't against slavery, any more than the Whigs," Allison responded. "They don't want to talk about it, that's all, so they preach all those lies about foreigners."

Aindreas felt a tingling pride for Mr. Allison, but a sharp rapping sound from the chief clerk's desk brought the discussion to a close. His ruler in hand, the chief clerk looked for certain the part of a stern schoolmaster. "That's enough," he said. "This is a business here, and business people shouldn't involve themselves with politics."

Grumbling, the group near the file cabinet broke up. Allison glared at Tom Williams before he turned to leave.

The chief clerk added, "Let each man do his job and all will be well. Nothing about this election has one single thing to do with us."

Though no business would be done for another twenty minutes, the clerks and factory hands went dutifully to their places. So did Aindreas.

2

On an errand, Aindreas crossed Water Street onto the levee early that afternoon. He scanned the line of steamboats from habit. He hoped Jack Graham had resumed his post on the *Ben Franklin* and that there hadn't been any change in the boat's schedule. Aindreas stepped inside the wharfmaster's office and handed the papers across the counter to the man in charge. No sign of Jack. "Mr. Graham not here anymore?" Aindreas asked.

The man muttered about the dry ink pad and stamped the papers. "Left a little over a week ago," he said. "Didn't you know he got his first-mate job back?"

Trying to appear unconcerned, Aindreas only shook his head.

The man slid a stamped copy of the bill over the counter. "Let's see," he said, scanning a ledger. "The *Ben Franklin* ought to back in here Saturday or Sunday."

Aindreas thanked him and walked away from the wharfmaster's office feeling more assured. The schedule hadn't been changed, and Jack Graham was aboard.

The garbage piles always smelled worse than ever in the midday heat. Wanting no part of that, Aindreas avoided Market Street on his trip back to the office. Up ahead on Main Street, children screeched and waved at someone in front of the Louisville Hotel. Aindreas stopped to find out the source of all the excitement. The spectacle in the street amazed him, at least at its beginning.

A big mule pulled a buggy with a single seat. It first appeared the the driver stood upright, but then Aindreas could see that the man was seated—his knees jutting into the air above the dashboard. The man wore a high hat and held a whip, in the fashion of a hack-driver. A very large man.

"Jim…Jim," the children cried. They squealed when the wagon pulled to the curb. A black hotel porter took hold of the mule's bridle. The driver rose from his wagon seat, and Aindreas realized he was looking at the gigantic Jim Porter.

The huge figure sported a dark frock coat with tails. His shirt had an old-fashioned standing collar, and the ends of his neck cloth hung at least a foot down his chest. Hotel guests clustered on the sidewalk, chattering along with the children. The giant seemed unsteady. He winced when he laboriously stepped down from the buggy.

One woman said, "My word, I never saw the like."
A grinning doorman from the hotel took the chewed cigar stub from his mouth, observing, "You should've seen the rifle he used to carry around."

The giant shook hands with each of the children in turn, then lifted one small girl up onto his shoulder. She smiled bravely, but shied away when he offered to kiss her cheek.

To make the encounter more memorable, Aindreas went clear around to the other side of the crowd in order to get up close to the giant. Standing as tall as he could, it seemed to Aindreas that the top of his head wasn't more than a foot or so above the towering man's belt.

One child's mother said, "So big and strong, just like America."

"You bet," the doorman agreed. "He's what this country stands for."

The giant leaned down and said hello. Aindreas gazed up into the long, homely face. The yellowish eyes looked sick and fearful, and the giant smelled of whiskey.

Walking away, Aindreas felt let down. *What would Mr. Knight have called such an experience? The giant as illusion?* The high hat, the long coattails, the whip, even the rifle the doorman mentioned, these were nothing more than props—such as an actor used in a stage play. If he really was what America was all about, did that mean the whole country was a collection of stage props? Aindreas shook his head. *Wouldn't do to dwell on thoughts like those.*

### 3

The chief clerk sent Aindreas to pick up a package of printed business forms late that afternoon. His legs ached, and he stopped twice along the way to rub them. Luckily, this would be the last run of the day.

The printer rooted among parcels and in several cabinet drawers, trying to find the right order. Aindreas sat back in a chair, resting, not unhappy for the delay. It was already too late for him to get back to Cawthon's in time to help clean up the office. The always eager William Williams would have this chance to sweep all by himself. This made Aindreas smile for the first time all day.

Coming from the printer's shop, he glanced across the street. A familiar-looking figure in a gray suit dawdled near a lamppost partway up the front steps of the Jefferson County Courthouse. The man puffed on a pipe and carried a paper case. Aindreas had to dodge between wagons halfway across Jefferson Street before he felt certain of the man's identity. By that time, Mr. Knight had looked up and waved him on.

"So, I finally see you again," Aindreas said.

Knight turned and started up the steps, motioning for him to follow. Aindreas stayed behind Knight as they passed through the rotunda and headed toward the back staircase.

"Where have you been?" asked Aindreas.

"Shhhhh...I've been here all the time," Knight whispered. "You always wanted to look around in here, didn't you?"

"Yes."

Knight made a mock bow. "Well then, lead the way," he said.

They silently climbed the stairs to the darkened third floor, which Aindreas had never seen. That level of the building had remained unfinished, though he believed the courthouse had opened to the public near the year of his birth.

They paused. Aindreas looked around nervously. From the looks of this level, they might have journeyed to some other place entirely, to some ruin illustrated in a history book. Slivers of light peeked through cracks in the unpainted and barely finished ceilings and walls. He signaled for caution, and they walked with care around broken or missing floor boards.

Several men came out of a lighted room near the rear of the building, casting huge marching shadows on the wall. They went down the stairs, talking among themselves in low voices. Aindreas followed Knight toward the room where the men came from. The door was closed, but no one had bothered to lock it.

Aindreas leaned his package against the wall, then went inside. Mr. Knight kept watch in the hall. Stacked cartons and a handcart loaded with ledger books nearly blocked the doorway, concealing part of the room. Aindreas opened several of the boxes and peeked inside. Ballot paper. Two other cartons overflowed with yellow badges and armbands, the same kind those men wore at the Fourth of July rally. He squeezed himself around the handcart and on into the interior of the room. A long table stretched out before him covered with pistols, clubs, and bowie knives. Muskets, maybe fifty of them, leaned against the walls, some with bayonets attached.

"Election supplies?" Knight asked dryly from the doorway.

Aindreas heard a noise and bounded out of the room in a panic, almost bowling over Mr. Knight. Then, nearly to the staircase, he turned and ran back to retrieve his package and pull the door shut. Yes, those men had started back up the stairs. Halfway down, Aindreas stepped to one side to make way for the men ascending. One of them, was a courthouse retainer he'd seen many times. Afraid the man would know his face, Aindreas wanted to turn his head away.

Mr. Knight whispered, "Keep your eyes straight ahead, as though you belong here."

Aindreas could feel the men looking toward him when they passed. They said nothing. He still carried the printed forms under his arm. *Maybe they thought he had come to deliver a package.* Once past them, he descended the remaining steps two at a time. The men paid no attention at all to Mr. Knight, who had

walked down the hall ahead of him. Aindreas hurried to catch up.

Up ahead, a slack column of perhaps twenty men stretched from the door of one of the offices. Rough-looking and boisterous, the men seemed spoiling for a fight. "Hey!" bellowed one of them from the rear of the line. "Do we get the goddamn meal tickets or not?"

They guffawed up and down the line, the same kind of

laughter Aindreas had heard a hundred times near the saloons and whorehouses down near the levee.

"Shut up," someone yelled from the front of the line. Another shoved the man beside him in line and said, "This mate ain't gonna need a ticket if he sticks his elbow in my ribs again."

Aindreas and Mr. Knight made their way past the men and out the side door of the courthouse without event. They paused at the corner of the grounds, where the master commissioner had sold the slaves. Aindreas balanced his package atop the low fence.

He took an envelope from his shirt and held it up for Knight to see.

"What's that?"

"A letter for Isaac," said Aindreas. "Thought I'd be prepared. If the plans all work out, I might not have the chance to say a proper good-bye."

What Aindreas didn't tell Mr. Knight was that Isaac could be running away that very minute. His thoughts returned to what he had seen inside the courthouse.

Knight asked, "What do you think will happen, Aindreas?"

"I don't know, but I've seen other men around town lately like those we just saw inside."

"Had you seen them before?"

Aindreas felt a hard knot in his stomach. *All those whispers. The hatred he felt every day in the streets. And what was that Tom Williams had said in the office this morning?* "No," he said.

"Maybe certain voters won't be allowed to vote in the election," said Knight, frowning, "and that could be a bad situation…could it not?"

"Very bad," said Aindreas.

They began to walk in the direction of Cawthon's Furniture. Aindreas's anger grew, and sadness settled over him, sadness near as bad as that day at the cemetery.

Knight broke the silence two long blocks later. "Will you try to warn people?" he asked.

"Who would believe me?" Aindreas kicked a rock so hard it skittered almost clear across the street. "But somebody must be smart enough to figure this out."

"Ah, if it could be so simple—just go find a smart somebody." Knight sounded weary. "Prentice and Bishop Spalding are supposed to be very smart. At least that's what everyone believes."

"Don't they have an idea what might happen?"

"Hard to tell about their ideas," Knight said. "You've read enough to know that each of them fell in love with his own words a long time ago."

They walked on without speaking for long moments. Aindreas shrugged in frustration then said, "I can't stop what is going to happen." It seemed so clear now. "I must help those who can be helped and not get hurt any worse than I have to."

"It occurs to me that maybe I'm not as necessary for you as I was when all this started," Knight said. "You're walking rather well on your own."

Aindreas stared down for a moment. When he looked up, Mr. Knight had gone.

4

**B**ack at the office, the others had gone. Aindreas saw a newspaper sticking out of the wastebasket by Tom Williams's desk. He picked it up and scanned the page, his attention drawn to an article Williams had underlined.

LOUISVILLE JOURNAL, 1855

> *We are glad that the Germans have made up their minds to go to the polls...Let the Germans go by all means to the polls, and if there is time for all to vote, let them be sure to vote. But...if there shall not be time, if a portion...must be barred..., every consideration...demands that the foreign-born citizens should of their own free accord*

stand back until the native-born freemen shall have recorded their suffrages. We hope, and we have the right to expect, they themselves...will take this view of the matter. It is the right view.

*Published and Printed by*
*Prentice, Henderson, & Osborne*

### 5

Heat wafted over the table when Kirsty took the cornbread from the oven. She lifted the lid to check the boiling pot of beef and cabbage. "With Da comin' home for supper tonight, I hope you won't make a scene about the meat," she said.

Aindreas had no further wish to offend her. Besides, Kirsty had repaired the torn knee in his trousers. "No speeches from me," he said.

"You mean it—you'll eat the beef?"

"No, but I promise I won't make a scene."

She set the plates and utensils around the table. Her eyes welled up and she bit her lip. It looked as if she might cry again. "Seems so odd," she said. "Five plates for years, and now only three."

Aindreas kept his tone light. "We only have three decent ones left, since Da threw Michael's against the wall. Plates don't last long in these temper-storms."

"Andrew!" Kirsty said, with mock severity, then "Well, the three of us are together, at least."

Aindreas thought it curious that Kirsty, who had so wanted her freedom, seemed less eager now that it stood close to hand.

Joseph Rivers came into the kitchen and went directly to the sink to wash up. Kirsty set the cornbread back on the stove top to warm while he scrubbed his hands and face. He sat down, and when Kirsty leaned over to fill his plate, he kissed her on the cheek. He even looked at Aindreas without scowl. Something in his life was making him a little more cheerful, at least on the outside. "Squire Travis caught up to me when I came down the lot," he said to Kirsty.

She asked, "What did he want?"

"All puffed up about the rent. Wanted forty-two dollars."

"Forty-two dollars!"

"That's what he told me."

Kirsty's voice quavered. "What can we do?"

Joseph Rivers shook his head and began to eat.

Aindreas felt it wise to keep silent, though his father's words certainly involved him as well as Kirsty.

Kirsty, not yet ready to let go of the subject, asked. "What did you tell the Squire?"

"Told him I didn't have that kind of money."

*Da had given up.* Aindreas kept his eyes averted. Slowly chewing a bite of cabbage and cornbread, he set aside several pieces of salty beef for König.

Joseph Rivers bolted down his food quickly. Kirsty carried the plates to the sink and poured more tea.

"Squire Travis gave me ten days," he added matter-of-factly. "Told me he'd put us out on the street if he wasn't paid by August twelfth."

"Then nothing can be done?" said Kirsty.

Aindreas heard the words he had expected all along. "I don't know if the family can stay together any longer," Da said.

Kirsty welled up. "Do you say that because you're never here anymore?" she said angrily. "Because there is someplace else you'd rather be?"

Joseph Rivers reddened. "Best mind your manners, miss."

Kirsty wailed, "Or did you say it because that's what your father did, and you haven't seen your sisters in thirty years?"

She shrank back when he raised his hand, but he did not hit

her. He looked down at his hands, then lowered them to his lap. They sat in silence until Kirsty left to clean up the supper dishes at the Travis house.

Joseph Rivers drummed his fingers on the table, then went back to his room. He whistled, obviously readying himself to go out. Whatever might have mattered in his life now didn't seem to include the family. Aindreas remained at the table, even when his father came back to the kitchen to comb his hair in front of the cracked mirror over the sink.

Joseph Rivers said, "Well, boy, if there's something in your head, say it. Mind you, your sister already tried my patience." Aindreas remembered all too well that he had never convinced his father of anything but wanted to warn him about what lay ahead.

"Be careful where you go on Monday, Da. Something very bad is going on."

His father gave him a thin smile, then turned back to the mirror. "You heard some things about the election, I imagine."

"Yes."

"Oh, I've heard some of that malarkey," Joseph Rivers said patiently. "But the Know-Nothings won't do anything all that bad."

Aindreas asked, "Why do you think that?"

"Because they already have it won, *ma bouchal.* They know how to count, and they have at least a third more votes than the rest of us."

"Oh," said Aindreas.

His father actually patted him on the shoulder. "I'm glad you wanted me to know," he said. Da moved toward the door, then paused in the doorway. "Don't you be worried about it," he said, then walked out toward Prather Street.

Aindreas sat at the table for a while. Then he took the bason from the cabinet. He unwrapped it in his room and stared at it for a long time. It seemed that no matter how long he rubbed and buffed, the bason did not glow as it had that day it was a gift for his mother.

Lately, he couldn't go to sleep. When he looked out the window to see if König had returned, the big dog sat silently waiting. Isaac was standing near him.

Aindreas eased over the window frame and dropped to the ground. König took the pieces of salty beef, one at a time, from his fingers. Aindreas whispered, "I'm glad you're here, Isaac. I would have been by, but you know how hard it is with Squire Travis wandering around all the time."

Isaac said, "I know. Tonight, Squire and Miss Travis both gone. Saw 'em go out right after supper. I figured this might be the last chance to talk to you."

Aindreas swallowed. *If Isaac and Tempie intended to run for it tonight, maybe he should go with them.*

"We goin' to wait on you and the captain," Isaac said.

"You will?"

"We know the squire sure to sell us. Took a chance by not runnin' two weeks ago, but we made up our mind."

Aindreas grinned. "That's the best thing I've heard in a long time," he said. "It will be Monday or Tuesday night, but don't go out in the streets Monday. If the squire wants to send you somewhere, try everything you know to get out of it."

Isaac looked puzzled. "Won't that get him to thinkin'?" he asked.

"Maybe, but do everything you can to stay close around here. Some bad things are going to happen, and you don't want to be in the middle of it, believe me."

"I believe you," said Isaac. "We be ready whichever night, Monday or Tuesday."

Aindreas leaned over and stroked König's broad head. "Looks like I won't be here much longer, either," he said. "We're behind forty-two dollars on the rent, and the squire put my father on notice that he will put us out."

Isaac whistled low. "Lot of money. How your daddy get in that shape?"

"Don't think he could help it," Aindreas said. "The more I figure on it, my mother was the one who made it work for all of us. When she left…." Aindreas's voice trailed off.

Isaac looked hurt. "Don't like the sound of all that, young Andrew. Things happen to us we couldn't do nothing about, but it hurt to see *you* goin' down."

"Hey, I'm not giving up," Aindreas said, trying to sound as reassuring as possible. "Once you and Tempie are safe, there are a lot of things I want to do."

Isaac smiled. "You mean that?"

Aindreas put his hand over his heart. "I promise," he said.

# 16

The *Ben Franklin* tied up at the Louisville wharf late Sunday afternoon, with no plans to start downriver until Tuesday evening. Aindreas was told to have Isaac and his family on Seventh Street near Prather right after dark that day. Jack Graham would pick them up in a wagon. Aindreas didn't feel certain what part the boat would play in the escape, for Captain Workman wouldn't elaborate on his instructions.

But those things were to take place on Tuesday. First, Monday must be survived, and Monday would not come. Aindreas leaned against the window frame, looking into a sky still black as a mocking crow. Flies buzzed and bit the way they did before a storm. He went back to bed. Still unable to sleep, he flopped onto his stomach. His taut arms and hands couldn't hold their grip on the sides of the bed any longer, and he floated numbly in a smoky, black underworld.

*Tall, strutting, his evil dreams will come true. Of all the foul murderers, the red-haired one is the most proud.*

*Must I watch another innocent person die? The red one holds the power of life and death, and smiles in triumph. He doesn't guess that I have the same power. Can it ever be right to kill another? No one has ever taught me. If I am wrong to do this, I'll see his evil face again in hell.*

*Lord have mercy...Christ have mercy...Lord have mercy.*

1

Sprawled half off the bed, Aindreas blinked in the brilliant sunlight. Monday morning had come, the sixth of August, 1855. Within moments, he was trotting up Seventh Street on the way to work. Seven o'clock, and the sun already felt hot. At the Walnut Street intersection a young fellow was rooting in a wagon piled with rags. As Aindreas drew closer, he recognized his old co-worker, Tim Lytle.

Aindreas waved. "Hey, Tim!"

His old running mate climbed down from the wagon, and they shook hands. Tim looked a little taller, more serious than Aindreas remembered, but his face was as blotched as ever.

"I seen a bunch of men with guns coming out of the courthouse," Tim said right off. "And my uncle told me he heard the Know-Nothings took over the polls before dawn."

"You better be careful today," Aindreas said.

Tim scowled, perhaps put off by such a mild reaction on Aindreas's part. He snapped, "The hell you say...I think they're the ones that better be careful."

Tim might only have been repeating something he had heard his uncle say, Aindreas thought. He felt tempted to ask Tim what connection he had to the broken windows at the Cawthon's Furniture office, but didn't pursue it. An awkward silence followed. As it turned out, two former co-workers who barely liked each other had barely anything to talk about, after all.

Tim abruptly climbed back up into the driver's box of the wagon. He released the brake. Before the wagon pulled away from the curb, he said, "Might run into you again 'fore the day's over, Lucky."

"Yeah, I hope so." Aindreas said, and waved. "See you Tim."

Sixth Street was out of the way, but Aindreas headed in that direction so he could pass near the courthouse and see for himself. He knelt down by a water trough on the other side of Jefferson Street and watched. Men clustered in small groups near the building entrances, and individuals milled about the grounds. Twenty-three of them altogether. Some wore yellow badges or armbands, and every one of them carried a club or some other kind of weapon.

A lone man hurried across Sixth Street toward the building. The courthouse had always been the polling place for the Sixth Ward, and he probably intended to cast his vote.

Three men in yellow armbands closed around him. One shouted, "You damn foreigner!"

Another yelled, "Kraut-sonofabitch!"

*Know-Nothings.*

Out of courage or ignorance, the man didn't turn and run. He tried to fight back when they closed in around him. Knocked to his knees, the man rolled into a ball and covered his head with his arms. The men with clubs methodically hit and kicked him. When they were finished, they sauntered back to their station near the door. The man slowly got to his feet, a hand covering one side of his bloody face, and staggered across the street into an alley. Some of the Know-Nothings catcalled after him.

Aindreas left then, headed for Cawthon's Furniture. He knew he hadn't imagined it but didn't want to believe what he had seen.

The office didn't seem the same that morning. The clerks leaned properly over their desks as they figured and copied, and their pens dipped from paper to inkwell to paper in the usual continuous repeated motions. But talk was buzzing, snatches of persistent mumbling just below the level of conversation.

The chief clerk must have heard it, too, and looked up from his ledger several times. Papers and packages usually rested on the front part of his desk, but today only papers. He shuffled them together and said, "Williams, Rivers, come up here." Then, loud enough to be heard by everyone in the room, he announced, "Too much talking in here."

For the moment, the buzzing stopped. Aindreas stood beside Williams in front of the desk. "Well," the clerk said in a low voice, "rumors are floating around all over the place this morning. Someone reported an American named *Burge* was killed down on Hancock Street. Then I heard the man was really *Berg,* a German cabinetmaker."

"My father told me they would start trouble today," Williams piped in. "I don't want to go in those foreigners' neighborhoods if I don't have to."

"Some of these are for Germantown and the Irish streets," the chief clerk said, leafing through the papers.

"How about you, Rivers?"

"I don't mind," said Aindreas, giving Williams a quick glance. "The Germans and the Irish don't scare me any-thing like the others."

The chief clerk handed him a sheaf of papers. Before getting on his way, Aindreas hurried back to the loading dock to warn Mr. Allison about what he had seen at the courthouse. Another driver told him Allison had gone on a personal errand and hadn't yet returned.

Aindreas started sweating less than a block away from the office, but he couldn't seem to slow down. He felt that he was hurrying to something unknown but important. The courthouse scene still fresh in his mind, it seemed wise to steer clear of Jefferson Street and he did.

The route Aindreas had figured out moved him northeast, from one delivery stop to the next. When he neared Beargrass Creek, a column of smoke rose several blocks to the south, maybe on Green Street. It looked to be a big fire, but he heard no bells ringing.

Aindreas had intended to end his morning deliveries in Germantown. That way, if he had time, he could warn his aunts and Mr. Adler about the trouble downtown. Dull, popping noises in the distance made him nervous. *Were those guns?*

He made steady progress, and by eleven o'clock he had only one paper left for delivery—for Stohler's Paint Shop on Wenzel Street, near the big brewery. He could smell the smoke he had seen earlier, and the popping sounds started up again. *No doubt about it now...those were gunshots.* The door to the paint shop had been locked and the windows shuttered.

Just as he turned onto Shelby Street, three men suddenly sprinted past him from the opposite direction. Even from more than a block away, the scene before him looked like something from a nightmare. Thick, black smoke billowed from two or three buildings. Aindreas began running south toward Green Street, past bloodied people lying in the street amidst broken glass and smashed furniture. The windows and doors of Meier's Coffee Shop weren't there anymore. The place looked as if it had been ripped apart by a cyclone.

A horde of men, maybe two hundred or maybe more, moved south on Shelby Street carrying torches, covering the street like a disorganized parade. Farther south, near Walnut, more men with guns lay in the street firing at the windows of homes and shops. Aindreas could see the puffs of white smoke; someone must have fired back at them. Soon, one of the houses under attack began to blaze and then another one.

Men and women came hesitantly from their homes near Meier's Coffee Shop to help the injured. A wagon rattled to a stop in Green Street, and the frightened horse reared in the harness. Georg Adler was the wagon driver.

Aindreas dashed toward the wagon. "Mr. Adler, it's me," he shouted.

Adler clung to the reins. "Just in time, my friend," he said. "Grab hold of this crazy animal."

The horse's eyes looked wild. Frightened himself, Aindreas

grabbed the bridle with both hands and held on with all his might so he wouldn't slip under those front feet. Over and over, he kept softly saying "Eeeeasy boy," the way he heard Mr. Allison do it, until finally the horse calmed down.

Adler tied off the reins and jumped down. "Good man," he said to Aindreas, and ordered those tending the wounded to load the seriously injured into the wagon.

Blood was everywhere. Blood from mouths, blood from eyes, from ears, blood from holes and cuts and slashes in the bodies. Some of the victims had been beaten, others shot or stabbed. So much blood coated parts of the street that Aindreas's boots made squishing sounds when he helped carry the wounded. He barely recognized Mr. Saatkamp, the baker, who had been hacked in the head with a big knife or hatchet. A young man had been dragged up and thrown down a flight of stairs repeatedly, and now he lay dying or already dead.

"Don't worry about your uncle Theodore and your aunts," Adler assured him. "I saw them going home earlier. They're safe."

"How did all this start?" Aindreas asked.

"I don't know. Some fool shot at somebody in a buggy, and the mob came from all directions. Some of the Irish and Germans tried to fight back, but they didn't have a chance."

Nine wounded had been loaded into the wagon. A loud, growing cheer came from little more than a block away. The gunfire had stopped, but flames engulfed more houses and shops. The mob continued south on Shelby Street.

"They'll loot and burn every place in the neighborhood," Adler said, "and who knows what else." The wagon tailgate secured, he climbed into place. Adler looked back at the mob's path again. "Try to get to Saint Martin's Church," he said to Aindreas. "They're headed right for it. Run down a block and go around the block, try to beat them there."

Aindreas nodded.

The wagon began to move. "Don't risk yourself, boy," Adler said over his shoulder. "Just try to warn them."

Aindreas ran down one block to Campbell Street. Muney's Grocery was ablaze. The window blew out as he approached. He dodged to the other side of the street and increased his speed. Sweat ran into his eyes. Walnut Street, Madison…his chest was heaving…Chestnut, finally Gray Street. He cut back over to Shelby Street, toward the towering green spire of Saint Martin's Church, still ahead of the rioters.

Aindreas looked up at the louvered windows near the tower clock and yelled, "Mr. Finkel! Mr. Finkel, if you're up there, you better get out of here."

Gunfire started again. The mob was barely a block away. Aindreas went through the front portal into the quiet dark. Down near the altar, a priest was watching over several men moving boxes. Maybe they were packing up some of the holy things.

"They're coming." Aindreas shouted. His voice echoed in the cavernous nave. "They're almost here."

The priest's only acknowledgment was a curt nod. Aindreas went back outside, coughing, his eyes burning in the smoke. The hundreds of men surging down Shelby Street looked like an army from hell. A man in a blue shirt, little taller than a child, must have resisted in some way and now tried to escape. He evaded the mob's vanguard, throwing aside a pistol as he sprinted ahead. He might have made it, but more men from the opposite direction blocked his way. They surrounded him near the front door of a gray house just across the street.

New recruits to the mob swept Aindreas along in their midst. A white-haired fellow came out of the house and stood in front of the small, scared man who had pounded on his door. Now, Aindreas recognized them both. The one who had tried to escape was John Murphy, and the man now protecting him was a carpenter named Felder. A lot of shouting, then a knife blade flashed in the sun. Felder grabbed his chest and fell back against the door. Two men slashed at him as he slid to the ground, and others closed in around Murphy. The little Irishman screamed. Moments later, some of the attackers dragged him across the street and draped the body on the churchyard fence.

The mob was growing even larger as men, women, even children came from all directions. One and all seemed giddy at the violence, drawn to the fun. Many carried torches, and almost everyone carried a knife, a hatchet, a scythe, something that could be used as a weapon. Aindreas kept silent. He figured he looked enough like the rest of these people that he would be in no special danger provided he kept his mouth shut. The throng overflowed the street and formed a semicircle around the front of the church. For the moment, there seemed to be no single leader of the rioters. They cheered and pushed forward a little closer to the church each time another person mounted its front steps and urged them on.

Shouts went up: "They got powder in there...guns."

"Yeah, guns."

"Burn the damn thing down."

"Yeah, burn it down...but first we go in and take what we want."

The crowd bulged toward the church, but something had gone wrong. The front ranks stopped abruptly. Caught in the press of bodies, Aindreas gasped for air. He struggled to keep from going underfoot.

Several men in dark suits, their arms in the air, stood facing the crowd. The mayor was one of those men. Aindreas figured several of the others were city councilmen. Another man with them wore a military officer's uniform and he held a pistol. The mayor tried to speak, but Aindreas couldn't hear his words over the din.

"You people up there get out of the way," someone near

Aindreas yelled, and a raucous cheer followed.

"They got gunpowder in there!" More cheering.

A chant began. "Burn it down. Burn it down. Burn it down."

They seemed ready to force their way into the church, and there seemed little doubt of what would happen to that priest or anyone else found inside. Shots were fired in the air. The chanting stopped. One of the councilmen bellowed loud enough to be heard above the noise. "Listen! I warn you to listen to me. I am speaking on behalf of the mayor."

The mass in the street stopped pushing, and the noisy clamor softened just a bit. Then, another shot was fired—and all movement stopped, save the silent, smoky flames of the torches. The will to grind the mayor underfoot had weakened, at least for a time.

"Mayor Barbee will search inside," the councilman announced in his booming voice. "We'll find out if the Germans are hiding anything."

Barbee and two of his men went into the church. A few more men in uniform joined those facing the waiting mob. At least ten minutes passed; it seemed like a long time. Soaked with sweat, Aindreas felt his chest might explode. He squirmed his way through sweating, dirty bodies to a place near the uniformed men. He might end up getting shot, but at least there he could breathe.

The mayor came out of the church. His expression gave no clue to what he had found, but all color had drained from his fleshy face. "No gunpowder!" he shouted, and shook his head. "No gunpowder."

Disappointment hung in the air. Murmurs went through the crowd. Aindreas felt enormous relief at the mayor's words, yet something in Barbee's face, perhaps the hint of fear in his voice, made him seem less believable.

"What'd he say?"

"He ain't telling the truth."

"Nothin' in there?"

"He's lying, goddamn it."

"Says they ain't hiding anything in the church."

"We ought to burn it anyway."

Barbee waved his arms for quiet. "I have a very important announcement. The American Party has won the election!"

A thunderous roar went up. Men waved torches, muskets, and knives. The mayor smiled, doubtless knowing he had told them what they wanted to hear. Aindreas wondered what could have prompted Mayor Barbee to say what he did. Unless the election had been called off, the polls weren't supposed to close for hours.

"Your candidates have been elected," Barbee added.

The mob stood with the mayor now. He let them cheer and carry on for a moment or two, but once the officers had quieted the crowd again, Barbee pressed on. "Now, I want you, all of you who don't live here in the First Ward, to return to your own neighborhoods." He reached over and raised the arm of the man dressed as a military officer. "You are under the command of Captain Lovell Rousseau here, and I authorize him to organize a company of volunteers."

The mayor and councilmen got into a carriage and left quickly. The uniformed men formed a wedge and cut their way through the crowd. Captain Rousseau waved a flag in the air and shouted "Follow me!" over and over again.

The mob moved sluggishly north, the direction from which it had come. Even as it moved, still more joined. The latecomers included a column of fifty men or so, carrying muskets with bayonets attached and pulling a small cannon.

Aindreas hung back. The street in front of Saint Martin's gradually cleared. Two stragglers stared for a moment at the contorted body hanging from the fence. Perhaps they didn't care for the fact that the Irishman had something of the look of a person who had been crucified. One of them knocked the body to the ground.

König lay watching from the yard between the church and the school. Aindreas wondered whether he should try to make his way directly back to Cawthon's. On the other hand, if he stayed on Shelby Street all the way to Jefferson, he might run into Adler and be of some help to him.

South on Shelby Street, another man was being chased, and he ran like the wind toward the church. Three pursuers, a half block behind, looked to be gaining on their prey. Aindreas recognized him, it was Finkel. He hadn't been in the church at all. Dawdlers from the mob apparently had flushed him out of his hiding place. Aindreas rushed over to the yard by the school and waved for Finkel to turn in there. The desperate man must have seen him and followed, the pursuers no more than fifty feet away by this time. König lagged behind, then turned to face them at a narrow opening where the school and the church nearly touched.

"Run on to Georg Adler's house and hide in the basement," Aindreas told him.

Staggering, Finkel had the look of one ready to collapse. He hunched forward, hands on knees, his body trembling. He seemed so shabby and small and afraid.

"Go on, go on," Aindreas urged.

Finkel didn't move. Aindreas looked back. König gave ground slowly, grudgingly. The massive dog was taking some blows, but most of the time he managed to keep just beyond reach of the clubs, and König saw to it that Finkel's enraged pursuers paid with hurts of their own for every inch they advanced.

Finkel stared down at himself dumbly. He had wet his pants. Aindreas's feelings of sympathy turned to fury. He shoved Finkel hard with both hands, then punched him in the face.

"Run, run, you damn crazy man," Aindreas yelled.

Holding his face, Finkel lurched around the corner of the school and out of sight. Aindreas ducked inside the school, locked the door behind him, then vaulted up a flight of stairs and hid on the second floor. From the window, he saw König suddenly dart away and disappear from view. The men cursed and threw stones after him, but fighting seemed to have lost its charm for them. After only a few moments, the bleeding conquerors were walking back out to the street, perhaps in search of violence less dangerous to themselves.

Aindreas waited for a while before he left the school, then headed north, back in the direction from which he had come. Smoky haze hung everywhere. It wasn't difficult to follow the trail of the mob. Charred shops and homes smoldered on both sides of Shelby Street, and looters had thrown down anything they couldn't carry or decided they didn't want. Those less-seriously injured wandered about in a daze. Several residents crowded around a woman standing in the street holding a baby. She had been wounded by a knife, and the baby in her arms had been stabbed as well.

Though several people told Aindreas they had seen Georg Adler, no one knew where he could be found. Aindreas decided he would stay on Shelby Street as far as Jefferson. He knew they would be wondering about him back at Cawthon's, but he couldn't leave yet. Fire bells rang in the distance. Just north of Jefferson Street, a ragged blaze fingered into the air above the rooftops. A fire company had already arrived at Garrety Coopering Shop by the time Aindreas got there. Though hose lines had been strung out, the firemen did nothing more than stand around and watch. Stacks of oak lumber and enormous half-finished hogsheads and butts fueled the flames.

No wounded people lay around; the Garretys must have known what might happen and fled, just as the people at Stohler's Paint Shop had done earlier. Looters rolled away barrels and smashed the few remaining undamaged windows with side axes. Children helped cart off coal scuttles, churns, kegs, and buckets. The fire burst through the roof, and the heat became so intense that onlookers moved across the street. One shop wall collapsed in a shower of sparks.

Aindreas asked a firemen, "Did you try to put it out?"

The fireman laughed. "We're here to make sure *American* property don't get burned down," he said.

Staccato gunfire and the boom of a cannon came from near Beargrass Creek. "Must be the brewery," the fireman said. "The damn Catholics got arms stored in there."

It sounded like Saint Martin's all over again, but this time nobody would be around to talk the rioters out of it. Aindreas trotted toward the sound of gunfire. Along the way, he passed the smoldering shell of Stohler's Paint Shop. Closing up the place hadn't done any good, after all. He patted his shirt pocket to be sure he still had the paper he had earlier tried to deliver there. He would give it back to the chief clerk.

The gunfire had stopped by the time Aindreas reached Ambruster's Brewery. The mob used a battering ram to knock down the main doors, then stormed into the sprawling brick building. A young woman with a baby in her arms stood watching on the other side of Wenzel Street. She smiled at Aindreas. He remembered her, the lady with the crying baby who had stood next to him at the Fourth of July speech.

Aindreas heard more gunshots, intermittent now. He crossed to the other side of the street. The woman trailed behind, then stood close beside him; her baby was still crying.

"It's finally happening," she said, her eyes aglow.

He didn't respond.

Brewery workers, pulled out of the building, were beaten to the ground. Only a few managed to pull free and run away.

Perhaps half-a-dozen women and one young girl walked out

on their own, carrying loads in their held-out aprons—the way his mother used to bring baked potatoes from the oven to the table. Aindreas knew the girl, ten-year-old Sophie Ambruster, from his deliveries to the brewery. Almost chubby-looking that day, she stared straight ahead, even when the toughs ripped away all the aprons. Papers and personal things lay scattered on the ground. The sullen crowd allowed the group through, committing no greater aggression than to grope at two of the women. The apron-less women cried in each other's arms, then set about to comfort those earlier injured. Little Sophie, on the other hand, chugged like a wet-heavy breeze to the next corner and then disappeared from sight.

"I kept hoping the Americans would come, and they did," the young mother of the crying baby said.

"Why did you want that?" asked Aindreas.

Some of the rioters came back out of the building, bringing as many bottles as they could carry. "Apple and peach brandy," they shouted. They passed and the mob clamored for more. "Brandy! Brandy!" was the demand.

"Hiding things," the woman said. "I know they was. Me and the neighbors told the police, but I don't think they believed us."

More brandy was passed around, and the rioters whooped it up in front of the brewery; they whirled and danced in celebration. Empty bottles smashed against the building and the street.

The woman fixed Aindreas in her dogged stare. "When the Americans come up Jefferson Street, the foreigners shot at 'em. That proves they was hiding something, don't it? So maybe they believe me now."

Aindreas backed away from her. The fire was spreading. He said a silent prayer that no one had been left inside. Two explosions blew out the window openings, and a towering column of black smoke rose ever higher as flames engulfed the building. Five dead men now lay in the street. No sign of any wounded. Maybe they had been taken away. The mob edged away, down the block, but showed no sign of breaking up.

Aindreas decided to leave. At the far edge of the crowd, he passed a man with a soot-covered face who leaned on his musket and drank from a dark-brown bottle. "Did you find any guns?" Aindreas asked him.

The man turned up the bottle and drank the last in it. "Nah," he said, "except two or three they shot at us with."

He gripped the bottle by the neck and threw it as high as he could, then ducked his head. The bottle hung in the air, turning end over end, then fell and smashed on the street in the middle of the celebrants. "We didn't find the gold, neither," the man said, then let loose a terrible laugh—his teeth indecently white in the blackness of his face. "Somebody carried off the goddamn gold."

Aindreas made his way in the direction of Cawthon's.

*Surely the madness had to be coming to a close. Mr. Knight had told him to help all he could, but he hadn't accomplished much. Well, maybe he'd done some good for Mr. Finkel, but it would have been better to help someone he liked. He needed to find some fish tonight and give König a special treat.*

The sun grew hotter. Aindreas wiped his forehead and dripping chin with an already-wet handkerchief. He noticed his hand was streaked with soot. He'd have to look in a mirror when he got back to Cawthon's, his face might be black, too. Exhausted by the time he got closer to the courthouse, he had forgotten what happened there earlier. The morning seemed like such a long time ago.

A running man bowled Aindreas to the sidewalk. Then, as many as ten men and boys chasing the running man charged around the same corner. One carried a pitchfork. Aindreas rolled out of their path. Several boys launched lead balls from their slingshots and brought the fleeing man down. A line of boys across the street yelled and laughed as they watched. William Williams was among the boys enjoying the spectacle.

*Perhaps the madness wasn't coming to a close, but had only begun.* Aindreas sprang up from the sidewalk. He vaguely recognized the victim, a peddler he had often seen on the streets. He lunged forward to help and then backed away as the thugs claimed their prize.

The man writhed on the ground, holding out his hands in appeal. They kicked and stomped on him with their boots, then pulled him upright. He was still conscious when one of them rammed the pitchfork nearly through him. The captors dragged him toward the jail. The leader of the parade, bloody pitchfork in hand, grinned at the applause and pumped his grisly baton up and down in march-time.

Aindreas felt ready to fall. He dropped to his knees by the water trough and splashed his face, then dunked his head in the water again and again, trying to wash away the dirtiness.

The Tibet Dog. (Youatt.)

KÖNIG

# 17

**The** men at the loading dock reported that Mr. Allison still hadn't returned. Aindreas went into the office by the back door. No one seemed to take notice of his appearance, his dripping-wet state. The chief clerk had been called out of the office and hadn't yet returned.

Between two lines of desks, William Williams's older brother, Tom, was entertaining his office mates. "...and the American Party voters all have yellow tickets, so they get to vote in a hurry," he explained, and smiled. "Now for the foreigners, it's different. Let's suppose one of them somehow gets to the head of the line and comes in to vote. Somebody like Mr. Allison. Oops, I'd better not say that, or he might come in here and spit on the floor."

The idling clerks laughed.

"We'll call him O'Brien," Williams continued. "Mr. O'Brien presents himself to vote. Two judges and one clerk are sitting there at the table. Now, the judges don't admit that he is a qualified voter, so they have to interrogate him."

"Does this really happen?" another junior clerk asked.

"You bet," Williams said. "And don't interrupt." He then pulled the clerk out of his seat. "You play Mr. O'Brien," he ordered, "and I'm the poll judge." Williams cleared his throat. "Mr. O'Brien, have ya resided in the state and in the county one year immediately preceding this election?" he asked. "If not, ya can't vote."

The young man nodded in the affirmative, and some of the clerks giggled.

"Oh, you did?" Williams said. "Well then, did ya reside in this precinct sixty days? If not, ya can't vote."

The imitation Irishman nodded again.

"Well, I hope ya brought your naturalization papers," Williams said. "If not, ya can't vote."

The young man gave him a look of mock disappointment, but then produced several sheets of paper and held them out.

Williams snatched the papers, then said, "We'll look at these when we have the time, Mr. O'Brien, so you'll have to wait outside." He paused. "Yes, it could be a long time, maybe the whole afternoon." Another pause, "Oh, ya can't wait out in the boilin' sun that long?"

Tom Williams raised his arms like the director of a choir, and all the clerks said in unison, "Well, then...ya can't vote."

The office front door slammed, and the clerks hurried back to their desks. The chief clerk hung up his coat and sat down. Aindreas went over to the high desk, and handed him the wrinkled, damp paper he had carried back from the paint shop. "Couldn't deliver this one, sir," he said.

The chief clerk's hand seemed unsteady when he took the paper. He didn't ask why it hadn't been delivered.

"They were burned out," Aindreas volunteered.

The chief clerk only nodded, then got down from his stool and went to the center of the office. He looked to be more shaken than Aindreas had ever seen him, even that time when someone broke out the windows. "Attention, everyone," announced the chief clerk. The horseplay and conversation diminished, but a few of the young men continued their joking around.

"One of our wagon drivers, Allison, left early this morning on a personal errand. When he still hadn't returned by dinnertime, the other drivers asked around whether anyone had seen him. About thirty minutes ago, the city authorities summoned me."

One of the young men gave a high-pitched laugh, and another punched him on the arm. "Allison's not all that bad," a third young man said. Others murmured agreement.

The chief clerk swiped a handkerchief over his face. He said, "Allison had been shot through the chest. He died at the jail."

The office fell to utter silence.

Aindreas slumped down behind one of the desks, feeling guilty. *Why couldn't he have warned Mr. Allison about what was going on outside the courthouse?*

"I don't understand," the chief clerk whined, wringing his hands. "We try to run a business here."

Aindreas couldn't keep his mind on what the chief clerk was saying. *Maybe those people were burning down houses on Prather Street by now. What would happen to Kirsty? König might be back home. He'd defend against them.*

Aindreas tried to blank out the image of Mr. Allison but couldn't. He clapped his hands over his ears and cried inside. He could still hear the man's chuckle, recalled his mentioning the "kiddos" at home, that he and his missus made do.

The chief clerk said, "And we always stayed out of affairs that didn't concern us."

Aindreas edged toward the door. No one seemed to care or notice. The chief clerk carried on. Though he had steadied himself, his tone bordered on panic. "Keep this question foremost in your mind, gentlemen. How did it come to this—that they would attack one of us? We're businesspeople, for God's sake."

1

The neighborhood where the Rivers family lived stood quiet, untouched by the madness. From the looks of Prather Street, the riots might be taking place in some other city entirely.

He saw Kirsty hanging wash. Short of breath from the hard run, he hurried in the back way. König panted in the dense shade of a maple tree. Aindreas pumped water for the hero and waited to watch him drink. In addition to that ever-present leg wound, the dog now had two nasty scrapes on his back. Aindreas stroked Köing's throat. Having such a friend made up for a lot. So gentle now, so ferocious this morning when he stood alone against those men. "If I still live tonight, you'll have fish, even if I have to beg it or steal it," declared Aindreas. "I promise."

He climbed through the window into his room. Considering that such a man as Mr. Allison could be killed for no reason, Aindreas's own chances for living out the rest of the day couldn't amount to all that much. He knew he must get squared away with Isaac, just in case. Aindreas found one of his mother's wooden closet boxes that would serve for what he needed. He lined the inside with crumpled paper to make it soft. When he had finished the job, he closed the box and tied it with string—only to have to open it again to put in the letter he had composed for Isaac.

His sister was folding laundry when he went through the kitchen. She dropped a shirt when she saw him. "Thank goodness you're all right, Andrew," said Kirsty.

"I'm going to see Isaac," responded Aindreas.

"I heard about the terrible things going on," she said in a voice that sounded so much like their mother's. "You won't go back down there, will you?"

He went out the door and toward the cabin without answering. Isaac rose from his workbench as Aindreas marched over the parched, brown grass.

"Glad you came, young Andrew," Isaac said. "Tempie's over there." The slight movement of Isaac's eyes indicated he was referring to the Travis house. "Says they gone to vote."

Isaac led the way inside the cabin.

This errand filled Aindreas with melancholy. "I...I know you'll be traveling light," he stammered, then thrust out the box at arm's length to Isaac. "But you and Tempie need to take this along with you." Embarrassed, he looked down. "And there's a letter in there, too, from a friend."

Isaac blinked, then turned and padded across the creaky floorboards to the far side of the room. He brought back a package wrapped in butcher paper. Isaac looked a little sad, too when he handed over the package. "That cover Tempie made with all the colors, the one your mamma liked so much? We want you to have it."

Aindreas recalled the huge tablecloth, the one Tempie had worked on for years. She and Isaac brought it out only at special times. His mother had once said the cloth made her think of that coat in the Bible, Joseph's coat.

"We was gonna give it to you tomorrow night when we leave," Isaac said. "Ain't nothin' wrong, is there?"

"No," Aindreas said, trying to keep the shakiness out of his voice. "Jack Graham will be waiting for you at Seventh and Prather just after dark. He's the first mate of the *Ben Franklin*. I wanted to ride along on the wagon, but you all get on out of here at dark ...if it should turn out that I can't make it."

They walked outside together. Isaac reached over and patted Aindreas's shoulder, who started at the unexpected touch. "You worried bad about somethin', but be with us long as you can," Isaac said. "We scared, too."

Aindreas turned away, not trusting his voice any further, and went back to the house. He put the package from Isaac on the shelf just under the picture of the Madonna, then covered it with a folded blanket.

Kirsty waited in the kitchen. "Please don't go out again, Andrew," she said.

"I have to. I work down there."

"Da came home on his dinnertime," Kirsty said, clutching her brother's arm. "He looked afraid…and told me he heard awful things about killing and burning."

Aindreas pulled loose and headed for the door. "You best tell Da to be careful, then," Aindreas said over his shoulder.

"Andrew!" she called after him.

He kept going and didn't even look back at Miss Flowers's window.

Even necessary talk sounded subdued when Aindreas got back to the Cawthon's Furniture office. The chief clerk remained distracted, vague. He absently handed Aindreas a few papers for delivery but said nothing.

Aindreas went back out on the streets. Sounds of gunfire came from one direction, then another. Columns of smoke lingered above the east end of town, where he had been that morning. He thought about Aunt Mary. She would be there in her home. And Aunt Margaret and Uncle Theodore, Georg and Marta. None of them would do anything foolish, he knew, but where they were concerned him.

For the rest of the day, he served as the sole messenger for Cawthon Furniture Manufactory. William Williams hadn't come back from his morning delivery runs. *Probably having too much fun,* Aindreas thought, relieved that he didn't have to look at Williams—so relieved he didn't mind at all sweeping out the office by himself after the clerks left.

Two watchmen with shotguns patrolled the sidewalks around the Cawthon property. The chief clerk apparently had asked for extra protection. Aindreas paused by the door.

*If that mob wanted to bring the place down, it would come*

*down. Twenty watchmen wouldn't make any difference.*

His skin prickled when distant, muffled blasts rattled an unbroken window across the street. Dirty thin rivulets of smoke twisted downward through the still air to probe the crevices in the street. All this seemed designed to frighten or to warn. The lesson seemed obvious enough: to pass this way involved risk; to stay invited great danger.

Aindreas started at a voice behind him.

Only the chief clerk. "Look, the outlaw dog came out tonight," he said.

König lay waiting on the other side of the street. The clerk locked the office door and looked up and down Jefferson Street anxiously. "Go home right now, Rivers," he ordered.

"Yes sir," responded Aindreas.

He watched the chief clerk walk away. Scared, Aindreas knew that he should get out of the neighborhood, as well, yet he had no intention of doing so. He could feel it in his bones, certain tasks remained to be done, though he had no clear idea what those might be. He crossed the street and joined König. Together, they started west toward the reddest of sunsets. Aindreas's feet eagerly took him forward, almost as if he were on a Sunday stroll, carrying him toward the fresh sound of guns.

He turned on Tenth Street and walked north, toward the river. Across the street from the Roundtable Livery, a column of twenty or so tramped along, some with small children in tow. Probably Irish being escorted out of the neighborhood for their own safety. Aindreas recognized the two military officers leading the group: Major Krauth, the man who had read the Whitman verse at the Travis party, and Colonel Preston, a candidate for Congress in the election.

Jack Graham was acting as rear guard for the column. The sober set of his expression broke when Aindreas fell in step alongside him. "Seems like you always turn up, Lucky," Graham said. But his smile faded soon enough. "You should go on home," he warned. "It's dangerous around here."

Aindreas didn't tell Graham what he had seen on Shelby Street earlier in the day.

The column stopped at the corner. Colonel Preston instructed the Irish to continue on to the cathedral on Fifth Street, which was under protection of the city government.

"Colonel Preston saved some lives today," said Graham.

Aindreas nodded, then gestured in the direction of the river. "What happened back there?" he asked.

Graham shrugged wearily. "A man named Rhodes and a couple of his pals were chasing an Irishman, and they followed him into Kennedy's store."

Aindreas nodded. "I've been in there."

"A few of the Irish had guns and opened up on Rhodes's bunch inside the store," Graham said. "They killed Rhodes, wounded the others."

"Then what happened?"

"The men who did the shooting ran up Chapel Street and hid in one of the buildings on Main. Know-Nothing thugs have been coming down here from all over the city. Must be several hundred of them by now." Graham smiled wickedly. "Maybe when they get another hundred or so, they'll get up the nerve to go after those three men."

"Have the police done anything at all?" Aindreas said.

"They're part of the mob, Lucky. I nearly got arrested as many times as I nearly got killed." Jack Graham laughed nervously. "Hey, know who else has been watching me?"

Aindreas thought he knew. Before he could answer, Colonel Preston called to Krauth and Graham.

"Have to go," Graham said. "I'll be on the lookout for you, but you need to get the hell out of here."

"And you better keep a lookout for Cooper," Aindreas said.

Eyes wide, Graham just shook his head.

Aindreas retraced some steps and resumed his north route on Tenth Street. König followed well behind him. The sound of gunshots died out. When he looked back, Graham and the others had disappeared. Approaching Main Street he saw no one but heard the low, rumbling sound of many voices. At the intersection, four armed men suddenly came around the corner with muskets at ready, then pulled Aindreas out into Main Street. Now, out in the open, Aindreas could see the mass of people.

"Hell, it's only a kid," a bearded lookout said. He sounded disappointed.

Then the man noticed König, less than half-a-block down the street. "Look...the killer dog!" he yelled.

König tore across Tenth Street in an instant. Only two of the men got off shots, but one bullet hit the bricks just above the dog's head as he disappeared into an alley.

"Damn," the bearded man said. "Thought I had him."

A cheer from the mob assembled near the corner diverted the attention of the sentries, and they turned to go. Satisfied that König has escaped, Aindreas trailed after the men with muskets into the crowd on Main Street.

There looked to be nearly as many here on Main Street as made up the mob that had ravaged Shelby Street that morning. *Had some of these men been in on the earlier violence?* Then he began to recognize some of the faces and realized that the noontime mob had never broken up, only moved from the east end of town to the west.

From behind him came new rounds of gunfire. He hoped Jack Graham and König weren't targets. Aindreas climbed the steps in front of a grocery store and stood atop the iron rail by the door to see across the street, where something was going on.

"We got one of 'em," a man in the uniform of a military officer bellowed. "We got Barrett."

Aindreas shook his head. *This many had been after three men and caught only one of them?*

Two men pulled the captive up the steps of the building across the street and displayed him, to the jeers of the crowd. "This here's Barrett," the officer shouted.

The guards holding the man sprang away from their prisoner at the sound of a shot from the crowd. The impact of the ball drove Barrett against a door. Several more shots hit him, making his limbs jerk about as though pulled by wires. Aindreas couldn't take his eyes away.

"Now, now!" the man in uniform cautioned. "Justice must be done." And then he laughed.

The guards dragged Barrett, still alive, down the steps. They threw a rope over a lamppost arm and slipped the hastily tied noose around his neck. Three men pulled at the rope. Barrett slowly rose in the air. Only one of his hands clawed at the rope, and he hardly kicked at all. Waves of laughter and cheers rolled up and down the street. Men in the crowd pointed at the hanging man and shoved one another playfully.

Fire bells were clanging. *When had they begun?*

A new speaker addressed the mob now, the policeman with muttonchop whiskers who smoked cigars, the one at the Free German rally. "Bring him down," the policeman ordered.

They lowered Barrett to the ground, probably dead.

"Listen to this," the policeman announced. "We heard they shot and killed the first mate of the *Henderson* on his way home."

There arose an enormous bawl of outrage. Aindreas didn't know the identity of the first mate of the *Henderson* packet and wondered if any of these people did.

The man with the muttonchops held up his arms for silence, then pointed toward tenement buildings only a block west on Main Street. "The shots came from there," he said.

Aindreas watched as the mob turned and like a gigantic slug

began inching toward Quinn's Row. If some collective will wished to roll over and crush the tenements, that wish was denied for the moment. Puffs of white smoke came from the tenement windows, and before they were heard, sparks leapt up from the street stones.

The sight of that mass coming toward them might have frightened the Irish enough to shoot. It seemed every man in the mob tried to hide behind another or scrape out a hole in the limestone and mortar with his hands. Aindreas hadn't forgotten the terrible power of that mob, and he knew the Irish in those tenements wouldn't last a long time—they couldn't, but he had felt a trace of pride that those Irish shots had for a few moments scattered the mob.

The attackers began shouting back and forth to each other. Aindreas heard the sense of it. They intended to attack the tenements, and they intended to burn them down.

Quinn's Row, actually two rows of wooden buildings, stood on the north side of Main. Aindreas had delivered to shops and homes all along Main between Eleventh and Twelfth Streets. He knew the neighborhood. A large number of men ran north to get around behind the tenements, while others remained huddled in protected positions on Main Street. Still more of them looped west on Market Street to attack from the Twelfth Street side. The cannon used earlier at Ambruster's Brewery had been pulled here through the streets. Four men strained to wheel it into position. The first shells hit Lang's Pedlar Shop. Almost immediately, the shop was burning. The fire soon spread to Riordan's Food Store and Charles Ryan's Boarding House. Fire companies stood all about, but the firemen made no move to contain the blaze. Arms folded, they stood and watched. A few forgot themselves and cheered some special action by the mob that fired their imaginations.

The cannon blasted away. Aindreas again worried what might

have happened to Jack Graham. Certainly no sign of him in all this. And Aindreas was beginning to feel real fear for himself. *Why hadn't he gone home as Graham told him to?*

Samuel Cooper led one group of the attackers. Convinced that Cooper hadn't noticed him, Aindreas acted on the urge to follow them.

Aindreas paused at Twelfth Street, long enough to listen to the shouts of those laying siege. He saw how it would end. From that spot, once the attackers got across Main Street, they could put Quinn's Row to the torch. Only the stubborn gunfire from the windows had held them back this long. A sharpshooter with a long rifle climbed to the second floor of a house directly across from the tenements. Each time the long rifle boomed, another Irish gun fell silent. Aindreas hated the sharpshooter but had to admire his deadly skill. He must have fired at the Irish muzzle flashes.

Finally, the mob had safe access to Main Street. Protected by withering gunfire from three directions, young men crawled along the bases of the tenements and threw torches under the buildings and through the window openings. One of the young men Aindreas recognized was Tom Williams, from Cawthon's. The younger Williams brother watched from the corner.

Mr. Hulbert, an elderly man who owned a shop on Portland Avenue, strayed too near the edge of the mob on Twelfth Street. Cooper's bunch grabbed him and knocked him about. Hulbert tried to explain that he was only going home and had nothing to do with any of this.

Hulbert's look was that of horror as one of the men rammed a pistol against his face and declared, "C'mon, you damned Kraut, you've got to die for the fun of it."

Cooper smiled at the victim's frantic attempts to pull free. They dragged Hulbert away from the crowd. Aindreas turned away when Cooper and the others raised their pistols. They left the old man's body sprawled across the curb.

Aindreas, mindless of bullets whizzing overhead, tried to run, but the mass of people now on Main Street had grown so thick he couldn't get through. Fire roared up through Quinn's Row. Screams came from the tenement windows. He tried not to hear.

The mob in Main Street responded. Their boots thudded on the stones as they alternately stamped and yelled. They eagerly waited for anyone still alive to come out of the inferno.

William Williams swaggered through the crowd, several of his minions trailing. "That's them," Williams yelled, and pointed at two young men. They're part of that Lang family."

Thugs grabbed two young men, with smudged faces and arms, who had gotten out of Lang's Pedlar Shop and unsuccessfully tried to melt into the crowd. The Lang brothers were shot where they stood, their bodies left to be trampled by those who hadn't been in on the kill so far.

Aindreas caught up with Williams and grabbed him by the arm. Williams's friends were watching as he tried to pull away.

"I saw what you did," said Aindreas.

Williams had a wild look about him, perhaps some of it was fear. "So, who cares what you saw?"

Aindreas spat in his face. "If you ever come back to Cawthon's, everybody will know," he said, expecting Williams to start punching.

To Aindreas' surprise, Williams's friends began to edge away. Williams yanked his arm free and stepped back from Aindreas, wiped his face with the back of his hand, then turned and scurried into the crowd.

The mass of people had become suffocating to Aindreas. He wanted to get away from Main Street but could barely move. The sights and sounds around him became more horrible, less real, and he felt sick. The smoke carried a faint hint of roses, and the right side of his face began twitching.

A wounded man covered with a blanket leaned on his wife. Red Cooper's group yanked the man away and executed him in front of her. They grabbed the crawling wounded by the feet and dragged them across the limestone on their faces. Cooper played the star in the midst of it all, an artist of human violence and misery.

Aindreas suddenly stopped struggling. Stunned, he now realized why he was there, standing on Main Street, why he had taken such risks. *He had come for Red Cooper. Cooper couldn't be aware of this. Aindreas hadn't realized it himself until that moment, but the two of them were bonded in a pact. The dreams of one must consume the dreams of the other. There was no other way.*

The rioters shot Patrick Quinn, owner of Quinn's Row, when he stumbled out of one of the front-row buildings. Aindreas knew him by sight, the brother of the priest who said words over Marcus. Attackers set upon Quinn, hacking and slashing with knives. Once they had their fill they picked up Quinn, carrying him over their heads for all to see, and heaved him back into the burning tenement.

"Lord have mercy…Christ have mercy," Aindreas mumbled over and over, as he probed for any way out of this mass of people. He had to get away from this madness, and from Red Cooper, until the fated moment.

Pressing his hand to his right cheek, Aindreas finally worked free enough to run. He had to make sure Jack Graham reached safety, had to get home. He sprinted east, skirting shattered things and bodies along the way. Only Shelby Street that morning could compare to what he just saw.

He slowed down, then stopped in the middle of the block, by a flour warehouse, when he saw Tim Lytle. Aindreas stood in place until he caught his breath, watching Tim. Such a pose, so typical that Aindreas couldn't help but smile. Tim was sitting, propped against the wall with his legs stretched out on the sidewalk. It's the way he used to sit by the wall at Cawthon's Furniture.

Aindreas approached. "Hello Tim," he said. "Looks like you were right about us running into each other before the day was over."

Tim's eyes stared back, but he didn't answer.

Aindreas knelt beside him. "I'm glad somebody carried you over here," he said. "Has to be more comfortable than the street."

He jabbed Tim on his arm. *Oh, Tim. If anybody was going to stub his toe, or say too much, or find a way to get in trouble, it would be you.* "You always had too many edges," Aindreas said. "But I guess you wouldn't have changed that if you could."

He gently touched Tim's face. The ever-present blotches no longer flamed but had grown faint and purplish. The small wound in his head had nearly dried. The hair at his temple had burned black, and powder grains pocked the skin. Whoever killed him had done it up-close, person to person.

It would have been good to cover him with something, but there was nothing. Aindreas took off his shirt and covered his dead comrade's chest and face. He rose and took a few steps, then stopped and turned around. "See you, Tim." he said.

He began moving faster. Little whiffs of that sickening, sweet smell hung about his face. It was coming. In his limbs, his face. It would take him down. *How much time? Get on home.* The bearded man and his cohorts were still hanging around the Tenth Street intersection. They got to their feet as Aindreas approached, but he broke into a run and simply waved his hand as he sped by them. Before he had covered the block to Market Street, he heard a shot behind him. Then König streaked past. The dog must have lain in wait for him up near Main, and those men had been unaware that he had hidden there. Aindreas cursed silently at himself. König could get killed now because of him.

Well up ahead, the dog barked furiously. König had stopped in the street by the Roundtable Livery. Aindreas glanced back quickly over his shoulder and kept running. He could not see those guards behind him, at least not yet. Two bodies lay in the street by the stable. The man on the right side of the street was twisted grotesquely in death. On the other side, near the stable, lay Jack Graham, who opened his eyes when Aindreas knelt down beside him.

Graham grinned, then said hoarsely, "I'll be damned... it's you again. Maybe they should start calling me "Lucky" if we get out of here."

Graham had a hole in his shoulder and couldn't bend his right leg. Aindreas folded over his handkerchief and tucked it against the shoulder wound. The leg appeared to have been broken.

Graham gestured toward the dead man across the way. "We got separated from the others and ran into some hooligans hired by the Know-Nothings. Cooper was with them. They heard all the excitement up on Main Street and ran off to get in on it. That's the only reason I'm alive."

"Yes," Aindreas said. "Cooper turned up on Main Street."

Graham grimaced when he tried to get up. "I wanted to get into the stable. Either you've got to hide me in there or find something to haul me away in."

Aindreas's eyes darted to the stable. It looked empty.

"You understand, don't you?" Graham said urgently. "Cooper will be coming back for me."

His face twitching again, Aindreas said, "Yes, Jack, but not just for you."

Graham looked confused, then frowned.

Aindreas pulled under Graham's arms, and the big man pushed with his good leg. Slowly, Graham scooted on his rear to the entrance. He leaned back against the wall, wet and exhausted.

Aindreas looked around the interior. No horses or equipment remained. Nothing. He fought the rising panic. The whole place reeked of roses, and König was growling.

"Someone's coming," Graham whispered.

Aindreas looked down the street. Those guards from the intersection were no more than a quarter of a block away. They must have followed him. He shoved König into the first stall and bolted the door, then piled straw around the small opening at the bottom.

The men walked over to the stable entrance. When they noticed Jack Graham, one of them asked, "What happened to him?"

Dizzy, unsure he could talk, Aindreas muttered, "Accident."

"Accident?" the bearded man said. "Is he a foreigner, or has he been takin' up for 'em?"

Aindreas shook his head.

"We got orders to take any that's hurt down to the jail."

"He's American," Aindreas said with some heat. "First mate of
the *Ben Franklin*. Captain Workman won't like anyone taking him to jail."

The guards chuckled. Aindreas guessed his words must have sounded garbled.

"All right," the bearded man said. "You seen that black dog around here?"

Aindreas wiped his mouth twice. "Not since it ran past me," he lied. With a jerk he pointed toward the south horizon. "Clear out of town by now, maybe."

The men snickered and rolled their eyes at each other. They walked away, back toward Main Street. Before they were out of sight, Aindreas collapsed in the straw.

His head hurt terribly when he came out of it. Slowly, the blurred image of Jack Graham became clear.

Jack was talking. "Lucky...Lucky. Are you all right?"

Aindreas sat up, his back against the stall door. He managed a nod, then a moment later he asked, "How long did it go on?"

"Not too long," Graham said. "Do you think you can get up? Maybe we can find a place to hide in here."

His ears still ringing, Aindreas thought he heard a horse's hooves. Yes...he had. There the sound came again, closer now. His heart beat fast. He struggled to his knees, straining to see through the darkness. A horse and carriage, just down the street.

"Hello," Aindreas cried. "We need help."

The carriage stopped. The driver stood up, a woman. She held the whip in her hand like a weapon.

"Andrew, is that you?"

Only one voice in the world sounded like that. "Yes, Miss Flowers, it's me," he answered.

Blanche Flowers pulled the wagon over and tied up the horse. She knelt and wiped Aindreas's face, then wrapped her arms around him and held him close. "Thank God I found you," she said, her words tumbling out. "Your father looked all over town for you. He and Kirsty have gone nearly mad. Isaac asked about you every ten minutes. Mr. Adler and your uncle Theodore came over to the house, and they're looking for you, too."

Aindreas told her what had happened to Jack Graham, and why they had to get away. Graham told them he felt game to try the carriage, if they could somehow get him up into it. Together, Aindreas and Miss Flowers hoisted Graham up on his good leg. Aindreas sensed someone watching. All the color drained from Graham's face then, and he slumped back down to the ground.

Aindreas turned to see the man he knew would be there. Tall, feet spread well apart, Cooper cut a powerful figure. His hair gleamed red in the lamplight and, for all he had done that night, his linen suit remained neat and clean, his shirt collar white. He tapped a long, heavy club against his leg.

"Who are you, sir?" Miss Flowers asked.

Cooper smiled crookedly. "We've met, Mrs. Flowers, at the Travis house. Now, I'll have to ask you to stand aside and be on your way."

Blanche Flowers crossed her arms. "I think not," she said, "and I doubt Squire Travis would approve of your manners."

Red Cooper's laugh chilled Aindreas.

The tall man gazed down at Jack Graham. "I knew you weren't much, Graham, but it surprises me that even you would hide behind a woman." Then Cooper glanced at Aindreas, "And your little idiot friend here."

Cooper fixed Aindreas in a malevolent stare. "Oh yes. I've watched your antics for the last twenty minutes from across the street. In fact, I've seen you all over the place tonight. You've been following me."

Miss Flowers stepped forward, and Aindreas joined her. When Cooper tried to barge past, they grabbed at his arms. One swipe with the back of his hand knocked Miss Flowers down hard. He grabbed Aindreas by the arm and flung him against the stall door.

Aindreas grabbed at the whirling images, the echoing sounds. Jack Graham clawed at the wall, trying to get up. Miss Flowers lay still. Cooper bent down and picked up his dropped club. He smiled at Graham.

Aindreas heard König growling from the other side of the stall door. The bolt, halfway up the door, seemed so far away. His right arm wouldn't move. He pulled himself to a sitting position against the door and stretched upward with his left arm, finally hooking a finger through the ring on the door bolt.

Knowing what this could mean, Aindreas hesitated. No more than two or three seconds passed, though it seemed like an eternity of hoping he would not have to make such a choice. He saw a solemn-looking Mr. Knight standing near the carriage dressed in black, as he had been the night of Doireann Rivers's wake. The needed approval was given by Knight with a single nod. Aindreas yanked the bolt on the stall door.

König lunged against the door, forcing it open far enough for him to wriggle through. Out in the open, he shook his coat as if he had been wet. Though obviously hurt from the injuries suffered that morning, his large, bushy plume of a tail curved proudly over his massive back. He moved between Cooper and Graham.

Cooper leaped forward with a shriek and brought the club down on the dog. The sound of the blow was frightening. König yelped loudly and for a second went down. Frenzied, the tall man swung the club down again and again. Konig rolled away from some of the blows, and others were glancing.

The frightened horse kicked at the buggy and tried to pull the reins loose from the rail where it had been tied. Aindreas crawled to a pitchfork lying in the straw. His hand closed around the handle. He struggled to his feet, his heart near bursting, determined that he would slay Red Cooper or be killed himself.

Blood came from König's nose and above one eye. He had fully regained his feet. Snarling, he backed up as far as he could go, to Graham's feet. Cooper closed in with a savage grunt, apparently intent on finishing it—but König sprang to meet him with movements so quick that Aindreas saw only a blur. Cooper recoiled several steps, then looked down at a spreading bloody place on the upper-right leg of his linen trousers.

Aindreas leaned heavily on the pitchfork to stay upright, thrilled at König's indomitable spirit. In addition to his hatred for the slave trader, Aindreas now felt disdain. There, right before him, stood a man opposing a fierce warrior...a man who only now was feeling the pain in his leg...a man desperately trying to convince himself that this was not the last moment of his life.

Cooper moaned, retreated another step, then another. The

club was loose in his hand. The wounded animal moved directly toward his prey; no circling or teasing as he had done with those robbers that night in the alley.

Only the first of Cooper's screams escaped his mouth when König leaped upon him and brought him to his knees. The great dog seized Cooper by the throat and violently wrenched his body back and forth. When it was finished, the man was dropped to the ground like a rag.

Aindreas stood unsteadily, some feeling coming back into his arm. König lay down only a few feet away. Miss Flowers sat up, holding a handkerchief against her face.

"Is Cooper dead?" asked Graham.

"I don't know," Aindreas said, then went over and helped Miss Flowers to her feet.

"Check to if his heart's beating," instructed Graham.

Aindreas knelt beside Cooper. The slave trader's eyes remained open, his head tilted at an unnatural angle to the side. Except for the trouser leg and his torn throat, he looked immaculate even now. Miss Flowers placed her fingers on the inside of the man's wrist, and Aindreas pressed his the palm of his hand on Cooper's chest. He was dead.

"We have to hurry," Graham said. "Get everything out of his pockets."

Miss Flowers retched, then went over near the carriage and sat down. Aindreas spread Cooper's handkerchief on the ground and rifled through his pockets. The small pile on the floor began with a watch and chain, then a wallet, a gold toothpick, comb, some coins and keys. The last thing Aindreas found, a tiny locket, held an untied curly lock of red hair. Whether from a woman or a child, perhaps it represented some part of the man's life that had not been monstrous. Aindreas tied up the kerchief and put it on the carriage seat.

"Can you manage to get him inside the stable?" Graham

asked.

Aindreas and Miss Flowers each grabbed an arm and dragged the heavy body into the middle of the stable. Aindreas piled armloads of straw over him.

Once they got Graham up on his good leg, it wasn't difficult to pull him into the carriage seat. König shook off efforts to help him, and managed to climb into the carriage and lay down on its floor. Her face still bleeding, Miss Flowers held the reins without the same authority as before.

Aindreas needed no instructions for what to do next. He lit the lamp from the outside wall and smashed it against the stable floor. Fire spread quickly, over Cooper's body and up the walls. By the time the carriage reached Market Street, flames had seeped through the stable roof.

Graham handed the bundle of things from Cooper's pockets to Aindreas. "Throw that in the river when we get there," he said, then looked back at the fire. "Tomorrow morning, they'll think they only found one more dead Irishman."

The carriage moved along briskly through deserted streets. Aindreas sat quietly, his eyes nearly closed. *König had broken the man's neck...but he, Aindreas, had willed the killing, and had been ready to do it with a pitchfork as he had seen it done. This could not be denied. Nothing would be the same after tonight. Not for this city. Not for him. How would he feel about it in the days to come? He only knew he wanted to be home.*

Miss Flowers turned the carriage north on Fourth Street toward the river. Soon they would reach the wharf and the *Ben Franklin*. Captain Workman would know where to find a doctor for Jack Graham, and he would send men along to escort Miss Flowers home. And he would have fish for König. Captain Workman understood things like that.

285

# 18

**Monday** night, Aindreas sailed a river…a wide river, a river teeming with dark dreams. *His mother cried. He searched far and near, but could not find the object of her heart's sorrow. He had become Mr. Knight, or someone very like him. König's eyes were pleading. He did not know what König wanted, and failed to think of a question he should ask. Miss Flowers, the beautiful black Madonna, cooed to her baby in the straw of the Roundtable Livery…then she turned harlot child of the street and for two pennies lay with a boy Squire Travis under Cawthon's loading dock.*

1

Tuesday, Aindreas again woke at dawn. He hurt in too many places to get up right away. Moreover, the prospect of going out into a world based on yesterday did not attract him in any way.

He propped himself up in bed and sat curled up, his arms around his knees. He gazed at the Madonna on the wall. How serene was the expression on her delicate and yet strong face. She hadn't always been black, he recalled. And of the three kings who brought gifts to the stable, one of them was black—the only other person of color he had ever seen in a holy picture. Had that wise man turned black, Aindreas wondered, or had he been born that way? The prior day revisited Aindreas's mind in bits and pieces. The flash of a face or the image of some horrible deed make him

286

groan and lower his head between his knees. When that happened, he tried to blank out that picture and start over. He got better at separating out the memories that he could smile at, or at least didn't make him weep, and on those he dwelt.

And Captain Workman—what an impressive man. When they had arrived at the wharf he broke out the medicine kit, poured whiskey down Jack Graham's throat and cleaned him up and then made certain the deck hands carefully, gently transported Graham to his cabin before the doctor arrived. The captain comforted Miss Flowers gallantly and assured her that her painful injuries were not serious. The doctor looked her over and confirmed the captain's diagnosis. Workman also helped Aindreas tend to the wounds of the not entirely cooperative König, who by that time walked with his right rear paw held off the ground.

And the captain had insisted that Miss Flowers and Aindreas have supper on the *Ben Franklin*. He personally got mackerel from the galley and served up a huge portion for König on the main deck. Even standing on three legs, the dog had wolfed it all down with impressive gusto.

Workman had listened patiently to the things Aindreas needed to say, then threw Cooper's bundled belongings far out into the river. He later sent two men armed with pistols to escort Miss Flowers and Aindreas to Prather Street.

As it turned out, Miss Flowers had used a carriage belonging to Squire Travis. Aindreas laughed out loud when he recalled finding out that Isaac had hitched up the horse for Miss Flowers last night, and that only Isaac knew that she and the carriage were gone.

Late in the night, back at home, Miss Flowers told all those in the room—his father, Kirsty, Uncle Theodore and Aunt Margaret and Georg Adler that he, Aindreas Rivers, was the bravest young man she had ever known.

Aindreas got out of bed, dressed and was out the door before his sister and father rose. König was nowhere to be seen. Aindreas left fresh water for him, then started for work. A newsboy on Sixth Street let Aindreas look at the front page of one of the newspapers he was selling.

*LOUISVILLE JOURNAL, 1855*

*We deeply regret to have to record the scenes of violence, bloodshed, and house burning which occurred in our city yesterday...when foreign-born citizens, with not the shadow of justification, assassinate American citizens in our streets, what can be expected but that the aroused spirit of our countrymen will rage and thirst for revenge?*

*The riots were occasioned by indiscriminate and murderous assaults committed by foreigners, chiefly Irish...*

*Published and Printed by*
*Prentice, Henderson, & Osborne*

Aindreas handed the newspaper back to the newsboy, who looked away, as if embarrassed that he was handing out such writing. A layer of smoky haze still hung over the city. Though Aindreas felt drawn back toward Tenth Street, he went directly to Cawthon's. He dawdled around filling the inkwells so he could keep an eye on the door, wondering if William Williams would dare show up.

A pile of boxes and envelopes stood near the door. The pile contained food, money, clothing for children, and varied personal items. Each man arriving for work left something there. Aindreas could hardly believe it when he learned that the staff had been asked to bring in donations for the Allison family. On the other hand, the chief clerk nearly always surprised him.

Tom Williams came in without his younger brother. He added nothing to the pile of gifts inside the door. Williams gave

Aindreas a cold look but didn't speak. Later, Aindreas saw him whispering to the chief clerk.

The clerk slipped a dollar into an envelope and put it with the rest. He surveyed the collection for the Allison family. "Gentlemen," he announced, "Mr. Cawthon, if he were here today, would be proud of your generosity." Two of the wagon drivers came into the office to pick up the collection. "Anyone else want to add anything?" the chief clerk asked the office at large.

Aindreas still had thirty-five cents left of the dollar he had won from William Williams. He put the coins in an envelope and gave it to one of the wagon drivers.

"Who will represent our office, to extend sympathies to Mrs. Allison?" asked the chief clerk.

He looked frustrated when no one responded. "Come now, we haven't got all day."

Aindreas broke the silence. "Send Tom Williams."

"Why me?" Williams snapped, plainly annoyed.

The clerk turned to Williams with a wry smile. "Because you talk more than anyone else, and we might as well put that trait to good use."

Tom Williams glared at Aindreas when he walked out with the wagon drivers.

The chief clerk signaled Aindreas to come to his desk. "Tom Williams told me his brother may not come back to work at Cawthon's because he can't get along with you," the chief clerk said sternly. "Is that correct?"

"I don't like him, but that's not correct," Aindreas said.

"Do you want him to come back?"

"No, sir."

"Why?"

"Because he spends too much time polishing apples and doesn't work hard enough at his job."

The chief clerk looked pensive. "We have to have somebody, Rivers. All right, so maybe young Williams does seek favor. Does that make him worse than someone like that no-good Tim Lytle?"

Aindreas looked down. "Actually, he's a lot worse."

"If you were me, what would you do about Williams?"

"I would find someone else," declared Aindreas. "Anyone else."

## 2

**A**ll that morning, Aindreas worried about the promise he had made the night before. He had told Captain Workman that he would go by her apartment and check on Miss Flowers. Aindreas wanted to see her and yet felt anxious about it, but a promise was a promise. He made his deliveries faster than he had ever done before, and by early afternoon he had time to go home for a while.

Mrs. Travis stood at her usual back-window station, apparently watching Tempie dig in the garden behind the house. This might have been a good time for a quick word with Isaac, but Aindreas did not see him anywhere around. Perhaps the squire had sent him on an errand.

After washing up in the kitchen, Aindreas climbed the outside stairs to Miss Flowers's rooms.

She might have seen him coming, or known about it ahead of time, and stood as if waiting near the open doorway. "I'm so glad you could come, Andrew," she said, and ushered him in to the table. "Will you have some dessert with me?"

Her light dress with white lace trim and her long hair, combed straight back and tied, gave her a look of simple beauty. She kept her head slightly turned away, but when she leaned to pour the tea, Aindreas saw her full face. Both lips had been split and a dark bruise stretched from above her right eye down to her neck. Miss Flowers had two faces, one light and one dark.

"Are you still hurting?" he asked.

"It's very sore," she said, touching her cheek. "How about your arm?"

"Still tingles a little, but I can move it around." He flexed his right arm. "See?"

"That's good. I felt so worried about you." She took the cloth from a long baking pan and held it out for Aindreas to see. "Look what Tempie brought this morning."

A beautiful cobbler. "Blueberry?" he asked.

"Yes. I think she knew you were coming."

Aindreas ate two large pieces. Miss Flowers ate but a little. Mainly, she watched him. They drank tea. It came to him that he felt less angry near her than he had in months.

"I'm happy we have this time together," Miss Flowers said. "We used to talk so often about everything under the sun," she said, smiling. "Remember?"

He nodded.

"Last night, Isaac and I talked for a long while," she said.

"What about?"

"So many things. Isaac is a wise man. The conversation somehow always wound its way back to you." Miss Flowers seemed to be choosing her words carefully. "So much has happened in these last few months. I thought I had lost you, my greatest friend. Did you know that's what you have been to me?"

Aindreas studied his hands, spread on the tablecloth. "No," he said.

"Perhaps I should have told you. Anyway, some things that I've done caused you unhappiness. Is that true?"

"I don't know," Aindreas said. "I guess so."

"After surviving last night, and even though we don't always understand each other, do you think we could still care about each other?"

Aindreas flushed. "You don't think I do?"

"Of course you do, but I'm not sure just how. I think I became your ideal, and perhaps I always was. I never deserved to be held in such an exalted position, Andrew, You thought of me as your white flower, not as flesh and blood."

Aindreas rose and stood by the window, hands in his pockets. He could see Tempie working on her hands and knees in Mrs. Travis's garden.

Blanche Flowers said, "I suppose my greatest weakness involved letting myself get hurt by foolish boys who never grew up."

Aindreas wheeled around.

Miss Flowers gently shook her head. "Not you," she assured him. "Johnny Flowers, for one," she said, a quaver in her voice. "And Squire Travis. I went with him on an afternoon riverboat cruise. He wanted to introduce me to a schoolboard member who might save my job, but it turned out there was no board member."

"You and the squire aren't…"

She waved a hand. "Don't be silly, Andrew. Social standing and all, Squire Travis will always remain a boy, and not a very bright one."

Aindreas returned to his chair, his head swimming. "I wish I was older."

"Please don't wish that," she said. "You have time to become what you choose."

The light and dark faces of Blanche Flowers blended into such beauty that Aindreas hardly dared look at her.

"What will happen to you?" he asked.

"I'll be fine," she said, and poured the last of the tea into his cup. "Did I tell you that I start a new job next week at Garfield's Music Shop?"

He shook his head.

"It's rather sad about the teaching job," she said. "I became a

Catholic because of Johnny, and now I can't teach because of my church affiliation. The school board assumes I am disloyal, or some such nonsense." Miss Flowers permitted herself a thin, ironic smile. "One thing I can promise you: no one will ever again get a free ride questioning my loyalty, or telling me where I can or cannot go to church."

Her look of determination gave Aindreas goose bumps. As for those other things she had said earlier, he needed to think. He rose from his chair. "I have to get back to work," he said, "but I'd stay longer if I could."

"Wait a moment," said Miss Flowers. She got a small white scarf from the closet and walked to the door with him.

"I won't stay away like I did," he said.

She tied the scarf around his arm. It covered the rip in his sleeve. "Come to the music shop next week and whenever you like," she said. "We'll sing songs together and we'll find the time to stroll down Jefferson Street to Stephen's Ice Cream Saloon."

"I would like that," said Aindreas.

He did not pull away when she brushed the hair from his eyes. She kissed him lightly on the lips.

"When I am gray and frail, I will yet be pleased that once you chose me for your lady fair," she said, as if reciting a verse from one of her books, "And when you grow old, I hope you will recall that to your lady fair you were a hero."

3

The day had passed so quickly, and only a few hours of daylight remained. König limping along behind him, Aindreas hurried over the creek bridge. It had been clear last night that Jack Graham would be in no shape to carry Isaac and his family to the boat. Captain Workman had asked Aindreas to find a way to do this, and he promised the captain that he would. Aindreas had thought about asking Georg Adler to do the driving but didn't want to involve his friend in such a risk. If Georg would just lend him his wagon, Aindreas would have to do the rest.

The aroma of baking bread wafted into the street. König went on ahead, and plopped down near the door of the Adler house. Marta answered Aindreas's knock. "Here you are," she said, wiping her hands on her apron. "Georg will be back in a few minutes."

When Marta saw König, she clapped her hands together. "Oh, he's been hurt!" she said.

König watched her every move.

"He remembers," Aindreas said.

"Wait," she said. She went back inside and then returned with a steaming bowl of scraps. "Give this to him."

When König began to eat, Aindreas went with Marta to the kitchen. He sat down by the table and leaned his chair back. Marta told him she had baked all afternoon, and plum duck boiled away on the stove.

"I'm not hungry," he said.

She poured him a glass of milk and placed before him an apple dumpling covered with heavy cream. "Of course you are," she said, and patted his shoulder. "You should come to live with us, young man, and we would put meat on your bones."

Aindreas chuckled.

"I'm serious," Marta said. "Georg and me talked about it."

She checked the pot to be sure that the muslin cover on the plum duck remained securely tied. "Georg loves this so, but it takes all day. Already boiled for two hours and needs to cook four more."

Aindreas absently held the spoonful of apple dumpling halfway between the dish and his mouth. *In four hours, Isaac and Tempie and their children would be gone.*

Georg Adler bustled into the kitchen, arms full. He carried a huge bag of onions and several fish on a line strung through their gills. Georg patted Marta's rear when she bent over to pull the bread out of the oven, then ducked under a missed slap that couldn't really have been intended to hit him.

It turned out that Georg wouldn't get off work at Dorrn's Saloon until ten o'clock. Aindreas tried to sound casual when he mentioned needing a wagon to get to the wharf, and that he would be going on the boat to Portland.

Adler looked curious. "You talk like this means nothing, but I have the feeling it's important," he said.

"Yes, it is important," admitted Aindreas.

"Maybe Dorrn would let me off tonight. I could drive you."

"I couldn't ask you to do that, sir."

Adler thought for a moment, then snapped his fingers. "Hah…we do it this way. You come get the wagon at Dorrn's when you're ready. After you haul your stuff, tie up the wagon at the wharf. Finkel owes you a big debt and he knows it. He will come later and pick up the wagon at the wharfmaster's office. He could even drive the wagon to Portland and bring you back."

The notion of dealing with Finkel didn't fill Aindreas with enthusiasm, but he quickly agreed with Georg' idea. Marta made Aindreas eat every bite of the dumpling before he left.

4

Time grew shorter while Aindreas sat at the table with Kirsty and his father. "I have the feeling I'll never see Michael again," Joseph Rivers said.

Aindreas nervously glanced out the window at the waning daylight. It wasn't that he didn't care about where his brother had gone, but there was nothing he could do about it, and he would have to start for Dorrn's Saloon shortly. As Kirsty cleared away the supper dishes, Joseph Rivers ticked off a list of places where he had searched for Michael. A few people claimed they had spotted the young man during the riots, while others said they hadn't seen him since the night of the wake. But none of them, not even his saloon friends, had any idea where he might be now. Da had inquired at the rail yards, of course, but Michael hadn't reported for work this morning. "But I'll keep looking," Joseph Rivers said. "A man can't just disappear from the face of the earth."

Kirsty agreed, "That's right."

Aindreas thought of Red Cooper. *Oh yes, his brother could have disappeared from the face of the earth easily enough.* To comfort his father, Aindreas said, "Michael may have got in a temper and left town. You know how he is."

Joseph Rivers nodded. "Yes, that could be it. Might've gone off to work somewheres downstate."

Aindreas looked out the window again. "There is something I have to do," he said.

"Me, too," his father said. "But listen, the both of you. We need to talk tomorrow night. I don't know what will happen, but as long as we can, I want us to stay together."

"That's wonderful," said Kirsty.

Aindreas nodded. "Tomorrow night."

5

**D**orrn's Saloon, now packed with customers, had suffered only broken glass in the riots. Aindreas walked straight over to the bar. A man in the corner led the singing and accompanied it with a squeeze-box. Georg Adler called the song *Das Mannlein* and explained to Aindreas that it concerned a little man in the woods.

Adler pointed out the window to the Madison Street side of the building. "The wagon with the empty whiskey barrels, that's mine," he said. "You helped to settle down that horse when we hauled the wounded. Remember?"

Recalling his fear of that wild horse, Aindreas nodded. "I haven't been truthful with you about something, Mr. Adler."

296

"Oh?"

"I'm not a wagoner," he blurted. "My grandfather loved horses and I don't understand this, but they've always scared me half to death."

Mr. Adler chuckled. "I know," he said, then added as they walked toward the door, "I'm not worried about you and the horses, Aindreas, but be careful in whatever you're up to tonight."

Outside, Aindreas slowly approached the wagon. The horse snorted. Tall and strong, his blaze caught the light when he tossed his head. Aindreas fished in his pocket for the lumps of sugar Marta had given him. He held one in the palm of his cupped hand, the way Mr. Allison had told him, and offered it. The horse blew noisily through its lips, then took the sugar. Aindreas patted the horse with his damp hand.

He drove the wagon west on Walnut, not yet wanting to be seen near Prather Street. The knobs in the west now concealed a small part of the sinking sun. The light looked as if it might hold out for about another ten minutes. Aindreas slowed the horse to a walk. Only streaks of light remained in the sky by the time he turned the wagon onto Seventh Street. Just short of the Prather Street intersection, he pulled the wagon to the curb. No traffic at all, not even anyone walking. Through the trees, he could see lights from the Travis house, indicating the direction from which Isaac would come. Aindreas set the brake and stepped back into the wagon bed. One of the whiskey barrels had been rocking back and forth on its side. He set it upright, then nearly jumped out of his skin at a question from the darkness.

"What are you doing, boy?"

Two men were standing on the sidewalk. Aindreas hadn't noticed them earlier. *Where had they come from?* With his knee, he nudged the barrel into the corner of the wagon. He began to feel sick to his stomach. "One of these got loose," he said, tying off the barrel with a rope.

Policemen. The big one wore his hat pulled low near his eyes. The other, the man who had spoken, had muttonchop whiskers. Both of them were smoking cigars. "Those barrels smell good enough," the same man said. "You don't have any bottles up there, do you?"

"No, sir," Aindreas said. "I sure don't."

Gripping the side panel, the man boosted himself onto the wheel and looked down into the wagon bed. Satisfied, he got back down and waved his hand in dismissal. By the time the two men started toward Prather Street, sweat was dripping from Aindreas's face onto his shirt.

*Would it be better to move or stay put?* He could drive around the block, but if those two saw him again they might be suspicious.

The policemen walked around the corner onto Prather and out of sight. Isaac and Tempie must have been watching and emerged from the bushes at that instant. Each carried a knapsack over a shoulder and held a child by the hand. Isaac looked terrified.

*Did it have something to do with those policemen?*

Aindreas jumped down and took the sacks. "Quick!" he whispered, "Lie down in the wagon, flat as you can."

They did as he said. Surely no one could see them from ground level except maybe the giant. Back in the driver's box, Aindreas felt thankful for the silent well-behaved natures of little Sarah and Aaron. "Giddup," he said, and turned the wagon west on Prather.

The two policemen continued walking up ahead. As the wagon rolled slowly past them, Aindreas waved. They didn't acknowledge him or the wagon with the least interest. Before he turned north on Eighth Street, he stole a quick glance back at the glowing tips of their cigars.

He kept the wagon moving at an even, slow pace. *If they were* caught, it would be bad for all of them. Isaac and Tempie would be whipped, the family probably split up and sold. And as for him, he could look forward to time behind bars.

Never had the river seemed so far away from Prather Street. The moments dragged by. Though it seemed they would never get to the wharf, Aindreas resisted the temptation to drive faster and risk attracting attention.

Finally, the wagon crossed Water Street and rumbled over the stones of the levee. The *Ben Franklin* lay near the foot of Second Street, slightly apart from the rest of the boats in line. Aindreas had the feeling someone was watching, but he saw no one. He whispered for Isaac and Tempie to stay put. He jumped down from the wagon. Captain Workman and Jack Graham waited on the main deck. Workman must have arranged for everyone else to have work below, for no deckhands were in sight.

The captain waved for them to come aboard. Aindreas urged Isaac and Tempie out of the wagon, then vaulted into the wagon bed and handed down the children and the knapsacks. They started for the boarding plank. "Walk natural," Aindreas cautioned.

As soon as they had boarded, Aindreas told Captain Workman that he needed to move the wagon over next to the wharfmaster's office. The captain hustled the family toward a cabin in the aft section of the main deck.

Back on the levee, Aindreas gave the horse the other sugar cube. When he started to climb back to the driver's seat, the feeling of being watched returned. *Someone had seen everything.* His heart hammered in his chest. A figure moved in the shadows.

"What do you want?" Aindreas demanded.

The figure came into the light. "I'm here to take the wagon," Herbert Finkel said.

Aindreas let his breath out slowly as he climbed down. "Thank you," he said. "I don't know how long my business will take."

Finkel shrugged. "Because of you, I have all the time in the world," he said, and climbed upon the seat. "I will wait in Portland."

Without another word, Finkel flipped the reins, and the wagon wheels started grinding over the stones and up the levee. Aindreas ran back up the plank onto the *Ben Franklin*.

Jack Graham leaned on his crutches, still acting as lookout. He gestured toward the cabin. "Go on in," he told Aindreas.

Captain Workman had already introduced himself. Sarah and Aaron shyly took cover behind Isaac and Tempie. The captain spoke rapidly, his voice full of authority. "Listen carefully because I won't have a chance to repeat this. Tied to the rear of this steamboat is a work yawl, a rowboat, about fourteen feet long. Only two things are in that boat—some canvas and oars. Can you row hard, Isaac?

Isaac nodded.

"Tempie?"

"Uh-huh," she said.

"Good," said the captain. "In a moment, when Jack Graham signals that the deck is clear, I'll take you back there. When you are in the boat, pull the canvas over you. Don't move around or talk. All right so far?"

"Yes, sir," Isaac said.

"You'll have to lie in the boat for some time," the captain went on. "I won't start into the canal until it looks clear from this end."

"Is there anything I can do, sir?" Aindreas asked.

"Jack Graham shouldn't even be on his feet," said Workman. "You, Aindreas, will have to release the rope. This is the most important job. Watch for my hand signal from the pilothouse when we move out of the canal and back into the river."

"We gonna try for Indiana in the rowboat?" Isaac asked.

"That's right," the captain said. "Aindreas, can you whistle?"

"Yes, sir."

"Let me hear you."

Aindreas made a shrill whistle from high to low.

The captain pointed to Isaac. "That's your signal. When you hear that whistle, count to five before you roll back the canvas and set the oars. It's dark, but you'll see Sand Island right in front of you and Portland to your left. Row past the tip of the island, and once you get around it, pull hard for Indiana."

"What will we see?" Isaac said.

"That's good," Captain Workman said, and smiled. "You're right with me. Forty-five degrees to your left..." the captain gestured with his arms, and both Isaac and Tempie nodded, "you'll see a lantern swinging from side to side. Don't row the boat straight for that light or the current will carry you past it. Keep well to the right of it, and let the current help you there."

Aindreas was having trouble swallowing. "Where will they go then?" he asked.

"They will shove the boat back out into the current and follow the man with the lantern up the bank to a church."

Something like pride swelled in Aindreas's chest.

The captain cracked open the door and watched for Graham's signal. Moments later, he said, "Let's go."

They moved together across the darkened deck. Isaac climbed down into the yawl first, then Tempie. The captain swung Sarah and Aaron down to them. Aindreas handed down the knapsacks. Isaac began to pull the canvas over the boat, over his family. There was no time left for words. Aindreas held on to the rail and leaned far over. He clasped his friend's hand for an instant, then Isaac disappeared under the canvas.

"Jack, I want you back in your cabin," the captain said. "The boy will release the rope on my signal."

Graham started to protest, then limped slowly toward his

cabin. Captain Workman started up the stairs to the pilothouse. Alone, Aindreas remained on the dark aft section of the main deck.

River traffic looked sparse. He saw one cotton packet, doubtless headed upriver for Cincinnati and Pittsburgh, and a small excursion boat inching along the Indiana shore. Noise from the *Ben Franklin's* engines grew louder. Twodeck hands came from below and cast off the lines. Three sharp blasts from the steam whistle echoed along the wharf. Captain Workman backed the boat out a ways, then swung it downriver. Aindreas leaned on the rail and watched the lights of the riverfront glide by. They quickly neared the Portland Canal.

Aindreas wondered what pretext Captain Workman had come up with to justify this extra trip to Portland. Most likely, he had intentionally failed to pick up something scheduled for the trip to Cincinnati.

The captain had picked his time well. The canal looked quiet and dark. The distant lights of the Tarascon Mill reminded Aindreas of the wagon ride to Portland with Mr. Allison and that strange visit to the churchwhere Isaac and his family would surely go tonight.

If they could get across that river, nobody could stop them, not even Mr. Bones. The locks weren't far ahead. Off to the left shone the lights of Portland, and past the end of the canal loomed the black shape that must be Sand Island. It was all happening so quickly.

Someone started whistling. *God! Isaac mustn't mistake one of those trills for the signal.* A man, doubtless a crew member, walked port side along the rail, hands in his pockets. Trying to appear unconcerned, Aindreas kept an eye on him.

The man wore round, thick glasses, and his cap was pushed back on his head. Aindreas remembered him. It was Mr. Brickhouse, the engineer. "Hello, young fellow," he said.

"Good evening, sir."

Brickhouse looked idly about the deck and continued in the direction of the aft rail.

"Lovely night, eh?"

"Yes sir, fine night," responded Aindreas.

The engineer looked down at the yawl trailing a few feet behind the *Ben Franklin,* and made a sound something like "Hmmm."

*What had Brickhouse seen?* Aindreas moved closer to the engineer and looked down; he could see obvious lumps under the canvas. One of them looked for all the world like the shape of a person. The engineer continued staring at the trailing rowboat. *Why didn't he say something?* Aindreas rammed his hands in his pockets.

Brickhouse peered up at the davit, the guy wires, and the pulley ropes, then back down at the boat. "Strange," he said. "I thought that davey had been fixed, but we're still pulling that yawl."

*Hadn't he seen the shape?"* Aindreas let out enough breath to respond with his own "Hmmmm."

The engineer checked to see that the rope from the yawl remained tied securely to the chock. "Seems like a good way to lose a boat," he said. "I'll have to mention it to the captain next time I see him."

Brickhouse leaned over the rail and peered closely at the yawl, then straightened up and shrugged his shoulders. "You with us when we head back upriver?" he asked.

"No, sir. Just riding along to Portland."

"Well, goodnight," Brickhouse said, and walked purposefully toward the engine room.

*How could a man as smart as Mr. Brickhouse miss something like that? Maybe it was so plain to Aindreas because he knew who lay beneath the canvas. Maybe knowing was easier than finding out.*

After the *Ben Franklin* moved through the locks, Aindreas kept his eyes trained on the pilothouse. When the boat neared the end of the canal, Aindreas took hold of the rope. The light of the Portland wharf shone ahead, and the *Ben Franklin* began to swing left, out into the river. The captain turned from the wheel and looked down toward Aindreas, then raised one hand above his head and brought it down sharply.

Quickly, Aindreas unwound the rope from the chock and threw it into the water. He leaned over the rail and gave his high-low whistle. The small boat began to fall back. Then he counted, *one...two...three...four...five.* Isaac and Tempie stripped the canvas away and struggled to fit the oars into the locks. The steamboat's engines slowed nearly to a stop. The captain let loose a couple of blasts from the steam whistle.

Up ahead, another boat started to back out from the wharf, then stopped. Perhaps the pilot couldn't anticipate what the *Ben Franklin* might do. The wily Captain Workman evidently intended to stall around in front of the wharf a little longer, to divert attention from what even now was beginning to move out in the river. The rowboat sloughed through the dark water near the tip of Sand Island. Oars flashed above the water. The engines of the *Ben Franklin* came alive again, and Captain Workman began to move the steamboat in toward the wharf.

Aindreas strained to keep the boat in sight. Light caught the oars again, and again, then the yawl disappeared behind Sand Island. The swelling in his chest turned painful. He could barely contain the joy and grief at having lost his friend to freedom.

6

Isaac spoke softly, "Pull." Then again— "Pull."

Tempie didn't know whether Isaac was talking to himself or to her. She pulled her oar in time with him. They worked well together.

Isaac looked over his shoulder. "I see it," he said. "I see the light."

The pain started in her belly soon after they cleared the edge of that island and spread to her back and thighs. Sarah and Aaron never took their eyes from her face. Tempie bit her lip to keep from crying. She could not cry in front of them. She wrenched the oar through the water.

"Getting closer," Isaac grunted. "Keep pullin' if you can, girl."

Her arms ached. Her belly knotted worse. *Was she killing her unborn child?* Pull...pull. *No...sometime it may seem that God don't care as much as we wish He would, but God ain't mean.* She pleaded silently. *Don't let this child die 'fore she take one free breath.*

"See behind you, Tempie? We past the middle of it."

She hadn't enough energy left to turn her head. *Help me, freedom child. Help me pull one more, one more.* They pulled together, again and again. Slowly, they made their way clear across the dark water.

"We made it," Isaac said finally, and patted her arm.

Hands grabbed the boat and pulled it close to the bank. Tempie slumped over the oar as Isaac lifted out the children and the knapsacks. She heard the whispers of two other men. One of them sounded like a white man.

Isaac pried her fingers loose from the oar handle. "Come on, Tempie," he said, "come on."

Tempie put one foot over the side into water up to her shin, then lifted over the other foot and pitched onto her face. The men pulled her up to the bank. She coughed and coughed, spitting muddy water. Now they had her upright and held her under the arms. The white man searched the boat to make certain everything had been taken out, then swung the boat around and shoved it hard. It drifted away from the bank, beginning to pick up speed in the current.

Isaac carried Aaron, and Sarah hung on to Tempie's hand. The Colored man doused the lantern. It looked as far as a city block up the riverbank to a wide building with a tower on the top. A halo glowed around a streetlight in the distance. "That's where we're goin'," the Colored man whispered. "They look after you tonight."

The other man gripped her elbow when they started up the bank. Glad for the support, she didn't mind. She nearly fell again as they trudged up the bank, but they made it to the rear of the building. Haltingly, she followed the white man down dark stairs. They were led to one of the rooms in a large basement.

Isaac sensed that they were under a church. After they all had been given food and water, Sarah and Aaron drifted off to sleep. Tempie sat with her eyes closed, leaning against the brick wall.

She felt better.

The big man who had held the lantern on the riverbank came back to see them. "Had plenty to eat?" he asked.

Isaac nodded. "How long we goin' to stay here?" he asked.

"Till tomorrow night. Then you ride on to the next depot."

"Where is that?"

"Don't know. Maybe Corydon…Palmyra."

Isaac asked, "Where we gonna end up?"

"Depends. Some Colored settled right here in Indiana, or up through South Bend to Chicago, or up east to New York or Boston. A few keeps right on goin' to Canada." Isaac wagged his head in wonder.

"Ain't no hurry; make up your mind as you go along," the big man said, and laughed. "Get some rest now."

Tempie opened her eyes. She leaned against Isaac, and they sat quietly. After a time, he took the wooden box from his knapsack and untied the string. Tempie watched as he removed the velvet covering from something in the box. Isaac held out the bason in the flickering lamplight. It seemed to give off a glow of its own that owed nothing to the lamp. He handed it to Tempie. There was also an envelope in the box, a letter.

AUGUST 7, 1855 LOUISVILLE, KENTUCKY

> Dear Isaac:
>
> You may have only gone a few miles when you read this. God willing, you read it a free man.
>
> Two things I hope you will do:
>
> First, don't stop until you get to Canada. Some people may tell you that you could settle in Ohio, Indiana, or Illinois. You can't. Captain Workman told me that butternuts and buckeyes want no part of you—and they have laws against Blacks moving there. It may not make you feel any better, but some states once had those kinds of laws against the Irish.
>
> Second, please don't change too much. You're the smartest man I ever met, and I will miss you. We may not meet again, but I will think of you and I'll look for you any place I ever pass through. Try to remember that good lived here, too. I hope in your dreams you come back, as I will, to Louisville and Prather Street.
>
> Your friend always,
> Aindreas Rivers

Isaac looked over at Tempie. Smiling, she cradled the bason in her arms like a child. She could not look away from it, as if in its glowing scenes she saw a future for the children, for the child to be, for Isaac, and for her.

7

As soon as the *Ben Franklin* had docked at Portland, Aindreas went ashore. Captain Workman saluted and shouted "so long" from the pilothouse. Jack Graham came out of his cabin and stood, waving, on the main deck. Even Mr. Brickhouse came down on deck. He leaned on the rail, smiling.

Good as his word, Mr. Finkel waited with the wagon. Aindreas had no desire to talk, and Finkel did not speak a word the entire trip back home. Such gratitude grew in his heart, that Aindreas decided he almost liked Finkel...almost.

Later, home at last, Aindreas slumped on the side of his bed. It was done. He got up and wandered into the kitchen. Through the doorway, he could clearly see the empty place where they would live no more. Supper fire smoke still curled from the cabin chimney. So hard to imagine what life would be like without Isaac. *Where was he now, and Tempie, and the children? What would Squire Travis do when he found out they were gone?*

Aindreas wanted to look at the table cover Tempie had made. He took the package from the shelf, untied the string and unwrapped the paper. He unfolded the cloth of many colors and spread it across the bed. It looked just as he had remembered it from back when his mother still lived. In its center, Aindreas found a heavy envelope. Money spilled out, and a note in Isaac's labored script.

*LOUISVILLE 1855*

*Andrew you leave and don't go owing that man nothing. You be free. Thank you for what you done and we carry you with us all the time—Isaac White and Tempie*

Aindreas wept. He couldn't stop, and sat there on the edge of his bed for long minutes. Amidst little sobs that came out his windpipe like hiccups, he counted the money—forty-two dollars.

A sound from out back of the building claimed his attention. Moving to the window opening, he looked out into the darkness. Amber crystals glittered in the lamplight. Aindreas dashed to the kitchen and returned quickly, carrying food scraps on a newspaper. With a joyful laugh, he scampered over the windowsill to the grass below, and to the waiting dog. Still holding the rear paw off the ground, König bore his many injuries with his customary, massive grace. Not believing his eyes at first, Aindreas knelt for a closer look at that cursed, eternal wound on the right foreleg. It had healed.

THE END

# MAP

# PERMISSIONS AND NOTES

# CHARACTER EPILOGUES

# CITY MAP OF LOUISVILLE 1855

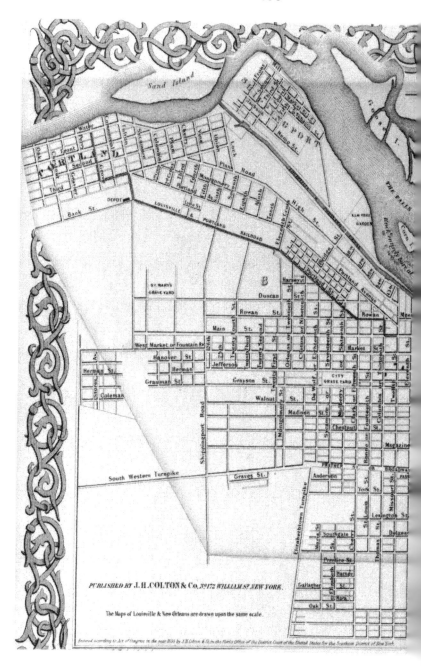

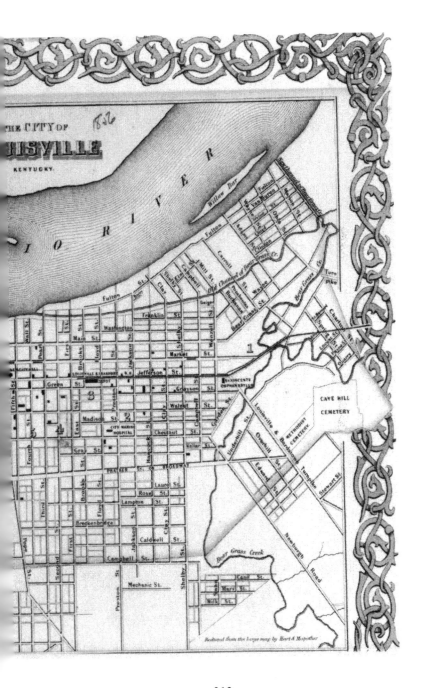

THE CITY OF
LOUISVILLE
KENTUCKY.

OHIO RIVER

CAVE HILL CEMETERY

Reduced from the large map by Hart & Mapother

313

**Color Lithograph Louisville, Kentucky 1855:** (Cover)
Courtesy of Bank One, Kentucky; Published 1855, J.T.
Palmatary, Cincinnati.

**Ben Franklin Row Boat:** Filson Club Historical Society,
Louisville, Kentucky. (Taken from the engraving of *Ben
Franklin and View of Louisville, Kentucky 1851*.)

**Bear Grass Creek at Preston's Landing:** Special Collections,
Ekstrom Library, University of Louisville.
**Note:** French engraving copied from *James River Guide
1856*. When the story begins Aindreas is coming out of a
seizure in the bottom right hand side of the engraving.

**Public Landing at Louisville, Kentucky:** Special Collections,
Ekstrom Library, University of Louisville.
**Note:** Stevedores loading boats along the warf in 1856.
Engraved expressly for the Progress of the Republic, and
entered according to Act of Congress.

**Speed Market:** Special Collections, Ekstrom Library,
University of Louisville.
**Note:** The enclosed market is located in the center of
engraving between 5th and 6th street on market Street. One of
the six enclosed produce stands in 1856.

**Customs House and Post Office:** Filson Club Historical
Society, Louisville, Kentucky.

**Note:** Erected at 3rd and Liberty in 1851 in the Anglo-
Norman style for $258,500.

**Court House:** Filson Club Historical Society Louisville, Kentucky.

**Note:** Construction began along Jefferson Street between 5th and 6th street in 1836 and *Guthries' Folly* was still unfinished in 1855. The sale of slaves in settlement of the Spencer estate took place on the lawn in the bottom center of the engraving.

**Ben Franklin and View of Louisville, Kentucky:** Filson Club Historical Society Louisville, Kentucky.

**Note:** Engraving published in 1851 depicts four modes of river transportation, steam boat, sail boat, row boat and log raft.

**Eclipse:** Courtesy of *S & D Reflector* published by the Sons and Daughters of Pioneer Riverman.

**Note:** Built in New Albany, Indiana, 1852, weighing 1,117 tons.

| | |
|---|---|
| Length of deck | 365' |
| Width of hull | 40' |
| Depth of hull | 9' |
| Paddlewheels | 40' dia., working 15' |
| Extreme width | 77' |
| Engines | (2) 36" cylinders with 11' stroke |
| Boilers | 16 in number |
| Smokestacks | 95' waterline to top,  85" dia. |
| Draft | 4.5' light. 10' loaded |
| Passenger capacity | 140 cabins, 60 on cots |
| Freight capacity | 1,600 tons |
| Cost | $375,000 |

Glassware for tables, bars, and other parts of the boat are designed and made in Switzerland. The carpet reaching from the gentlemen's hall to the large mirror at the end of the ladies cabin is seamless, and woven in Brussels, with eyelets on each sides, to be button down[sic] instead of being laid permanently, consequently always spotless clean. The cabin is Gothic and Norman styles. The ceiling is divided into diamonds and half diamonds by the crossing of Gothic arches, and at the points of intersection hang pendant acorns entwined with oak leaves of rich gilt, the whole giving the appearance of two vast, arched colonnades. The intervening spaces in the ceiling are decorated with frescoes; each stateroom door is embellished with a landscape; and over the forward entrance to the cabin are two large paintings of the patron cities, Louisville and New Orleans. The large stained glass skylights above and the six massive and richly gilded chandeliers are objects of wonder as well as sources of light.

**Town Clock Church:** Courtesy of New Albany Floyd County Public Library.
**Note:** Center section of a 50" x 39" painting of New Albany in 1851 by George Morrison. Isaac and his family escape to the basement of Town Clock Church, a station in the Underground Railroad in 1855.
**König:** Drawing of a Mastiff of Tibet from 1848 book *Dogs* by Youatt.

**Boat used by Isaac, Tempie, Sarah, and Aaron floating down the Ohio River.**
**Note:** River people found the *Ben Franklin* boat upriver from Paducah, Kentucky not far from the Mississippi, and

returned it to Captain Workmen.

**City of Louisville, 1855:** Filson Club Historical Society Louisville, Kentucky.

**Note:** Colton's 1855 map of Louisville.

**Aindreas Rivers:** Aindreas subsequently lived with George and Marta Adler. In the following years, Aindreas haunted the libraries in his quest for self-education. He served a short enlistment as a medical attendant in the Union Army during the American Civil War, prior to his first writing job at a newspaper—the *Scribe*.

**Mr. Knight:** Not seen again for a decade.

**König:** Vanished sometime in the night of August 7, 1855.

**Captain Carl Workman:** Remained captain of the *Ben Franklin* until it went to Confederate registry in 1861. He became captain of the river packet *Alexander Hamilton*.

**Samuel 'Red' Cooper:** His disappearance caused a stir in American Party circles, but he was forgotten in their euphoria over election victories.

**Mr. Raskin:** Perished in the Mississippi River. No trace of him was ever found.

**Jack Graham:** Continued as first mate umder Captain Workman, later movimg with him to the *Alexander Hamilton*. Served as a boat pilot with the Union Army and received a decoration for bravery at the siege of Vicksburg.

**Know-Nothings (American Party):** Swept all the local elections. Won the governorships and legislatures of New Hampshire, Massachusetts, Rhode Island, Connecticut, New York, California, and Kentucky. By 1856, eight states had American Party Governors: The party faded into oblivion with the rise of the Republican Party and Abraham Lincoln.

**Doireann Rivers:** Buried in St. Mary's Cemetery, grave unmarked for years.

**Blanche Flowers:** Remained in Louisville to better fortune, undefeated by her husband's abandonment and the loss of her teaching job. She would forever be the female ideal to Aindreas, the standard by which he would measure all other women.

**Michael Rivers:** Rumored to have become a patroller on plantations near New Orleans.

**Kirsty Rivers:** Taken in by Aunt Margaret and Uncle Theodore. Worked as a domestic for the insurance agency owner, Mr. Jones.

**Joseph Rivers:** Lived with Lila. Together they started and owned the Limerick Saloon.

**Isaac White:** Cared for Tempie after the loss of her newborn daughter, Andrea, in Canada. Took his family to New York City in 1861.

**Tempie White:** Suffered ill health and severe melancholy for years after the death of her newborn child.

**Sarah White:** Assumed many of Tempie's duties in the family, and acted as a mother to Aaron.

**Aaron White:** Apprenticed to his father from the age of eight. Became a zealous protector of his mother and sister.

**Chief clerk at Cawthon's Furniture Manufactory:** Labored on with Cawthon's in the service of commerce.

**Tad Englender (Master Commissioner):** Convicted of misappropriation of public funds and served time in state prison.

**Say-Nothings (*The Sag-Nichts*):** Active until the demise of the American Party, then disappeared as a political organization.

**Mister Bones:** His home became a national shrine. His specter continued to appear at the courthouses and other public places.

**Emily Travis:** Her husband forced her to sell many of her family heirlooms and move with him from Louisville. Insignificant among the society flowers of the South, she remained unfulfilled.

**Squire Travis:** Enraged by the loss of his own slaves, and determined to avoid the coming violent conflict over slavery, he sold his properties and moved the family to Atlanta, Georgia.

**The two policeman (the tall man with the hat pulled down, and the man with the mutton-chop whiskers):** Continued to serve those in power, later including the Union Army.

**Calvin:** Sold down river in August, 1855.

**Marcus McFate:** His bones rest in an unmarked grave in the City Cemetery.

**Tim Lytle:** Body claimed by his family at the City Jail.

**The Union of Free Germans:** These authors of the *Manifesto of 1854* were absorbed into other labor and political organizations.

**Johnny Flowers:** Killed in a hotel room fight over a woman in New Orleans in 1858.

**George Prentice:** Became even more powerful in the years to come. Had a reputation as a staunch Unionist until Lincoln's Emancipation Proclamation.

**Herbert Finkel:** Saved enough money to open a stationer's shop. Became a notary, and continued to write poetry.

**Georg and Marta Adler:** Took in Aindreas as a son. Their home prospered as marriage of cleverness and industry.

**Dr. James MacIntosh:** Went on as a respected member of the medical society in Louisville. Formed a surgical unit for service with the Union Army.

**Reverend Cole:** Moved to New Albany, Indiana in 1856 and started a Baptist church.

**Watchman at Cawthon Furniture Manufactory:** Died of consumption in 1860.

**William Williams:** Studied for ministry, and became an Episcopalian priest.

**Tom Williams:** Fled Louisville after rape charges were filed against him.

**Mr. Pritchett:** Became a prolific buyer of cheap rental properties around Louisville.

**Mrs. Greene:** Moved to Paducah, Kentucky with her children for a new start.

**Curly:** Rumored to have gone to Paducah in pursuit of Mrs. Greene.

**Major Krauth:** Killed at the battle of Shiloh.

**Libby Krauth:** Active in literary circles in New York City after the death of her husband.

**Mayor John Barbee:** Served out his term as maor, and was succeeded by another Know-Nothing mayor in 1857.

**Young woman with the crying baby:** Within a year, the baby disappeared. She begged for money on the streets.

**Aunt Mary Zimmer:** Moved in with her sister, Margaret.

**Aunt Margaret and Uncle Theodore Herdrich:** Took in Mary as well as Kirsty Rivers.

**Lila:** Lived with Joseph Rivers, sold the grocery store and put up the money to start the Limerick Saloon.

**Father Joseph Callaghan:** Became the parish priest at St. Martin of Tours Church.

**Mr. Brickhouse, engineer of the *Ben Franklin*:** After the departure of Jack Graham, he became first mate of the *Alexander Hamilton*.

**Mr. Allison:** Body claimed at the City Jail by his wife and six children.

**Dicey:** Scrubbed on the *Eclipse* until its destruction in the great storm at New Orleans in 1860.

**Jim Porter:** The "Kentucky Giant" died of heart failure in the 1859, age forty-nine. Buried in Cave Hill Cemetery.

**Capt. Lovell Rosseau:** Practiced law, and became a Major General in the Union Army.

**Catherine and (little) Sophie Armbruster:** After these two young heroines saved the Armbruster gold, carrying it away strapped under their petticoats, their family files suit against the City of Louisville.

**Colonel Preston:** Lost his bid for re-election to Congress. Later rose to the rank of Major General in the Confederate Army.

**Mr. Barrett:** Body claimed at City Jail by family.

**Mr. Hulbert:** Body claimed at City Jail by family.

**Patrick Quinn:** Remains claimed from the ashes of Quinn Row by family.

## ACKNOWLEDGEMENTS

*Aindreas the Messenger* is dedicated to Kim, my wife.

Friends and colleagues helped—acted as sounding boards, made critical suggestions, and encouraged. My gratitude to DiAnn and Don Miler, the late professor Leon Driskell who gave unselfishly of his time, Reah Cobb, Walter Collins, Mary Sue Ewing, Joe Grove, Pat Jacobson, Prudence Todd Moffett, Don and Lynn Renau, Maggie Riley, Patrica Seitz, Gayle Shields, Tom Tichenor, and Mary Lawrence Young.

Working on historical background and detail, I received gracious assistance form the Louisville Free Public Library, the Floyd County Indiana Library, the University of Louisville Library, University of Kentucky Library, the *Courier Journal,* Howard Steamboat Museum, the Portland Museum, and the Louisville Historical League.

For their published works, lectures, and knowledge with respect to the time time and setting of this book, my thanks and admiration for our historians, archivists and writers—including Thomas Clark, Father Clyde Crews, Tom Owen, Samuel Thomas and George Yater.

Gerald McDaniel

# A WORD FROM THE AUTHOR

Why would one write a story set in Louisville, Kentucky in 1855? Because in that city in that year, as in other cities and other years, the frailty of the human spirit was stripped naked for all eyes to see. Ethnic and religious targets bore the brunt of injury, degradation and death heaped upon their *kind* as those before and after them.

Walk down any street. The past reveals itself to no more than glimpses and imagination. But we must avidly imagine, for the past contains our present just as surely as our future is molded now. Since the beginnings of talking, drawing, singing, and writing, the storyteller has defined our world.

Whether a subject of fiction or non-fiction, middle 19th Century America often draws writers to the Civil War. While this first industrial war was a dramatic culmination of failed institutions and fallen gods, I was not drawn to it. Dwelling upon victory or defeat in wars, or the lives of great men, I leave to others. I chase the ordinary individual making moral choices.

In my clouded perspective, the most telling glimpses of the past have been directed toward the human heart and mind, rather than at the deeds of great men. Humankind has yet to evolve beyond the acquisitive, cruel nature of its genes and inclinations.

Yet, we know that in the face of adversity and sorrow, a

man, a woman, or a child can find in the pocket of the soul the grit and vision to reach for that beyond reach.

# AN EXCERPT

## *AINDREAS THE SCRIBE 1865*

### Book two in the Aindreas Rivers Saga

MIDNIGHT
WEDNESDAY, JANUARY 11, 1865

**The** packet *Alexander Hamilton* lay docked at the Louisville wharf below the foot of Fifth Street. Lantern in hand, Captain Workman led the way across the main deck. Aindreas Rivers followed a few steps behind, head down in the eye-watering breeze off the river, his writing folder under his arm and his hands buried in his coat pockets. The *Alexander Hamilton* didn't inspire in him the same affection as the other packet Workman had captained for years, the *Ben Franklin*. In appearance and spirit, the two boats were as unalike as their namesakes.

A solitary white flake fluttered down just off the side of the boat. Aindreas looked up; clear night stars still shown above. But it had looked like a snowflake. From a boat somewhere down the line a steam whistle shrieked, an ungodly sound at such an hour. A brief shower of white flakes descended in a ghostly dance over the riverbank. One settled on Aindreas's sleeve, crumbled to nothing on his fingernail when he tried to lift it. Ash

They reached the boarding plank. "Goodnight, Captain," Aindreas said, patting the shoulder of the man nearly a head taller than he.

"Thanks for listening to an old man's tale of woe," said Workman. He held out the lantern at arm's length and looked up and down the line of river boats, apparently trying to pick out which boat had caused the commotion.

"Wonder what that was all about," he groused.

Aindreas said nothing about the ash, which might have come from nothing more than an upwind trash fire. He walked down the plank and onto the levee. The cobblestones, thinly glazed with ice, had turned into a wide slope of slippery knobs. Perhaps a third of the way up the levee, his feet came out from under him. Even if he had looked like a circus clown, he hadn't fallen on his face and had nothing worse to show than skinned knuckles."

Careful now," Workman cautioned from the deck.

Writing folder now clutched in his left hand, his arms held out for balance, Aindreas moved forward deliberately. He rarely drank liquor and knew he shouldn't have tonight. It had been months since the last seizure, but one could come right out of a blue sky, a lot more likely than a snowflake. Halfway up the incline, he peered back over his shoulder. The lantern light had disappeared; Captain Workman had returned to his cabin.

It had been a somber evening and would have been more cheerful had their old friend and former first mate of the *Ben Franklin*, Jack Graham, arrived on leave from his duty station on the Mississippi. But Jack hadn't made it. The *Alexander Hamilton* was scheduled to leave for New Orleans in the morning, heavy with furniture and industrial pumps, and would bring back a full load of coffee. If all went well, Captain Workman would make a nice profit. A celebration in advance would have been the thing to do this evening, but a week ago the captain's wife of forty-two years had died in Cincinnati. Without laughter, Aindreas and the captain had exchanged wry toasts and downed rye whiskey.

Wind at the top of the bank stung him, icy, right through his overcoat and shreds of whiskey numbness still hanging on. He turned up his coat collar and put on his gloves. Steam- whistle blasts were coming from the line of docked boats. From the higher vantage point he could see the source, a packet near the bottom of Pearl Street, two blocks away. He moved in that direction, east on Water Street while piercing whistles continued, the shrieks only seconds apart now. The sullen, gray underside of a low-moving cloud carried in it sparks as bright as lightning bugs. Shadowy figures hustled ashore from several boats along the line, the men slipping and staggering up the levee toward Water Street. Aindreas began to run, past Fourth Street, past Pearl, and didn't pause until he reached Second Street. Smoke was coming from the Galt House, and from the roof of the building, a brief towering flame curled up into the darkness like one of those sun storms astronomers wrote about and others thought were omens, and maybe they were. *The Galt House. Dickens once spent the night there. My God, what a wounding sight.*

He drew nearer to the hotel, his head clearing, taking in the street chaos as he walked. Smoke was billowing out of the upper windows. He'd never noticed before that the hotel stood only four stories high in the rear, one less than the front entrance on Main Street. At least twenty firemen were stringing hoses at the rear of the structure, and another company of ten or more arrived amidst a lot of bell-ringing.

He moved on up the bank. Men and women in work clothes, perhaps on dinner break, watched mutely from Second Street; some weren't even wearing overcoats. No one had any idea how or when the fire had started. A woman screamed in the distance. A noisy crowd milled around by the Main Street entrance, getting in the way of the newly arrived firemen. Knots of neighborhood people clotted near the door gawking at hotel guests coming out—most of them walking but others being helped or carried. Flushed youngsters dashed about with their big eyes; it was beginning to take on the look of a street fair.

"Get back, dammit," a fire chief shouted at spectators surrounding the front door.

Those who had gotten out of the building wandered about in a daze, coats or bedspreads over them like Roman senators. The crowd drew closer when hotel porters carried out an elderly man and woman; they laid them on a pad spread over the icy street. Wheezing through open, thin-lipped mouths, their faces and bodies smeared with black smudge, but for the length of their nearly naked bodies, they looked more like wrinkled, barely alive babies than a man and a woman. A hotel assistant manager, wearing a wing collar and a cutaway coat, hovered anxiously over them. Shortly, other hotel employees bundled the two unfortunates in blankets and carried them to a wagon.

The firemen were pumping water through one hose, but the stream barely reached above the second floor. Judging from that soaring plume of flame Aindreas had seen a moment earlier, the situation was looking worse by the minute. He grabbed at the assistant manager's arm. "There are still more people inside, aren't there?"

"I...uh, I don't know," the man stammered, but then nodded his head. "Maybe a few."

"Has anyone died?"

The man cast a quick look at the upper floors. "I hope not," he said.

Both ducked their heads at a gunshot-like sound from overhead. Small pieces of broken glass rained down. A window on the fifth floor had blown out. Most of the onlookers backed away toward the other side of Main Street.

A woman's voice rang out. "Somebody please help us up here!" A young woman was leaning out a window on the fourth floor. "The door is jammed...we can't get out."

A few of the spectators looked to be fresh from a saloon, and acted it. One of the rowdies held out his arms and bawled, "Jump, dearie. I promise to catch you in me arms...at least by the first bounce!"

A younger fireman, a husky fellow with a full mustache already coated in ice, shouted, "How many are up there?"

"Four," she said. "Five, counting my dog."

The fireman wagged his head, apparently at the dog reference. "Volunteers?" he asked loudly all around.

No one stepped forward. The fireman pulled on a knit cap, then emptied a full bucket of water over his head. He grabbed an axe and started toward the front entrance alone. The assistant manager lagged behind him.

Aindreas, standing near the door, watched the two men approach. He felt afraid, but the woman's voice…and the notion of those people trapped in their room wasn't something he could have lived with in the morning. After a false start, he stuffed the writing pad inside his coat and stepped in front of the fireman.

"I'll go with you," he said.

The fireman laughed, as though as joke had been made, then noticed the hotel's assistant manager also at his side. "All right, you two heroes," he said, and pulled them over next to a pumping wagon. Without preamble, he poured a bucket of icy water over each of them. Hefting the axe over his shoulder like a bat, the fireman led the way inside. The three of them moved quickly through the empty lobby, which seemed darkened even though all the wall lamps were still alight. Aindreas trailed the others. He was shivering; all the warmth from the whiskey was gone. No flames were visible yet, but smoke veiled the high ceiling like moving clouds. Aindreas stopped shivering and began to unbutton his heavy overcoat so he could peel it off.

The fireman glanced back over his shoulder and shook his head no. "You'll be glad to have that on you in a little while," he growled.

They clambered up the staircase and reached the mezzanine level without difficulty. Halfway up the next flight, gasping from the smoke, they had to retreat. The manager hacked furiously into a handkerchief, his whole body quaking. The fireman held him by the shoulders.

"Is there a service stairway, man?" Aindreas demanded.

The manager confirmed there was. Aindreas received a grudging nod from the fireman. Having collected himself quickly, the manager led them back deeper into the building—closer to where the fire had to be raging. The narrow staircase felt hotter yet, but maybe there was a little less smoke. All three of them doubled over, keeping their faces as low as possible, and climbed again.

The fireman glanced at Aindreas. "Who the devil are you?" he asked.

Aindreas answered between short breaths. "I write for a newspaper."

"Jesus," the fireman snorted and then looked away.

The smoke grew heavier after they reached the second floor. Aindreas wondered whether the hurt came from breathing the smoke or out of the fear in his chest. It was looking as if they might have a chance to reach the stranded guests. A thunderous, crashing sound came from the rear of the building.

"Get going—. Get going!" the fireman shouted.

They rushed into the stairwell. Darkness completely. enveloped them for a moment on the next flight of stairs. They climbed by feel, on hands and knees, the fireman urging them on from the rear. Aindreas doubted more than once that he would make it. Finally, they paused to rest a moment at the landing. Then on up the next flight of steps, which was easier. The fourth floor.

Glad to be still alive, a certain giddiness took hold of Aindreas and he asked the fireman, "And just who the devil are you?"

Another crash came from the back of the building. "Thorson," the fireman said.

The notion that he had come into this thunderous hell with a man so named seemed   absurd, and Aindreas laughed out loud like a madman.

Toward the rear of the building, no more than fifty feet away, the hallway was smoldering. Black smoke curled above their heads as they proceeded down the hall in a crouch, leaning away from the parts of the walls actually afire—on toward the rooms that fronted on Main Street. Aindreas's watch slipped from his pocket. He put it back, astonished to realize they had been inside the hotel for barely more than five minutes. The first room they reached stood empty. In the hallway they could now hear the muffled barking of a dog. The same strong voice they had heard from the street rang out again. "We're in here and the door won't open."

The stranded guests occupied a suite two doors down and must have heard the men tramping down the hall. The manager lunged against the door with his shoulder, but it didn't budge. Lower to the floor now, smoke crept like fog down the hallway.

"Stand aside in there," yelled Thorson, and struck at the door with his axe and then again.

The barking had become furious. It wasn't that deep König-like bark but that of a smaller dog.

"Come on...hurry!" said the woman. "Get your back into it."

Thorson's compact, powerful swings with the axe shattered the panels and lock rail of the door. Aindreas noticed that the door had been locked. Thorson kicked out shards of wood clinging to the lintel and the outside rails and the three of them entered the room ahead of the heat and smoke.

The four hotel guests made the room seem full to bursting with dramatic characters in a stage play or heroic painting. In the center, commanding attention by her mere presence, stood a strikingly sensual-looking young woman with strawberry-blonde hair and eyes green as Gulf water close to shore—she was the one who had yelled from the window. Clutching her hand, his gaze oddly focused on her, stood a tall, middle-aged man in trousers and open shirt, his face chalk white. A petite, refined-looking woman, apparently his wife, pressed her face against his chest and clung to him with both arms. A dark-haired young woman knelt in the middle of the room trying to quiet a black-and-white spaniel.

Aindreas helped Thorson strip the sheets off the beds.

"Is there a bathroom?" Thorson asked the manager.

"The adjoining room," the manager responded, and pulled the door open.

"Get some water in the bathtub," Thorson shouted after him.

The assistant manager and Aindreas soaked the bedding, so that everyone would have a wet sheet or blanket for protection.

Thorson tossed one to the woman kneeling by the dog. "Wrap this around yourself," he ordered.

Apparently, she didn't pick it up quick enough to suit him.

Thorson said, "Move, goddammit."

"Don't take God's name in vain," the blonde woman snapped. "My father is Reverend Sharpe, and he doesn't allow that kind of talk."

"It doesn't matter what your father allows," barked Thorson. "If we don't get out of this room right quick, we're not going to get out."

The green flash of her eyes was more arresting than Aindreas's fear and the smoke in his airways; he couldn't look away from her. Though flushed pink with the heat, her skin had not even the hint of a freckle or blemish.

Aindreas watched as Thorson and the manager picked up some of the traveling cases near the window. After shouting a warning to those below, they tossed the cases out. A couple of them shattered when they hit the street.

"What are you doing?" the blonde woman asked.

"They're trying to save some of our things, Lorelei," the kneeling woman said just before   the dog pulled free from her arms and bolted from the room.

"Abigail!" the blond woman wailed, and moved toward the doorway. "Damn you, Faith," she said.

Thorson grabbed her arm and swung her around. She wrenched free and slapped him, her fingers leaving white marks on his sooted face. The man, Reverend Sharpe, picked pieces of ash from his white mane and seemed near to smiling.

Mrs. Sharpe stumbled to her daughter. "Lorelei...Lorelei," she cooed. "What will these brave gentlemen think?"

With all of them arrayed in wet sheets and blankets, they appeared to Aindreas like a gathering of Dickensian ghosts.

"Follow me in single file," Thorson said. "Let's go!"

Lorelei gestured toward the remaining trunk, a strapped suitcase, and two carpetbags gathered near the bed. "What about the rest of our things?"

Thorson paused for a second, then simply shook his head and ducked out through the doorway into gray smoke in the hallway.

Reverend Sharpe gave an anguished look back at the remaining luggage, then he and his wife followed. Daughter Faith was between them, guiding her mother. The manager went next.

Only Aindreas and Lorelei remained in the room. Her eyes were glued on the luggage. She began to sob, the way a little girl might when she can't have her way. Though this annoyed him under the circumstances, her sounds and the streaks made by her tears made him captive; the clinging wet sheet accented her shape in a way that made him less aware that the hotel was burning down around them.

He had to somehow clear his mind and forced himself to nod toward the remaining luggage. "I can't carry that trunk," he said. "Which of the smaller ones is most important?"

She gestured toward the suitcase with the straps around it. "We can't leave that case. Some of my father's papers are in it."

Aindreas grabbed the case, which wasn't as heavy as he had feared, and lurched out the doorway. She followed, toting a carpetbag.

The rolling smoke in the hallway had become nearly unendurable. They pressed forward on hands and knees, following Thorson. Aindreas pushed Lorelei in front of him so that he could drag the suitcase. His heart sank when he saw that flames had made the service stairway impassable on that floor. They turned and crawled toward the main staircase. Thorson led the way, constantly looking back to see that the line hung together.

Mrs. Sharpe kept up a steady moan, and she screamed in terror once. "Be still, Mother," snapped Reverend Sharpe. The first words he had spoken.

Though trying to keep her mouth covered, Mrs. Sharpe wailed again.

Lorelei called up to her, "If I have to come up there and quiet you down, Mother, I'm going to be very mad at you."

"Leave her alone," said Faith. "She's no more scared than the rest of us."

Though he didn't care for the tone and the way Lorelei had talked to her mother, Aindreas realized that he had never seen anyone like her.

Fortunately the main stairway was not burning, and they ran down to the third-floor landing. They could go no further, because below that level the stairway was burning. Panic squeezed Aindreas's chest again. Were they trapped? Something heavy crashed on the floors above. Shaking and soaked with sweat, he wondered if he could take another step.

"Go back...make a run for it down the hall," Thorson ordered. They stumbled once again toward the service stairs, each holding onto the sheet in front. The competence of this man Thorson was suddenly clear to Aindreas. Thorson had realized that the fire's descent through the building wasn't even, and he was gambling their last energy on the chance that the service stairs at this height might not yet be ablaze.

The hallway ceiling flamed over their heads. Burning pieces of wood dropped upon them and the singed bedding they wore crackled in the heat. A terrifying moment passed before they saw the narrow service stairs were only filled with smoke. Choking, coughing, they began rushing down the winding steps. Thorson's instincts had proved correct.

Just before they reached the second-floor landing, Reverend Sharpe collapsed against the wall, spent, unwilling or unable to go further. Aindreas stepped down and shoved him with all his strength. Sharpe tumbled down several steps before he was able to regain his footing. But he did go forward. When Aindreas fell back to his place in line, Lorelei slapped his shoulder. Somehow he didn't mind. He had done what needed to be done and even in anger, her hand felt good on him.

They reached the mezzanine floor and started down the final flight of stairs. Not until they were staggering through the doorway and into the hotel lobby was Aindreas convinced they had made it, they had escaped. A group of waiting firemen helped them. They hurried out the front door and into the cold, Aindreas dragging the suitcase behind him. Coughing uncontrollably, he let go of the case. Volunteers moved forward to cover them with blankets.

Aindreas became separated from the others and shuffled toward a bonfire across the street. Shivering, he stood close to the flames. So ironic, this fire thing, he couldn't seem to live with it or without it. He glanced up at the roof of the hotel, at the flames across the width of it. The efforts of the fireman with their puny hoses hadn't much effect except to keep the fire from spreading beyond the hotel. The Galt House itself was going to burn to the ground. He stood by this small fire, across the street and among strangers, watching in silence for some moments. Someone reported to the group at large that maybe as many as a half-dozen people had been killed. From the looks of some of the guests he had seen earlier, Aindreas knew that others had been badly burned. But for Thorson and some luck, he could have been one of those who hadn't gotten out.

Later, he retrieved the suitcase and came upon the Sharpe family. Lorelei had her head turned away from him as he approached. Surrounded by curious gawkers, the family clung together, their faces nearly as dark as if smeared with burnt cork, apparently waiting for a carriage. The reverend eagerly took the strapped case from Aindreas, then simply handed him a card.

REVEREND PAUL MASON SHARPE
SOUTH CHRISTIAN CHURCH
THIRD AND ST. CATHERINE STREETS
LOUISVILLE, KENTUCKY

Faith came to him with a kind, wet-eyed smile. "Thank you for saving us," she said.

Hearing her sister's words, Lorelei looked around and then eased herself between her sister and Aindreas. She pressed his hand, more nearly stroked it. He wanted to say her name out loud, 'Lorelei Sharpe.'

"Those rag-tags stole a few of the cases thrown out the window," she said. "We didn't have people like that in Lexington, people who would steal the nicest fitted clothes off your back. What will they do...sell them? Well, that's not your fault," she said in a softer voice. "You must come to see us tomorrow at the church."

The prospect stirred his blood. "Tomorrow?" he said.

"Yes, perhaps in the afternoon." She had the kind of gaze that could make one feel he was the only other person in the world. "You were very brave," she went on, "and we must thank you."

Aindreas absently stuck the Reverend's card in his shirt pocket. "Thorson, the fireman, he's the one we all need to thank," he said, admitting to himself that his fear had nearly paralyzed him but at the same time pleased that this woman would think of him in that way.

"Oh, him," Lorelei responded, and waved her hand as if in dismissal of an unwelcome offering from a waiter. She nodded toward the burning building. "You see, we're new here. They didn't have our home quite ready, so we had to stay at this terrible hotel tonight."

Aindreas tried to smile. "A grand place, actually. Charles Dickens mentioned it once."

She raised an eyebrow. "Oh, I didn't know that."

He could have looked at her face the rest of the night. A murmur went through the crowd when a black-and-white spaniel darted across the street and wriggled its way into Lorelei's arms when she knelt to receive it. Having lost her attention, Aindreas shifted uncomfortably.

"Oh, Abigail," Lorelei exclaimed," "you've made me the happiest person in the world."

The dog's bare skin showed through a few burned spots in her coat, but she looked little worse for the ordeal. Whimpering, Abigail buried her muzzle in Lorelei's shoulder. Aindreas needed to get to the newspaper office and reluctantly turned to go. He shuffled over the now frozen water that had been brought to put on a fire and had ended up on the street. When he looked back, the dog's tail was frantically fanning the ice.

# THE AINDREAS RIVERS SAGA

The *Aindreas Rivers Saga* is a four-part series that follows the life of Aindreas Rivers from 1855 through 1918.

## *AINDREAS THE MESSENGER: LOUISVILLE 1855*

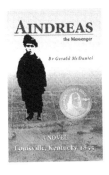

## *AINDREAS THE SCRIBE: 1865*

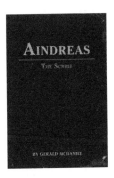

## *AINDREAS THE ODYSSEY: 1876-1892*
Coming Soon

## *AINDREAS THE DISSENTER: 1918*
Coming Soon

*Gerald McDaniel*

# OTHER BOOKS BY MCDANIEL

## *NIGHT SWEATS AND GRAFFITI*

A thriller, *Night Sweats* is the first book in a two-part *Graffiti* series featuring Daniel Francis Saul, a set-in-his-ways attorney who is forced, after the murder of a wealthy socialite, to become a reluctant hero.

## *TRANSFIGURATION BLUES*

Book two in the *Graffiti* series, takes our reluctant hero, "Sol" to a new level of danger and intrigue.

# ABOUT THE GERALD MCDANIEL

Gerald McDaniel, an attorney and an award-winning author is a lifetime resident of Louisville. Gerald received both his B.A. and J.D. degrees from the University of Louisville, then practiced law in a private firm for a number of years and is a former prosecutor.

*Aindreas: The Messenger,* and *Aindreas: The Scribe*, are McDaniel's first and second book and both are in their second printing. *Aindreas: The Messenger* received the Benjamin Franklin award from the Independent Book Publishers Association and the Jesse Stuart Award from the Kentucky Association of School Librarians (KASL).

*The Messenger* and *The Scribe* feature the life and times of Louisville native Aindreas Rivers, a courageous underdog pushed by political and cultural forces beyond his control. Both books are a part of a four book series called *The Aindreas Rivers Saga*.

McDaniel's third book and his first thriller. *Night Sweats and Graffiti* is the first book in a three-part series featuring his central character, Sol, a set-in-his-ways skeptic, who becomes a reluctant hero and protector of the innocent.

The author invites you to read his blog called *walkin' and talkin'.*at www.GeraldMcDanielAuthor.com. The blog features unique stories about interesting people, places, and things, focusing on Louisville neighborhoods.

McDaniel is available to read or speak with your organization or group. To schedule a reading, send an email to Gerald@GeraldMcDanielAuthor.com, or leave your contact information on the comment bar at his website.

## STAY CONNECTED WITH GERALD

If you enjoyed reading this book, I hope you will take a moment to write a short review on Amazon. If you are curious about Louisville history, or have a question about the Aindreas Rivers books, please visit my website and contact me by email.

To join my email list and receive an advance copy of the next Aindreas Rivers Saga book, please email me or sign up using the form on my website.

**Web:**
www.GeraldMcDanielAuthor.com
**E-mail**:
mailto:Gerald@GeraldMcDanielAuthor.com

Made in the USA
Middletown, DE
08 November 2023

42219956R00205